REMBERTON

Other novels by D.J. Meador

His Father's House (1994)

Unforgotten (1999)

REMBERTON

A NOVEL

D. J. Meador

iUniverse, Inc.
New York Lincoln Shanghai

REMBERTON

Copyright © 2007 by Daniel J. Meador

All rights reserved. No part of this book may be used or reproduced by any means, graphic, electronic, or mechanical, including photocopying, recording, taping or by any information storage retrieval system without the written permission of the publisher except in the case of brief quotations embodied in critical articles and reviews.

iUniverse books may be ordered through booksellers or by contacting:

iUniverse
2021 Pine Lake Road, Suite 100
Lincoln, NE 68512
www.iuniverse.com
1-800-Authors (1-800-288-4677)

Because of the dynamic nature of the Internet, any Web addresses or links contained in this book may have changed since publication and may no longer be valid.

Certain characters in this work are historical figures, and certain events portrayed did take place. However, this is a work of fiction. All of the other characters, names, and events as well as all places, incidents, organizations, and dialogue in this novel are either the products of the author's imagination or are used fictitiously.

Cover illustration by Ann Cowden

ISBN: 978-0-595-46000-7 (pbk)
ISBN: 978-0-595-90300-9 (ebk)

Printed in the United States of America

Dedicated with affection to
long-time friends who enjoy thinking they
recognize characters here and in my previous
novels, all works of pure fiction

Chapter 1

▼

A stranger stood at the registration counter in the lobby of the Cedar Ridge Motel. He was a middle-aged man of medium height with black, gray-flecked hair. His undistinguished face of weathered complexion and deep-set dark eyes could have been a face among many in a truck stop. It did not match his attire: gray pinstriped suit, silk tie, and white starched shirt.

No one was at the counter, but sounds of a TV soap opera floated in through an open door to the rear. He tapped a small bell.

In a moment an overweight, middle-aged woman in a sack dress, bedroom slippers, and beehive hairdo came through the door. "Good afternoon. Can I help you?" She exuded good cheer.

"Yes. I have a reservation. Rooter's the name. Jesse Rooter." He spoke with a surly impatience.

The woman bent behind the counter and rifled through some papers. From the TV came an agonized female voice breaking up with a boyfriend.

"Look's like we've got you." Her eyes ran over the paper. "Chicago! You're a long way from home. Ever been to Remberton before?"

The question caught him off guard. "Er, yes … but it's been a long time." She laid the paper on the counter. "You're lucky. You got the last room in the house, maybe the last in town."

"My secretary said she tried two other motels before she found this room. Is something special going on?"

"Big wedding this weekend. Folks already coming in from all over." She was filling out a form.

"I'm surprised Remberton has so many motels."

"They're chains—came with the interstate. We were here a long time before that, but the new places get most of the business now."

"How long has the interstate highway been here?"

"About six years—came in 68. Changed a whole lot of things."

"I noticed." He pulled a credit card from his wallet and slid it toward her. She made an imprint with a noisy clanking and handed the card back. She took a key from a rack behind her and laid it on the counter.

"Room 107."

"Is the county still dry?"

"Went wet five months ago, but we haven't gotten around to thinking about a bar."

"Is there one nearby?"

"Spiffy's, just across the interstate. You can't miss it, Honey."

He picked up his key and turned to go. Then he paused and turned back. "Do you happen to know a lawyer here named Noble Shepperson?"

"Oh, everybody knows Mr. Noble. He's the biggest lawyer in town."

"Can you tell me how to find his office?"

"Just go along this road here for a couple of miles." She waved her hand. "And you'll hit Center Street. Then take a left. The post office is on the corner. Go about three blocks and you'll see it on the right, on a corner, a block before the courthouse."

"Is the bank still by the post office?"

"Yes sir, but it's not the First National anymore. Some chain took it over."

Jesse Rooter moved away from the counter toward the front door. "Can I pull my car around to the room?" He was breathing heavily.

"Yes sir. Just go on around this side. Are you all right? Do you need any help?"

"No. I'm OK."

As he opened the door, letting in the distant sound of interstate traffic, she called after him. "We've got coffee and doughnuts here first thing every morning."

The late afternoon shadows were lengthening across the front lawn as Noble Shepperson pulled his Buick into the two-car garage. Nan's Chevrolet station wagon was parked in the other slot. They had built the house a couple of years after the war, out on a new stretch of School Street, one of Remberton's older streets extended beyond the edge of town to provide for new residential construction in the post-war upsurge. The house was one-story brick, traditional in architecture, with a touch of the ranch style then popular. Azaleas, planted across the front, were now putting on their finest spring show, a profusion of red, white, and lavender. Camellias lined the driveway, some still exhibiting their last-of-season blooms.

Nan was in the kitchen cutting up something on the counter when he walked in. She was about five six in height and had developed a middle-aged chubbiness, but retained a reasonably good figure. Her ear-length wavy brown hair framed a roundish face, at times sunny and cheerful but sad and morose at others. At this moment it was somewhere in between. She wore a casual skirt and blouse.

"Well, how did it go today?" she asked matter of factly, the same question she had asked almost every day for years.

"Oh, about as usual. Judge McKnight treated me all right in that bank case. How about you?"

"Book club and some errands around town. Tonight's my bridge group's supper. I'm leaving you a salad and ham sandwich. There's ice cream in the freezer."

"I can manage—with the help of a little gin and tonic."

Noble moved on through the kitchen. In the bedroom he ripped off his lawyering clothes—suit, tie, dress shirt—and put on a short-sleeved sport shirt and casual slacks.

Back in the kitchen he found a glass, filled it with ice, and mixed a gin and tonic. Nan was putting some things away in a cabinet. Then she moved toward the garage door, saying, "I'm on my way. Probably be back around nine."

He headed toward the porch with glass in hand. The early April evening was mildly warm, but not hot. The smell of spring was in the air. Good screened porch weather. Daylight was waning. The setting sun was masked from the porch by a stand of pecan trees, from which came the raucous sounds of blue jays. Off to the right was Nan's flower garden, now a profusion of color, and in the far rear was the vegetable garden, not yet in full production. Beyond was a solid wall of pine and oak trees, land owned by a timber company, making it unlikely anything would ever be built on it. He sat down in a white wicker rocker, stretched out his six-foot two-inch frame, and took a long sip.

These were now quiet years for Nan and Noble, with both of their children, Kirk and Martha, grown and married. Kirk lived with his wife in Mobile, where he was in the trust department of a bank. Martha was married to a medical doctor and lived in Nashville, where she did freelance editing. Each had a baby boy.

On the whole, life had been good to Noble Shepperson—a still-intact marriage—not perfect, of course, but overall not bad—two grandsons and children who had worked out well, a remunerative law practice, a reputation as a solid, outstanding citizen, and fully credentialed genealogically as a member of one of Remberton's oldest and most respected families.

But that outwardly harmonious world around him—and the tranquil evening scene—belied an inner disquiet. This spring of 1974 had brought over him an odd feeling of restlessness. He didn't know why, couldn't identify any reason. At 65, he was at the point where many men retired. But he was in excellent health and had no desire to stop work, to do nothing but play golf and piddle around the house. Time was passing, though, and he had begun to wonder whether he was missing out on something, whether there was one remaining challenge he should confront, some last great noble deed he could perform for his fellow man. His wartime experiences had for a long while satisfied his taste for high adventure, but they were receding ever more into the past.

He had begun to replay his life, wondering whether he had done the right thing in coming back to Remberton. He could have stayed in the regular army, seen the world, maybe ended up wearing stars. Then there were opportunities with major city law firms he had passed up, a good shot at the state supreme court, too. All of that he had foregone to remain in Remberton, a spot on the map inhabited by 8,000 souls. This place, carved out of the Alabama wilderness in the 1820s by his forebears and others; this place where four generations of Sheppersons before him had lived, worked, and died, where he himself had grown up and knew every nook and cranny of town and county; this place had exerted an extraordinary pull on him, like an irresistible magnetic force. And so he had come back, not simply to enjoy the good life but to do what he could to improve life there for everyone. But had he done that? He was plagued by late-life second thoughts.

Rocking and sipping gin and tonic, he mused over his law practice and the Remberton lifestyle—golf every Wednesday afternoon, church on Sunday morning, Rotary Club luncheon on Tuesday, and occasional parties. Was he getting bored with it all? Possibly tired, too?

A life in the law carried with it a certain stress from living with other people's problems; having responsibility for resolving them, protecting clients against disastrous financial ruin or the threat of prison. He had been at it for forty years, had seen the full range of human failings and virtues—greed, lust, skullduggery, meanness, love, generosity, charity. It was the fate of the small town general practitioner to know some of the darkest aspects of human existence. Maybe he had had enough, needed now to be freed of all those burdens and responsibilities, freed from the routine of life in Remberton.

Twilight was setting in. The last chirpings of sparrows had died out. Frogs in the creek beyond the woods croaked away. A multitude of insects had begun their nightly chorus. The ice rattled in his glass. He got up, went to the kitchen, refilled it with gin and tonic—he never used a jigger—returned to the wicker rocker and stretched out again.

He thought about Nan, as he often did in these moments of reflection. Forty-one years ago, he had been propelled into the wedding by the notion that he had to get married. Everybody was doing it; it was a required next step when he graduated from

West Point. At that moment Nan was the most promising and attractive prospect available. She was the only non-Southern girl he had known, and he was captivated by her perky personality and accent, so different from the girls back home. He had tried to pretend then that he was in love with her, but in his innermost being, he knew that he had not been. Fond of her, yes; infatuated with her, yes. But the spark that distinguishes those sentiments from real love had not been there. He knew this because two years earlier, he had truly been in love with a girl from Montgomery, and he had been heartsick when she married his competitor. But what difference had it made? Nan had been a good mother, raised two successful children, and kept a well-organized house. There had been some rocky stretches—mainly mood swings that caused her to be cool and aloof for a time. All in all, though, she had been a good wife. But the fun and companionship he had seen and heard about in some marriages had not been there.

Stimulated by the infusion of gin, he wondered what life might have been like with some of the other women he had known along the way. He took his wedding vows seriously, though, "For better, for worse…. till death do us part," meant what it said. For him, divorce was unthinkable. So whatever their ups and downs and whatever the attractiveness of other women, ending this marriage was never an option.

There had been opportunities—he was a man who attracted the attention of women—and there were continuing blandishments from youngish and not-so-young-widows. But he had always resisted—that is, with one long-ago war-time exception, which now crept out of his chamber of memories. That memory always brought with it a mixture of pleasurable fantasy and guilt.

The evening had grown dark, almost too cool to stay on the porch. His reverie was broken by Nan's voice from the kitchen.

"I'm back!"

He called out, "Aren't you early?"

She came on to the porch. "Some of them had spring colds and didn't feel good, so we decided to eat early and leave. Have you eaten?"

"No. Just enjoying the evening. Not much hungry." He rose, heading to the kitchen. "But I think I'll have it now."

He pulled the salad and sandwich from the refrigerator, fixed another drink, and sat down at the table by the window.

"How many is that?" she said.

"I don't keep count. Two or three."

"Well, if you're having another, I'll have a nightcap."

"O.K." He rose and went to the bar. "What'll it be?"

"Bourbon on the rocks."

"Must have been a bad day."

"Not bad," she said, "Just hectic."

He handed her a short glass filled with ice cubes and bourbon. He sat down and began eating salad. Sitting across the table, she sipped the drink and looked vacantly beyond him.

Then she said, "Kirk called this afternoon."

"What did he want?"

"Just wanted to talk. Nothing in particular. They're getting along all right."

"He's always liked to talk to you more than me."

"Maybe you've always been too busy."

He ate more salad. Feeling moved to make conversation, he said, "What went on in book club?"

"I think I told you the theme this year is novels between the wars. Today we did *For Whom the Bell Tolls.*"

"What did the good ladies think of it?"

"We agreed it's a man's book."

Noble chuckled. "There must be some women's stuff in that period worth reading."

"Oh, yes. Virginia Woolf and Katherine Anne Porter are on our list."

Didn't you tell me that Lucille got out of the club?"

"She did. Ann Simmons says the only things Lucille reads are magazines in the beauty shop and some trashy novels."

"Right now," Nan said, "Lucille's consumed with getting ready for the wedding on Saturday." Then added, with a hint of sarcasm, "That should be quite a show."

As a native of Newburgh, New York, Nan was something of an oddity in Remberton, amidst a sea of locally born and bred sons and daughters. She and Noble had met at a West Point Hop during his last year in the Academy, when she was a student at Vassar. She would have graduated in 1934 had they not married right after his graduation. She thought she was getting a regular army officer for a husband and had visions of tours of duty in far-flung and exotic places. Soon after, though, he decided to leave the peacetime army, which he found boring, and attend law school and then come back to Remberton and go into practice.

And so it was that, instead of seeing the world as an army wife, she had found herself wife of a small town Deep South lawyer—and very far from New York. She did not adjust easily. Four years later, when Noble left for overseas during the war, she took their two small children and went back to her parents' home in Newburgh where she stayed for close to three years.

Readjusting to Remberton after the war had not been smooth, but she eventually more or less reconciled herself to the situation. At first, folks said she "talked funny," an exotic creature from another world. The sharp "r" in her voice forever marked her as a Yankee. But the cachet of coming from somewhere else, especially New York, held an irresistible attraction, and the women of the town took her in. Or at least they made a pretense of doing so. After all, she was Noble Shepperson's wife and thus could not be ignored. Noble often wondered how much her relationship with Remberton contributed to her mood swings.

He finished the salad and reached for the sandwich. The telephone in the den began to ring.

"I'll get it," Nan said, rising. In a moment she returned. "It's for you."

"Who is it?"

"Didn't say. It's a man. Didn't talk like anybody around here."

Noble went to the den and picked up the phone. "Hello."

"Mr. Shepperson?" came a hoarse male voice.

"Yes, what can I do for you?"

"My name is Jesse Rooter. You probably don't remember me. No reason you should. I grew up around here, but left years ago."

"Are you in town now?"

"Yes sir and I'm wondering whether I can see you tomorrow."

"Tomorrow?" Noble paused, thinking over the next day's agenda. "Well, I don't have any appointments in the morning, so I could see you then. Can you give me some indication what it's about?"

"It's a long and complicated story. I'd rather explain it in person."

"All right. Would nine o'clock suit you?"

"Yes sir. I'll be there then."

Noble went back to his sandwich and drink.

"Who was it?" Nan asked.

"Name of Jesse Rooter. Says he used to live here and wants to see me. That name does have a faint ring of familiarity, but I can't quite place it."

"Must not have been among Remberton's first families," Nan said, in the tone that usually infected her voice when she commented on Remberton life.

Noble smiled slightly. He was mildly amused by her cynical attitude toward the place. "Rooter is not a name that readily comes to mind."

He finished his sandwich and drained his glass. Nan's glass was empty. He looked at her across the table. Some people around town called her cute. He saw it now in her curly hair, her large brown eyes, naturally pink cheeks and slightly turned up nose. He was stirred by the allurement that had attracted him to her in the first place.

He pushed back his chair and said, "Why don't we just go to bed."

When Jesse Rooter hung up the telephone he leaned back against the pillows on his motel bed to reflect on tomorrow morning. Earlier he had found Spiffy's, just the other side of the interstate. He took a seat at the small bar and ordered a scotch on the rocks. The bartender was a thin young man with a crew cut, a hair style Jesse had not seen in Chicago in a long time.

"I gather this is a new place," he said to the bartender.

"Yes sir. The first bar in Rembert County. Nobody ever thought they'd see liquor served here. But then folks voted it in. Got tired of running fifteen miles up the road across the county line."

After two drinks Jesse moved over to the restaurant section where he found an all-you-can-eat buffet for $2.95. Most of the tables were filled with vigorous eaters, their plates piled with fried chicken. He saw more fried chicken than he had seen in decades. He took a couple of pieces, passed up the black-eyed peas and turnip greens and settled for French fried potatoes.

Reclining now in his motel room, Jesse Rooter tried to absorb the fact that he was back in Remberton for the first time in nearly thirty years. Nothing out here around the interstate had been there in his time; he could be anywhere, the commercial strip on the edge of a thousand American towns. The Remberton he remembered was another mile or two farther on. He was beginning to wonder whether he really wanted to see it, whether he should have come on this trip. But it was not curiosity that had brought him back. He had a mission in mind. He had gone a very long way from here, geographically, economically, and socially—maybe too far to come back.

He lived on the North Shore of Chicago, where from the city northward up the western side of Lake Michigan the suburban towns stretched endlessly, one after another—Evanston, Wilmette, Kenilworth, Winnetka, and on and on. Running through them, close by the lake, was Sheridan Road, and along it mile after mile were spacious houses—even mansions—opulent manifestations of the wealth generated in by-gone decades in this mid-western metropolis.

In one such house—an immense gray stone edifice, with a medieval castle effect, one of the most imposing along Sheridan Road in Winnetka—lived Jesse Rooter. Except for a housekeeper, he was there alone, his wife having died three years ago. A mild stroke and heart attack had caused him to slow down. So he went into his brokerage firm in the Loop only two days a week, leaving him plenty of time to think and brood over the past.

In recent drab and overcast days he had sat for hours, staring through tall, drapery framed windows across an expanse of lawn to the wind-chopped waters of Lake Michigan, stretching away to the horizon. No sign of spring greenery had yet appeared. The frothy chunks of ice along the shore had melted, but the weather was still too chilly for any but the hardiest of sail-boat enthusiasts.

In his lonely brooding, his thoughts had drifted back to the distant past, to the painful and desperate scenes of his childhood, scenes he had for years put out of mind as he had advanced into the different world of high-powered business deals and North Shore society. Those memories had generated in him an emotional mixture of sadness, bitterness, and anger. He had developed a fierce resolve to do something about it, to get even, to force that society to remember the circumstances it had never known and didn't want to know. This resolve had now propelled him back to his place of origin, a trip that for thirty years he had sworn he would never take. His first step was to see Noble Shepperson, the only man in Remberton from whom he could hope to get some help. To explain why he was here he would need to lay before Shepperson all those unhappy memories that motivated his burning resolve, memories that he now found himself reviewing again.

✻   ✻   ✻   ✻

On a dirt road, two miles from the blacktop highway, sat a three-room plank house, unpainted and weathered brown. The small front porch sagged forward into three wooden steps, the bottom one broken and flat on the ground. On one side of the porch was the frayed back seat of an old car, its springs broken down. On the other was a wooden bench. Through the middle of the house ran an open-ended dog trot. Two rooms were on one side, and one room was on the other, with the kitchen tacked on behind it in a kind of lean-to fashion.

In each room was a small fireplace where on cold winter days a log fire sizzled, often sputtering and hissing from rain falling down the chimney. The roof leaked in several places during heavy rain. In summer the house sat airless under a hot and humid blanket.

Without electricity or other lighting, the occupants went to bed when darkness came. They drew their water with a bucket from a well fifty yards to the rear. Off in another direction, thirty yards from the house, was the outhouse, a one-hole privy. The yard in the front and rear was swept clean, hard-pack whitish sand bereft of even a single sprig of grass. A half-dozen scrawny chickens scratched for worms and insects around the edge.

In his earliest memories there, Jesse had two older sisters, Lida Belle and Bessie Ann. His father, Lem Rooter, was a tenant farmer, raising, or trying to raise, cotton and corn on seventy acres of the thinnest and poorest soil in Rembert County. His mother, Sadie May, seemed always to be having children. Although he didn't really remember the arrival of the next child after himself, another girl named Peggy Sue, he did recall the birth of his brother, Grady, followed by another boy who never had a name; he died a week after he was born.

Jesse learned early how babies ate, as he watched them sucking at his mother's breast. "Ain't he cute?" she would say, "going at it like a hog at slop." Always barefooted, she wore a home-made flour sack dress, cut low and loose, making her large, pendulous breasts readily available. After Jesse, the babies came so close together that one had not finished nursing before the next arrived. So there were times when she had to feed two at once. In hot weather she would sit on the front porch, with dress dropped down to her waist, holding a baby to each breast. "Just like a litter of pigs," she would say, laughing at the two gasping, slobbering, and sucking infants. She seemed to have an inexhaustible supply of milk, the only plentiful thing on the premises.

That milk saved Jesse's life once in the winter when he was four years old and became seriously ill. For days he lay in bed, too weak to get out. There was little food in the house, and his mother got in the bed with him and fed him from her breast.

In the crowded house, he came to know even more about the female anatomy, as his older sisters sometimes wore little or nothing on the hottest summer days, and the rest of the time were careless in how they dressed or undressed around others. He had noticed a difference early on between their bodies and his, but as they grew into their teens he became entranced by the newly emerging differences. He tried not to stare at them when they were nude, but found himself doing so anyway. Sometimes Lida Bell would say, "Jesse, what are you looking at?" She would call out and say, "Mama, tell Jesse and Grady to stop looking at us." Grady had gotten old enough to be interested. He and Jesse wondered about what seemed an irresistible attraction, but at the same time a little frightening.

Grady was especially precocious in this connection. Once when he found Lida Belle standing naked he wrestled her on to the bed. Her screams brought Lem running in to break it up. He gave Grady one of the worst thrashings he ever got. After that, Grady left his sisters alone and directed his attention to girls at school.

On Sundays they hitched up their mule to the wagon and drove three miles along the dirt road to the Shiloh Church. It was a Hard-shell Baptist congregation, meeting in a one-room structure, long in need of paint.

When Bessie Ann died at the age of thirteen, she was buried in the cemetery there. His father placed a pine board at the head of her grave, and the preacher printed her name on it with a crayon. Neither Lem nor Sadie May could write.

They all ate at a table in the kitchen, which took all the room left in that small space by the iron wood burning stove. They lived mainly off corn bread, biscuits, corn, and fried strips of fat back—salted white pork, sometimes with a streak of lean in it. Lem had an ancient twelve gauge shotgun with which he sometimes shot a rabbit or squirrel to supplement the diet. Shotgun shells were expensive, so that was not often. In the rooms of the house there hung always a distinctive and unpleasant smell, a unique blend of old fried grease, unwashed bodies, mildewed mattresses and quilts, and wood smoke.

As soon as Jesse was large enough to hold a hoe, he was in the field, along with father, mother, and sisters chopping cotton. In late summer as the bolls opened, revealing the white fleecy fiber, they were all out there picking from earliest light until dark. There were many days during spring planting and fall picking when he missed school.

During the rest of the school year, he and his sisters—and later his younger brother, Grady—walked the two miles in rain or shine to the black-top road where they were picked up by a school bus for the eight-mile ride to Remberton. Most of the other children in the school came from another world, wearing a variety of colorful trousers, sweaters, and dresses. They came from town, the sons and daughters of merchants, bankers, doctors, and lawyers. They paid little attention to the Rooter children. In his worn overalls, Jesse felt different, shut out, and embarrassed.

Nevertheless, he liked school. It got him out of the field and away from the drabness of home, and he found that he enjoyed the studies. When he brought home report cards showing above average grades, he had to explain them to his parents. Lem showed little interest, but his mother always quizzed him about what he was studying. From time to time, Lem would say, "Jesse, if something happens to me, you got to take hold here." When his father was not around, his mother would say, "Jesse, I want you to finish high school and then get out of here. This ain't a life for you. You got to do something better."

On Sundays when they went to church and on those Saturdays when they went to town, Jesse and his father and brother got out of their overalls and put on their one pair of pants and shirt. His mother and sisters, instead of dresses made of flour sacks or unbleached domestic, got into homemade gingham or cotton dresses. They all put on shoes.

Going to town on Saturdays was the biggest event in their lives. They would leave the house at daylight for the two-hour trip in the mule-drawn wagon. They sat on planks laid across the wagon sides, listening to the wheels creaking on the ungreased axles and the clopping of the scrawny mule's feet on the blacktop. In town, they would pull the mule and wagon into a large lot a block off Center Street, behind the hardware store. On a busy Saturday two or three dozen wagons and their mules would be parked there, while the tenant farmers and sharecroppers from south of town roamed up and down Center Street and did a little shopping. White and black jostled together on the crowded sidewalk and in the ten-cent store.

If it were one of those times when Lem had some cash, he would set the family up to soda crackers, sardines, and Coca-Colas. He hoped to have enough cash every few months to replenish their food by buying a hundred pound sack of flour, a fifty pound can of lard, and a slab or two of white side meat.

Standing around on Center Street, they heard talk about what the government was going to do to help the country get out of the Depression. "They say they's going to help the farmers, but I ain't seen no sign of it yet." There was talk that President Roosevelt—they pronounced it Rooz-a-velt—might even get electricity out into the country. But there was skepticism.

A man, his left arm missing, wearing an army cap from 1918, said, "I don't look to see no light bulb in my house in my time."

When Jesse was 13, the cotton crop was almost done in by bad weather–rain and drought at the wrong times. The family faced near-desperate prospects for the coming winter. One day Lem said to Jesse, "I ain't got no choice but to go to the bank and see if I can borrow some money."

So they found themselves in the two-story high, marble lobby of the First National Bank. They stood off to the side, Lem not knowing what to do. All the men coming and going wore suits and ties, men of substance with actual money. The place represented all that the Rooters were not. The marble walls and floor, the low hubbub rising from the various transactions, exuded financial solidity, a world as alien to Lem as the planet Mars.

Lem approached a man standing behind a counter and looking through a window with small bars on it. "Please, sir, can you tell me how to get a loan?"

"You'll have to see the president. He makes all loans. He's over there at that desk behind the wall." He pointed to a man at a desk in the far corner beyond a low marble wall. Two people sat facing him. "He's busy right now, but just wait and he'll see you."

Lem and Jesse stood by the wall, feeling ill at ease and vastly out of place. Shortly the president walked over to them. He was a tall, elderly, gray-haired man, "What can I do for you?"

"I need to borrow some money," Lem said.

The president led them to his desk, walking now on a deep green carpet. They sat down across from him, Lem on the edge of the chair, nervously twisting his old felt hat.

"How much do you want and what do you want it for?" the president said.

"Just enough to get me through the next crop. We ain't got much to eat, and winter's coming on."

"What kind of collateral can you put up?"

"Collateral?"

"Yes. Something for security. The bank has to have security for the loans it makes."

"You mean some kind of property?"

"Right. Something the bank could look to if you were to default on payment of the loan."

"There ain't much out there. I got a mule and a wagon and a plow."

"How about your house?"

"Ain't mine. I just a tenant. It belongs to Mr. Funchess."

"I see. Can't Mr. Funchess help you out?"

"I done been to him, and he says he can't do nothing. Says he's had a bad crop year himself."

"I hate to say this, Mr. Rooter, because I sympathize with your situation, but it would not be prudent for me to authorize a loan under these circumstances. I have to be responsible to our depositors and stockholders. It's their money, not mine. Mr. Funchess insists on strong collateral for our loans."

"Mr. Funchess? What's he got to do with this?"

"He's the chairman of the board. Since you're his tenant maybe he'll make an exception. I'll give him a ring."

The president disappeared into a room in the rear and was back in a few minutes. "I'm sorry, but Mr. Funchess says the bank ought not to take this risk."

Lem sighed. "Look's like he's got me coming and going."

"I hope you can work out your difficulty," the president said. "We've got welfare now. You ought to try that."

As they left the bank, Lem said, "I ain't surprised. When you ain't got nothing, you can't get nothing. The welfare ain't no good. I done tried that."

Standing in front of the bank, they looked far up Center Street, to the courthouse sitting at its head, a high brick Victorian eminence, dominated by its tower whose round clock face looked down the street like an all-seeing eye. Just as the bank symbolized money and its power, so the courthouse symbolized The Law, that mysterious force presided over by judges and sheriffs, with power to hold you to your debts, to put you in jail, to put you off the land. Between the bank and the courthouse, Lem Rooter was nobody, and Jesse knew it, absorbed it into the warp and woof of his being, never to be forgotten.

When Lida Bell was 16, she married the son of a deceased tenant farmer who lived five miles away. Her husband had to support his sick mother and two younger sisters, so Lida Bell moved there to help take care of that family. This was a loss to Lem of a good field hand.

In the fall, an assistant to Mr. Funchess, a lean, underfed looking young man, came to the house and announced that Mr. Funchess was going to make a change and would be getting a new tenant for the next season. They could stay until after Christmas but then they would have to vacate.

"But where we gonna go?" Lem asked.

"I don't know," the assistant said, "but you've got a couple of months to figure that out."

The fact was there was nowhere to go. There were no jobs anywhere. Men were out of work all over the country. Lem couldn't find any other landowners willing to take him on. The grim weeks passed, and in the middle of January they were still there.

Cars rarely passed along the dirt road in front of the Rooter house. So it was a matter of considerable note one day when a shiny black Ford pulled up into the yard and stopped. A tall man in dark suit and tie got out—a figure of that sort could only mean trouble. The whole family quickly gathered on the front porch. The fifteen-year-old Jesse would never forget this moment.

"Are you Mr. Rooter?" the man said.

"Yes sir."

"My name is Noble Shepperson. I'm a lawyer representing Mr. Sam Funchess. He's given you notice to vacate by the end of December, and you haven't vacated."

"Well," Lem said, slowly, "we ain't got no place to go."

Shepperson said nothing for a moment, looking over the forlorn group—humanity reduced to its lowest level, their malnourished faces gaunt and expressionless, the toll of the Great Depression in microcosm, standing in flour sack dresses and threadbare overalls, destitute and helpless before his eyes. "I'm sorry to hear that, and I wish I could help you." There was genuine sympathy in his voice. "I'm afraid that Mr. Funchess has got the law on his side. He's got a right to reclaim his land. I'm just here to carry out his instructions." His voice regained a business-like tone. "So I have to tell you that you've got to move right away."

"Since we ain't got nowhere to go, suppose we don't go."

"Then the only recourse Mr. Funchess would have would be to get the sheriff to come out and evict you."

They all stood silent for a long minute, just looking at Noble Shepperson. He finally spoke.

"I'm terribly sorry to have to bring this news, but you'll have to go by next week or the sheriff will be out."

Shepperson turned and walked to his car, started the engine and drove off.

Sadie May said, "What we gonna do, Lem?"

He sighed. "I don't know, I don't know."

Three days later Shepperson again pulled up at the house in his shiny black car. Peggy Sue was the first to see him. "Daddy," she called out, "here come that lawyer man again."

"Oh, my God," Sadie May said, "I guess he's come to put us out."

All the family flocked to the front porch.

Shepperson said, "Mr. Rooter, I've got some news. My firm represents the cotton mill. I was just talking to the manager, and he told me one of their loom operators got his arm crushed yesterday and they're going to have to replace him. I told him about you, and he's willing to take you on. It pays $18 a week. Is that something you could handle?"

"Eighteen dollars a week!" exclaimed Sadie May. "We ain't never seen that kind of money."

"I don't know nothing about no cotton mill," Lem said, "but I'll take it."

"There's a company house in the mill village you can move into. If you want the job you need to move right away."

*   *   *   *

"Enough of that!" Jesse muttered to himself, finding the recollections too painful to dwell on any longer. He got up from the motel bed and turned on the TV, just in time to catch the late night news from a Montgomery station. It was filled with the never-ending news of the Watergate investigation and possible impeachment of President Nixon.

CHAPTER 2

In Remberton, from time immemorial the law offices had been upstairs, over stores along Center Street near the courthouse. But now the lawyers had all migrated down to ground level. When the shopping center at the interstate exit had forced many of the old main street businesses to close, their premises became available at bargain rates. The first lawyer to move down was looked on as some kind of maverick, not quite like a real lawyer. Real lawyers were upstairs. A second moved down, then a third. The herd instinct took over, and suddenly they were all abandoning the upstairs.

Noble held out until the last. Then he was being thought of as antiquated, as a man not keeping up with the times. So he reluctantly yielded. After years over the drug store, he was now down in a small corner building previously occupied by a cut-rate clothing store.

He had gutted it and renovated the space to provide an efficient, comfortable, modern, air-conditioned set of offices. It was fancier than anything he had had before. But it lacked the mellow ambience of the old upstairs office where for decades he had practiced with his brother-in-law, Ed Kirkman.

In his new combination library and conference room, he maintained the two largest sets of books—the most recent 200 volumes of the *United States Reports* and 275 volumes of Alabama Supreme Court decisions. Here, too, were dictionaries and reference books of various kinds, including the *Encyclopedia Britannica*. The lower shelves held a miscellaneous assortment of books that Ed Kirkman and Noble had accumulated over the years but were of little use now. Noble couldn't bring himself to get rid of them. The collection included a valuable early edition of *Blackstone's Commentaries* that Noble had found in a rare book store in Washington. All of the currently useable legal texts were shelved in Noble's office.

That was a spacious room carpeted in a soft blue-gray. Harmonizing draperies hung at the one large window. Through the window Noble could see the courthouse tower and clock that had boomed out all the hours of his life in Remberton. Nan had picked out the carpet and draperies.

"I'm glad to see you get out of that old tacky upstairs," she had said, "and into an office that doesn't make you look like a run-down country lawyer."

"A country lawyer is all I claim to be," he had said. "But I hope not run down."

"Oh, you know what I mean."

She got lots of compliments on her taste. One lawyer told Noble, "You're lucky to have a wife who takes some interest in where you are. Mine wouldn't care if I were in an outhouse."

Half of his office wall space was covered with shelves filled with law books. On a small bookcase on rollers, which he kept near his chair, were the *Alabama Code* and *U. S. Code*.

The rest of the wall space was taken up with an array of framed items—his West Point and law-school diplomas, bar admission certificates, and Second World War memorabilia.

Planning to get some work done before his nine o' clock appointment with Jesse Rooter, Noble had come to the office early. But he was unable to focus on his cluttered desk. Instead, he leaned back in his swivel chair, eyes closed, his reflections from last night continuing. What was this restiveness that had him in its grip? He had never before found himself thinking back so much over his life. He had always disputed the proposition that the unexamined life was not worth living. Those in the arena didn't have time to examine their lives. He had been too busy helping build a better community, taking care of clients, and fulfilling his obligations as a lawyer. Surely his life had been worth something, he reassured himself, if only to this small patch of earth—his work on the school board to strengthen the schools, his efforts to overcome or at least lessen the impact of the interstate on downtown and uptown, his moderating influence during the stressful years of desegregation.

He had been too busy to think back over wartime experiences, but now, looking at the photographs on the wall, he found himself reliving that supreme adventure of his life. There he was, in Ike jacket and overseas cap, in front of an 18th century English manor house, his regimental headquarters, flanked by his executive officer, adjutant, and other staff officers. The picture had been taken only a week before D-Day. Two of the men in the group would be dead within a month, done in by German 88 millimeter shells.

His eyes lingered on the next photograph, taken at a reception for him and his officers in the county hall in the nearby town of Bramton. He, Lt. Col. Noble Shepperson, six feet two inches tall, dwarfed the mayor standing beside him—a portly but diminutive English gentleman in a cutaway coat, the symbol of office draped around his neck—who could not have been more than five feet six. They were surrounded by members of the Ladies Hospitality Committee, a collection of mostly middle-aged, overweight, dowdily dressed but cheerful English women whose self-appointed mission was to make the American soldiers in their vicinity feel at home in those months before the event they all knew was coming sooner or later—the invasion of Europe.

Third to his right in the picture stood a woman, younger and considerably more stylish and attractive than the others, wearing a wide-brimmed hat that concealed much of her luxuriant chestnut hair. Her lips were parted in a broad smile and there was no mistaking those eyes, still sparkling, he thought, across all those years. A loose, wintertime dress hid the figure he knew to be there. She was the only reason that this otherwise unremarkable photograph hung on his office wall.

Early in the reception she had come up to him, smiling with her green eyes glinting, and said in a lilting English accent, "Col. Shepperson, I'm Jennifer Cromlyn. We welcome you and your men to our little corner of this island."

He took the hand she extended. It was warm and soft. "Thank you very much. The hospitality could not be better."

Tea was served and they all stood around talking in the high-ceilinged, wood-paneled room, the ladies asking the Americans, "From what part of the States do you come?" and in turn answering the Americans' questions about the town and surrounding countryside. The hubbub was remarkably cheerful considering the wartime circumstances under which these ladies had already been living for four years and what the Americans knew to be coming.

To make conversation, Noble asked Jennifer Cromlyn, "Have you lived here all your life?"

"Yes, except for my years away at school and in London after I married."

"And where is your husband?"

"He's an army intelligence officer posted in North Africa." She went on to explain that he had become a barrister before the war and that they were married just after the war started. "So for the duration I'm back living in the family place I inherited. It's just a short way from your camp."

Other ladies drifted into the conversation and Noble mingled with the crowd. As the reception was breaking up, Jennifer Cromlyn came up and said, "Col. Shepperson, I'd be delighted to have you and some of your staff to tea some afternoon, if you can break away from those arduous training duties."

Her melodious English voice was abruptly interrupted by the repeated buzzing of the intercom on Noble's desk. Jolted back into the present, he leaned forward and pressed a button, "Yes?"

The voice of his secretary, Alice Hawkins, came out loud and clear. "There's a Mr. Jesse Rooter here to see you."

"Send him in," Noble said, quickly adding, "And, Miss Alice, how about making up a little coffee?"

Noble stood up and moved around his desk to greet Jesse Rooter as he came in. He was shorter and stockier than Noble, and his leathery face and black eyes contrasted with Noble's fair skin and blue eyes. They shook hands, and Noble motioned Jesse to one of the two deep cushioned chairs facing his desk.

Noble said, "You say you grew up around here?"

"Yes sir. But this is the first time I've been back since right after the war."

"Where have you been?"

"Chicago. Became a stock broker, had a fortunate marriage."

From the Brooks Brothers suit, oxford button-down shirt, and silk tie, Noble surmised that he had indeed done well. But the face didn't go with the clothes. The face was that of a working man long exposed to the outside.

Noble smiled and said, "You may have changed your residence, but I still detect a touch of a Rembert County accent." What Noble thought, but didn't say, was that the accent hinted ever so slightly of an uneducated countryman from the southern part of the county.

"That's right," Jesse said, with a light chuckle, the only break in an otherwise somber countenance. "I straightened out my grammar. Got rid of double negatives. But that old accent is hard to erase. At the same time, I notice I don't any more talk like people around here. They think I'm a Yankee."

"I'm trying to figure out how I might have known you or your family."

"I'll explain the whole thing, if you have the time."

"There's nothing pressing right now. So take whatever time you need."

"Let me say right away that I want to compensate you for your time because I want your advice."

"O.K. Tell me what your problem is."

"While you may not remember me or my family, I've never forgotten you. It's not too much to say you saved our lives."

"Oh? That's quite an accolade," Noble said, his interest picking up.

"To tell you about it will take a while, but it all relates to why I'm here."

The door swung open and Miss Alice came in with two cups of coffee on a tray. "Would you like sugar or cream?" she asked Jesse as she put a cup in front of him.

"No, thank you," he said, "black is fine."

Miss Alice, widow of an insurance salesman, had been with Noble since the early fifties, entirely reliable and competent. With gray hair pulled back in a bun and horn rimmed glasses, she looked exactly like what she was.

After taking an initial sip from his cup, Noble said, "Go ahead. You have my curiosity up."

Jesse proceeded to describe his miserable and impoverished childhood in that run-down cabin ten miles from town. Listening intently, Noble had leaned back in his chair, coffee cup in hand wondering what all this had to do with anything now. Suddenly he heard his name mentioned. Jesse was telling of the day that Noble came to their house to say that Mr. Sam Funchess meant business, that they had to get off his land, and then how Noble had returned a few days later to bring word of the cotton mill job.

Noble sat up straight. "You know, I do now remember that. We're talking more than thirty-five years ago, way back before the war. What I do remember is that I was nearly sick at my stomach, standing there looking at your family, telling them that they had to go when they had no place to go. But representing Sam Funchess, I felt I had no choice. The law was with him. Then I remember how relieved I was to hear about that mill job. God, it's hard to believe you're that boy who was standing there then."

"That mill job is what saved us. I do not know, can't even imagine, what we would have done if that hadn't come along. I remember Sam Funchess as a ruthless man."

"He could play hard ball, no doubt about that."

"I'm reluctant to say this, because he was your client, but to me he represented pure evil."

"Ed Kirkman and I did represent him for a little while before the war. But then we gave him up. He was a difficult client to work with and frankly, between you and me, I didn't care for some of the things he did. He died about ten years ago. But I don't think I knew anything about what happened to your family after you moved to the mill."

"Bear with me and I'll give you the rest of the story," Jesse said. And he proceeded to do so, talking on without interruption.

* * * *

The small, narrow-fronted, unpainted company house in the mill village was exactly like three dozen others, grouped close together along dirt streets. Men coming home drunk late at night sometimes wandered into the wrong house. There was no way to tell them apart. But Lem Rooter his family now had, for the first time in their lives, electric lights and indoor plumbing.

The village, surrounding the mill—a sprawling two-story brick structure—was right on the southern edge of town. Town and village were separated only by a road along which were a couple of filling stations and a small grocery store. But the village might as well have been surrounded by a twelve-foot high wall, hermetically sealing it off from the rest of Remberton. It was a distinct and separate social and economic world, with a life of its own. Its inhabitants had little or no association with the town's more fortunate citizens. They were at or near the bottom of the white pecking order, economically just a notch above tenant farmers and sharecroppers.

The main contact with the outer world came through the mill village children who attended school in Remberton. With Lida Bell married and Bessie May dead, only Jesse, Peggy Sue, and Grady remained with their parents. A year after they moved in from the country, Peggy Sue ran off with a boy in the village who was five years older. They got married and he took a job in the shipyards in Pascagoula. So for the last few years of school only Jesse and Grady were left at home, and they walked together to school every morning.

Grady got on the football team, and that kept him at school in the afternoons during the fall. Jesse worked every afternoon at a filling station. In the summers, both boys worked full time at a variety of jobs.

With a free house, Lem's $18 a week paycheck, and the money the boys made, the family, though still near the bottom of the economic pile, was far better off than it had ever been. They still had no car, but they didn't need one. The boys at last were out of overalls. Each one had two pairs of pants and several shirts, and they stayed clean through their mother's never-ending washing in a tub on the back porch. They felt a little less conspicuous at school, but had no doubt they were outside that magical circle—children of the town's merchants and professional people and the county's large landowners.

For part of their way to school in the mornings, the boys went along shaded streets, lined with substantial residences behind neat lawns, architecturally a mixture of Victorian, 1920s, and antebellum. There was a car for every house. There were Fords, Chevrolets, and Plymouths, but also here and there an Oldsmobile or a Chrysler.

In several houses, there were girls they knew by name. Often, as the boys walked along the sidewalk, they would see a car pulling out of a driveway, a mother or father at the wheel, taking the girls to school. They were never offered a ride. Indeed, no sign of recognition was ever manifested. It was as though they were invisible.

Grady, much more talkative than Jesse, didn't hide his feelings. "Those stuck-up bitches," he would often say, as the girls passed in their cars, looking straight ahead, "think they're better than anybody. Some day I'll show 'em who I am—show 'em I'm just as much a man as those highfalutin boys they run around with—actually more of a man."

"How are you going to do that?" Jesse asked.

"We'll see. I'll figure it out some way."

Jesse was rather plain and unimpressive in appearance, but Grady was turning into a handsome young man. He was right at six feet, had sandy blond hair with a slight wave in it—movie star good looks. By the time he was sixteen, he had developed a reputation as a ladies man, but not with those girls passing by in their cars. He operated with girls in the village and on the fringes of town. He began to stay out late at night and would sometimes come home drunk. Lem and Sadie May would get into heated arguments with him about this, but they had little effect. Sadie May would tell Jesse, "I just hope we can get Grady through high school. But you the one I'm counting on to make something out of yourself."

At school Jesse began to notice something he thought he would never see. During lunch hour Grady would actually be talking to some of those self-important girls—standing close to and speaking to the forbidden fruit. He had an ingratiating smile and was an easy talker, coming up with witty remarks. The girls would laugh and giggle with him. He seemed to have singled out two or three of the best lookers, those more physically advanced.

One day Jesse happened to be standing unnoticed near several of them. He overheard one say, "That Grady Rooter is really cute."

Another said, "He surely is. Too bad he's from the mill."

Walking to school a few days later, Jesse said, "I've seen you talking to that Craighill gal and the MacKnight gal."

"They look like pretty hot numbers, don't you think?"

"I guess so. You don't think you're going to get anywhere there, do you?"

"Wait and see."

Grady's next move was to begin meeting Julia McKnight clandestinely at the picture show on Saturday afternoons, where they would sit together in the dark, sometimes holding hands. When he finally got up his nerve to take the ultimate step and ask for a date, he came up against hard unyielding reality. "Grady, I'd love to, but you know you can't come to my house. Mama and Daddy wouldn't hear of it."

Grady vented his anger on Jesse. "Who do these bitches think they are? Giving me the come-on and then telling me I ain't good enough to come to their house." He went into an imitation falsetto: "'Mama and Daddy wouldn't hear of it.' Do they think if I get in their house I'll get in their sweet little girl's pants?"

"That's what you got in mind, ain't it?"

Grady smiled. "Well, I wouldn't say I hadn't thought about it. Talking about that, have you noticed that Funchess number? Lucille's her name. She's going to have what it takes. Look at those sweaters she wears. Already filled out."

"You better give that a few years."

"By then she'll be a bitch like the rest of them. She's already showing signs of being high and mighty. And where does she get off with that? I've heard folks say that her old man come into town from the piney woods just like us. You know he's the one who throwed us off out there. The only difference between him and us is money."

"That's a pretty big difference," Jesse said.

"Well, I'd like to find a way to get at him," Grady mumbled.

In the spring of 1940, Jesse graduated from high school. About the only jobs around Remberton were at menial labor in filling stations or grocery stores or possibly in the mill. His mother was insistent. "Jesse, I don't want you to get bogged down like we been all our lives. There's more to you—you got to make something of yourself."

In school they had studied the war in Europe, and he knew that the army was building up. He decided that was the best way out—all food, housing, and clothes, plus $21 a month, with possibilities for travel and training of some sort. So he enlisted, leaving Remberton, to return thereafter only for infrequent short visits. After undergoing tests that showed he had some potential, he was assigned to the Air Corps and sent to radio operator's school. Every month, he sent home $5 of his pay.

When the attack on Pearl Harbor came, he was stationed at Randolph Field, Texas. Shortly thereafter, he was ordered to an air base in Puerto Rico, where he began flying as a radio operator on patrols to find and sink German submarines in the Caribbean and Atlantic.

Grady finished high school in 1942 and enlisted in the Marine Corps. He went through boot camp at Parris Island and was then sent to San Diego.

Returning one day from a flight, Jesse was handed a telegram: "Mama very sick. Come home." He obtained emergency leave, found space on an Air Corps plane headed for the mainland, and wound up at Maxwell Field. He caught a Greyhound Bus to Remberton. From the station there, he walked to the mill village.

It had been nearly two years since he had left. Now he could hardly imagine ever having lived there. The narrow dirt streets, the small, unpainted houses, crowded close together, presented a scene of unbelievable drabness. He had been gone too long, had seen a world totally unknown to these people.

Several neighbors were sitting on the front steps when he walked up. "Jesse," one of them said, solemn faced, "I hate to have to tell you this, but your mama died this afternoon." He found out that she had had pneumonia for over a week. He was inclined to think that she had just worn out, that after years of hard field work from dawn to dusk, giving birth to six babies, cooking and washing all the time, she was too tired to go on.

Along about dark, Grady arrived from California, wearing his Marine Corps dress uniform, resplendent in blue and red, looking far more glamorous than the son of a tenant farmer and mill hand had ever looked.

One of the men on the front porch said, "Grady, the women gonna be falling all over you in that fancy outfit."

"Worse things could happen," Grady said.

A little later, one of his old drinking and carousing buddies came by in a second-hand Model A Ford, and Grady took off with him. They called after him from the porch, "Grady, don't forget the funeral at two tomorrow."

The next day, as that hour approached, Jesse and his father and a little knot of mill hands and their wives, along with the preacher, were gathered outside the Shiloh Baptist Church on the lonely dirt road a little beyond the house and sorry land where Sadie May had spent so many years. Lem looked tired and bent, wearied by time and toil. Jesse, in his army khakis, now sporting sergeant's stripes, had gone from a boy to a man since he was last here in this godforsaken stretch of country. They had all come out on a company truck.

Lida Bell, her enormous pregnant belly encased in a billowing cotton dress, was there with her husband. "Bo's mama's taking care of the children right now," she said. "There's three, soon to be four." She smiled and patted her great bulge.

Peggy Sue, also pregnant and only a little smaller in girth, stood by holding the hand of a three-year-old boy. "Joe Tom couldn't get off at the shipyard. With the war and everything, they working around the clock."

The plain wooden coffin rested nearby on the ground. They were waiting for Grady.

"Ain't nobody seen him all morning," one of the men said.

Another said, "That boy what picked him up last night just lives a little piece on down this road. Maybe he's down there."

"If he don't show up in a minute or so, I'll get in the truck and go down there and see."

It was late spring, and the day was hot. The sun beat down out of a clear blue sky. The land around them was deserted, still and quiet, except for crows cawing raucously somewhere in the distance. A light wind played mournfully in the tops of the pine trees surrounding the little cemetery.

Then somebody said, "I think I see him coming."

They all looked westward along the road to where it disappeared over a low hill about half a mile away. A lone, hatless figure was walking toward them. As he drew nearer they could see he was in a light brown shirt, sleeves rolled up above the elbows and no tie. He wore Marine Corps dress pants, blue with a red stripe down each side.

The breeze kicked up little swirls of dust in the road as he came on, angling toward one side and then the other.

One of the men mumbled, "Looks like he's drunk."

Another said, "Ain't the first time."

He came up to Lida Bell first. "You ought to be ashamed of yourself," she said, in a low angry voice. His shirt was wet with sweat. He was unshaven and exuded an aroma of stale liquor. He seemed oblivious to the crowd.

The preacher moved out in front of the group. "All right, sisters and brothers, let us proceed with the service."

Four men picked up the coffin and followed the preacher toward the freshly dug grave on the far side of the cemetery. The rest moved along after them.

The men wrestled the coffin down into the grave, while the others gathered around. The preacher read from the Scriptures, prayed, and read on.

"The Lord is my shepherd. I shall not want...." He was interrupted by a wretching sound at the rear of the group. Grady was throwing up—three prolonged heaves. Heads turned to look, but the preacher continued, hardly missing a beat.

"He leadeth me beside still waters ..." He thanked the Lord for the life of Sister Sadie May and asked that she be granted a well-deserved and eternal rest.

Jesse stood by, cap in hand, hearing his mother saying, "You got to get out of here. You got to make something out of yourself."

※   ※   ※   ※

Jesse stopped. "Excuse me, but would it be possible to have another cup of coffee?"

"Oh, sure." Noble picked up the phone and asked Miss Alice to refill their cups.

Then he leaned back in his chair, exhaled and said, "That's quite a story. Looking back on it all, it's hard to believe those times."

"The remarkable thing is that I was able to put it out of mind for so long."

The two said nothing for an interval, reflecting on it all.

Then Noble said, "You mentioned a Craighill girl. I assume that's Catherine, the daughter of Dr. Lucius Craighill."

"That's my recollection."

"And that McKnight girl, Julia, was the daughter of Judge McKnight."

"I'm not sure who her father was. But I did know that Lucille was the daughter of Sam Funchess. He was the real villain in our lives."

"You might be interested to know that Lucille's daughter is getting married this Saturday. Those other two girls, Catherine Craighill and Julia McKnight, are still here. All this is interesting, but I'm wondering what it has to do with anything now.

"I apologize for taking so long. I thought it important to give you the background so you would understand what I'm going to ask you. I'm getting to the point, if I can lean just a little more on your patience."

He hesitated as Miss Alice came in with the pot of coffee. She refilled their cups and left.

Jesse went on. "Grady was in some pretty hard fighting in the Pacific—Iwo Jima and Okinawa. But he got through it all. He came home and went back in the house with our father, who was still working at the mill. He got a job with a building contractor—Denkens by name."

Noble interrupted. "I knew the outfit well—Denkens Construction Company. In fact, our firm represented Denkens for a while."

"Well," Jesse said with a touch of sadness, "Grady didn't live long. A year later I got a message he had drowned. Never heard any details."

Noble straightened up. "You know, I now remember that. What I recall about it is that Will Denkens, who was then our client, said it was a strange accident. He was sorry because he said Grady was a good worker, but—I hope you'll excuse my repeating this—he was something of a hell raiser."

"A womanizer, too, I gather." One of the fellows in my Air Corps squadron was from Chicago and he persuaded me to go there when we were discharged. I went because I didn't have anything to come back to in Remberton. First worked for a trucking company, on the loading dock. But I was driven by my mother's urging that I make something out of myself. So with the GI Bill, I enrolled in Northwestern University and graduated there with a major in economics. I went with a bank but after a couple of years I joined a brokerage firm and stayed there until my health forced me to cut back a year ago. I made a lot of money and was lucky in investments."

Noble was shaking his head. "A real Horatio Alger story."

"But my greatest financial break came when I married Isabel Stephan." Jesse explained her inheritance of millions and how it all came down to him when she died three years ago.

"Are you living alone now?"

"Yes, in the Stephan mansion on the North Shore, right on the lake. Twenty rooms to myself, with a housekeeper during the day. But I don't know how long that will last. Had a slight stroke a year ago and a heart attack before that. To put it mildly, I'm not in robust health. And this gets me to the reason why I've come to see you."

"Good," Noble said, smiling and hiding his relief at finally getting to the point-or at least he hoped so

Chapter 3

The clock in the courthouse tower boomed ten. Jesse Rooter had been there an hour telling his life's story. Noble was beginning to get impatient, wanting to know the purpose of this visit.

He said, "To be perfectly frank—and I think we should be—I would say that I detect a tone of bitterness."

"Bitter is an understatement."

"It's understandable, but what's that got to do with seeing me?"

There was a knock on the door. Noble said, "Come in."

Miss Alice strode in, saying, "I thought you might like some fresh, hot coffee."

"It would hit the spot," Noble said.

She refilled their cups. Looking at Jesse, she said, "Mr. Rooter, wasn't Grady Rooter your brother?"

"Yes, he was," Jesse said.

"I thought I saw a resemblance. He was two years ahead of me in high school. Played football. The girls all flocked around him. It was sad what happened to him."

"Yes, it was. I appreciate your comment."

Miss Alice left, and Jesse resumed. "It was the way this place treated me and my family. We were nobodies, non-persons. It was as though we didn't exist." Jesse's voice took on an angry tone.

Having heard Jesse's background, Noble now understood his face. In the eyes and complexion he saw traces of what he had seen in hundreds of faces over the years, the faces of men who grew up on pellagra-and-hookworm-ridden hard-scrabble farms, laboring in the field from dawn to dusk, that flotsam and jetsam of poor whites out of the trauma of war and Reconstruction and decades of eking out a bare living under the one-crop cotton system on infertile land, taken to new depths by the Great

Depression. The experience etched itself so deeply in the face—even an otherwise handsome face—that not all the years of Chicago stock brokering and North Shore living could entirely eradicate it.

Noble said, "In retrospect I see it clearly. There was a pretty firm class structure in place—the town and the mill, the well-off and the poor, black and white. I have to admit I was part of it. I simply grew up with it and didn't think about it. It was just there, like the trees and the courthouse."

"But, as I told you, you were the only person who ever did anything to help us. That's why I'm here."

"Well, what can I do for you?"

"I had sworn I'd never come back after Grady died. But in recent weeks an idea has been growing in my mind, been building up and has finally brought me back." Jesse paused and sipped coffee.

"Go ahead," Noble said.

"It's revenge. I'd like to get back at this place in some fashion, to pay them back, to force them to recognize my family, to make up for the way we were treated."

"You're here to tell me you are plotting revenge on Remberton?"

"It's not that simple. The revenge I want would not harm the place. On the contrary, it would confer a benefit. But it's got to be something that will get this bitterness and anger out of my system."

"Revenge that will confer a benefit," Noble said, as though talking to himself. "A novel concept."

"Get back at these people in some way that will force them to recognize the Rooters and relieve my bitterness. Money is no concern. I may not have much time left on this earth, and I've got more money than I know what to do with."

"Not a bad position to be in," Noble said, with a slight smile.

"This bitterness is like a hot coal burning in my stomach. I've got to get rid of it."

They sat in silence for a few moments, Noble pondering the oddity of Jesse's idea. Then he said, "I think what you have in mind could be called a constructive revenge, maybe a benevolent revenge."

"You've got it."

"But why are you telling me this? What do you want me to do?"

"I would like to ask you to think about it. If possible, to come up with a good idea."

"To figure out how to wreak revenge but without doing harm?"

"You're the only person I can hope to get help from," Jesse said.

Noble, not addressing Jesse but looking at a row of law books beyond him, murmured, "Benevolent revenge? A fascinating concept." Then turning to Jesse, he said, "O.K., I'll take you up on it, but I don't promise results."

Jesse rose. "Good! I'll call you back tomorrow or the next day. I expect to be here for a little while, looking around."

When the door closed behind Jesse, Noble stood by his desk for a long minute. He was perplexed by this man, a man who had come out of nothing, and was now a multi-millionaire, running with the North Shore social set. Thirty years ago they would hardly have spoken to each other, certainly would not have sat down as equals in a law office discussing some big money transaction. Now, this meeting left Noble with the feeling that he liked this man, a feeling that they could get along well together. After all, they both came out of the soil of Rembert County, although under radically different circumstances.

But most of all, Noble was fascinated by Jesse's unique and creative idea, and he wanted to see how it might play out. Maybe he could steer it toward something truly good for the town.

Outside on the sidewalk, Jesse looked up at the courthouse, a formidable brick structure on a circular island, presiding over the head of Center Street like a giant mother hen. It was the seat of nothing good in his life. It looked the same as he remembered, unchanged among all the surrounding changes. The tall clock tower seemed to bear down on him oppressively.

It was a warm spring morning. Only a few white fluffy clouds punctuated the deep blue sky. He had forgotten the easy feeling of early spring in Alabama, such a contrast with the frigid weather he had just left in Chicago.

Now, with mixed feelings, he would look at some of the sites of his youth.

He got in the Ford he had rented at the Montgomery airport and started the engine. In cars, as in other matters, his taste was simple, unpretentious. He drove away; circling the courthouse and heading back down Center Street. Many of the stores were empty and locked, victims of the shopping center out on the interstate. He passed the bank, bringing back memories of the humiliating scene when his father, desperate for money, had been turned down by Sam Funchess. The very thought of that man caused him to grit his teeth.

When he stopped at a traffic light, the motor died. This had happened earlier. Although it started again, he decided to have it looked at. He headed back uptown. A block down from the courthouse on a side street he found a Ford dealership. He pulled in the service entrance.

A stout man in greasy coveralls approached. "What can I do for you?"

Jesse explained the problem. The man agreed to take a look at it within a couple of hours. He motioned Jesse over to a waist-high counter.

He pulled over a form on a clipboard, picked up a greasy pencil, and said, "What's your name?"

"Rooter, Jesse Rooter."

The man scribbled on the form. He looked up under shaggy eyebrows and thick gray hair and said, "Right after the war I worked with a fellow named Grady Rooter. You any kin?"

"He was my brother."

"Well, I'll be damned. Yeah, we worked together on some construction jobs."

"Was that with the Denkens Construction Company?"

"That's right. He was a good worker when he was sober. He'd get drunk on the job sometimes, and old man Denkens would ball him out. Almost fired him several times. Too bad what happened to him. I never did understand it."

"What do you mean?"

"Well, you know they say he drowned in Possum Creek. But that didn't make no sense. Him and me went up the road that night to the beer joint in his car. He had this convertible he bought when he come home from the war. When we got back from the beer joint he let me out around ten o'clock. We'd had a good deal to drink, but he wasn't drunk. What in the hell would he be doing twelve miles out of town on the creek after he let me out?"

"I never did hear any details," Jesse said. "What did they say happened?"

"The sheriff said they found his car parked near the creek with empty beer cans on the floor and an empty fifth of bourbon on the seat. But when I got out, there weren't no cans or bottle in the car."

"What do you think could have happened?"

"I don't know. It just all looked funny to me."

"Was there an investigation?"

"All I know is what the sheriff said."

"Was there an autopsy?"

"Never heard of one."

"Well, I appreciate your telling me this," Jesse said. "By the way, what's your name?"

"Earl Scroggins. I'm head of the service department." They shook hands, and Jesse left, saying he'd be back in a couple of hours.

Deciding to use the time to walk around town, Jesse headed out along Oak Street, a block over from Center Street. He thought back on his meeting with Noble Shepperson. He had been apprehensive over what his reception might be. Would he be met with a cold indifference, with no interest in his problem? After all, Shepperson was a member of the class that had so looked down on his family, had treated them as dirt. Jesse had been banking on that touch of humanity Noble Shepperson showed thirty-five years ago out at that Godforsaken house—and he had not been wrong. He sensed that this was a man he could talk to, one who was not hung up on that old class structure. He had a glimmer of hope that this trip might not be in vain after all.

Oak Street had seen better days. On one side were the backs of the commercial buildings that fronted on Center Street. On the other were dilapidated old houses, mostly Victorian but a few dating from the antebellum era. Deferred maintenance was everywhere obvious.

He was about to turn and walk over to Center Street when he noticed a sign just ahead reading "Remberton Public Library." Something made him stop and contemplate what he saw. The sign was in front of a small two-story frame house, probably built around the turn of the century. He walked ahead and stood in front of it for a moment. Then, on impulse he went up the short walk to the small porch and went in.

He was in a medium-sized room with book-filled shelves on all walls. Two small tables were piled high with books. Straight ahead was a desk, behind which sat a woman, wearing large tortoise shell eyeglasses. Her blond hair was pulled back into a ponytail. She was affixing tape to the spine of a book.

"Good morning," Jesse said.

She smiled and said, "Good morning."

"I'm from out of town. Just passing through," Jesse said. "Is this the main library for Remberton?"

"It's the only library," she said, "small as it may seem."

"May I look around?"

"Certainly. Anything special you'd like to see?"

"Well, maybe. Do you happen to have a collection of Remberton High School yearbooks?"

"We surely do. In the local history section. I'll show you."

She got up and led Jesse into a rear room. He thought her more trim and shapely than she had appeared behind the desk. She was trailed by a faint rose petal scent.

In the back room every square foot was filled with books. They lined the walls and filled two large tables.

"As you can see," she said, "we're a little crowded for space. Sorry we don't have room for a table where you can work. But at least here's a chair. Now right here we have the *Remberton Echo*, dating back to 1930. I believe that's when it began to be published." She pulled the chair over near the shelf.

"Thanks," he said. "I'll just sit here and look at a few."

She retreated to the front room, saying, "If you need any help, let me know."

He sat down next to the shelf, moved his finger along the spines, and slid out the *Echo* for 1940. He and Grady had never bought a copy of their yearbook because it cost $10. He opened the book and saw in alphabetical order pictures of the senior class. And there in the right order was himself—Jesse Rooter in his high school incarnation. Unlike most of the other class members, he had no organizations or activities listed with his name. He had always worked after school and had no time for anything else. The face was thin and nondescript, not that of one who would be picked out for any distinction in life. Rifling through the pages, he recognized many of his classmates, faces he hadn't seen or thought of for over thirty years. He had no real friends among them and didn't know what had become of them.

He slid the book back on the shelf and pulled out the volume for 1942. Among the graduates he found Grady Rooter. In these high school pictures there was a noticeable family resemblance between the two brothers. But Grady was the more handsome. Here in the yearbook Grady was smiling broadly, which, together with his open-collared shirt and thick wavy hair, gave him a devil-may-care look. Varsity football and the R Club were listed with his name.

Jesse perused the pages depicting earlier classes. In the class two years behind Grady he came across the three girls who had fascinated his brother: Lucille Funchess, Julia McKnight, and Catherine Craighill. Then there was Amanda Harris, and several other girls who ran around together in that tightly knit social set in a world unknown to and inaccessible to the Rooter boys. Some innocent looking, others with a sensual air. All, he mused, now had to be post-menopausal.

Jesse sat for a few minutes, reflecting again over those years of his youth and the mill village. Then he rose and went forward to the front room.

"Do you have more rooms in the library?" he asked the woman at the desk, still taping up broken spines.

"One more in the rear and two upstairs. All packed just like these."

"She paused, studying his face, and then said, "You look familiar. Could I have seen you before somewhere?"

"It's possible. I grew up here. Could you tell me your name?"

"Catherine Craighill."

"Catherine Craighill?" he repeated, incredulously. She bore little resemblance to the sexy teenager he had known and whose picture he had just seen. She was now a matronly middleager, but not bad looking. He recovered himself and said, "Yes. I remember you. In fact, I just saw your picture in the *Echo*."

"No wonder you didn't recognize me. There's a lot of change and not for the better."

"You weren't wearing glasses in the picture."

"Now that's a sweet thing to say. And what's your name?"

After an instant's hesitation, as though he might not respond, he said, "Jesse Rooter."

"Jesse Rooter! My lord. You're Grady Rooter's brother! I can see the resemblance."

"That's right."

"Well, I declare. You look like you've done pretty well, gone a long way from RHS."

"Can't complain." Jesse felt all the old distaste for her and her crowd—one of those high and mighty girls, as Grady used to say, but not looking so high and mighty now. He didn't care to prolong the conversation. "I'd better be going." He left her sitting there with a puzzled look.

Jesse walked over to Center Street, looking for a place to eat lunch, shaking his head over the extraordinary happenstance of encountering one of those girls. He had never expected to see anyone of that crowd. It made him wonder again why he was here.

Going toward the railroad station—or what had been the railroad station—he passed two places that were restaurants, but both were dark and locked. Up a side street he saw the open ground where a sea of mules and wagons had parked on Saturdays. It was now empty. The sidewalks, back then overflowing with country folks in for the day, were nearly deserted.

He turned around and headed back up the street, passing again the bank, the post office, the park with the Confederate statue. Finally he found a small dingy sandwich shop behind the courthouse. Sitting on a stool, he ate a grilled cheese sandwich and Coca-Cola, mulling over what Scroggins had said about Grady. It was disturbing. Jesse wanted to know more. He got up and walked back to the Ford place.

He stood inside the service entrance for a few minutes until Earl Scroggins saw him.

"Got you all fixed up to go," Scroggins said. "Carburetor just needed a little adjustment."

"How much will that be?" Jesse said.

"No charge. It just took a minute."

"Well, I certainly want to pay you for your time."

"Don't worry about it. Glad to do something for Grady's brother."

"That's mighty nice of you. I appreciate it. If you don't mind I'd like to ask you a little more about Grady's death. Is anybody still living around here who would know something more about it? How about the sheriff?"

"He died ten or twelve years ago."

"Did the prosecuting attorney look into it?"

"I don't know, but he's still around. You could ask him. He's the judge now—Judge McKnight."

"How about the coroner?"

"I don't remember who the coroner was."

"The whole thing does sound strange," Jesse said, looking vacantly into the shadows of the garage. "But it's been nearly thirty years ago, so there's probably not much we can do about it. Can you think of any reason why anybody would have wanted to do Grady in?"

Scroggins said he didn't really know of any. Every now and then Grady would get in a fight up at the beer joint, but, Scroggins said, he didn't think anybody would want to kill him. He added that Grady was a hell raiser and ran around with a good many women. It was possible, he speculated, that somebody might have gotten crossed up with him on that account.

"Do you know who any of those women were?" Jesse asked.

"Only one I heard of by name was Gladys Kinston. She worked out at the glove factory."

"Is Gladys still around?"

"I think so, but I ain't seen her in several years."

"Anyway," Jesse said, "I'm glad to have met you, and I appreciate hearing what you've said about Grady."

They shook hands, and Jesse backed his car out and pulled away.

He was again having second thoughts about this trip. There was no joy in it, no fun. Nothing here brought back happy memories. There were no happy memories to bring back. He was a stranger in what was supposedly his home town. But he had never really felt part of the town, never integrated into its life. The disquieting question about Grady's death had cast an even darker shadow over it all. Why was he punishing himself?

He swung the car on to Center Street, through downtown and under the railroad, and up the hill to the road that led south to the mill village. Shortly, on his right, he saw the sprawling, dark brick structure where his father had labored for $18 a week. But had it not been for that building, he would not have known where to turn. Everything else was different. The old store and a filling station that had stood at the corner had been replaced by a Laundromat and a shiny new station.

He turned in and was met with an even more changed scene: the street was now blacktop; the small frame houses where he and all the other mill families lived had vanished. It was hard to believe that they had ever existed. In their place were a couple of one-story office buildings, a maintenance shop, and parking lots. The mill itself was now a shirt factory. He thought he found the spot where his house had stood, but he was not sure. The era of the cotton mill with its looms and clanking machinery run by unlettered refugees from the piney woods and hill country "lint heads" was gone, a demise that, as far as he was concerned, was unlamentable.

Jesse circled back on to the main road. Eight miles south of town, he turned his car off the highway into a small county road, blacktopped now. But there were no farms left. Tall longleaf pines lined the road for miles, all owned or leased by paper mills. The land had been given back to what it was naturally suited for. The Rooters' ramshackle cabin where Noble Shepperson had pulled up so long ago with an eviction warning had disappeared absorbed into endless rows of pines. He couldn't even tell where it had been. Though the scene was different, he could almost taste the memories, as though they were a tangible substance that he could neither swallow nor spit out.

But the Shiloh Church was still there, an island in the pine woods, in use, but unpainted and in need of maintenance. He parked off to the side on the clean-swept, hard-baked ground. The only sounds were the distant cooing of doves and the soft murmuring in the tops of the pines, stirred by the light April breeze. The world seemed devoid of life, human and animal. Even the buzzards that once floated lazily overhead had disappeared.

He walked past the frame church building into the small, deeply shaded cemetery. He remembered the Rooter graves as being on the far side, so he moved through the rows of graves. Some were unmarked mounds of dirt, some marked by hand-lettered wooden boards, some with regular head stones, but nothing elaborate. He thought of Gray's elegy: "Nor you ye proud impute to these the fault if memory o'er their tombs no trophies raise …"

At the rear he found them—four side by side, each with a small granite headstone bearing the name and dates of birth and death: Lemuel Rooter, Sadie May Rooter, Bessie Ann Rooter, Grady Rooter. Years ago, after he had made some money, he had contacted the undertaker in Remberton and arranged to have these granite stones put here, to replace the hand lettered wooden markers.

As his eyes fell on Grady's grave, he was brought up short. Right beside the headstone was a bunch of purple and white gladiolas and green ferns. The container was wrapped in colored tinsel and ribbon, like that provided by florist shops. The flowers were bedraggled and wilting but not yet dead, obviously put there only recently— maybe for Easter Sunday, just a few days ago. But by whom? Jesse puzzled over the startling sight. Nothing gave any clue of the flowers' source. As far as he knew, no Rooter kin were left anywhere in these parts. But obviously some living person remembered Grady fondly enough after all these years to go to the trouble of placing flowers on his grave in this forlorn cemetery. Who could it be? How could he find out?

Chapter 4

At mid-morning the next day Jesse Rooter and Noble Shepperson again sat facing each other across his desk, cups of coffee in hand. After a few pleasantries, Jesse said, "Do you remember anything about my brother Grady's death?"

"Only that he drowned. I recall that because my firm represented Denkens where he was working, and I had to fill out some papers for their records. Why do you ask?"

"Yesterday I stopped by the Ford place to get my car checked. It turns out that the service manager, a fellow named Earl Scroggins, knew Grady, worked with him on some construction jobs. Do you know him?"

"Known him for years. Represented him once in a divorce case."

"I was awake half the night thinking about what he said. He was with Grady the night before they found his body in the creek. Says it doesn't make sense, why Grady would be way out there in the country by himself in the middle of the night. He's always thought there was something peculiar about the whole thing. If it wasn't an accident, then we're talking about foul play of some sort, even murder."

There was silence for a few moments. The word murder hung in the air. It startled Noble. In this quiet town murder was not something contemplated or often encountered. He thought Jesse must be overreacting, too edgy about the local scene.

Then Noble said, "Does Scroggins have any facts to suggest that?"

"Apparently not. It's just a feeling."

"Feelings don't usually get us very far. What could have possibly been the motive?"

"I asked Scroggins the same question. The only thing he can think of is that it might have been connected to Grady's womanizing. He got around a good bit. Maybe an irate father or brother or husband wanted to get rid of him."

"Well, I guess that's a possibility."

"I doesn't feel right just letting it go. Would you be willing to investigate it, find out everything about it, get to the bottom of it? Of course, I'll pay whatever your fee might be."

Noble sat still for a long moment, taking a swallow of coffee. Then he spoke slowly and reflectively. "Folks have died, memories faded. And this womanizing thing could get us into some ticklish territory. If I did an investigation, what would you do with what I found?"

"Depends on what it is."

Noble hesitated again, gazing out the window. He felt sorry for Jesse, felt that maybe Remberton owed him something. He turned to face him.

"In my judgment, it's unlikely we'll find much after all this time. You need to understand that. But if you want to pay for the trip, I'm game to try."

"Good. I realize it's a long shot. Just keep me posted. Now let me get on to what we talked about yesterday. Have you come up with any ideas?"

"Afraid not. I can think of ways you could zap the town, and I can think of ways you could benefit the place. But to do both at the same time strikes me as a near impossibility."

"I'm not giving up. Something may come to me as I look around. The more I see of this place, the more it all comes back, and—I hate to say this—it all feeds my desire for revenge."

Noble saw no light side to this man. He was somber and bitter. Yet he did not dislike him. In fact, found him interesting. "Do you plan to be around for a while?" Noble said.

"I may drive down to Mobile for the weekend to see Bellingrath Gardens. Some friends of mine in Winnetka were there last spring and said they're well worth visiting. But I'll be back and would like to talk with you some more." Jesse rose and Noble came around to shake hands.

"O.K., Jesse," Noble said, "have a good weekend. Let me know when you're back."

Jesse left, and Noble stood by his desk for a long moment, reflecting on the man. Something about him made Noble slightly uneasy. It was a vague far off feeling that Jesse's return bode no good. A year later he would remember this moment and this feeling, wishing to God he had heeded it and gotten Jesse to turn around and go back to Chicago and forget Remberton.

When Jesse returned to the Cedar Crest Motel after lunch, he was handed a message: "Please call Catherine Craighill," with a phone number. He couldn't imagine what she wanted. It occurred to him that times had really changed if a Craighill was calling a Rooter. He was not enthusiastic about talking to her again, but he nevertheless dialed the number.

The answer came in a smooth, husky voice. "Hello."

"Catherine Craighill?"

"Yes?"

"This is Jesse Rooter."

"Oh, I'm glad you called. I had to track you down through three motels. I was wondering whether you could drop by for a drink late this afternoon. I know this is short notice, but I would love to chat with you some more."

Jesse could hardly have been more startled. He was tired and had no desire to see Catherine Craighill again. Yet something made him pause. "Let me call you back in a few minutes," he said.

"All right. I hope you can make it."

He mulled it over. It would be a novel Remberton experience. He had always wondered what those houses were like on the inside. Now here was a chance to see and to get insight into this slice of Remberton life today—and possibly learn something helpful for his revenge scheme.

So he called back and accepted, adding, "Where should I come?"

"To my house, the house I grew up in. Do you know where it is?"

"Passed it hundreds of times. Always wondered what it was like inside." His voice had a sharp edge that he tried to minimize.

"Well, now you can find out."

So it was that at five o'clock, Jesse, having driven along the tree-shaded street lined with old houses and well-tended lawns where he and Grady had walked through their high school years, pulled his rental car into the driveway under the oaks surrounding the Craighill house. A Cadillac was parked at the far end. The frame structure was built high up off the ground in what was referred to as the raised cottage style, popular in the 1850s. Red azaleas, now in full bloom, lined the walk to the front steps. Sounds of birds, not yet heard on the icy shores of Lake Michigan, filled the balmy air.

Catherine answered the doorbell promptly and led him into the parlor. It was a spacious, high-ceilinged room crowded with antique sofas, chairs, and tables. An oriental rug in deep reds and blues covered the floor. "Please sit down," she said, motioning him to a sofa behind a marble-topped coffee table.

He could hardly believe this was the woman he had seen at the library yesterday. Gone were the eyeglasses and ponytail. Instead, she wore a fuchsia cocktail dress, form fitting and short. Her wavy blond hair—possibly out of a bottle, he thought—came down just below her ears. A string of pearls hung against her pale skin in the v-neck cut of the dress. She gave Jesse the impression of a woman several years younger than he knew her to be.

"Now," she said, "What would you think of a martini?"

"If you're having one, I'll join you." Jesse had determined to put on his best diplomatic style.

"Martinis are among my favorites, but I mix them only on special occasions. Excuse me for a minute."

Jesse surveyed the room, bathed in late afternoon sunshine. So this was what it was like inside the home of the renowned Dr. Lucius Craighill, premises that in his youth had belonged to another world. He felt awkward, not knowing what they would or could talk about.

She came back with two oversize martini glasses, filled to the brim. "Martini glasses in most bars are too small," she said, as she placed one on the coffee table in front of Jesse. "I found these in a little shop in Atlanta."

She sat down opposite him in a wing chair and crossed what Jesse observed to be quite shapely legs, skirt coming up just above her knees. "Here's to having you in Remberton after all these years," she said, extending her glass toward him.

Being served a drink by this unreachable stuck-up bitch—as Grady used to call her—was almost too much for Jesse to absorb. But in the spirit of the moment, he responded, lifting his almost overflowing glass and then bringing it to his lips. The ice-cold gin—he couldn't detect any vermouth—created a fiery stream down his throat.

He said, "I can't imagine why you wanted to see me. To be frank, and I hope you don't think I'm being rude, I can't see what we could talk about, what we would have in common."

"We were in high school at the same time. I knew who you were, knew you were Graddy's older brother."

"That didn't mean anything back then. I don't remember that you ever spoke to me. We were in different worlds." He suddenly thought he had gone too far, was being unnecessarily curt. After all, she had invited him to her home.

She said, "Let's just jump over that. I'm very much interested in where you've been, what you have been doing. First, are you married?"

"No, not now. I was married up until three years ago when my wife died. We had no children."

"Oh, I'm so sorry. So you're living alone?"

"Yes, in a house far too big for me."

"Well, tell me what you've done since you left Remberton. You've obviously been a success."

Jesse began with his army service, then to Chicago, through college, and into the brokerage business, the gin propelling him to talk at greater length than he had intended. By the time he reached the point where he was living on the North Shore and a partner in his firm in the Loop, their glasses were empty.

"Time for a refill," she said, picking his glass up off the coffee table. She disappeared into the hall.

Jesse felt strangely relaxed on the deep-cushioned sofa. The room was aglow with light from the setting sun, filtering through the curtains. He himself was suffused with a glow from what must have been the equivalent of two normal martinis. Catherine Craighill didn't seem too much of a bitch after all.

As she came back with two refilled glasses, Jesse asked, "Who is that?" pointing to an oil portrait hanging over the mantel. It depicted an elderly gentleman with a neatly trimmed beard.

"Walter Craighill. My great grandfather. He was a doctor here. Also surgeon in an Alabama regiment in Virginia. He's the one who built this house."

Emboldened by the martini, Jesse felt impelled to get out some of his true feelings. "I want to be honest—and I hope this doesn't offend your hospitality—but I hated this town and just about everybody in it. Swore I'd never come back."

"Did that include me?"

"Sorry to say, but it did—you and your friends, riding along in fine cars, going to school, passing Grady and me on this street as though we were invisible."

Ignoring his charge, she said, "I remember Grady at school. He was cute, a good talker, a big flirt."

"But, of course, you and the others would never have considered dating him."

"I guess you're right. You know how it was—the mill village and all that."

"I know it all too well." Reminding himself again that he ought to suppress his irritation—after all, he was her guest—he took a larger than intended swallow of the martini.

"Well, look," she said, "all that was a long time ago. Let's forget it and start with now. Feeling the way you did, why have you come back?"

"That's complicated, so if you don't mind I'd rather not get into it right now. Anyway, I've been doing all the talking. How about telling me about yourself? What happened to you after high school?"

"I went off to Randolph-Macon. Lucille Funchess—you may remember her—now Brentson, went to Sweet Briar, so we always traveled up on the train together. I eventually graduated and then went to Emory to get a master's in English. That's where I met my husband." She sipped her martini.

"I gather he's not in the picture now."

"Hasn't been for a long time. We were living in Atlanta, had two daughters. Then he got going with this floozy in his office. I took those vows seriously, said them right here in St. James Episcopal Church, he did too—talking about till death do us part. Ha!" She laughed derisively. "What a joke. Didn't mean anything to him. He took off, got an apartment, and she moved in." She seemed to be warming to the subject. "What a son of a bitch!" She sighed in disgust.

"What did you do then?"

"Lived on in Atlanta for a few years, got our children through high school. By then Daddy had died, and Mama was living here alone and not very well. So I moved back."

"How long has that been?"

She finished sipping the martini and then said, "Five years. Too long, I'm thinking. Mama died two years ago. Been by myself since then."

"Then you and I are in the same boat. How does it work for you?"

"Oh, I don't know," she said, letting out a sigh. "Lonesome sometimes. I work half-time at the library. Have some old friends here. There are folks around town who say I've let myself go. But what the hell. I don't care what they say."

"I don't see anything let go," he said, but immediately regretted it, realizing it was two martinis speaking.

"Thank you," she said.

They were both quiet for a moment. Only the chirping of birds and the ticking of the hall clock could be heard. Then she said, "I see your glass is empty and mine is too. I mixed up plenty more."

"I think I'm all right," Jesse said, feeling a considerable buzz from the two drinks. He doubted his ability to drive to the motel if he had another.

She was back in a couple of minutes with a full glass. "Sometimes when I'm drinking martinis I need a cigarette." She went to a chest of drawers, opened the top drawer and pulled out a half-filled pack. She sat down in the chair and shook out a couple. They dropped on the rug. She picked them up and said, "Would you like one?"

"No, thanks. Doctor took me off them after my stroke and heart attack."

"They're just tobacco. I don't go in for the other stuff. Now where in the hell is the damn lighter?" She went back to the drawer and found a silver-cased lighter. Back in the chair she lit up and inhaled deeply.

Jesse was shocked at her language. Here was the daughter of a supposedly refined family using language his mother, wife of a mill hand, would never have used. He wondered if she talked this way only when she was drinking.

Picking up the drink off the side table, she said, "Now, where was I? Oh, the divorce. I'll say this about it. He paid plenty for it. I inherited a good bit from my parents, so I'm not hurting financially." She stopped as though to reflect on the matter, drew on the cigarette, exhaled, recrossed her legs, and took a swallow from her glass. "How about you?"

"Not hurting. My wife's father was a packinghouse mogul, and he left everything to her, and she left it all to me. Not bad for a tenant farmer's son."

"Oh, you've got to get over all that. Think now, not then."

Jesse was quiet for a moment and then said, "I still don't understand why you invited me here. You would never have thought of it thirty-five years ago."

Sitting still, legs crossed, cigarette in one hand, glass in the other, she said slowly, "I wanted to see what another Rooter was like—to see how much the older brother was like Grady."

"Sounds like you knew Grady better than I thought you did. Did you ever see him after high school?"

"Did I see him?" She uttered a scoffing laugh. "Did I ever see him! Let me tell you. Or maybe I shouldn't." Her voice was slowing and slurring.

"Please do," Jesse said.

"It was the summer of '46. I was home from college. That place was like a damn convent, so I was in the mood for some excitement. Daddy had a construction company adding a family room on to the rear of the house. So who shows up on the crew but Grady Rooter. Ha!" She took a long pull on the cigarette, exhaled, and turned up the martini for a swallow.

Jesse admired her capacity. He thought he should go before she became outright drunk. Twilight was well advanced. But his curiosity was now peaked.

He said, "You say he showed up here on the construction job?"

After pausing as though her mind had drifted off on something else, she said, in her now labored and slowed speech, "He began to make eyes at me. I hadn't seen him since he left high school. But here he was, not a boy, but a real grown man, a Marine Corps veteran, even more handsome. Had a fancy red convertible. My parents would have had a fit if they had thought that I was fooling around with him."

"Just a nobody from the mill village."

"There you go again," she said. "All right, that's what they thought. But that was years ago. Forget it." Then slowly, after a pause, "I shouldn't be telling you this, but, hell, it's been a long time ago and you're his brother, so I might as well get it all out."

She crushed her cigarette in an ash tray and leaned back in the chair, looking beyond Jesse into space. Then he saw tears welling up in her eyes. Suddenly she burst into crying, holding her face in her hands and sobbing. Unsure what to do, he picked up a napkin and went over to her.

"Here, take this."

She took the napkin and began patting the tears. "Please excuse me. Don't know why I did that." She regained her composure so he sat back down on the sofa.

Then in a soft, dreamy voice she said, "Grady drowned not long after ... after ..." Her voice trailed off.

Jesse waited a few moments and then said, "After what?"

She sighed, then a long drawn out, "Nothing. Just heard he drowned in Possum Creek." She emptied her glass.

It was now dark. No light had been turned on, but Jesse could still see her indistinctly in the gloom. He stood up, saying, "Thanks for the hospitality, but I must go."

She got to her feet unsteadily. "The pleasure has been all mine. Whoever thought a Rooter would show up here after all this time. We need a little light." Sniffling and wiping her eyes, she fumbled at a lamp switch and turned it on. He came from around the coffee table to go.

She came close, studying his face. He felt the warmth of her body. She exuded a mixed aroma of cigarette smoke, gin, and sharply sweet perfume. "I see Grady in the hair and eyes." She touched his cheek.

He let her comment pass, "Well, I doubt we'll see each other again, but I'm glad for this visit."

"I hope you think better of me now than you did."

"You're not the person I knew then, but I didn't really know you then. Anyway, thanks for the drinks." He headed toward the front door.

She followed unsteadily and said, "Listen," taking his arm as they reached the door, "we need to talk again."

"Even with a boy from the mill?"

"No." She dragged out her words, squeezing his arm. "A gentleman from the North Shore." She looked at him, imploringly. "Need to talk some more. You can't just go."

"Maybe sometime, but I must leave now. Goodnight." He went quickly down the steps.

Jesse was lying in bed half awake in his motel room the next morning when the phone began to ring. His watch read ten minutes to nine. He roused himself, picked up the receiver, and said, "Hello."

"Jesse, this is Catherine." The voice was vibrant and alive. He was surprised to hear from her and amazed at her apparent recovery.

"How are you?" she said.

"I'm fine. Just waking up. Thinking about heading out to Mobile."

"Don't do that. There's something here you need to take in this evening."

"What's that?"

"Lucille Funchess, that is, Lucille Brentson, has a daughter getting married this afternoon. She's having a massive reception at her house afterwards. I don't want to go by myself, so I'd like you to go along."

Jesse was so taken aback he couldn't think of what to say. He hesitated. "Is that the big house Sam Funchess built?"

"Yes, but what's that got to do with it?"

"You don't realize what he did to my family."

"Sam's long dead."

"Aside from that, I can't go uninvited to somebody's wedding reception."

"You won't be uninvited. I'll call Lucille and tell her you're in town. Over three hundred people are coming, so one more won't make any difference. She knew Grady, and I'm sure she'd be extremely interested to see you."

"Maybe and maybe not. But I've got a lot of bad memories of her father. It wouldn't be very enjoyable."

"Oh, come on now." She switched into a pleading voice. "Be a good sport. You may never be in Remberton again. I'll take care of you."

After protesting a bit more and turning it over quickly in his mind, he reluctantly agreed. His martini evening with Catherine had mellowed him a bit on her—and, he had to admit, stimulated a mild interest.

"Good," she said, "I'll pick you up at the motel at 5:30."

Chapter 5

On the lawn and under the trees in the rear garden of Lucille Brentson's house some three hundred guests mingled with high spirited conviviality. The wedding had been at four o'clock in the Methodist Church and now the reception was in full swing. Under an expansive blue-and-white striped open-sided tent, a wooden dance floor had been laid, and the Capital Six, a dance band from Montgomery, pounded away. Round tables for eight, covered with white cloths and bearing arrangements of cut flowers, ringed the lawn, some occupied by guests drinking and feasting from the copious offerings spread along buffet tables. Other guests stood and chatted, many crowding the three bars. On the slower numbers the dance floor was filled with the older crowd, but when the music accelerated the floor was packed with the younger set, including the ten ushers in cutaway morning coats and the ten bridesmaids in peach-colored, form-fitting tea-length dresses.

Noble Shepperson turned away from the bar, a fresh gin and tonic in hand, and strolled over to the hostess, who was animatedly talking with anybody in earshot. Lucille Funchess Brentson was a woman of average height, with a busty, sensuous build, a lot of brown hair with pleasantly encroaching gray. Although she had a prominent nose and cheekbones and a slightly hard look, the face was not unattractive.

"Well, Lucille," Noble said, "It doesn't get any better than this in Remberton."

"It's good of you to say that, Noble." She laughed and added, "Can the handsomest man here give the bride's mother a big hug?" She threw her arms around his neck and pecked him on the cheek. He gave her a quick, unenthusiastic squeeze around the waist.

Noble did indeed cut a handsome figure, as tall and erect as he had been on the Plain at West Point four decades ago, iron gray hair only slightly receding from his widow's peak, and waistline under control, helped by Wednesday afternoons on the golf course.

Lucille said, "Some people may think this reception is too much, but with just one daughter this is my only chance."

"Whatever they think, they're not reluctant to take advantage of the food and drink."

"Well, I want everybody to have a good time. I really don't care what they think." She took a swallow of white wine. "Isn't Ellen just beautiful?" She was looking across a short stretch of lawn at her daughter, in a white hoop-skirted dress. "That's my wedding dress, you know."

Ellen had sandy blond hair and rather sharp facial features. She was more petite and overall prettier than her mother.

"I suppose I should say she's as beautiful as her mother."

"Only if you mean it," she said, smiling coyly.

"I guess Jack Palmer's quite a catch for Ellen."

"I should say so. There're better looking men, but no better family in Montgomery."

"You mean no richer one, don't you?"

Lucille smirked. "That helps." Then, looking toward the house, she said, "Who's that man coming this way with Catherine?"

Noble's jaw dropped. It took a second for his brain to absorb what he saw. He managed to say, "His name is Jesse Rooter."

From laughing jocularity, Lucille's face went blank. "Rooter? Rooter?" she gasped incredulously.

Noble could not have been more surprised if the Queen of England had appeared. How could Jesse Rooter, son of the cotton mill, gone thirty years, be at this reception? And with Catherine Craighill? He said the first thing that came to mind: "He's just passing through town. Does the name mean anything to you?"

"My God," Lucille murmured under her breath, staring at the approaching stranger as the couple drew nearer.

Catherine came up and said, "Lucille, here's a ghost out of the past. Jesse Rooter. He just showed up unexpectedly and I thought you wouldn't mind if I brought him along."

Lucille, thrown off stride, fumbled for words. "Well, er, of course …" There was no smile, no extending of a welcoming hand. "Are you Grady Rooter's brother?"

"Yes," said Jesse, his eyes locked on hers. "I apologize for intruding on your reception. Catherine insisted I come."

Other guests crowded in to speak to Lucille, and Catherine and Jesse were jostled aside. He turned on her irritatedly. "Hadn't you prepared her for me?"

"I'm sorry I forgot to tell you I hadn't been able to reach her. But it's all right. Let's go have a drink."

"It may be all right with you, but not with me."

Noble appeared at Jesse's side. "Thought you were in Mobile. You said you didn't know anybody in Remberton, much less Catherine Craighill."

Catherine intervened. "We got acquainted in the library. I thought this would be a great way for Jesse to have something to do in Remberton."

"Well," Noble said, "Jesse, you do get around fast. Let's move over here to the bar."

In his navy blue pin strip suit, Jesse fit right in with the crowd. Catherine was a standout in a low cut, lime-green satin dress. It occurred to Noble that she looked better than he remembered, although he seldom saw her.

The band had slowed down and was now doing "Moonlight Cocktail." The surging crowd at the bar shoved Noble aside just as he was handed a gin and tonic.

He came face-to-face with Ben Harris, the physical opposite of himself, pale and slouched, with black horn-rimmed glasses and receding gray hair. He had the largest private library in the county. In addition to being the best-read man around, he was also well informed on local history and gossip and not reluctant to talk about it, including his own genealogy—he, Benjamin Tyler Harris, being a scion of one of Rembert County's oldest families.

"Has it occurred to you, Noble, to wonder what old man Sam Funchess would make of this show?"

"No, but now that you mention it, I doubt he would care much for it. For a man with as much money as he had, he surely didn't like to spend it. But his daughter's making up for lost time."

"He did break down and build this house, but I think that was at his wife's insistence."

The house was a huge two-story brick pseudo-Greek revival structure, the most impressive—some said the most ostentatious—residence in Remberton. Sam Funchess had built it in the late thirties, just before the war, at the edge of town. It sat well back from the street, behind a gently sloping lawn. A horseshoe drive swept up to the front portico. To its rear, where the reception was taking place, were two acres of lawn, trees, and a variety of plantings. This palatial spread was on a stretch of Jeff Davis Road where, since the war, numerous fashionable houses had sprung up, but none that could match the Funchess place, which the only child, Lucille, had inherited.

Ben said, "I'm probably one of the few people still around who remembers Sam when he hardly had a dime. Came out of nowhere, somewhere down in the county, below Shiloh, I think. But he was smart enough to buy a lot of cheap land, actually borrowed money to buy what looked like no-good land that turned into a gold mine when timber got going. He told me once, when he had bought a long stretch of empty land at Destin, that he believed in buying by the acre and selling by the front foot. That Gulf coast land turned out to be another gold mine."

"Before the war I represented him on some piddling matters. He was shrewd and could be ruthless. You probably remember he got into oil down in South Alabama and Mississippi. It's amusing to realize that some of these folks here wouldn't have given him the time of day in 1930, probably would have thought he was white trash. Now they think Lucille is the cream of society."

"Some memories are short," Ben said.

"Bob Brentson was more than willing to help Lucille spend Sam's money. He'd really be enjoying this occasion. Too bad he had to drop off so early."

They stood there, sipping their drinks and surveying the scene, nodding to various guests as their eyes met across the way. Noble knew Ben was one of those old Remberton folks who looked down on this opulent display of new money. To Ben, money was not the determining standard for one's position in society. What he wanted to know was who was your grandfather, or, better, your great grandfather. For him, there were people around town living in genteel poverty who were at the top of the social ladder because of their forebears. But he had to admit to himself in more rational moments that what gave those forebears the required status was, at least in part, money. He also privately recognized that in these parts there was very little genuinely old money. Whatever there had been had mostly gone down the drain during the war and Reconstruction, and if that didn't get it, the Great Depression had.

Noble fully understood the Ben Harris view about ancestral significance, had grown up with it, came out of the same background. But he took a more relaxed attitude, not greatly concerned with origins, ready to see through some of the hypocrisies and pretensions. If a man can come out of nowhere and make it honestly, he thought, more power to him.

The crowd swirling around him was indeed a mixture. There was old money, new money, and little or no money. There were those who doted on great grandfather, and there were those who knew nothing of their ancestors and cared less. Lucille obviously wanted to throw the biggest party anybody could remember and was not particularly discriminating in the guest list. Ben Harris had commented, "If you weren't invited to this wedding you're really out of it."

In the midst of noisy laughter, animated talk, and the throbbing band music, Noble felt strangely detached, looking at the crowd around him in a new and odd way, as though he were apart from it, as though he were sitting on an observation platform off to the side, all because Jesse Rooter filled his thoughts—Jesse with his strange idea of doing something to benefit the town and at the same time taking revenge on it, and then his notion of reopening inquiry into his brother's long-ago death. There was a delicious and amusing irony in this scene. Here were Jesse and Lucille whose fathers had identical origins, both coming out of dirt-poor tenant and sharecropping circumstances. The difference was that Sam Funchess had made a lot of money and Lem Rooter had made nothing. But now, a generation later, Lem's son, Jesse, had caught up. Indeed, judging from what Jesse had said, he could probably buy out this entire crowd.

In the distance, Noble saw Jesse and Catherine talking with Ben Harris' daughter, Amanda—a small, thin woman with bleached blond hair, making an obvious effort to be glamorous. She lived in Birmingham with her husband, an insurance company vice-president. She had been swept up in the Birmingham social scene, so it took a special occasion like this to get her back to Remberton. He smiled at imagining her reaction to encountering a Rooter here, if she remembered the name at all.

Noble said to Ben Harris, "I better find Nan. Have you seen her?"

"I think she's at that table down there at the far end," Ben said, motioning off to his left.

Noble edged his way through the crowd, many of whom were the bridal couple's out-of-town friends he didn't know. The band was now in a rock-and-roll style. Like the party swirling around him, the afternoon was perfect—the sky a blue canopy, the early spring sunshine warm but not hot, the air moving slightly, filled with the scent of flowers and freshly turned earth.

Noble was suddenly face to face with Judge Andrew McKnight. He had a rotund build, a fleshy face, and shock of still-dark hair. He had long been in the state senate before being appointed to the bench by the governor ten years ago.

"Noble, it's good to see you," the Judge boomed, exuding good cheer and extending his well-padded hand to shake. His left hand jiggled the ice in a glass of bourbon, the color of strong iced tea. "One of my father's rules was never let the sun shine on your whiskey. That's generally good advice if you want to stay away from AA. But, as we in the law appreciate," he chuckled knowingly, "there's an exception to every rule, and this afternoon has got to be one."

"Right," Noble snapped. "If this isn't it, I don't know when there'd be one."

"Well," the Judge said, enthusiastically, looking to Noble's side, "here comes Julia." Noble turned to face the Judge's daughter.

"Hello, Daddy," she said, patting him on the arm, and then, "Noble, you're looking mighty fit."

He nodded with a smile and said, "You're looking pretty sharp yourself."

She had married a local boy, Jimmy Goodson, while he was in medical school. He decided to come home to practice, and they had been back for many years. Their daughter was one of the bridesmaids. Julia was tall, comfortably filled out, with long dark hair and dark, deep-set eyes. A man would turn around twice to look at her.

"Ginger looks mighty pretty in that bridesmaid's outfit," the Judge said, referring to his granddaughter.

"Naturally we think so," Julia said. Directing her gaze across the crowd, she said, "Who's that man with Catherine?"

Noble looked that way and saw Catherine and Jesse talking with someone he didn't know. "His name is Jesse Rooter. He lived here years ago and is back on a brief visit."

Judge McKnight and Julia stared in that direction, said nothing for a long moment. Then Julia spoke up, "Jesse Rooter? Do you know him, Noble?"

"Just met him for the first time a couple of days ago."

"What do you know about him?" she said.

"Only what he told me. He lives in Chicago."

"Well," she said in a disdainful tone, "he had a brother named Grady—lived in the mill. What in the world is he doing here?"

Following up, the Judge said, "Noble, do you have any idea why he's here?"

"Not really. I'm just as surprised as you." He added, half jokingly, "Do you all want to go over and speak to him?"

"Not right now," the Judge said. "I'm about to head over to the bar."

Julia exclaimed, "Oh, there's Amanda. I haven't had a chance to talk to her yet, so excuse me." She turned and moved quickly away.

Judge McKnight took a swallow from his nearly empty glass and said slowly, obviously changing the subject, "Looking at all those cute bridesmaids makes a man wish he were forty years younger."

"You don't have to be forty years younger. I've known a lot of men your age who've taken up with some sweet young thing, got their batteries recharged, and went on for years."

"That may be all right for you friskier fellows, but it's too late in the day for me. The action would be a little swift." The Judge's wife had died five years ago.

"Now, there's Lucille over there," Noble said, with a whimsical smile. "A lot of folks think she's eligible. Not only eligible but interested."

"Maybe for somebody, but—I speak diplomatically—not my cup of tea."

Noble, though, couldn't get his mind off Jesse Rooter. "Judge," he said, "do you remember the incident when Grady Rooter drowned?"

The Judge was turning to go to the bar, but he stopped, face now serious, and said, "Vaguely. What about it?"

"As I recall, you were the solicitor then, and it occurs to me that you might recall something about it."

"That's been a long time ago. How does this come up now?"

"Jesse came by my office, out of the blue. I had never known him. He said he never had an explanation as to how his brother died and was curious whether I could shed any light on it. Of course, all I could say was that I just recalled the incident. I thought you might be able to give him some details."

"Afraid not. My recollection is that the sheriff found him drowned in the creek. Just an unfortunate accident." Turning away, he said, "My system is calling for a refill," and he moved toward the bar.

Noble sipped his gin and tonic and surveyed the crowd. Far across the way he saw Catherine and Jesse talking with some of the bridesmaids. He smiled inwardly at the thought that, in addition to Catherine, the McKnight, Harris, and Funchess women had all been mentioned in Jesse Rooter's recollections of his brother. But he was getting the impression that no one of them had any interest in such recollections, indeed had a distinct distaste for the subject. They were dealing with Jesse like the proverbial bastard at a family reunion. That is, all except Catherine, who seemed to be enjoying herself immensely.

Indeed she was. She and Jesse were again at the bar and she was getting her fourth gin and tonic. Jesse marveled at this woman's capacity but was now concerned about getting her home.

They filled plates with shrimp, cheese, crackers, hot meatballs, and crab dip, found two empty chairs off to the side, and sat down. After three bourbons on the rocks, the scene for Jesse was taking on a surreal quality. At all those years of black tie balls and dinners for the Chicago Symphony and at the Indian Hill Club, his past was behind him, out of mind. But here in Remberton he could not shake the thought that he was just the son of Lem Rooter, tenant farmer and mill hand. At the same time, he had difficulty comprehending that what he saw before him was in Remberton; it was not the Remberton he had known. This Remberton scene was as alien to him as a ball in Buckingham Palace. He tried to ward off the inferiority he had always known in Remberton by reminding himself that he was a multi-millionaire and a graduate of Northwestern University.

White-coated waiters moved about with trays of champagne. Catherine and Jesse each took a glass, and they sipped and ate without talking.

The band had switched from rock-and-roll and was now into "Sentimental Journey." "Oh," she said, "do I ever remember that piece. Why don't we dance?"

That was going too far for Jesse. He said, "Let me off on that. I haven't danced in years."

"Oh, all right, I won't insist," she said. "Confidentially, I don't like champagne. Let's get something better."

So they were back at the bar. She was handed another gin and tonic. Although his concern was rising, he figured he might as well go along. When would he ever be back in Remberton? This Remberton! At Sam Funchess' house! The thought brought him close to nausea. He ordered another bourbon on the rocks.

Around them was the jostling hubbub—shrieks of girlish laughter emitting from the bridesmaids, male guffaws here and there, music in ever-rising tempo and volume—waiters with flutes of champagne, and on all sides, chatter, chatter, chatter.

The spring twilight had passed and darkness set in as Noble and Nan drove home through the streets of the town. The bridal couple had finally cut the wedding cake and toasts had been made. Then they had disappeared into the house to change clothes, emerging to make a dash to the car, amidst showers of birdseed and rice and a cacophony of cheers and jokes and good wishes.

After Noble and Nan had ridden in silence for a few minutes, she spoke up with a weary sigh. "I thought the bride and groom would never leave."

"Different from us," Noble said. "Remember how we couldn't wait to get going. He laughed and slapped her lightly on the knee.

"We had something to look forward to. For this couple, tonight is just another night and another party."

Noble turned the corner near the Craighill house and slowed to look at the colorful array of azaleas, illuminated by the porch lights. Nan said, "I'll have to give Catherine credit for keeping this place up in good style."

After the war Nan had taken serious interest in gardening and had become especially interested in camellias, being fascinated by such colorful flowers in the middle of winter. She had learned about the numerous multi-colored varieties, but she particularly liked the pure white of the Alba Plena and the solid red of the Professor Sargent. It was her idea to have camellias planted all along their driveway. "I do believe that camellias are the best thing Remberton has to offer," she had said.

"How about your husband?" Noble had said.

"Well, next to him."

A moment after they passed the Craighill house, Nan said, "Incidentally, who was that man Catherine was with?"

Noble smiled. "None other than Jesse Rooter."

"Jesse Rooter? Isn't that the man who called you the other night?"

"The same. Why he was there tonight I haven't the foggiest notion. He hasn't been back in thirty years. He came to see me on a little business, but I had no idea he knew Catherine or for that matter anybody else here."

Nan said, "This sounds catty, but it seemed to me that Catherine had too much to drink."

"She was in a high mood. I wondered whether it was liquor or Jesse Rooter."

"By the way," Nan said, "I noticed that a lot of those snobs who look down on Lucille were taking plenty of her liquor and food."

"I guess you'd say that's an example of the hypocrisy around here. Which reminds me—because you'll think this is just another example—I heard several people this afternoon say how beautiful that dress is and how good you look today."

"You know how these folks talk."

"They're right. You look as good today as when I first saw you." He was making special efforts these days to behave in a way that belied his disquieting inner thoughts.

"Now don't you go lying too. Or maybe you've had too much to drink."

He pulled the car into their driveway and edged it into the garage.

As he cut off the ignition, Nan said, "Just sit here a minute. I want to ask you something."

Her tone of voice made him uneasy. "Go ahead."

"Recently you've seemed terribly preoccupied. Is something wrong?"

Noble was caught off guard and hesitated for a long moment. "Oh, nothing out of the ordinary. You know how I sometimes get worried about cases. Some have knotty problems." He tried to affect a casual air.

"I've seen that before, but you seem more distracted than usual."

"Well, anyway, it's not something you need to be concerned about." Opening the car door, anxious to change the subject, he said, light heartedly, "Let's go on in. I guess you'll say Lucille's spread takes care of supper."

"It certainly does."

"Then I guess there's nothing left to do but go to bed."

"I love your enthusiasm," she said, with barely concealed sarcasm.

Holding the door open, he said, "Come on. We'll see about that."

Chapter 6

▼

Jesse Rooter pulled the Cadillac into the Craighill driveway and shut off the engine. He had taken the keys from her as they left the reception. It was dark now, but under the porch lights they made their way to the front door.

As they entered the house, she stumbled against a hall table and mumbled, "Need a light." He maneuvered her into the parlor, found a lamp, and switched it on.

"Now," she said, standing unsteadily in the middle of the room, "we want a little brandy to top off this fine evening."

My God, Jesse thought, does this woman have no limit? He was about to object, but she was already moving into the hall. He followed her into what appeared to have been a butler's pantry. She opened a cabinet door. "There, see if you can find it."

Jesse had been relieved to get her out of the reception upright and without an embarrassing incident. But now that she was home he figured it didn't matter how drunk she got. He found the brandy and some snifters in another cabinet. He poured an inch into each glass and they went back to the parlor.

She plopped down on the sofa. "Sit down here," she said. "Tell me what you thought about this show. You have to understand this was a big day for Lucille—a very big day." She dragged out the words. "Jack Palmer is from an old Montgomery family with plenty of money. Lucille thinks that really makes her social position. I know Lucille. She can't fool me. She's mainly interested in money and men." She paused, laid a hand on Jesse's knee, and said, "But, you know, I like her anyway. She can be a little crude, but we've been friends a long time."

Jesse, sitting beside her, felt a fiery pool forming in his stomach as he took a sip. It suddenly occurred to him that he didn't have his car here. How was he to get back to the motel? It was at least two miles out on the highway. He could hardly undertake to walk, especially in his condition. Was there a taxi in Remberton? His blurred judgment told him that he should go now, but he leaned back on the sofa, snifter in hand.

He said, "Lucille could hardly have been colder. I thought you had explained me to her."

"Sorry I didn't get her. But it didn't matter. Actually, it was funny." She giggled.

"Not to me. I was a real fish out of water. Did you see the reaction of those other women when you introduced me? I had no idea the Rooter name would be remembered. How do you account for that?"

Her head rested dreamily on the sofa back. "Grady, that's it. I guess you didn't know him in those days."

"No, I was in Chicago."

She spoke in a labored fashion, as though special effort was required to enunciate each word. "He was a real rounder on that construction job. Worked in other houses." She stopped and closed her eyes for a few seconds. "I told you something about Grady last night, didn't I?"

"Yes."

"What did I say?"

"You just said he was making eyes at you while he was here on the job."

She sipped the brandy. "Well," she said very slowly, "there was more to it. Maybe I shouldn't tell you."

"Tell me everything you know about Grady."

"Now here's something nobody knows." She punched him in the arm. "I'm telling you, just you, 'cause you're his brother."

When she didn't continue, Jesse said, "Well, what is it?"

"One thing led to another. One day I was here alone, and he was the only one on the job. Somehow we ended up in the guest room down here." She motioned off to the side. "Next thing we have our clothes off—then we're in bed."

Jesse felt the impact of a hand grenade. Grady Rooter from the mill village here in this very house in bed with Catherine Craighill! A long silence ensued. Then, fishing for something to say, Jesse muttered, "Was that the end of it?"

"No. A week later we were at it again. Mama came home and found us. She pitched a fit."

"What happened then?"

"She told Daddy, and he got hold of Mr. Denkens, said he didn't ever want Grady back in this house again."

"Was that the end of it?"

She finished her brandy and closed her eyes. In a moment he saw tears rolling down her cheeks. Gasping, she said, "I can't talk anymore about it."

Jesse pulled out his handkerchief and mopped her face. He put his hand on her shoulder and said, "I'm sorry I got you into this. We don't have to talk about it."

She calmed and closed her eyes again, head reclining on the sofa. Jesse stood up. "I really must go. Is there a taxi in Remberton?"

She opened her eyes and murmured, "Don't know. Never use them."

"I'll check the phone book." He went to the telephone on the hall table. In the yellow pages of the slim directory he found one taxi. He dialed. After ten rings, he hung up.

When he returned to the parlor he saw that she was asleep. He shook her gently by the shoulder, but her heavy breathing continued.

He stood, uncertain what to do, aware that his mental processes were struggling through an alcoholic haze. Should he call for help? Who could he call? Should he just quietly walk out into the night and hope somehow to make his way to the motel?

He leaned over and pulled her into a reclining position lengthwise along the sofa. Could at least make her comfortable. He put a pillow under her head. He felt voyeuristic as he stood looking her over. He admired her pretty face and wavy blonde hair. His eyes traveled down her well-tapered legs to her high-heeled shoes. How can a woman walk on those spikes? He slipped them off. Then, thinking she might get chilly, he searched for a blanket and found one in a hall closet. He laid it over her, tucking it in around her feet and her rhythmically rising and falling bosom.

Tired and woozy, he wandered down the hall, went through a door, and saw the shadowy outline of a bed. He climbed on it, stretched out, and fell sound asleep.

"Are you awake?" The husky feminine voice caused Jesse to open his eyes. Though half asleep, he saw Catherine Craighill standing beside the bed, in her party clothes from the night before. Then he realized that he himself was still fully dressed in suit, tie, and shoes. Confusion and embarrassment swept over him. He blinked at the early morning sun spilling through the curtains.

She said, "I'm not much on breakfast. I can give you orange juice and coffee."

Stretching and struggling to sit up, now realizing what had happened, he said, "That's fine. God, am I embarrassed! Give me a few minutes to pull myself together."

She left, and he got up and went into the adjoining bathroom. "My God," he mumbled to himself, "how in hell did I get in this predicament?"

His head was throbbing. In the mirror he saw red eyes, unshaven face, sallow skin. He wondered about his heart. How much more of this could it take? Another night like the last two might do him in.

He took off his coat and tie and washed up. As he was drying with a towel, the startling thought struck him: He had slept in the same bed that Catherine had shared with Grady, at least according to her account. She surely would not be lying about such a matter. The two Rooter boys spending the night in the Craighill house—an almost unimaginable fact! But more than that: Catherine actually in bed with Grady! What kind of woman was this?

He shortly appeared in the kitchen. Catherine was now in a simple cotton dress. Her face looked freshly scrubbed, with no makeup. "There's juice," she said, motioning to a place at the small table. "Coffee's on the way. Would you like toast and peach preserves? That's about all I have."

"Anything sounds good, mainly coffee." His headache had not diminished. He marveled at her ability to recuperate; it seemed to be unlimited.

She poured their coffee, put some bread in the toaster, and sat down at the table. "I guess I really tied one on last night," she said sheepishly.

"I wasn't in much better shape. Don't worry. We got out of the reception all right."

"I want you to know that I don't do that very often. Remberton does get boring, and I hadn't been anywhere in a long time. So I just let it all out. Hope I didn't embarrass you."

"Oh, no. There were plenty of others well oiled, including me."

"I'm ashamed to ask this, but what did I talk about when we got home?"

"A little about the reception and Grady."

"What did I say about Grady?"

Jesse felt ill at ease telling her the truth, but he went ahead. "You said the two of you got in bed together here, twice."

"I said that? My Lord! I must have been really drunk."

"Maybe my presence pushed you over the edge."

"Might have. Brought back all those old Grady memories. Anyway please keep that confidential. I've never told anyone else. What else did I say?"

"That your father forbid Grady to come back here. You started crying. Is there more?"

She looked out the window toward the garden and said, slowly, "I don't mean to be rude, but I just don't want to talk any more about it."

"I'm sorry. But you brought it up."

"I know. In my drunken stupor. You must think I'm a lush."

Before he could comment, the toaster popped up. She rose and in a minute was back with a plate of toast and a jar of preserves. "Help yourself," she said. She sat down and resumed sipping coffee.

As he was spreading preserves on a piece of toast, she said, "I will say this. I had suspicions about Grady. Denkens was doing projects at other houses—a patio for Funchess, a kitchen for McKnight, remodeling the den at the Harris's. Those gals and I ran around a lot with each other and they all dropped some casual comments about seeing Grady for the first time since high school. I didn't say anything. We just didn't talk about him much. But there was something about their expressions and the way they talked that made me think something might be going on."

"Did you ever hear anything more specific?"

"Well," she paused, "I remember hearing that Julia McKnight had been seen a couple of times riding with Grady in his convertible. But I don't know anything else about that."

She got up, brought the coffee pot over, and refilled their cups. "To change the subject, I still don't understand why you're in Remberton."

"Had a little piece of business to take care of. But since I've been here I've gotten interested in finding out what really happened to Grady. The accidental drowning theory doesn't make sense."

"Why would you want to get back into all that?"

"I would hope the guilty would be prosecuted."

"Isn't it a little late?"

"Never too late for murder. I've retained Noble Shepperson to investigate. He'll probably want to talk with you."

"I'd rather not get mixed up in this …"

"I know, but he'll speak with everybody who had any contact with Grady that summer."

Jesse had finished his coffee and toast.

"I've considerably over-extended my welcome, so I really must go."

"Stay as long as you want. I have no plans."

"Thanks, but I'm thinking of driving down to Mobile to see Bellengrath Gardens."

"They should be at their height." She drained her coffee cup. "Well, if you insist on going, I'll drive you to the motel."

When they reached the front door, she laid a hand on his arm and said, "Just a moment." He turned to face her as she said, "I want to thank you for your visit. Most enjoyable weekend I've had in a long time. I hope you'll try to come back before another thirty years."

"Maybe so. I had never imagined my trip to Remberton would be anything like this. The place may not be as bad as I remembered."

He turned and they went out the door into the bright sunshine of the April morning.

By the time he showered, shaved, took aspirin, and put on fresh clothes Jesse had revised his plan. Something more insistent than Mobile was pressing on his mind.

Looking in the Remberton telephone directory he found only one listing for Kinston. It was Joe Kinston, with an address on Dalton Street. After eating a cheeseburger and milkshake at one of the fast food places surrounding his motel, he got in his car and headed into town.

Dalton Street was a fringe strip on the southern edge of town, the last white street before the black section known as Liberty Hill. He found Joe Kinston's house and parked.

He was in front of a small, one-story frame dwelling, in need of paint. An antiquated refrigerator, its door missing, stood on one side of the front porch. The weedy patch of ground in front of the house had not been cut in some time.

He mounted the steps and knocked. The screen on the door bulged outward as though someone had lunged into it. From somewhere inside came a rough male voice: "Yeah?"

Jesse said, in a raised voice, "Is Joe Kinston here?"

"Hold on," came the response.

In a moment a middle-aged, barefooted man appeared in the door. His face, hard and weathered, sported a two-day growth of beard. He wore a khaki work shirt with sleeves rolled up, wet under the arms and besmirched with dirt. "What do you want?" he said, in a tone suggesting he resented being interrupted.

"I'm looking for Gladys Kinston," Jesse said. "I saw your name in the phone book and am wondering whether you're kin to her, whether you can tell me how to find her."

Joe Kinston took in Jesse through the screened door, slowly and uncertainly. "Are you some kinda government man?"

"No. I just want to talk with her for a few minutes on a personal manner."

"You don't look like you're from around here." Jesse was suddenly conscious of his pinstriped suit, wishing he'd dressed more informally.

"Not now, but used to be. Anyway, can you tell me how I can find Gladys Kinston?"

"I don't want to get her in no trouble."

"She won't get in any trouble." Jesse pulled out his wallet and extracted a hundred dollar bill. "Here's something if you can help me out. All I want to know is how to find Gladys Kinston."

Joe Kinston pushed open the screened door and reached out. But Jesse held back the bill, saying, "First, where's Gladys?"

"She ain't Kinston now. Married a man named Houston. They're at the end of Locust Street, last house on the left, just before the filling station."

Jesse gave him the hundred dollars and left.

From fine houses close to the center of town, Locust Street petered out into much more modest habitations. The Houston house was where Joe Kinston said it was, next to a filling station, where town dribbled into country. It was a cut better than Joe's—painted and with a well-maintained yard.

In response to his knock, a middle-aged woman appeared in the doorway. Jesse said, "Are you Gladys Houston?"

"Yes, sir."

"My name's Jesse Rooter. Could I talk with you for a few minutes?"

"Jesse Rooter?" She emphasized the last name. "I declare! You're Grady's brother? You look a little like him."

"That's right. Been gone a long time."

She pushed open the screened door and said, "Let's sit out here."

They sat down in two wooden rocking chairs. The day was sunny and warm, but the shaded porch was cool. She wore a plain but neat dress over a slim figure. Her graying brown hair was short and well groomed.

"I can't get over it," she said. "After all these years. Jesse Rooter." She stared at him as though trying to convince herself that it really was Jesse Rooter. "I hope you don't mind if I say You're more dressed up than any Rooter I ever saw."

"Well," Jesse said, with a touch of embarrassment, "I've been pretty lucky. Hard to believe, but it's been nearly thirty years since I was here, on my way out with just the shirt on my back."

"I admire you, a very long way from that mill village," she said. What brings you back to Remberton?"

"It's complicated but one thing I'm trying to do is find out how Grady died. My impression is that you knew him after he came home from the service. Is that right?"

Her mouth spread into a faint smile. "Yes, I knew him all right. In fact, you'd have to say I was in love with him. I wanted to get married but he didn't."

"What was your situation?"

"Living at home, with Mama and Daddy, working at the glove factory. I left that a year or two later and trained as a nurse. Still doing that, working at the hospital."

"Why didn't Grady want to get married?"

"Oh," she sighed, "he probably had too many wild oats to sow. I knew he was running around with other women."

"Do you know who they were?"

"Not specifically. I did pick up some gossip that they were some high society girls. But I didn't believe it. I couldn't imagine those girls giving Grady the time of day, him coming from the mill. But he and I had a lot in common. Same sort of folks."

Yes, Jesse thought, the same sort of folks—you, Grady, and me. Just mill village boys and glove factory girl. Their genes, their origin, were the same, yet he no longer felt that he belonged to his beginnings. Strange as it seemed, it came over him that he felt more comfortable with Catherine Craighill than with Gladys Houston.

He asked, "Were you and Grady still seeing each other when he died?"

"He'd been drifting away. Seeing less and less of me. I don't know if I ought to tell you this. Don't anybody know it except my husband and Joe—he's my brother. Mama and Daddy are dead."

"I wish you would tell me whatever it is."

"Since you're Grady's brother I guess you're entitled to know. Anyway, it's been such a long time, and it don't really make much difference now." She paused, looking off toward the open field across the road. A car swished by in front of the house.

When the sound of the motor died away, she said, slowly, "Well, to get right to it, I was pregnant. Been three months pregnant." Again there was silence, as though she found it too difficult to continue.

Jesse sat rigidly still, absorbing the bombshell. After a few moments he said, "Did he know?"

"Yes. I told him after two months."

"What did he say?"

"He was upset. Mumbled something about figuring out what to do. I told him the only thing to do was to get married, but he didn't want to."

"What then?"

"I was young and scared. Had to talk to somebody. So I told Mama. Then she told Daddy. He got madder than a wet hen, saying Grady would have to marry me. Called him all kind of names."

"Did you tell him that Grady had said he wasn't going to marry you?"

"Yes, and he said we'd see about that. Then Grady came by the house one night—I hadn't seen him for a couple of weeks—he'd been drinking. He wanted me to go out with him. Daddy met him at the front door and there was a terrible scene. My God, I'll never forget it." Her face twisted into a scowl.

When it seemed that she might not continue, Jesse said, "What happened?"

"They were yelling at each other. Daddy saying you got to marry my daughter and Grady yelling that nobody was going to tell him what to do. Daddy cursed him. I thought they would start hitting each other. My brother, Joe, was there, and he came up right by Daddy. Grady backed out the door saying he didn't have to stay there and listen to all that. He drove off in his car. Joe wanted to take off after him. He was yelling something like, 'I'll show that son of a bitch. But Daddy held him back."

"Then what happened?"

"I never saw Grady again. He drowned a week later."

They sat in silence. A couple of cars passed by. Finally Jesse said, "What did you do after that?"

"I was just sick, out of my mind; three weeks later I had a miscarriage."

Jesse couldn't think of what to say.

Studying her closely, he now saw in her face compassionate warmth, reflecting something in her make-up that must have drawn her into nursing. She had obviously lifted herself a considerable notch above her brother.

He said, "I'm terribly sorry about the trouble and heartache he caused. I wish I could do something about it."

"There's nothing to do. All over long time ago. In fact, I hadn't thought about it in I don't know when until right now. I've got a good husband and two grown children doing all right. So I've got a lot to be thankful for."

"What do you know about how Grady died?"

"Just that they found him drowned in Possum Creek. Must have been drunk."

"Do you have any reason to think it wasn't an accident?"

"I remember Earl Scroggins—he worked with Grady—telling me that he didn't see how it could have been accidental. But I don't know any more than that."

Jesse wanted to linger. She was an easy-going, down-to-earth woman, comfortable to talk to. But he thought he had gotten from her all that she was likely to say about Grady.

So he rose and said, I'm mighty glad to have had this chance to talk to you. I'm sorry for all the trouble Grady caused you. If there were any way to make it up to you, I would."

"No, there's no way." She had a wistful, far away look. "Are you here for a while?"

"Not long. I'm hoping to find out more about how Grady died. But it's been so long ago, I'm not likely to learn much."

With that, Jesse shook her hand, and they said good-by.

Driving away from Gladys Houston's house, Jesse felt the need to get out of Remberton to assimilate what he had seen and heard. His perception of the place and of Grady was now quite different from what it had been four days ago. He had seen more of Remberton society in that one night at the wedding reception than he had seen in all of his growing up years. And now with Joe Kinston and his sister Gladys he had seen the other side, actually his side. He was puzzled over what to make of it all and where he might go from here. He marveled over—had a grudging admiration for—Grady's ability to operate across a huge class divide, in bed with both the upper crust Catherine Craighill and the glove factory Gladys Kinston. At least with the latter there was a motivation for murder and two possible suspects. One living and one dead. Was there still more he hadn't yet heard?

He went back to the motel, put a few things in a bag, and took off down the interstate to Mobile.

Chapter 7

It was Monday morning. Noble Shepperson was in his office preparing for an upcoming oral argument in the State Supreme Court. He enjoyed those occasions, standing at the podium, facing nine black-robed judges arrayed behind the bench. In this process a lawyer was directly involved in shaping the law, as well as in resolving a dispute. His challenge was to convince at least five of those judges that the legal theory he was arguing was the correct one. He had won this case in the local circuit court, and the other party had taken an appeal. So Noble was in the preferred position of defending what had already been decided. The case was a controversy over title to land worth several hundred thousand dollars. The question dealt with an unusual aspect of the law of adverse possession. It was novel, and there was no prior decision directly in point. It was the kind of juicy, unresolved legal question that Noble loved. At this moment, he was engrossed in reading an Alabama Supreme Court opinion from the 1930s, thinking it didn't help him very much.

His reading was interrupted by the buzzer and Miss Alice's voice over the intercom. "There's a man on the phone who says he's General Toby Kendrick. Wants to speak to you."

It took a long second for the name to sink in. Not because it was unfamiliar, but because it had been so long since Noble had heard it, a name belonging to another time and place. Orienting himself to that world far removed from Remberton, he said, "Put him on."

"Noble, how in hell are you?" The voice was crisp and official, clearly not of southern origin, the voice of Lieutenant General Tobias Kendrick, West Point '33, Noble Shepperson's cadet company commander at the Academy.

"Hanging in there," Noble said. "How about you?"

"Taking life easy. Marla and I do a lot of traveling. Is Nan still there?"

"She is, but we don't get around a whole lot—too much law practice."

"Well I'm calling to see if we might do something about that." They exchanged a few remarks about their situations, but the General was not given to small talk, and he moved on briskly. "To get to the point, as you know, the thirtieth D-Day anniversary comes up in a couple of months. I'm putting together a small group of Academy graduates—bird colonels and up—who were actually there, to go over and help out with the celebration. I've discussed this with the Supe, and he likes the idea. We'd like you to go along—you and Nan. We'll have a good time of it."

Thirty years! Is it possible? He never expected to go back. "That's a bolt out of the blue. Sounds good, in fact, a great idea. But I'll have to take a look at my docket."

"O.K. Let me hear within a few days. We can get some special hotel rates, and there'll be some entertainment by the Brits, but I regret to say you'll have to pick up most of the tab yourself. Unfortunately, we can't travel at government expense."

After they hung up, Noble leaned back in his chair, images of Toby Kendrick flashing through his mind. He saw him over forty years ago, on the Plain out in front of the company, a rather dashing figure under a shako, in full dress with a red sash, shouting orders, saber in hand. Then there he was, a decade later, the assistant division commander, wearing a single star and steel helmet, in the hedgerows of Normandy, on the banks of the Rhine. The two hadn't seen each other since the war, although there had been sporadic contact. Noble felt a swell of excitement over this unexpected prospect of a reunion, of seeing England again, and—not least—getting away from Remberton for a stretch. He leaned back, eyes closed, memories flooding his mind.

* * * *

England, November, 1943. Autumn chill had set in; days gray and damp, intermittent mist and rain. But the grass was still green—green, green, green, so green it looked painted on. A vast mechanized, armed, and armored armada from the new world beyond the sea had been incongruously jammed in amidst the villages and thatched-roofed cottages of the West Country for one purpose: to prepare for the invasion of Europe. No one knew when or where it would be. They knew only that its coming was inevitable and that when that day came they had to be ready for a massive assault against the legendary Atlantic Wall.

The thundering roar of tank engines shattered the early morning tranquility of the English countryside. With their tracks clanking and creaking, the steel monsters, ninety-millimeter canon protruding forward like long metal snouts, resembled beasts from another world. They lumbered past Lt. Col. Noble Shepperson, standing with his staff officers, all in steel helmets, OD field jackets, and combat boots. Next came half-tracks filled with steel-helmeted soldiers, heading for a practice exercise.

When the last half-track passed, Noble turned and walked with his executive officer, Major Willis Dumfries, a couple of hundred yards across a field toward the eighteenth century manor house that had been taken over as regimental headquarters. Major Dumfries was a chunkily built man with a broad Midwestern face topped by crew cut red hair. He came from Topeka, Kansas, had gotten an ROTC commission from the state university, had returned home and gone into the insurance business, and had been called up after Pearl Harbor. He was amiable and efficient, and he and Noble worked well together.

In general, Noble liked his staff officers. Some, of course, were more engaging than others; he doubted, though, that any would have been his close friends back home.

The cool, moist English air brushed their faces as they walked, the raucous roar of the motorized force receding in the distance. Noble inhaled deeply, feeling invigorated in this post-dawn hour and looking forward to another cup of coffee. "If we're going to keep up this training we've got to have more ammo soon," he said.

"Division G-3 says the supply will pick up in a few days," Major Dumfries said. "Everybody's asking for more."

"Well, keep at it. You know the old adage about the squeaky wheel."

They walked up the stone steps into a hall. Noble went through the first door on the right into a spacious room that had served as a parlor. The room was filled with half a dozen folding tables, all army issue OD, behind which sat enlisted men with typewriters and in-boxes and out-boxes. Normally enlisted men were expected to snap to attention when an officer entered, but Noble had given orders that the formality was to be dispensed with here. There was too much coming and going and too much to do to be bothered with that. He walked through to the far corner and sat down behind his own folding table with piles of maps and mimeographed orders and SOPs.

A master sergeant approached. "Sir, here's a message for you. Left with the guard at the gate a little while ago."

Noble took the small, cream-colored envelope. The stationary and handwriting were feminine, and the paper emitted a faint fragrance. He read:

> My dear Col. Shepperson,
>
> On behalf of our Ladies Association, I want to say what an honor and pleasure it was to have you and your officers at the recent reception. We wish to do all we can, limited though that may be, to make your stay here as pleasant as possible, despite what must in the nature of things be somewhat onerous con-

ditions. Meeting and chatting with you was for me particularly enjoyable. I would be honored to have you and two or three of your staff come to tea some afternoon if you can break away, at least for a short while, from your training duties. May I propose this coming Sunday afternoon at 4? My home is only two miles from your encampment.

You may respond by sending a note to me at Hedgely Farm near Tiltham's Corner, Bramton.

Sincerely,

Jennifer Cromlyn

He remembered her immediately from the reception at the county hall two weeks earlier. She was the only one of the good ladies who had any youth, style, and attractiveness about her. Normally the prospect of having tea at some Englishwoman's home would have no appeal to Noble, and he would have politely declined on the ground that his duties allowed no time for such diversions, however pleasant they might be. But this fragrant note gave him pause. He remembered the warm, soft hand when they shook, the large bright eyes, the pink-flushed cheeks, the full head of wavy chestnut hair, the generous smile. How old was she? From what she had told him, she might be thirty, give or take a year. Husband with the British Army in North Africa. No children.

There are moments in life when one faces a choice to do or not do something, something ordinarily regarded as trivial and of little consequence but which in fact is of momentous import. Sometimes such a moment is accompanied by an ever so faint tick in the mind, as though it were a signal beamed in by some distant early warning system, an alert that this is no ordinary fork in the road. He heard it now, and heard it again … and again. His heartbeat accelerated ever so slightly.

He looked over the schedule for the days ahead. Sundays were usually light. Lots of weekend passes were issued. Disregarding the warnings, he took a pen and sheet of paper and wrote, almost involuntarily, as though some external force were propelling his hand. He thanked her for the kind invitation and said he and two of his staff would appear at her home at the appointed time.

Sunday afternoon had turned surprisingly mild. The sun was shining, and white clouds high up in the azure sky moved hurriedly from west to east. To accompany him, Noble had chosen Major Dumfries, partly out of obligation, he being the exec, and his supply officer, Major Dillon Waters, a South Carolinian, and graduate of the University of Virginia who went by the nickname "Bo." Noble had picked him because he thought he would add a desirable touch of sophistication to the occasion.

After the Jeep turned off the narrow country road at a small sign reading "Hedgely Farm," they passed along a lane, with no house in sight, a thicket of trees on one side and a fenced patch of pasture on the other where a half dozen wooly sheep looked up at them from their grazing. The lane turned and abruptly they were in front of a nondescript farmhouse built of dark red brick. The central portion was two-story but there were one-story appendages.

The lane circled up to the front door. The Jeep stopped and they dismounted. Noble told the driver to relax and stand by. A few seconds after he rapped the knocker on the solid wooden door, it was opened by an elderly woman in a simple black dress and white apron. "Come in, gentlemen," she said, "Mrs. Cromlyn is expecting you."

She led them through a small hall into a cozy sitting room crowded with a sofa and several overstuffed armchairs in a mixed blaze of floral prints. An electric heater—an "electric fire," as they learned—projected heat from the fireplace. Prints of hunting scenes hung on the wall. In the corner was a teacart.

The men stood in the center of the room, looking around but saying nothing. They were dressed in wool ODs, wearing Ike jackets, a waist-length fitted jacket that looked good on the lean build of Shepperson and Waters but went less well with the stocky Dumfries. With shiny brass insignia on the lapels, it was the dressiest outfit available in this wartime situation.

In a moment, Jennifer Cromlyn came through the door, smiling and radiating good cheer, her presence felt as well as seen. She wore a snugly fitting blue dress and cardigan sweater and seemed to be weighted down by necklaces and bracelets giving off a metallic jingle as she extended her hand toward Noble.

"Col. Shepperson, welcome to Hedgely Farm," she said. Her lilting, polished accent was entrancing. The pungent sweetness of her perfume extended well ahead of her. Her green eyes had a luminous intensity that made Noble slightly uncomfortable.

"This is certainly generous of you," he said. "Let me introduce two of my staff. This is Major Dumfries and this is Major Waters."

She shook hands with each, saying, "I'm delighted to have you. Now why don't all of you sit down?"

They let themselves down into the low, heavily cushioned chairs. Bo Waters, smiling, said, "It feels mighty good to be in a house again, somebody's home. Haven't been in one in months." He spoke in a husky low country accent.

"Certainly beats tents and Quonset huts," Dumfries added.

"This is just an ordinary English farmhouse, nothing pretentious," Mrs. Cromlyn said. "It's comfortable, though. Been in my family for over a hundred years. There used to be cows and hogs here, but now we have only sheep."

The elderly woman in black dress and white apron appeared in the doorway. Mrs. Cromlyn said, "This is Miss Sheffield. She's been with my family since I was a little girl." The gray-haired Miss Sheffield smiled slightly, and nodded her head at the group and moved to the teacart.

"I assume you'd like some tea," Mrs. Cromlyn said.

They all nodded and murmured assent, Noble adding, "I can't imagine an English afternoon without it."

Miss Sheffield proceeded to fill the cups, asking each of the officers if he would like sugar and milk or lemon. She passed them out and then distributed plates of scones, clotted cream, and tiny sandwiches with a filling they did not recognize.

"This is a refreshing relief from the chow line," Noble said, after biting into one of the sandwiches. "You said this place had been in your family. Are any of them here now?"

"No. I am holding down the fort with Miss Sheffield. My parents died some years ago. I have one brother who lives with his wife and two children in Winchester. He's an RAF fighter pilot. As far as I can tell, he has no intention of returning here. So it's left to me. Normally I would be in London with my husband."

"I'm wondering what you and your neighbors think about this huge American military presence in your midst," Bo Waters said.

"You may imagine what a drastic change it has been. All of a sudden within just a few miles we have these thousands of soldiers from another land with all of their motorized equipment—tanks, lorries, and guns everywhere." She smiled, poised to take a sip of tea. "But in spite of some complaining here and there we don't really mind. We know why you are here. I suppose you don't know when you're leaving."

"That's right," Noble said. "And even if we did, we couldn't say."

They chatted about the locale, its history and how the war was affecting it. She asked each about his home and family. Noble reported on his wife and two children, now at her home in Newburgh, New York. Bo Waters was unmarried but was engaged to a girl back home, where he had been in his father's mercantile business. Major Dumfries had a wife and small son and was looking forward to getting back to his insurance company. Miss Sheffield replenished their tea and passed the sandwiches and scones.

Mrs. Cromlyn sat opposite Noble in a straight chair, her legs crossed, skirt hitched slightly above her knees. He noted that her stockings were the cottony wartime variety. They covered legs that tapered down nicely into comfortable walking shoes.

In response to Noble's questions, she explained that she had attended Lady Margaret Hall at Oxford, had then gone to work for a small literary magazine in London, and there had met Edward Cromlyn, a barrister in the Middle Temple. They married but were together only a year before he shipped out to North Africa. The magazine she worked for shut down, so when he left she returned to Hedgely Farm.

"It must seem mighty quiet here, and lonesome, after London," Dumfries said.

"It can be so," she said, in a slightly wistful tone, "but I keep busy in Bramton with the Ladies Association doing what we can for the war effort. And then I need to keep an eye on the farm, although I have a long-time man who does a good job of running it for me."

Noble stood up, saying, "Mrs. Cromlyn, this is most enjoyable, but I'm afraid that duty calls. We're lucky to have this little time for a visit. We do appreciate your hospitality."

Dumfries and Waters rose and thanked her profusely. They all moved into the hall and toward the front door. Dumfries and Waters went ahead and aroused the sleeping Jeep driver.

Noble, lingering at the door, turned to face his hostess. "I can't tell you how good of you it is to have us out." His hand met hers—that soft, warm hand.

"It has been my pleasure," she said. "You'll have to come again." Her voice took on a hushed tone. "Even if the other men can't get away, perhaps you could pop out sometime for a brief respite." She stood close to him, continuing to hold his hand, their eyes meeting.

Noble hesitated, breathing in the sharp sweetness of her perfume. "That would be nice," he said quietly. "Maybe I can work it in one day."

Releasing his hand, she said, "You have my address, and you now know your way here."

He turned and moved swiftly down the steps, putting on his overseas cap. The Jeep motor started up as he slid on to the front seat.

"Not a bad looker," Bo Waters said from the rear seat, as the Jeep moved down the lane. "If I weren't already engaged I could get interested."

Noble looked straight ahead, saying nothing, but Dumfries said, "Didn't you hear her say she's got a husband?"

"Right," Waters said, "but he's in North Africa."

Autumn moved on toward winter. The chill and dampness were penetrating, making it seem colder than it was. The Bramton mayor told Noble, "There's a pint of water in every English mattress."

He and Nan had promised to write each other at least once a week and they held to that schedule. Her V-Mail letters arrived with regularity—small photocopies taken off microfilm—reporting on the children, then five and three. It was clear that she was enjoying life back in Newburgh, compared to that in Remberton, causing Noble to wonder how things would be after the war. His letters to her were short, mainly saying how much he missed them and asking that he be remembered to the children. There was not much else he could talk about.

His days were long, beginning at first light when he rolled off his folding canvas cot and pulled fatigues on over his thermal underwear and buckled on his combat boots. The days often ran far into the night. There were constant training exercises, regimental and divisional staff meetings, logistical problems, and efforts to keep morale up among the men. They all assumed that the invasion would not be launched until winter had passed, but they could not be sure. Their route to the Channel coast was worked out in detail so that when the order came they could move on short notice. He had little time to think about anything else.

One afternoon in early December, he and his driver were coming back in his Jeep from a meeting at division headquarters. At a crossroads he saw a sign reading "Tiltham's Corner," with an arrow pointing to the right. On sudden impulse, he said, "Corporal, take that right turn." In half a mile appeared a small sign announcing Hedgely Farm. "Turn in here," he said, "I've got to make a quick call."

His knock on the door was answered by Miss Sheffield. "Col. Shepperson! Come in."

As she closed the door behind him, he heard the voice of Jennifer Cromlyn from the rear. "Who is it?"

"It's Col. Shepperson," Miss Sheffield called back in a raised voice.

There was a long second of silence. Then, "Do show him in. I'll be there in a moment."

Noble was led into the room filled with floral printed armchairs. He stood wondering why he had stopped. In fatigues and field jacket, he was not dressed for a social occasion. Also, he was uncertain about what he would say, having given no thought to the matter.

She breezed into the room, smiling, hand extended, her thick chestnut hair looking a bit wind blown. "Col. Shepperson, what a pleasant surprise! Please pardon my appearance. I'm afraid you've caught me in my work clothes, but I'm delighted to see you." She wore a plain, long-sleeved housedress and no jewelry. She was about five feet six, not heavy but well filled out.

"You can't be dressed any worse than I am. I apologize for dropping in on you this way, but I was passing by and on the spur of the moment thought I would take you up on your invitation to pop in, as you put it." He became aware that, without thinking about it, he was continuing to hold her hand, that distinctively warm and smooth female flesh.

"Well I'm certainly glad you did. Would you like some tea?" Her English-accented voice had a musical quality.

"Thank you, but I can't stay long."

"Then at least sit down for a few minutes." He released her hand.

They sagged in the deep armchairs. "How have things been?" she asked. He was amused over the way she pronounced "been" as "bean."

"Busy, busy. Hardly a minute to spare. The build up goes on. Pretty soon your island might just sink under the weight of all this equipment."

"We do wonder where it can all be put. I noticed that another American unit of some sort has just moved in north of Bramton. I know you can't talk about what you're doing, but I would be interested in hearing more about you, your life before the war."

Noble studied her. She had an expressive face. He wanted to know more about her and not to talk about himself. But to answer her questions, he briefly told how he and Nan had met, how he got out of the army and moved back to Remberton to practice law, a big cultural adjustment for Nan. "Now what about you?"

"Not much to tell beyond what I mentioned the other day. My husband's been gone nearly two years now. I doubt that he minds, because I don't think married life really suited him. Maybe after the war when he's back it will all work itself out."

Noble was surprised at her frankness, but he made no comment.

She added, "Do you believe in that old saying that absence makes the heart grow fonder?"

"Sometimes it does and sometimes it doesn't." They lapsed into silence. The only sound was the ticking of the hall clock. Then he spoke. "The war has done strange things for lots of people, brought some together, pulled some apart. I would never be sitting here in this room if war had not come."

Her face had lost its usual cheerfulness, as though the sun had gone behind a cloud. "Yes," she said slowly, "That's an interesting point."

Noble couldn't figure where this conversation was going. He stood up. "I would like to stay longer, but I have to get back to my headquarters. Just wanted to say hello."

She too rose and said, "Thank you for stopping by."

They walked into the hall. As he reached for the door handle, she said, "Sunday after next our children's choir is giving its Christmas concert at the church in Bramton. They sing really well. Could I entice you into coming?"

She stood close to him, and he looked into her face—those large eyes, high color in her cheeks, wide moist mouth. Her smile was gone.

"It would be nice to have a touch of Christmas, but I'll have to check our plans. We could be off on maneuvers. Can I let you know later?"

"Oh, certainly. I could pick you up. It's at three in the afternoon."

The gray stone church stood on the corner of a crossroads in the middle of Bramton. Its square-topped tower emitted a peal of multiple bells, bass and tenor notes ringing interchangeably.

"This church was built in the sixteenth century but has been renovated twice since," Jennifer Cromlyn said, as she and Noble walked up the front steps. The December day was somber and chilly. Although it was only mid-afternoon, dusk was already setting in.

Inside, a center aisle ran the length of the sanctuary to an elevated altar, flanked by choir stalls. The walls were milky white, surmounted by heavy wooden beams across the ceiling. People streamed in and the pews filled rapidly. They sat down in one near the rear, uncomfortable with its perpendicular wooden back and uncushioned bottom. It creaked loudly as each new arrival sat down, gradually filling the pew to capacity, pushing Noble tightly against Jennifer, bundled up in a winter coat.

The organ, which had been playing quietly, suddenly ceased. A hush fell over the assemblage. Then the organ erupted with "O Come All Ye Faithful." Everyone rose. Down the center aisle came a procession of children, perhaps ten and eleven years old, more than two dozen in white robes, one of them bearing a cross and leading the way with the Rector. The congregation joined in the singing as the children took their places beside the altar.

The Rector opened with a prayer. Then the children sang a series of familiar Yuletide songs—"O Little Town of Bethlehem," "It Came Upon the Midnight Clear," and others. One of them read Matthew's version of the Christmas story in a high, thin English voice of one who had not yet reached puberty. Then came more singing—Christmas songs all well known to Noble, except "Once in Royal David's City," which he had never heard.

Noble was transfixed, his thoughts far away from this English village. Foremost in his mind were his children, just at the right age for Christmas at its most enjoyable and exciting. He should be there with them. These years would pass all too quickly. When, if ever, would he see them again? Christmases past filled his mind, those when he was growing up in Remberton, and, more pressingly, those with his little son and daughter—and with Nan. When the choir began "Silent Night" his eyes grew moist.

His mind came back to his surroundings as the Rector was delivering the closing prayer, invoking the blessings and care of the Almighty at this special season on the men who were far from home and family in the service of their country. The organ leaped into "Joy to the World," and the choir sang its way up the center aisle and out the back, the assembled throng lustily joining in.

Col. Shepperson and Mrs. Cromlyn came out into the chilly December dusk. They stood around for a few minutes, as she spoke to friends and introduced Noble as "one of the commanding officers from our nearby American encampment."

As they turned and walked toward her car, his eyes fell on a tall obelisk in the center of the square. "What's that?" he asked.

"A memorial listing all those from the county who fell in the Great War. The list is depressingly long. My uncle's name is there. He was killed on the Somme in 1916. I was a baby then and don't remember him."

They walked on. Noble had seen similar memorials in other English villages. He had become increasingly appalled at the loss of that generation. The American casualties paled by comparison. Would the lists be as long this time? Or longer? This war was far from over and the worst probably lay ahead.

She spoke up. "Could I entice you back to my house for tea? Or perhaps something stronger. Edward left a good supply of whiskey and I've scarcely touched it."

The prospect was inviting—the deep cushioned armchair, the warmth of the electric fire on this damp evening, a glass of Scotch, and most of all, he didn't like to admit, would be Jennifer Cromlyn's company, which he was finding increasingly congenial and attractive. But there again was that little warning tick from somewhere deep down inside. He hesitated, debating with himself. Then his resolve stiffened, and he said, "That's very good of you, and I do appreciate the idea, but I'm afraid I need to get back. We have an early move tomorrow."

"I'm sorry but I understand. Next week I'm going to Winchester to spend Christmas with my brother and his family. Perhaps you can drop out before then for at least a short Christmas drink."

He hesitated, then said quietly, as though thinking out loud, "Maybe I can. I'll be in touch."

Late the next Sunday afternoon, Noble found himself where he had been thinking about all week—in Jennifer Cromlyn's cozy sitting room in front of the electric fire, his second glass of Scotch in hand. She was drinking sherry and had just poured herself another glass. Instead of the armchairs, they were on the sofa sitting side by side. He had arrived by Jeep at four and told the driver to be back at 1730. He glanced at his watch: fifteen minutes to go.

Over the last hour the conversation had ranged widely. They had discussed the war, its effects on America and Britain, how it might all end, and what might lie ahead after it was over. She seemed starved for conversation and curious to know more about Noble—details about where he grew up, his schooling, his family. He was reluctant to talk about Nan, not sure whether to gloss over the situation with a few generalities or to level with her about the tensions and problems. He decided it was inappropriate to say much about his wife and instead deflected the talk to her, eliciting her recollections of growing up here on the farm, of her days at Oxford, and experiences in editorial work in London.

He was again surprised at her frankness. "It's peculiar, being married but without a husband. Most of the women I know around here who are my age have a man away in the war. It puts a lot of strain on the marriage. Some of them handle the situation by taking up with other men. Some go on with their lives. You get the impression they are rather relieved to have the husband gone, and then there are those who just pine away."

"And how do you handle it?"

She stared for a moment at the bottom of her empty sherry glass. "I try to keep busy with the Ladies Association and doing my bit, knitting, rolling bandages, and …" She paused and looked at Noble with a slight smile, at the same time placing her hand lightly on his knee. It was a gentle, almost unnoticeable motion, but the touch sent something equivalent to electric currents through his body. She added, in a softer voice, "Trying to boost American morale."

He took a swallow of Scotch, wondering what to say. "Well, I'd say you're doing a pretty good job of that. Here's one American whose morale has been boosted." Their eyes met, and they both smiled uncertainly, one of those exchanges that may portend a meaning that neither is quite willing to express in words.

She removed her hand and said, "Would you like another drink?"

Before he could answer, they heard the sound of a motor coming down the lane. Noble looked at his watch. "My driver is a little early." But as the motor grew louder and turned in front of the house, he said, "That's not a Jeep engine."

The vehicle came to a stop, engine idling loudly. "What on earth can that be?" she said, rising from the sofa and putting down her sherry glass.

The sound of muffled voices came over the engine noise. Then the vehicle pulled away. Immediately there was a loud knocking on the front door.

She went into the hall and pulled open the door. In a loud and startled voice, she exclaimed, "Edward! What a surprise! I thought you were in Africa."

"They shipped me out on short notice. No chance to let you know. How about a hug and kiss for the returning soldier?"

Noble could hear the rustling of clothing. Then the sound of a bag being dragged through the door.

"There," the male voice said. The door slammed shut.

"This is just too startling," Jennifer said. "I can't get over it, after nearly two years."

"You're looking the same, I'm pleased to say," he said with no particular enthusiasm.

"You look well, no worse for wear."

"Let me get out of this coat," he said. "I'll leave it here on my bag for the moment."

In a calm, low voice, she said, "We have a visitor in the next room. He's an American officer from the unit near here."

"Oh?"

"He's here to discuss plans for our Ladies Association program for his troops. Come in and meet him."

She came through the door from the hall, followed by a stocky man, not much taller than she, in a British officer's uniform. "Edward, this is Col. Shepperson." Looking at Noble, she said, "This is my husband, Major Cromlyn."

The two advanced toward each other and shook hands, coolly and formally. Neither man seemed to relish the encounter.

"Well," Edward said, "Colonel, I hope you're enjoying my wife's hospitality."

"It's generous of her and her organization to be looking after these foreigners."

"Yes. No doubt. She's good at things like that."

"Edward," his wife said, "may I get you something to drink?"

"Er, no thanks. Not at the moment."

"Col. Shepperson had just said he'll have to leave very shortly. But tell me, Edward, what's next? Are you here for long?"

"I'm to report to London for reassignment. Don't know what it'll be. The most I can hope for right now is a short Christmas leave." He turned to Noble. "Colonel, what sort of outfit are you with?"

"Armored infantry battalion."

"Here, I assume, to get ready for the big show?"

Jennifer said, "I think I hear a motor."

"That's my Jeep, I imagine," Noble said. "I must go. It's good to meet you, Major. I hope you have a decent Christmas leave."

"Thank you. We're counting on the Yanks, you know, so best of luck. I hope my wife can keep up your morale." Was this upper class English accent tinged with sarcasm or did Noble imagine it?

Before Noble could speak, she said, "I'll show you out."

They stood in the open doorway, Jeep engine idling nearby. He took her hand. "It's been a great pleasure. Have a Merry Christmas."

She smiled wistfully and looked into his eyes. Her bright luster had gone. "I know this must be a difficult season for you. Perhaps we can all look forward to better times. We can discuss the plans some more later."

"Yes," he said, quietly. "That will be fine." Squeezing and then releasing her hand, he said, "Good night." On impulse, he leaned over and kissed her quickly on the cheek.

* * * *

Miss Alice's voice on the intercom jolted Noble back from those long-ago events. "Amos Brewer is here for his appointment."

Amos Brewer, Amos Brewer … Noble thought hard to pull himself into the present. "Oh, yes. Send him in."

A heavy-set man in his early fifties, Amos Brewer had sharp, rugged features, weathered by years in the fields. He wore an old khaki army shirt—he had been a supply sergeant at Fort Benning for most of the war—and non-descript work trousers.

The highway authorities were poised to condemn a slice of his land to widen and straighten a county road. He was here to get Noble's help to block it or at least to minimize the amount of land taken.

"My place fronts on the road for a quarter of a mile," he said, as he drew a crude map on a piece of paper he laid on the desk. "It runs all the way back to Possum Creek, a half section altogether. Now if they take what they're talking about, the black top road'll come just fifty feet from my front porch. That'll put traffic right in my face. Then they want to take the whole corner here," he said, as he drew a diagonal line, "to straighten the road. They could do most of this by working on the other side of the road and leave me alone. Nothing much over there but woods."

Noble sat listening, asking a few questions. "Who's on either side of you?"

"On the north side there's the Timmons place. On the south side there's a dirt road back to the creek. You've probably been down there. It's a good fishing spot. You may remember that's where that fellow drowned, fellow named Grady Rooter."

"Grady Rooter? Did you know him?" Noble's alert system switched on.

"No. I think he worked somewhere here in town."

"Do you remember anything about the circumstances? It was August, '46, right?"

"Yes, sir. Hadn't been home from the army very long. I was out around the barn one morning when a man pulls his car in and says he's just been down to the creek and there's a red convertible with the door open and liquor bottles on the floorboards but nobody around. He thought somebody ought to call the sheriff. So I did. The sheriff and a deputy got out there in about half an hour, and we all went to the creek. Sure enough, there was the convertible with the driver's door standing open, but the top was up. There was an empty fifth of bourbon on the front floorboards and seven or eight empty beer cans in the back. The keys were in the ignition. The deputy went up and down the creek bank looking in the brush. About fifty yards downstream he found a man's body caught in some tree limbs up against the bank. He was lying face down in the water, dead."

"Did anybody know who he was?"

"The sheriff recognized him right away. Said he was Grady Rooter. Said he'd been a hell raiser ever since he got back from the war."

"Do you know what they determined to be the cause of death?"

"I heard later it was drowning."

"Do you know anything else?"

"Well, there is something I wondered about. The night before they found the body, I was sitting on my front porch with my wife. It had been a hot day, and we were glad to get some cool air. It must have been around eleven o'clock. A car passed in front of the house and turned in the road to the creek. In about five minutes another car comes along and turns off. I didn't think much about it because the spot on the creek was a favorite nighttime parking place for couples. So I figured these were some young folks heading for a little necking. In about fifteen or twenty minutes a car comes back out of that road and heads toward town. We went on to bed, and I never heard the other car come out."

"Was either car a convertible?"

"Couldn't tell. It was a dark night, no moon or stars, and I wasn't paying much attention."

"Do you know whether there was any further investigation?"

"Never heard of any."

They were quiet for a moment, Noble thinking. Then he said, "Well, O.K., let's get back to your condemnation problem."

Chapter 8

Noble Shepperson greeted Jesse Rooter as he walked into his office on Tuesday afternoon. "What in the hell have you been up to around here? I thought you were on your way to Mobile, but there you were at the wedding reception." He motioned Jesse to the chair in front of his desk. "I'll say this—you get around. For a man gone thirty years to show up at Remberton's fanciest social event accompanied by Catherine Craighill is going some!"

Jesse recounted how he had wandered into the library and met Catherine and how she had stunned him with the invitation to her house and then roped him into going to the reception. "It was strange, even weird. I couldn't get my resentment for her and all her friends out of my mind, but there I was, going along with the whole thing. Then, to make matters worse, she hadn't told Lucille I was coming. Did you see that frosty reception I got?"

"She did freeze up."

"Anyway, it's over. I came by here now to bring you up on what I've learned about Grady."

He told Noble what Catherine had said about her suspicions that Grady was up to some hanky panky with other girls, but he said nothing about her bed romps with Grady, thinking he ought to respect her privacy. He then went on to relate his meeting with Gladys Houston.

Noble said, "A fellow like her father, old Hubert Kinston—I knew him a little bit—could react pretty violently to a situation like that."

"Her brother Joe looks like a pretty tough customer."

"I've seen Gladys Houston for years at the hospital," Noble said. "She's one of our best nurses. This is pretty startling stuff. Does this mean that you've got a niece or nephew somewhere around here?"

"No. She had a miscarriage. Fortunately, I think."

"You have to wonder," Noble mused, "with a womanizer like Grady, whether there might have been other pregnancies."

"Can you investigate what happened on those construction jobs?" Jesse asked.

"You're talking about four pretty prominent families—three by ancestry, one by money. That's pretty delicate stuff."

"Aren't we wondering whether there might be any motive to do Grady in? That is, aside from Gladys' father and brother."

"So you're suggesting that Dr. Craighill, Judge McKnight, Ben Harris, or Sam Funchess might have had something to do with Grady's death?"

"I'm not suggesting anything except a thorough look into all possibilities, assuming nothing and letting the chips fall where they may. We know now that Gladys Houston's father had a motive, Also her brother, Joe. But were there others?"

Noble considered whether to tell Jesse about Amos Brewer's story, but decided for the moment not to do so. Instead, he said, "I'll have to give more thought to it all."

"I'm still thinking about the idea I mentioned, to see whether I can come up with a good scheme."

Noble laughed. "That combination of charity and revenge?"

"That's right."

"I'll tell you about a pet project of mine I've thought about for a long time. It may not fit your idea, but I'll just mention it. It would be to create a monument to the mule."

"A monument to the mule! Why would you want to do that?"

"The mule saved the South. After the war and during Reconstruction and the decades after it was the mule that plowed the fields, pulled the wagons, kept the whole economy going. Faulkner has a great tribute to the mule in one of his novels. I can see that as the inscription on the granite pedestal surmounted by a life size bronze statue of a mule."

"I have to say my memory of mules is not good. We had a bony, sour faced one called Job. I associate him with all those bad times of my childhood. And I don't see how the revenge element would fit in."

"You're probably right. But it would be a real tourist attraction here—the novelty of it, like the boll weevil monument down in Enterprise."

"An idea has occurred to me since we talked the other day. I'm still mulling it over. It has to do with the library. It looks pretty cramped. I don't know yet how it would fit my objective, but I'll be thinking about it."

"The library," Noble muttered, contemplating the thought. "That's not a bad idea. I know some people around here are concerned with its antiquated shape."

"I'll be thinking about it. But I don't want to give up on Grady. I have a growing hunch that there's more there than we know. Anyway, I think I'm about ready to get back to Chicago."

Jesse rose, and they shook hands. Noble walked with him out to the front sidewalk. They agreed that Jesse would call when he was ready to talk again. He got in the rented Ford and pulled away toward the courthouse.

Noble stood for a few minutes enjoying the April sunshine and thinking it all over. Only a few cars passed. Unlike a decade earlier, there were plenty of empty parking places up and down the block. Across the street, half the store buildings were unoccupied, including what used to be the town's leading department store, all victims of the shopping center out on the interstate. Abbott Drug Store, diagonally across the street, was about the only uptown business still thriving. Downtown the scene was the same. The railroad station, too, stood empty, passenger service gone. The three-block, oak-lined stretch of Center Street separating uptown from downtown, once filled with handsome two story residences, was now punctuated with an automobile dealership and a filling station, neither doing much business. The town had deteriorated architecturally. Was the place actually dying or was its life and heartbeat simply shifting out to the interstate? Maybe, Noble brooded, this was the end of one long era for Remberton and the beginning of another. Was there a parallel with his own life—one phase ending, a new one beginning? Inexplicably, he had a foreboding that something big lay ahead, that he might be on the brink of some sort of life-changing event.

Thrusting itself back into his mind was Jesse Rooter's hunch that there was more to Grady's death than they knew. He found himself agreeing, especially in light of Amos Brewer's report. Could there be some connection between Grady's death and his alleged dalliances on construction jobs? Noble could identify those jobs because he had represented Denkens back then and had a lot of the company's business records in his file storage room. The courthouse clock striking three reminded him to get back to work.

Late the next afternoon Noble was sitting on the screened porch at the rear of Lucille Brentson's house. It opened onto an extensive patio, beyond which was a long stretch of lawn, trees, and gardens, site of the recent wedding reception. Spring was now well advanced. The early green tint on the trees had turned into dark green leafage. The day was unusually warm; a ceiling fan rotated slowly overhead.

Noble was here as the result of a telephone call from Ben Harris telling him that the library board had just met and decided to launch a fund-raising drive to construct a new building and asking him to talk with Lucille. "Now that she's got that wedding behind her you might be able to get her attention," he had said. So Noble, not eager to take on this project but being the good citizen that he was, had called Lucille and set up this appointment. It was a happy coincidence that also served his other purpose.

She had just placed a gin and tonic in Noble's hand and sat down in a wicker chair beside him. "Now can you tell me to what I owe the honor of this visit? You were mighty secretive over the phone. But anytime Noble Shepperson wants to come by, the welcome mat is out." She smiled. "But before you get to that, I want you to tell me why in holy hell Jesse Rooter was here and why Catherine Craighill had him in tow at the reception."

"All I know is what he told me—he met Catherine at the library and she invited him to go."

"Well she had a nerve to bring him—and to make it worse—uninvited. I didn't appreciate it one bit."

"What's the problem with Jesse?"

"I knew his brother and I...." Her voice trailed off.

Noble interrupted. "I was looking through some old records and saw that Grady worked on building this patio in the summer of '46, was employed by Denkens. Do you remember that?"

"Yes. He was around. Why do you want to know?"

"As you may recall, he was found drowned that August, and I'm wondering whether you know anything about that."

"Of course not. All I ever saw of him was around here on the job. Why does this matter anyway?"

"Jesse was never told anything about Grady's death, and he's curious to know more about the circumstances. Several people seem to suspect it was not an accident. Jesse has engaged me to investigate."

"Well, I can't help you. Now that's not what you came to talk about, is it?"

"No. So I'll get right to the point." He explained that the library board had decided the library needed a new building and was determined to mount a substantial fundraising effort. "I would like to help if I can, and I agreed to talk with you to see whether you might get interested."

"Did Ben Harris put you up to this?"

"This is a board project. He's on the board, but there are four others."

"Sending you here sounds like something he'd do. He wouldn't lower himself to see me in person. But he'll damn sure take my money!"

"You have to understand this as a civic effort, for the good of the town and county. The fact that Ben Harris is connected with it shouldn't affect your attitude."

She finished swallowing a sip of gin and tonic. "How much money are they trying to raise?"

"The goal is three hundred thousand dollars."

"My God! In Remberton? They've got to be kidding."

"They know it's ambitious. Actually, more is needed to have a really first class library. But they think this is a realistic goal, and they can make it with the help of folks like you."

"And how much did they tell you to ask me for?"

"The fundraising experts say that for any campaign to succeed ninety percent of the money has to come from ten percent of the contributors, and they say that two or three large kick-off gifts are essential."

"And I'm guessing they've got me spotted as one of those."

"As a matter of fact, yes."

"Don't beat around the bush. How much?"

"$100,000."

She slammed her glass down on the table. "A hundred thousand dollars! Do they think I'm made out of money?"

He smiled. "No, but they think you've got a good deal of it. And they're right, aren't they?"

"I live comfortably, but I've got to think about Ellen, and maybe grandchildren too."

"Of course, you're the only one who can decide what you might do. I just wanted to put the idea in your mind so you can think about it."

She calmed down. "Well, you've put it there. Now you can tell Ben Harris if he wants some of my money for the library he'll have to come to see me himself." She smiled broadly and added, "Now let's have another drink and talk about something more pleasant than money."

When she returned in a few minutes with two fresh drinks, he asked her what Ellen's situation would be in Montgomery. That triggered a voluble description of the new house Ellen and her husband would move into when they returned from their honeymoon and the social life she could expect. Then she said, "Let me hear something about what you're up to these days, aside from library fundraising."

He told her about the D-Day observance in England and how he and Nan planned to go, what places he hoped to visit, places at which he had served in those weeks before the invasion.

"That lucky Nan! What a trip."

"You've done England, haven't you? I have a vague recollection that you and your mother went over there once."

"Yes. Daddy thought we ought to have a version of the grand tour. But that's been a long time ago. Haven't been back since."

Noble's glass was empty. He said, "I have to run."

"Oh, you married men do have problems."

Noble said jokingly, "Speaking of marriage—and we know each other well enough for me to be perfectly frank—folks around town think you might have gotten hitched again by now."

"I'm certainly not against men, but I like to be a little picky." She again smiled. "And there aren't many Noble Sheppersons around."

He didn't know quite what to say to that, so he stood up. "This has been pleasant. Sorry I do have to move along."

They walked through her spacious hall to the front door. She gave him a quick hug and said, "Come back anytime, even if you have to carry messages from Ben Harris."

As he started down the porch steps, she called out, "Why don't you go see Catherine Craighill?"

He turned and paused. "Do you think she'd be interested?"

"Ought to be. She works there. And Ben Harris might like that money better. It's old."

"New money spends as well as old. But maybe I'll look into that." He laughed. "I'm not letting you off the hook though."

Noble was alone in his office the next morning when the intercom buzzed. "General Kendrick is on the line," Miss Alice said.

"Things are shaping up," Toby Kendrick announced, getting, as usual, quickly to the point. "We are all booked at the Savoy. There's a reservation there for you and Nan. We'll be guests at a reception in Guild Hall on the night of the fifth. Plans are underway for a special service in Westminster Abbey. Some other events are being worked on. We're trying to line up a group trip out to our old area near Bramton."

"Sounds good," Noble said. "Our airline reservations are all set."

"I'll keep you posted when I get more details."

The Savoy Hotel! How extraordinary, Noble thought. Of all the hotels in London where they might have been booked, it had to be the Savoy!

✳   ✳   ✳   ✳

England, February 1944. The morning as usual was rainy, gray, and chilly. Lt. Col. Noble Shepperson sat at his folding table in the converted parlor of the eighteenth century manor house, catching up on paper work. His battalion had returned the night before from a training exercise on Salisbury Plain. Incoming mail from the states had just been distributed, and Noble was engrossed in reading the small photocopied V-Mail letter from Nan, his first word from her in two weeks.

After giving her usual account of the two children's activities, she reported that she and several of the women in Newburgh with whom she had grown up had formed a bridge club and met once a week. "It's good to be with women I can understand." She was continuing to roll bandages with the Red Cross. Her parents enjoyed having their grandchildren there and tried to take them out for a short ride every week, but gas rationing kept this down. Even though her father, as a physician, had a "C" sticker, there was little gas for pleasure. Sometimes they went to the drive-in where there was only orange juice, tomato juice, coffee, milk, and tea, never Coca-Colas or other soft drinks, because of sugar rationing.

As he finished the letter, the executive officer, Major Willis Dumfries, came up. "Sir, you remember we have an inspection at ten hundred."

"Yes. Too bad about the weather. Not ideal, but we have to keep going."

"Looks like its getting worse. Good thing we finished the exercise."

"O.K. Let's head out in ten minutes."

A corporal appeared and handed Noble an envelope. "Sir, this was delivered to the guard last night."

Noble immediately recognized the cream-colored paper with its familiar scent. It had been two months since he had left Jennifer Cromlyn's house on the night her husband returned. He had thought of her many times but had assumed he would never see her again. He opened the envelope with surprising eagerness.

> My dear Col. Shepperson,
>
> You have probably forgotten me by now, but I want to let you know that I have not forgotten you. Edward, who has been in London for most of the time since Christmas, left a few days ago for an assignment in the Mediterranean, not expecting to return for some months.
>
> You are no doubt busier than ever, but if you can find a moment for a visit, I would enjoy having you come by. Several days a week, I go to Bramton, but I am usually home by mid-afternoon and am always here on Sunday afternoons.
>
> Fondly,
>
> Jennifer Cromlyn

He was still staring at the note when Major Dumfries' voice cut in. "Sir, time to go."

He crammed the note in his pocket as he stood up and reached for his field jacket on a hook behind his table.

For several days Noble brooded over the note. He felt an acute pulling and hauling on his emotions. He could not deny that he would like to see her. Despite being in the midst of his fellow officers and hundreds of men, he felt lonely. He had never before experienced such a prolonged absence of female companionship. But this situation was fraught with danger, like striking a match in a room filled with gasoline fumes—he a married man far from home and she a married woman with husband far away. It would be better, he argued rationally to himself, to leave well enough alone. It would be easy not to see her again. On the other hand, he would not likely be here more than a few more weeks and then be gone forever. What would be the harm in innocently having a bit of her company along the way?

On a Sunday afternoon two weeks later, Noble Shepperson found himself in Jennifer Cromlyn's sitting room, the electric fire warding off the chill of the encroaching dusk. His plain wool Ike jacket was dressed up a bit by a silver leaf on each shoulder and a US and pair of crossed rifles on each lapel. He sipped from a glass of scotch—no ice, of course

"With all respect to this land of tea," Noble said, "I have to say this is better."

"It's easier than making tea. Something I appreciate with Miss Sheffield off today."

She, having obviously dressed up for the occasion, wore a black dinner dress, pre-war, like all clothes these days, accompanied by the array of jewelry of which she seemed to be particularly fond—gold necklace and bracelets and diamond earrings. Nylon stockings had disappeared for the duration, but her smooth cotton pair showed her legs off quite well. Her short skirt always hitched itself above her knees when she sat down. She radiated that sharp sweetness that had been imprinted on his mind since they first met.

For a while they chatted about what they had been doing—his routine of paper work and training exercises, and her activities in town with the Ladies Association. After she had replenished his Scotch and her sherry, she sat down on the sofa beside him.

For a moment they sipped, saying nothing. Then she spoke, slowly and hesitantly, "Col. Shepperson …"

"I would feel more comfortable if you called me Noble."

"All right. If you'll call me Jennifer."

"That seems fair enough."

"As I was about to say—I don't quite know how to say it. Somehow it seems inappropriate, but I feel the need to explain Edward. You no doubt recall the night he arrived here unexpectedly."

Noble nodded, saying nothing. Her expression had grown serious, the usual sunshine clouded over.

"After you left, he made a bit of a scene. He wanted to know how often you had been coming here and whether I thought it appropriate to entertain men in his house while he was away helping to defend the country. He didn't seem to be convinced by my explanation. We went to Winchester to see my brother at Christmas, but Edward was rather cool. After that he spent most of his time in London."

She paused and sipped sherry. To break the silence, Noble said, "Where is he now?"

"Somewhere in the Mediterranean. Malta, I believe, but I'm not sure."

"When I was here last time, you said something that led me to think the relationship between you two was not ideal."

"That's putting it mildly. It was a bit strained before he left the first time. Now it's even more so."

"I'm sorry to have contributed to the problem."

"Don't be concerned about it. He would have been the same. I don't know what his problem is. For a while I thought it might be another woman. But I now think he's simply not cut out for marriage. I don't know what to do about it. Nothing, I suppose, as long as the war is on. It's terribly lonely here, but I'm no different in that respect from millions of other women."

In the silence, the ticking of the hall clock sounded unusually loud. The electric fire glowed red in the fireplace. Noble took a long swallow. He looked at her and saw a tear trickling down each cheek. He had never known what to do around crying women.

Suddenly she leaned against him, putting her head on his shoulder. "Oh, Noble, I just don't know. I shouldn't be telling you all this, but I can't help it." More tears flowed.

He put his glass on the table, pulled a handkerchief out of his pocket, and gently dried her cheeks. At the same time he slipped his arm across her shoulders.

He said, "This damnable war has got everything messed up. I should be home with my children. They're growing up without me. But here I am, three thousand miles away getting ready to go into God knows what."

"And what about your wife?" She sniffled.

"She seems to be pretty happy where she is, back where she grew up. She's never liked living in Remberton."

With her head leaning back against Noble's arm, her upturned face was only inches away. Her large, sad eyes bored into him. Without thinking—indeed, thought was suspended—Noble moved down and kissed her lightly. She ran her arms around his neck and pulled him down against her, holding him in a prolonged kiss.

When she released him, he straightened up.

Looking at him dreamily, she said, quietly, "That was nice."

"Yes," he half whispered.

Neither spoke for a moment. Then he said, "The trouble with these visits is that they have to be too short. I do, after all, have a military command. So I'm afraid it's that time again—I have to go."

"Don't you have something like weekend passes or …" She hesitated, light returning to her eyes, "perhaps an overnight pass?"

"We give them to the men from time to time for a fling in London. It's good for morale."

"How about your morale?"

"I'm in a little different position, to say the least."

"Surely the commander is as much entitled to a break as the men."

"I hadn't really thought about it." He smiled faintly. "But maybe I ought to."

Brigadier General Tobias Kendrick stood at the far end of the Quonset hut with a long wooden pointer in hand. He was a muscular six-footer with a commanding presence. He had brown crew-cut hair and a chiseled face that conveyed intensity.

Beside him, a large map of southern England rested on a three-legged stand. On a celluloid overlay, a black grease pencil line had been drawn from Bramton southward, with some twists and turns, to the channel coast.

Facing him, seated on wooden benches, were the division staff and the regimental and battalion commanders, all still in field jackets in the unheated space. They were gathered to get a briefing on some recent changes in D-Day plans.

"As you know," Gen. Kendrick said, "we won't be in on the initial landings. We'll begin to move out at about 0800 on D-Day. There's no change in that respect. By that time, if all goes well, the first wave should be ashore. There have been some small changes in our movement route."

Using the pointer, he traced the division's line of march, south, along the black line, identifying the towns and villages along the way, into Hampshire and to the marshalling area just outside the port of Southampton. "Given these English roads, the best we can figure on is about fifteen miles an hour. We'll begin loading the ships at around 1400 on D-Day plus 1. If the first wave has done its job, we should have a relatively peaceful landing on the beach. But we have to be prepared for the worst. You'll get details of the movement in writing at the appropriate time."

He took questions for a few minutes and concluded. "You know as well as I do, and I have said it at least fifteen times—it can't be stressed too much—absolute secrecy is essential. In this whole D-Day operation, surprise is our greatest weapon. If any word gets out to the Germans we've got a whole new ball game on those beaches."

The officers stood, mingling and talking with each other and drifting toward the back door.

"Well, Noble," Toby Kendrick said, as the two met up front. "To loosely paraphrase Stonewall Jackson at Chancellorsville, the Class of '33 will be heard from soon."

"I hope we pull it off as well as Jackson did."

"Things are looking good. We're up to full strength now and the training is shaping up."

They were alone now in the Quonset hut. Noble said, "Toby, you know I haven't had a break since we got here last fall. Looks like we may have a little quiet time just ahead. What would you think of my taking a night in London? May never have another chance to get there."

"I didn't realize you hadn't done the town. Pretty beat up but still worth the trip. Yeah, go ahead, but check with the G-3 first to be sure nothing's up."

"Thanks. I'll do that."

"And by the way," Kendrick said, as Noble turned to go, "if I were you I wouldn't wait long, if you know what I mean."

The well-known Savoy Hotel is on the Strand as one proceeds east from Trafalgar Square toward the law courts and Temple Bar. On its south side it overlooks the Thames River and the Embankment. Gazing out from his room in that direction on a Saturday afternoon in March, Noble Shepperson was nervous and uneasy. He had been lucky to get this room—to get any room in London—as hotel space was extraordinarily tight. He had been able to arrange it only after getting help from a West Point classmate, Col. Tim Jenkins, stationed at supreme headquarters. Having gone to considerable trouble to set up this night in London, he was now uneasy and beset with second thoughts. What was he doing here? What was he thinking about? He, a pillar of the community back home, a lawyer of unblemished character, a family man, Presbyterian Elder, an officer and gentlemen, caught up in what now seemed a tawdry scheme. It must be that a sense of rectitude and responsibility diminished in relation to the distance from home. Maybe the normal rules of behavior were suspended during wartime—an overseas exception to what was otherwise expected. If it didn't exist, he had made it up to excuse what he was doing. But he wished there were some way to call the whole thing off, to get back to his battalion. His only comfort, and it was slight, was the realization that no one he knew would ever know.

A barely audible knock came from the door. He walked to it and, without opening it, said, "Who is it?"

A soft female voice said, "It is I."

He opened the door and Jennifer Cromlyn came in wearing a buff-colored raincoat and carrying a small suitcase. Her cheeks were flushed from the damp, cool English air and her thick chestnut hair was windblown. Her eyes had that lively luster that had so entranced him from the moment he first met her. With her came the familiar perfumed aroma.

"Welcome to the Savoy," Noble said, ill at ease but inwardly feeling a rush of excitement.

"My, what a beautiful room," she said, looking around and then walking to the window. "And what a magnificent view!"

"Let me take your coat." She unbuttoned it down the front, and he slipped it from her shoulders and hung it up. He placed her suitcase against a wall.

They sat down in chairs beyond the bed, flanking a table near the window. Noble sensed awkwardness in the situation. She seemed as nervous as he felt.

In a moment he said, "Did you have a good trip in from Bramton?"

"Yes. For a change the train was not overcrowded."

"I have some gin here. Why don't we have a little drink to celebrate your arrival?"

"Why not?"

Noble poured gin into two glasses. He sat back down and said, "It's about three hours till dark. When we finish these drinks, how about taking a walk? I'd like to see at least a few of the sights."

She agreed and they talked about where they might go. Noble was again charmed by the melodious English accent. The gin trickling down his throat created a pool of warmth in his stomach. His anxieties were rapidly diminishing.

Twenty minutes later they were out on the Strand walking toward Trafalgar Square. They came to Nelson's Column, symbol of Britain's victory in another great, long-ago conflict, pitting her, as now, against a continental power. They stood for a while watching the innumerable pigeons and surveying the rest of the square—St. Martin's in the Fields, the National Gallery, Charring Cross Station.

Jennifer knew London well, and she led him down Whitehall. They paused at the Cenotaph, the simple monument to the First World War, ended only twenty-six years earlier, with unbelievable casualties. Now the Americans were back again, in far larger numbers, to join with the British once more to do it all over.

Signs of the blitz were everywhere—the House of Commons in ruins, open rubble-strewn spaces where buildings and houses had stood. They walked on, and she pointed out historic sights he had read about all his life and had always wanted to see, but, of course, could never have imagined he would be seeing them amidst the devastation of war.

They came eventually to Piccadilly Circus. The sidewalks were filled with uniforms—mainly British and American, but sprinkled with Canadian and Australian and a touch of French and Polish. In this military mélange, all branches were represented—air, sea, and land, all readying for the greatest amphibious operation in world history. Only a few at the very top knew when and where, but all knew it was coming, that it would not be far off, that there would be casualties, perhaps many. There was a palpable sense of wanting to live life to the fullest, for no one could know what lay ahead.

As dusk came on, they stopped at a pub and had stout and a sample of the limited wartime fare.

"If you would like, we can supplement this back in the room," she said, "with some cheese and biscuits I brought along."

When they reached the room it was fully dark and the blackout curtains were in place.

"Some of that cheese might taste good," Noble said. "We can wash it down with gin."

As they sat munching on cheddar and sipping gin, she described London before the war—all the lights on, no air raid concerns. "I guess that day will come again," she said. "You know the song." She sang the first words softly and slowly: "There'll be blue birds over … the white cliffs of Dover … tomorrow … just you wait and see."

Noble, moved by her soft, wistful voice and feeling a warming from the gin, was now ever more at ease. He said, "I can see why the English like gin. It cuts through this everlasting dampness."

"Yes it does," she said, as she took another swallow.

"It tastes like more. Here, let me top up these glasses, as the English say."

He reached for the bottle. "This is a fantasy. I haven't been in a civilized bedroom for months. Nothing but a hard canvas cot. Add to that a beautiful woman and it's unbelievable."

"It does seem a bit like a dream."

As he picked up the bottle, he was stopped short by a loud knock on the door. Startled, he said, "Who can that possibly be? Does anyone know you're here?"

"No, not a soul."

He went to the door and said apprehensively, "Yes?"

"Noble"—it was a strong masculine voice—"It's Toby."

Here was the unimaginable. Someone he knew! Embarrassment engulfed him. He didn't know what to do or say, but there was no time to think. He pulled open the door. "Come in. This is a surprise!"

Gen. Kendrick entered briskly, followed by Tim Jenkins, wearing a silver eagle on each shoulder. With short black hair and a wide, Irish face, he was smaller than Toby.

"A double surprise!" Noble exclaimed, shaking hands with each.

Noble saw that both visitors had focused their eyes on Jennifer, sitting across the room. They looked quizzically at Noble.

Making an effort to appear calm and matter of fact, Noble said, "Er, I want you to meet an English visitor. This is Mrs. Cromlyn. Her husband is a British intelligence officer. I met them some time ago, and she offered to show me some London sights."

Jennifer arose. Noble said, "Mrs. Cromlyn, this is Gen. Kendrick, my assistant division commander, and Col. Jenkins, stationed here in London."

"How do you do, Mrs. Cromlyn," Toby said, giving her an intense examination.

She extended her hand and shook lightly with both men. "How do you do?"

Toby looked at Noble, the two acting equally awkward. "I just came in on the spur of the moment to see Tim. He told me he got you a room here. We were wondering whether you might come along with us for the evening …" He paused, glancing at Jennifer. "I gather you're already occupied."

Before Noble could say anything, Jennifer spoke up. "My husband and I had a couple of theatre tickets, but he had to go off on assignment, so I thought Col. Shepperson might enjoy a taste of the London stage."

"Well, we certainly wouldn't want to interfere with that," Toby said.

Tim Jenkins added, "No, we don't want to interrupt your plans." He gave Noble a knowing glance. "But it's good to see you, Noble. It's been a long time. Glad I could help you find a room."

"I really appreciate it. Can you stay for a drink?"

"Thanks, but we better get on."

They all said goodbye. The two officers left, and Noble closed the door and came back toward Jennifer standing beside her chair. "I hadn't heard about the theater tickets."

"Neither had I," she said, smiling broadly. "Would you rather join your friends?"

"What do you think? Let's have another drink and forget it."

But before he could move, she took a step toward him, put her arms around his neck, and looked up into his eyes. Her voice became a whisper. "Noble, I hope you've looked forward to this night as much as I have."

They kissed and held on to each other tightly. All his concerns, embarrassment and guilt, were no more. It was as though someone had switched off all those circuits and turned on one that lifted him far away into ethereal space.

As the weeks passed, Noble was caught up in intensified preparations in his battalion. Spring had come to the West Country with its milder air and new greenery. Oh to be in England now that April's there. Browning's line replayed in his mind, underscoring the irony of what he saw around him—hundreds of soldiers armed with rifles and machine guns, endless lines of half tracks, tanks, two and a half ton trucks, 105 millimeter howitzers—mechanized, destructive weapons of twentieth century warfare in this ancient, green, and pleasant land.

Since that night in London, in the intervals when he was not absorbed with military duties, his mind was obsessed with thoughts of Jennifer. Every week since, he had been able to slip away on either Saturday or Sunday afternoon. Those visits were short—an hour or two—but intense and emotion-filled. At first he felt a special need to be circumspect in light of the encounter with Gen. Kendrick in the Savoy. Yet caution was abandoned as the weeks passed. He realized that his Jeep drivers must wonder—or in fact know—what was going on. But Jennifer held such a grip on his heart and mind that he no longer cared. Gone were his hesitations and sense of guilt.

April turned into May. Increasingly Jennifer was distressed over the inevitable end of the relationship, crying almost every time they were together.

"Oh, Noble, I've said it a thousand times, but I don't know what I'll do when you're gone."

"It won't be any easier for me."

"I know you should go back with your wife and children …"

Although there were snippets of talk like that, there was not much conversation during his visits. The time together was too brief, emotions too high. Words were useless, out of place.

At twilight one afternoon in late May, as they walked toward her front door to meet the Jeep coming to pick him up, he said, "It can't be long now. When the moment comes, I won't be able to let you know. The security lid will be clamped down. So there'll be no goodbye. You understand that, don't you?"

"Yes. That means that every time we part may be the last."

They stopped just inside the front door and faced each other. Her face was wet with tears. They clutched each other desperately, acutely aware that they might never be together again.

"Gentlemen, this is it." Gen. Kendrick stood in front of key unit commanders gathered in the Quonset hut. "The division commander is still at corps headquarters for some last minute instructions. He's asked me to brief you." He explained that D-Day was now set for tomorrow, 6 June. "We move out at 0800 along the designated route. Detailed orders will be distributed within the hour. From now on, maximum security will be observed. No one is to leave the area. No outgoing mail will be sent. No communications of any sort with the outer world."

✳   ✳   ✳   ✳

"Mr. Noble ... Mr. Noble," said Miss Alice, standing in the door, her voice rising. "Have you forgotten you have a hearing in ten minutes in that will contest?"

Abruptly shaken back to the present, he mumbled, "Er ... yes, time slipped up on me."

Chapter 9

The next day, as Noble emerged from the probate office into the main courthouse corridor, he encountered Judge Andrew McKnight on the way to his chambers. "Judge," Noble called out, "can I see you for a few minutes?"

"Any time," the jovial judge said. "Come on in."

They passed through the secretary's room into the judge's inner sanctum. By comparison, the usually unruly lawyer's office looked tidy. Court files and miscellaneous papers a foot deep covered the desk and a nearby conference table. Other piles of briefs and papers were stacked on the floor to the rear of his chair. Seeing Noble looking at this mess, the Judge said, "When our summer recess gets here I've got to clean this up. The docket this winter was heavy, and I'm a little behind." He went around to the massive high-back leather chair. "Have a seat," he said, waving toward a chair in front of the desk. "What's on your mind?"

"You can relax. It's not about a pending case. I'm following up on that little conversation we had at the wedding reception about Grady Rooter."

"Have you found out why Jesse Rooter was at the reception?"

"Catherine Craighill's peculiar idea. I'm bringing Grady back up because I've learned something related to his death I didn't know. Since you were prosecutor at the time I'm wondering whether you ever heard it."

The Judge's fleshy face was expressionless—a face the color of a dove's foot, the product of legislative years of whiskey and steaks in Montgomery at the hands of lobbyists. He said slowly, "Probably won't remember. I don't carry in my head all the details of every incident that came to my attention."

Noble then related what Amos Brewer had told him about two cars going into the creek late at night and only one returning. "Do you recall hearing that?"

"Don't think so. But I wasn't involved in investigating. That was up to the sheriff." The Judge's usual affability had gone. He was now the serious public official, on guard lest there be something here that might impugn his integrity or performance of duty.

"Unfortunately," Noble said, "The sheriff's dead."

"And so is this case, I would think," the Judge said. "Look, Noble, I don't understand why you're spending any time on an accidental drowning back in the forties."

"Accident is the question. I hadn't thought much about it until I heard what Amos Brewer said. But whatever I think, Jesse has retained me to investigate."

"Brewer doesn't know whether one of those cars was Grady's, does he?"

"No. But if two cars go in and only one comes out in the middle of the night and early next morning Grady's car is found at the creek, it's a fair inference that one of those going in was his."

"So where does that take you?"

"From those facts I infer that whoever was in the car coming out were the last folks to see Grady alive. They either had something to do with his death or at least could provide relevant information."

"And how do you propose to find out who they were?"

"I was hoping you might have looked into this back then and could shed more light on it."

"Sorry, I can't."

"Do you think there would be any files in the sheriff's office on this case?"

"I doubt it. There've been three changes of sheriff since then. I suspect that files that old are long gone."

"Speaking of files, I went back into some old Denkens Construction records, left in storage from the time I represented the company. They show you had Denkens redo your kitchen in the summer of '46. Do you recall that?"

"Yes, but what's that got to do with this?"

"Grady Rooter was on the crew working at your house and was working right up to a day or two before he died. Do you remember seeing him on the job or anything about him at that time?"

"No. I was never there during the day. Didn't know who was on the job. I dealt with Will Denkens."

"Julia was home from college that summer. Did she ever say anything about Grady?"

"I wouldn't think she even knew him."

"They were acquainted in high school."

"Oh well, I suppose the students in Remberton High School all knew who the others were. But I can't imagine she would have really known a boy like that."

"You mean a boy from the mill village?"

"Well, yes, if you want to put it that way."

"Would you mind if I spoke to Julia about this?"

"About what?"

"About anything that might bear on Grady's death."

"I'd rather you didn't get her involved in an old case like this. She couldn't know anything of value."

Noble rose, smiling and extending his hand across the desk. "Judge, I won't take any more of your time."

"Always glad to see you, Noble."

Wanting to depart on a light note, Noble said, "Haven't seen you on the golf course lately."

"It's these damn cases. With spring here I hope to be out there more. A man's got to have some break from the grind."

Walking out of the courthouse, Noble headed along Center Street toward his office. It was a fine spring day—blue sky overhead, with hardly a cloud in sight. The courthouse clock was striking ten. Across the street the morning coffee crowd was gathering in the Abbott Drug Store. It was a daily ritual. Occasionally he joined them, but on most days he was too busy. Also, he found much of the conversation boring, and there was less incentive to go there since he had installed the latest coffee-making apparatus in his office.

If he did go over, he knew exactly what would happen. It never failed. Jim Abbott, owner and pharmacist, would be behind the prescription counter in the rear, a wiry little man in shirtsleeves and large glasses, with a big voice, always exhibiting good humor. From that vantage point he kept the entire place under constant scrutiny. No one could enter the front door quietly or unannounced. "Good morning, Noble!" he would boom out from sixty feet in the back.

"Come on in! What can we do for you?"

When he entered his office, Noble found Ben Harris sitting in the reception room reading the morning's *Montgomery Advertiser*. Putting the paper down, he said, "Good morning, Noble. Can you spare a few minutes?"

"Sure. Come on back," Noble said, as he walked toward the rear.

When they were seated at his desk, Ben Harris said, "I came by mainly to find out how you did with Lucille."

"Not too well, as you might guess."

"Does she have a problem with me?"

"No doubt about it."

"I'm not surprised."

Noble smiled. "She has what I would describe as an accurate view of what you think of her and her family."

"I don't want that to get in the way of this fundraising campaign. Is there anything I can do about it?"

"Two things occur to me. You could go by to see her yourself. I think she wants to hear you personally ask her for money. The other is that you might consider naming the new building for her father, if she would give at least a third of the cost. She's always admired him and that might just do the trick."

"Name the building for Sam Funchess? Good Lord! It's unimaginable."

"Even if that would spring loose a hundred thousand dollars?"

"Some things aren't for sale."

"In the fundraising literature I get from various institutions, they offer to name a building or a room or a scholarship for gifts of certain amounts."

"I know that. That doesn't make it right. Look, Noble, what possible case can be made for naming a library for Sam Funchess? He comes into town from out of nowhere, makes a lot of money, builds a big house, and then dies. You could probably count on one hand the books he read. What did he do for Remberton or for humanity? A man who makes that much money is bound to have walked over a lot of folks along the way. I suspect he did things a gentleman wouldn't do."

"Sam did establish a huge sawmill and a couple of other small businesses that employed a good many people. I suppose you could call that a contribution. In any case, this is just a suggestion you and the board ought to think about."

"I've duly noted it."

"Now," Noble said, "let me ask you about something else. At the wedding reception did you meet Jesse Rooter?"

"No. Didn't see any point in meeting him. I was told he was the man Catherine Craighill was pulling around."

"You probably recall back in the summer of '46 Denkens Construction Company was doing some work at your house."

"Yes, building a den. But what's that got to do with anything?"

"Jesse's younger brother, Grady, was one of the men working on that job. I'm wondering whether you saw him then or know anything about him in that time."

Ben Harris hesitated, choosing his words carefully. "A little bit. On two or three occasions my wife saw Amanda and him talking and laughing together. She mentioned it to me, and we agreed that this was something our daughter ought not to be doing. So my wife had a talk with her. As far as I know those incidents stopped."

"You're aware, I assume, that Grady died that August. Did Amanda say anything about his death?"

"I don't recall anything. Why are you asking about this anyway?"

Noble explained that a question had arisen about the accidental nature of Grady's death. Jesse had engaged him to get the facts. So he was trying to talk to everybody who had any contact with Grady that summer.

"From what I recall hearing," Ben said, "Grady was a rather despicable fellow. Why does Jesse want to get back into all this?"

"He's no admirer of his brother, but he thinks that if murder was committed the guilty ought to be found and prosecuted."

"Well," Ben said, standing up, "I've got to run along. I'll think about what you said about Lucille."

"Oh, one thing I forgot. Lucille says we ought to approach Catherine Craighill. What do you think?"

"Can't hurt. She's a little idiosyncratic and unpredictable. Bringing Rooter to that reception! Would you be willing to talk to her?"

"Wouldn't it be better if you did?"

"My main hesitation," Ben said, "is that she and Amanda didn't hit it off too well. I think it would work better for you to approach her."

"My problem is that I don't really know her. Dr. Loosh was my doctor and also my client but Catherine was never around. Since she moved back I've seen her only occasionally at some big event. But if you want me to see what I can do, I'll give it a try."

The next afternoon Jesse telephoned Noble to say that he was back home in Chicago. "I want you to stay on the Grady case, to see what you can come up with."

"You still believe there's something there?"

"My instincts tell me something's fishy. Anyway, I want you to dig into it more."

"It's going to be hard. I don't have the power of subpoena. If people don't cooperate voluntarily, there's nothing I can do."

"Couldn't a grand jury be convened? Then witnesses could be subpoenaed and made to talk."

"A grand jury would be up to the district attorney, and he's not going to do that on mere guesswork to satisfy your hunch."

"Well, do what you can. I'll be back in touch."

After they hung up Noble sat for a while, thinking about where he might go from here. Then he had an idea: *The Remberton Progress.* Knowing the paper's editor back then, the late Herbert Winston, and his penchant for printing only good news and avoiding items reflecting adversely on the town or its citizens, Noble doubted he would find anything useful. He would look, though, more out of curiosity than with the hope of learning anything significant.

"Come on back and we'll set you up at this big table," Frank Brandon said, as he led Noble to the rear of the office of *The Remberton Progress*, only a block down from Noble's office. He was a tousled-haired chubby fellow in his forties, originally from North Alabama, who had married Herbert Winston's daughter and then had assumed editorship of the paper when Herbert died. He had a more irreverent approach to local news than his father-in-law. When the store next door to the old *Progress* office went out of business he took it over, enlarging his quarters considerably. But Herbert Winston's collection of photographs still adorned the walls of the front room—the dominant one being Major John Winston, founder of the paper in 1866 after coming home from the war in Virginia. He was flanked by his heroes: Woodrow Wilson and Hilary Herbert, Colonel, CSA; Congressman; Secretary of the Navy. Then there was a shot of Alabama editors gathered around FDR in the Oval Office and numerous other pictures of events in the life of the paper and the town.

"I've organized these back issues into three-month clumps, usually twelve issues to the clump," Frank said, when they reached a small back room. "Here's the clump for July, August, and September 1946."

Noble sat down and began to turn the pages of the first issue. In July 1946 he had been back from Europe only a few months and was working hard to pick up the threads of his law practice. He was also becoming reacquainted with his two children and struggling with Nan's readjustment to Remberton after nearly three years in Newburgh, New York. The paper brought back long-forgotten events of that year. He found himself surprisingly absorbed in some of the news items, often trivial.

The society pages were tedious. Mr. and Mrs. So-and-So had just returned from visiting relatives in Birmingham. Miss Somebody had spent three days in Remberton visiting her aunt. The family of So-and-So was spending two weeks in the Smoky Mountains. And on and on. It would have been difficult in those days for anyone in what was considered respectable white society to arrive in or leave Remberton without catching the hawk eye of society editor Thelma Parker.

His eye fell on this: "Col. and Mrs. Noble Shepperson spent last week in Mary Esther with their children, Kirk and Martha." Herbert Winston followed the custom from the 1860s: once a colonel always a colonel. Noble now remembered that week, their first family vacation since before the war—romping with his children in the Gulf surf, water-skiing in Santa Rosa Sound, cocktails with friends at sunset. He now saw those post-war years as a happy and optimistic time, some of the best years of his life.

On the front page of the issue of August 8, 1946, he came to this item near the bottom of the page:

LOCAL MAN DROWNED

Last Tuesday morning the body of Grady Rooter was discovered in Possum Creek a quarter mile off County Road 23. His car was parked nearby.

Sheriff Norman Turner was called to the scene when a fisherman reported an abandoned car. The coroner concluded that death resulted from drowning.

Rooter had been working for the Denkens Construction Company since returning from service with the Marines in the Pacific Theater. He was a graduate of Remberton High School in the class of 1942. He has no known relatives here.

Good old Herbert Winston, Noble mused, wouldn't report such disparaging information as the presence of empty liquor bottles in the car. But maybe he didn't know about them. This newspaper story reported all that anyone knew at the time—that is, all except Amos Brewer, the sheriff, and perhaps a few others. Others? The murderer?

He paged on, finding no further mention of Grady Rooter. The man had passed unceremoniously from life and history with that brief notice. Gone and forgotten—except not forgotten, judging from the reactions to Jesse Rooter's startling appearance last week. And not forgotten by Gladys Kinston Houston—and who knows how many others with similar experiences.

His eyes were almost glazing over when they fell on this entry amidst the trivia on the society page: "Mr. and Mrs. Andrew McKnight and their daughter, Julia, spent several days last week in New Orleans enjoying the historic sights of the Crescent City." In the next issue he saw this: "Dr. and Mrs. Lucius Craighill and daughter, Catherine, were in Chicago recently to attend a meeting of the American Medical Association." Two weeks later he found the following: "Mrs. Samuel Funchess and daughter, Lucille, left this week for a grand tour of Britain and the continent. They expect to visit the major capitals and other historical spots and will be away for several months."

What, if anything, was he to make of these items? Nothing on their face. Yet a life in the law had trained him to be skeptical, even cynical, about human behavior, making a man more inclined to believe in the doctrine of original sin. So he wondered—all those trips in the weeks immediately after Grady Rooter's death, trips by those with daughters in whose houses he had been working.

Catherine Craighill met Noble at the door of her house and ushered him into the parlor. "This is a real pleasure. I haven't seen you in a long time," she said, "except for the wedding reception."

They sat down facing each other. Noble felt as though he hardly knew her. She was at least thirteen years younger and had been away from Remberton in Atlanta until recent years.

"Life is just too busy," he said. "Speaking of that reception, I nearly fainted when you walked in with Jesse Rooter. Later on, he told me you inveigled him into going. He said he met you in the library."

"He wandered in off the street. Talk about fainting. I nearly did when he introduced himself. I guessed he had an interesting story, and he looked respectable, so I asked him to come over and get acquainted."

"I imagine you heard his rags to riches saga."

"I did. He's got a problem getting over his origin. He's interesting, but not much personality. Incidentally, I'm afraid I embarrassed myself at the reception. Too much to drink."

"You weren't the only one. Don't worry about it."

"Well, since then I'm pretty much on the wagon. How's Nan?"

"This time of year she gets heavily into gardening. Still loves golf."

"I used to see her on the golf course, but I've about given up the game."

"You know," Noble said, "I was just thinking of all the times over the years that I've sat in this room, talking with Dr. Loosh. It seems odd now to be here without him. And there's Walter Craighill up there, still looking out over the passing scene."

"This place is filled with ghosts and memories, but I've gotten comfortable with them all. I do all of my reading and lounging around in an upstairs sitting room. I come in here only when I have visitors."

"It's heart warming to be back here," Noble said, "the first time since your mother died."

To get to the point of his visit, Noble said, "I don't have to tell you what the library needs. You know far more about it than I do." He explained he was here at the request of Ben Harris to discuss the fundraising campaign.

"I've heard about it," she said. "How's it coming?"

"Just getting started. No money in hand yet."

"So I guess that's why you're here." She laughed.

He smiled back. "Yes. We thought we might interest you in making one of the pace-setting gifts."

He discussed the amount of money that would be required to build a decent building, though not as much as everyone would ideally desire. Large kick-off gifts were essential, he said, telling her what he had told Lucille. Her reaction was not unfavorable, but she said she would have to give it a lot of thought.

"Talking about the library," she said suddenly, as though she had just remembered, "the other day I was going through that bookshelf back there"—she pointed toward a corner of the room—"and I came across this history of Rembert County." She handed the book to Noble.

"Oh, yes. I gave my copy to Kirk a couple of years ago."

"I'm sure you're familiar with it. I mention it because I am impressed with the discussion of the Craighills and Sheppersons in chapter two—how they came in from South Carolina in the early days and helped establish this place. A little further on it talks about your grandfather, Adrian."

Noble flipped through the pages. "I remember reading this a long time ago. Here's a section—I guess you know this—on Walter Craighill—his medical practice and his time with the 5th Alabama during the war." Then closing the book and handing it back to her, he said, "looks like we've been around here quite a while."

"Daddy was one of your great admirers. Said it was too bad that you were probably the last Shepperson here."

"Time is rolling on, no doubt about that," Noble said, standing up to go.

As they walked toward the front door, Catherine said, "I've heard you're investigating Grady Rooter's death. Is that true?"

"Yes, but I'm not getting very far."

"Did Jesse say anything to you about what I said about Grady?"

"A little bit."

"Would you mind telling me what it was?"

"He said you told him that Grady was making a pass at you while he was here on a job, or words to that effect. Also said you had suspicions about what Grady might be doing with your friends on his other jobs."

"Is that all?"

"Is there more?"

She hesitated. "Nothing that would help you."

"Even if it meant it would help catch a murderer?"

"Do you think Grady was murdered?"

"Anything's possible—that's the point of the investigation."

At the door, Catherine said, "Just because Daddy's gone ... well, what I mean is that you needn't think you have to stop coming by. You're welcome anytime. My schedule isn't heavy."

He felt himself looking at her in a way he had not before. She had blue eyes and a slightly sensuous face surrounded by luscious blond hair. The simple, cottony summer dress she wore revealed a figure more impressive than he had previously noticed.

He said, "Thanks. We'll probably be talking again about the library."

As he drove away, he mused over these two women on whom he had made his library call. High school classmates, both widows—one grass and one sod, as his father used to say—both well fixed financially, both good looking, but otherwise vastly different. Lucille—brash, assertive, sensual, materialistic, and only a generation away from the sharecropping world in the south end of the county. Catherine—softer and warmer, more subtly alluring, daughter of one of Remberton's oldest and most distinguished families. In a moment of fantasy, it occurred to him that if Nan weren't around and he played his cards carefully he could probably make some time with either one.

Two weeks later Noble was on a jetliner taxiing up to a gate at O'Hare Airport. He had flown up in response to a phone call from Jesse. "I've finally got an idea I need to discuss with you in person," he had said, "and I also have a thought about the investigation." He urged Noble to come up—"At my expense, of course, so you can see how a tenant farmer's boy is living these days."

When Noble emerged from the jet-way Jesse Rooter was there to meet him. They made their way along the crowded concourse, jostling through hundreds of passengers coming and going, passing through the vast terminal building and into the street, crossing over to a parking garage.

Jesse maneuvered his Mercedes through the traffic and maze of roads leading from the terminal on to the toll-way northbound. After some miles, they exited onto Willow Road, heading east, toward the Lake. Soon they were moving along the shady streets of Winnetka. Turning onto Sheridan Road, Jesse drove a short distance and then pulled the car through a pair of stone gateposts, entering a semicircular drive that swept up to a set of steps leading into a two-story stone mansion resembling something out of medieval Europe.

Noble got out and stood there, looking around, taking in the import of what he saw. "Amazing" was all he could say. A lawn spread out on both sides of the mansion, just beginning to show a faint green tint. The leafage on the trees likewise exhibited that pale green of early spring. The air was chilly, a temperature Noble had not felt since winter.

"We're a good month behind Remberton," Jesse said. "The Lake's on the other side. You can see it from the library."

They mounted the steps. Jesse pushed a bell button and at the same time inserted a key in the lock on a huge wooden door. As he pushed the door open, they were met by a gray-haired, middle-aged woman wearing a white apron. "Come in," she said.

To her, Jesse said, "This is Mr. Shepperson." Turning to Noble, he said, "This is Mrs. Schneider. She runs the place. Has for many years." They shook hands.

She led them down a long hall into a large room. One wall was covered with bookshelves. The other walls were in dark wood paneling. A stone-framed fireplace was on the wall opposite the bookshelves.

"This is where I spend most of my time," Jesse said. "Here's my desk and over there is a TV."

Through two tall windows, Noble looked across a hundred yard expanse of tree-studded lawn to Lake Michigan. "Quite a view," he said, entranced by the sight of such an enormous lake, running all the way to the horizon, like the ocean. Far out he saw a freighter, evidently headed for Chicago.

Turning to Jesse, he said, "Folks in Remberton will never believe this."

A self-satisfied smile crossed Jesse's face. He asked Mrs. Schneider to serve them tea. She left, and the two sat down in well-cushioned, high back wing chairs, facing each other across a low table.

Jesse talked about the history of the house, how his father-in-law had made his money in the meat packing business, had built the house in the twenties, and through skillful maneuvering had survived the 1929 crash. He talked about his wife's interest in the symphony and in giving parties here at the house. He went along with all of it, he said, but with her gone, he found little appeal in that style of life.

Noble thought that Jesse's countenance was even more a mismatch here in this opulent setting than it had seemed in Remberton. If he had been in work shirt and pants, his hard, coarse-textured look would have made him indistinguishable from a man come to repair the plumbing or put on a new roof. His origins and the Great Depression had left an ineradicable mark on the man.

Mrs. Schneider came in with a tray holding a pot of hot tea, cups and saucers, sugar, lemon, and milk. For a fleeting moment it reminded Noble of tea at Hedgely Farm, a memory recently revived by the prospect of the D-Day trip to England. Noble said he would take sugar and lemon. Jesse took milk.

When she left, Jesse said, "Well, maybe we should get down to business. Putting some distance between me and Remberton was good. When I was there I felt like a diver coming up from the depths too fast. Now I have a clearer perspective." He paused to sip tea. "Are you ready to hear my idea?"

Noble, teacup in lap, said, "I can't wait."

"This is all tentative, mind you, but what I want to put out for consideration is this. That I give two million dollars to Remberton for the construction of a new public library and for fully equipping it. There would be one condition: that the building be named for my mother. It would be known as the Sadie Mae Rooter Library, and that name would be prominently emblazoned over the main front entrance."

The room was quiet for a long interval. Jesse lifted his cup and sipped. Noble was motionless, looking at Jesse but with unfocussed eyes.

Jesse said, "The folks there do want a new library building, don't they?"

Suddenly Noble broke into laughter, prolonged, hearty laughter. He put his cup down on the table and then laughed some more. Trailing off, he said, "It's beautiful. Ingenious. An inspired combination of revenge and benevolence."

"I thought it was pretty creative myself."

"I can just see some members of that library board when they hear this. I mean no disrespect to you—and I hope you understand what I'm saying—but it's going to be hard for them to contemplate that name on what will be the most prominent building in the county."

"The illiterate wife of a tenant farmer and mill hand. I know exactly what you mean. That's why I'm proposing it."

"It presents a beautiful dilemma," Noble said. "Two million dollars, far beyond their wildest dreams, will be almost impossible to resist. But swallowing that name will be almost too much for some of them." He laughed some more. "They're thinking about $300,000 as an ambitious goal. Two million! It's fantastic. We could have the finest library in the state. Tell me this, though. Why are you interested in bestowing any benefit on Remberton?"

"My recollection is that the good book teaches forgiveness. Isn't that right?"

"Yes, but it's mighty hard for us flawed humans to practice."

"For a long time after I left Remberton I was bitter and resentful. Then I got married and went into a whole new life here and pretty much put it all out of mind. But since my wife died and I've halfway retired, that old resentment started coming back. I had too much time to think and brood. I finally decided that bitterness was eating away at me. I was the victim of my resentment. I had to do something to purge it. Forgiveness, I decided, was the only way to get rid of it."

"Two million dollars worth of forgiveness! That's putting your money where your mouth is."

"I'm not quite ready to announce this as a firm proposal. Before doing that I want to see how your investigation of Grady's death turns out."

"I'm afraid I haven't made much progress," Noble said. "There is one new development you don't know about." He then went on to tell him about Amos Brewer's story.

"That buttresses my hunch that something unusual was going on," Jesse said.

"It looks that way."

"Do you think a reward would do any good? I'd be willing to put up whatever might smoke out somebody."

"Well, I suppose it couldn't hurt."

"How about putting a notice in the paper? The amount could vary with the importance of the information, going up to, say, $25,000."

Noble whistled. "That's more money than most people in Rembert County would see in half a lifetime."

"I want it to be enough to get results."

Noble leaned forward and recovered his teacup from the table. "Let me think about it."

"I'd be willing to pay multiple rewards, not just one. Remember, I told you money is no concern. I'll spend whatever it takes."

They talked about how the announcement of a reward might be worded and how rewards could be administered. Then Jesse, looking at his watch, said, "Time's moving on. We better head out for lunch. I'm taking you to Indian Hill. That's the club here. I'll get you back to O'Hare in time for your flight."

Chapter 10

For the next few days Noble moved uncomfortably around town, aware that he was carrying a secret two-million dollar time bomb. He craved to communicate this dramatic news, but was reluctant to do so pending a green light from Jesse.

On his return from Chicago, Nan had said, "You look even more preoccupied than ever. Did something upsetting happen?" She had just come in from working in the garden, face wet with perspiration and was standing in the kitchen wearing Bermuda shorts and a loose fitting T-shirt besmirched with garden grime.

"It's just this business of trying to find out what happened to Jesse's brother."

"Why don't you just give up and tell Jesse you're at a dead end?"

"Can't do that right now. On a more pleasant subject, are you getting yourself ready for the big trip?"

She was at the sink, washing her hands. "Definitely. Getting clothes together. Have some books from the library."

"It'll do us good to get away for a while. Get Jesse Rooter and his brother out of mind."

She smiled coyly and said, "It'll be like a second honeymoon. Maybe better than the first."

"That would be going some," he said, smiling and looking her over. "But we can give it a try."

After a couple of days, his frustration mounting, Noble called Jesse and got permission to present his proposal to the library board to determine whether it would accept the money subject to the condition. He would stress its tentative nature, pending the outcome of the investigation. So at Noble's request, the board convened in his conference room.

The five members—upright citizens selected by the City Council because of their assumed interest in things literary—seated themselves around the table. As they gathered, Noble looked them over one by one, trying to imagine how each would react when he sprang the startling news.

The board chairman, Melba Robinson, sitting at one end of the table, was Noble's age, had grown up with him in Remberton. The widow of a local dentist, she had taught English in the high school for many years but was now retired. She was a cheerful, chubby woman; the round lens of her eyeglasses tracked the circumference of her face. Her gray-streaked brown hair hung straight below her ears.

To her right sat the bookish Ben Harris—Benjamin Tyler Harris, representing one of Remberton's oldest and socially most prestigious families. His small frame seemed swallowed up by the oversized conference room chair. His library included an extensive collection of writings by the Fugitives and Agrarians. He took pride in making it known from time-to-time that during his student days at Sewanee he had met and conversed with William Alexander Percy. He referred to him as "Mr. Will." On arriving he had said, with an air of expectancy, "Noble, I hope this is some good news on the matters we discussed."

On the other side of the chairman sat Norma Armistead, one of the grand old ladies of Remberton, amply able to match Ben Harris' pedigree. A white-haired, bird-like figure in her late seventies, she was public spirited, still vigorous, not reluctant to speak her mind, and a member of more organizations than one could count—among them the historical society, a book club, the garden club, the Episcopal Church, UDC, DAR, and Colonial Dames. She could equal Ben's accounts of his Percy meetings with stories of sessions with H. L. Mencken when she was a student at Goucher. Her late husband, one-time president of the bank, had been the most influential businessman in the county.

Beside her sat Judge Andrew McKnight, the county's leading public figure, greeting all with his usual cheerfulness. "Noble," he had just remarked, "I wish you could do something to get the judge's chambers fixed up as fancy as this office."

The baby of the board was Ann Simmons, wife of Dr. Bartow Simmons. In her forties and stylishly dressed, she came from Nashville and thus had the cachet, like Nan, of being from somewhere else. She and Bartow met when he was a medical student at Vanderbilt. They married when he graduated and eventually ended up in Remberton, his hometown. He was Noble's family physician since the death of Dr. Lucius Craighill. Having been an English major at Vanderbilt, Ann was familiar with the Fugitives and the Agrarians, giving her something in common with Ben. But unlike Ben, she was an avid reader of current bestsellers.

After all had exchanged pleasantries, Melba, presiding like the well-organized schoolteacher she was, said, "Noble, we thank you for having us to such posh quarters. We're all ears to hear what you have to say, so I'll turn it over to you."

Sitting at the other end of the table, Noble said, "Thank all of you for coming out. I think you'll be extremely interested in what I'm going to present, so I'll move right along. I have here what is probably the most dramatic news ever to hit this town, at least since Pearl Harbor. It involves a man named Jesse Rooter. Ben and the Judge are aware he was in town recently. Before getting to the point, I need to fill you in on his background.

Noble proceeded to summarize Jesse's life, beginning with his impoverished early years in the country, then in the mill village, the army, and onto Chicago and Northwestern University and into business and, finally, his marriage to a multi-millionaire's daughter. "I've been to his house. You wouldn't believe it—a mansion on the North Shore, right on Lake Michigan."

Melba spoke up. "I remember Jesse. He was in my English class. Seems to me he had a younger brother."

"He did," Noble said. "Named Grady. I'll get to him in a minute."

Norma said, "I'm bound to say I never heard of them and I've been around here forever."

"I'm not surprised," Noble said. "As the expression goes, they didn't amount to much."

"That's an understatement," Ben said. "This is a mildly interesting rags-to-riches story of a poor white boy, but I'm sitting here anxious to know what this has to do with the library."

"All right," Noble said, "let me get to the point. Here it is. Jesse Rooter proposes to give two million dollars for the construction and equipping of a new building for the Remberton Public Library."

He stopped, leaned back in his chair, and awaited reactions. Nobody said anything. The courthouse clock struck the half hour.

The silence was broken by Melba who blurted out, "My stars! Two million dollars?"

"It sounds too good to be true," Ben said. "Is there a catch?"

"There's one essential condition. You may or may not regard it as a catch. The condition is that the building be named for Jesse's mother. It would have to be known as the Sadie Mae Rooter Library." He paused and again leaned back in his chair to let this item sink in.

Again there was silence. Then Norma said quietly, "Sadie Mae Rooter? I thought public buildings were named for distinguished citizens, persons who had accomplished something, had contributed in some important way. Somebody whose memory should be preserved."

"Miss Norma," Ann said, "that's often the case, but I've seen a lot of buildings named for the one who gave the money and money was the person's only claim to fame."

"But Norma's got the right principle," the Judge said.

Melba said, "A building of this magnitude would be the most prominent structure in town. If it's named the Sadie Mae Rooter Library, what's that going to say to future generations? What example is that for our children and grandchildren? Suppose someone growing up here in future years asks, 'Who was Sadie Mae Rooter'?"

"You'd have to say," Ben said, "the wife of a tenant farmer and cotton mill worker."

"And," Ann quickly added, "mother of the man who gave the money for the library."

"Noble," Norma said, "what is the board supposed to do?"

"I see only two choices. One is to accept the gift, build the building, and name it as Jesse directs. The other is to reject the gift, refuse to accept the money."

"If we could raise the money from other sources," Melba said, "we wouldn't have the problem."

"As I understand it," Noble said, "you've set a goal of $300,000 through a fund-raising effort. So far you don't have a dollar. Jesse's gift would be more than six times that amount."

They all lapsed into silence. Then Noble looked at Judge McKnight and said, "Judge, what are your thoughts?"

The Judge cleared his throat and said, judiciously, "Well, I think we need to proceed carefully and not make a hasty decision. Did he say why he was doing this? What's his motivation?"

"It's a curious mixture of charitable impulse and desire for revenge."

"Revenge for what?" asked Norma.

"For what he considers mistreatment of his family. He thinks the town treated them like dirt, like poor white trash."

Ben said, "It sounds like that's what they were."

"Whatever the facts," Noble said, "Jesse feels pretty bitter about it. The only way he could figure to get back at the people here was to confer a benefit he thought they couldn't reject and put his mother's name on it. That would force the town, he says, to accept her and the name Rooter as real people. At the same time, he wants to forgive and get at peace with his bitterness."

Ben said, "Noble, you won't be surprised at my reaction in light of the little talk we had the other day about names."

"I remember your point. But before we go any further with this discussion let me say that Jesse does not want this to be regarded as a firm proposal. As I mentioned a moment ago, he had a younger brother named Grady. He came back here after the war and worked for the Denkens Company. In August 1946, he was found dead in Possum Creek. The coroner ruled it accidental death by drowning. Jesse has developed the notion that foul play may have been involved, and he wants it thoroughly investigated. He considers the two million gift for the library tentative until he gets the results."

Melba said, "Who's to do the investigating?"

"He's retained me, an assignment I must say I do not relish."

Ben said, "This gets more bizarre. I'm wondering whether Jesse Rooter is a little demented. What basis does he have for thinking this was anything but an accident? How can there be a meaningful inquiry after nearly thirty years?"

Ann said, "The more important question is how the investigation bears on his library gift."

Noble said, "That's a good question, and I don't have an answer. I don't think Jesse himself knows. He seems to want to wait and see what turns up."

Melba said, "I remember reading a short notice about Grady in the paper. It struck my attention because I had known Jesse in school. But I don't recall any suggestion of foul play."

"There wasn't any," the Judge said.

Norma said, "Noble, will you do this yourself or hire a private investigator?"

"Not sure. Jesse is considering offering a substantial reward to see if that'll bring somebody out of the woodwork."

All was momentarily quiet. Then Ann said, "So where does this leave us?"

Noble said, "The board needs to think about whether it is willing to accept Jesse's money with the condition attached, assuming he finally decides to give it. The question is whether you will take a two million dollar Library or possibly no new library at all—certainly not one of that size and quality."

"Well," Melba said, "it seems to me we have time to think about it."

"I agree," the Judge said. "We don't want to rush ahead."

Ben said, "I suggest we adjourn and meet again at the call of the chairman. Noble, I assume you'll keep her informed."

"You can be sure of that. I should add—because of the tentative nature of his offer—Jesse does not want publicity now. So please keep this to yourselves."

"With that," Melba said, "I think we'll adjourn. Thank you again, Noble, for this earth-shaking news."

A week passed. Noble continued to stew over how to proceed. He fiddled with drafting a notice of a reward. He located an elderly former employee of Denkens who had known Grady there in the summer of '46, but he knew nothing of him outside working hours. Meanwhile, Noble had to attend to other aspects of his law practice.

Then a phone call came from Lucille Brentson. She wanted to see him but preferred not to come to his office. He agreed to be at her house after lunch the next day.

When he arrived, Lucille's greeting was formal and serious, none of the coquettishness she usually displayed for Noble. The two sat on the screened porch overlooking the patio and garden. Spring was moving on and the early warmth was turning into days that were downright hot, alleviated now by the faint breeze from the slowly rotating ceiling fan. They engaged in a little chitchat about Ellen and her new husband.

After the maid brought out iced tea, Lucille said, "I've heard a rumor that Jesse Rooter is proposing to give two million dollars for a new library building to be named for his mother."

Noble was startled. Hadn't he told the board members this was confidential? But he should have realized that telling five people in Remberton was almost like telling everyone. Now, though, he saw no point in denying it, so he said, "That's correct."

"The idea of naming a big public building for a Rooter is, to put it bluntly, ridiculous and repulsive. It would be a disgrace."

"It'll be up to the library board to decide. You can let them know your views, but I don't know anything else to do."

"Well I do. I can top the offer. And here it is. I propose to give two and a quarter million dollars for the library building to be named for my father."

Noble whistled softly, rolling his eyes. "While back, you balked at $100,000. That's quite a leap."

"It's worth it to have a Samuel Funchess Library instead of a Sadie Mae Rooter Library."

"In the interest of full disclosure, I should tell you Jesse's offer is not final and absolute. He's reserving decision until he learns more from my investigation of Grady's death."

"Isn't that a fruitless venture?"

"Maybe and maybe not. We'll see. Suppose Jesse withdraws his offer. Would yours still stand?"

"You mean there wouldn't be any Rooter library?"

"Not if he withdraws."

"I'd have to think about it."

"Do you mind telling me why you're so upset over the idea of a Rooter library?"

She sipped tea and hesitated. Blue jays squawked in the nearby trees. "It just doesn't seem right. The Rooters didn't amount to anything. I guess you've heard some things about Grady. He was pretty bad."

He had to restrain himself mightily from pointing out that her father's origin was identical to the Rooters. He almost said it, but held back. Instead, he said, "Are you authorizing me to present your proposal to the board?"

"Yes, conditionally. I want to see what Jesse does."

"O.K.," Noble said, rising. "I have to run along. I hope you'll think about going through with your extraordinary offer, whatever Jesse does. It would be a magnificent addition to city and county."

She smiled and said, "What do you think Ben Harris would say about the Funchess name?"

Noble laughed. "Two and a quarter million might make it look better."

At the front door, she hugged him in her usual style, saying, "You're a good sport, Noble. Let me hear what the snobs have to say."

Over the next several days Noble was engrossed in preparing for a trial scheduled for the following week. The client was a discount clothing store located adjacent to the shopping center and owned by a national chain, the very kind of store he resented. When he had been approached a couple of years earlier by the chain to represent it with legal matters involved in setting up the store, he had initially resisted. But then he thought more about it. Commercial activity out on the interstate was the contemporary life of Remberton, and likely to be more so as time passed. Would he contribute to it by avoiding all involvement, or would it be better to be involved and try to shape matters in the best direction he could? If he didn't take on the representation, another lawyer in town would. Moreover, the new discount store would not have an adverse effect on stores along Center Street because all those clothing stores had already closed. So he had agreed to be retained by the company. Right now he had little time to brood over what Lucille had laid on him or the Grady Rooter investigation.

At the last minute, the clothing store case did settle so he found himself lying awake at night thinking about Grady. The only thing left to do, he concluded, was to publish notice of a reward, hoping money would spring something loose. But he had too much else to do before leaving for England. He would wait until his return.

Before his departure, however, Noble did want to inform the library board of his meeting with Lucille. At his request, the board again convened in his conference room.

"Last time we met," he began, "I thought Jesse's proposed gift to the library was about as dramatic a piece of news as there could be. But now there's an even more startling development—actually a two step development. Lucille Brentson somehow heard of Jesse Rooter's two-million dollar proposal. How she did I'll leave unexplored. It's a remarkable tribute to the concept of confidentiality. Anyway, for reasons best known to herself, she apparently cannot tolerate the thought of the library bearing the Rooter name."

Ben interrupted, "Lucille has more taste than I thought."

Noble ignored the comment and continued. "She wants to stop it, and the way she wants to do so—hang on—is to top his offer by herself giving two and a quarter million dollars for the library building with the condition it be named for her father."

Noble stopped, and again, for a few moments there was not a word. Then Melba spoke up. "I hardly know what to say. After years of starvation the library is about to be overrun with money. More money than Remberton has ever seen."

Judge McKnight said, "So we would shift from a Rooter library to a Funchess library."

"Good Lord," Ben said.

Norma said, "I can't help wondering whether the image would be improved."

"I don't know about the image," Noble said, "but the library would be a quarter million dollars better off. But wait, I'm not through. I told Jesse about this. The next day he called back to say he now proposes to give two and a half million dollars, with his mother's name on the building. We're having an incredible bidding war!"

"I can't believe it!" Exploded Melba. Others were shaking their heads.

"Is this a firm offer," Ann asked, "or does he still want to wait and see what you turn up about Grady?"

"It's the latter," Noble said.

The Judge asked, "If Jesse decided not to go through with his gift would Lucille's offer still hold?"

"That's not clear," Noble said. "I would hope so, but if the threat of the Rooter name were removed she might back off."

"If her offer did become firm," Norma said, "we would then face the same sort of question we had at our last meeting—whether we are willing to accept the money with the name attached."

"The Samuel Funchess Library!" blurted out Ben. "How much difference is there between Rooter and Funchess?"

"In this case," Ann said, "a quarter of a million dollars."

"That does seem to make the name go down a little easier," said Melba. "Then, too, Sam Funchess was a prominent citizen here for many years, whatever we think of him."

"It would help me," Norma said, "if someone would describe his contributions to the town or county. All I ever saw was that big house he built for himself."

There was a long silence. Then Ben said softly, "I'm afraid we're down to nothing but money, the almighty dollar."

The Judge said, "This is not something we need to decide now. The question may never arise."

"That makes sense," Melba said. "We can come back together when Noble has something new." She smiled and added, "Noble, is there any chance Lucille might raise her offer to top Jesse again?"

"I don't know. She doesn't know about Jesse's new proposal. I'm pretty busy getting things cleaned up before my big leap over to England. So I'll take it up with her after I get back and let you know. Please say nothing about this to anyone."

Melba said, "We'll all take a vow of secrecy, won't we?" Heads nodded sheepishly.

Then she said, "With that I think we should adjourn until further notice. Noble, have a grand trip!"

Chapter 11

▼

Six miles above the North Atlantic, Noble Shepperson leaned against the back of his seat, pushing it to full reclining position, hoping for a short nap before Heathrow. Dinner had been served and the trays removed, the cabin lights lowered. The small window was black against the night. Nan, beside him in the window seat, was already asleep. She had exhibited an almost child-like excitement about this venture, exclaiming, "It'll be the best trip since our honeymoon."

But sleep eluded Noble. Remberton was behind, fallen out of mind, and he felt a rising excitement about what lay ahead. Who among the old comrades would be there? Toby Kendrick and Tim Jenkens, of course, but who else? Some had not survived, and of those who did, time had taken a toll. Memories of those pre-invasion months in the English countryside were vivid—the greenness of the grass, the cool dampness, the fast, high-moving white clouds, those villages untouched since the middle ages, the training exercises on Salisbury Plain. Seeing that green and pleasant land for the last time on June 7, 1944, as his troop landing craft moved down Southampton Water, past the Isle of Wight, heading for they knew not what—death or an everlasting place in history or both. The emotions of that hour were unique, unlikely ever to be replayed. But thinking about that supreme adventure, as he rapidly neared the place where it all happened, revived deep within him something profound and stirring.

Then, inevitably, there was Jennifer Cromlyn. She had come out of the deep recesses of memory into the forefront of his mind ever since Toby Kendrick's initial telephone call. After considering over and over whether he should attempt to look her up, he had finally decided against it. The practical difficulties were substantial. Was she still married to Edward Cromlyn? If not, was she remarried? If so, what was now her name? In any case, how could he find her? She might even be dead. Then there was Nan along. Their relationship had been warming lately, and he now had less interest in seeing Jennifer than he had when Toby first called. He had concluded that Jennifer Cromlyn had to be considered a closed chapter, one of those long-ago episodes in life that may be savored—as he did occasionally with mixed pleasure and guilt—but could not be relived. So with that put behind, Noble was looking forward to having a good time with Nan and his old wartime buddies.

Out of the window, he saw the first hints of dawn. Racing eastward at more than five hundred miles per hour, he watched the sunrise come on quickly, as though it were a speeded-up movie. Nan stirred to wakefulness.

"Looks like you had a good sleep," Noble said.

"I did," she said, yawning. "I was tired after all the getting ready."

Flight attendants moved along the aisle, distributing orange juice, coffee, and croissants.

Nan said, "I hope there's not a lot on the schedule today."

"Nothing official. We'll just relax and recover."

The plane was descending now, on the approach to Heathrow. Nan, looking out the window, said excitedly, "There's Windsor Castle down there. Can you believe it! I can't wait to see all these places."

Three hours later, having worked their way through customs and immigration and the vast expanse of Heathrow Airport, traveling by coach to Victoria Station, and taking a taxi to the Savoy Hotel, they were at last in their room.

"Oh, Noble," Nan said, "this is beautiful." She threw her arms around him. "It's all like a dream."

He hugged the warm contours of her body against him and whispered, "It is."

Fortunately, Noble thought, the room did not look out on the same view that he had seen on that memorable thirty year ago night. Instead, from the window they looked up the Thames toward Westminster.

"Well," he said, "let's get unpacked and take a little rest."

They slept a bit, showered, and then went to dinner at Simpson's, just a block away on the Strand, where they enjoyed roast beef carved from a cart brought to their table.

They had arrived three days before D-Day, so they took advantage of the time to tour London and environs—by coach through the City and the West End and by boat along the Thames and by coach out to Hampton Court and Windsor Castle. Noble was struck with the contrast between what he saw now and what he remembered. Gone were the ruins, the piles of brick, and the gutted walls. Here and there were traces of the war, but they were few. The grim darkness of London in '44 was replaced by bright lights and bustling crowds far into the night. Could the new generation believe it ever happened?

Then Nan wanted to explore Harrod's and other stores, an outing that held little interest for Noble. So she went off on her own, and he decided to visit the courts.

It was a pleasant day and he passed up the waiting taxis in front of the hotel in favor of walking. He proceeded eastward along the traffic-choked Strand. Red double-decker buses rumbled alongside him, slowing and moving in spurts as traffic permitted. He followed the bend of the street around Aldwych, then past St. Clement Danes, the church of the RAF. Ahead he saw Temple Bar, where the Strand ended and Fleet Street began.

Then he came to the cathedral-like, dark stone Victorian structure housing the Royal Courts of Justice. Across the street began the Inner Temple and Middle Temple with their maze of buildings and gardens stretching down to the Thames. Behind the courts, just off Chancery Lane, was Lincoln's Inn, and beyond that, Gray's Inn. He was in the heart of legal London. He stood in front of the court building for a few moments, thinking about the centuries-long history that lay behind the law that he practiced, more than three thousand miles away. He felt a strong sense of legal kinship with this place where it all began.

Inside, he came into a long open space, with a soaring roof, the architecture and soft milky light suggesting a cathedral, perhaps the symbolic reminder of the ancient connection between the law and the church. To the rear, courtrooms lay off multiple corridors. There was a quiet bustle of people coming and going—barristers in their wigs and black gowns, accompanied by solicitors and clients.

In the center stood a row of postings of today's cases, on a permanent waist-high easel. He ran his eyes down the row. A separate sheet for each case showed the court, the judges, the barristers who were appearing. Some cases were in trial courts, others in the Court of Appeal. He had long heard of the way English appellate courts disposed of cases efficiently by hearing them orally and then deciding them on the spot, without waiting months to deliver a written opinion, as American courts did.

He moved to the Court of Appeal postings, glancing at each. Suddenly he froze. There, in an appeal against conviction, in the spot listing the barrister representing the defendant was the name Edward Cromlyn.

The sluice gates of memory opened. He saw that December evening at Hedgely Farm when Edward burst in unexpectedly, after two years in North Africa, the chilly introduction, and Jennifer's later account of their strained relationship. His resolve to forget Jennifer diminished, at least to the extent of taking this out-of-the-blue opportunity to learn of her current situation.

He found the courtroom designated for the case and slid into the banked rows of seats reserved for the public. High up on the bench were three judges, all in wigs and red robes, red always being worn by judges in criminal cases. The wigs and robes obscured the personal differences, rendering the judges relatively impersonal, symbolizing that they were the voice of the law and not that of individual human beings. One of the judges was in the process of summarizing the facts in the case just concluding and announcing the court's decision to dismiss the appeal. There was then a flurry of activity, a shuffling of papers, a departure of the barristers and solicitors in that case and a readying for the next.

The judge in the center then announced, "You may proceed, Mr. Cromlyn." In the front row of pew-like seats a stocky man arose. He wore the usual short gray wig and black silk robe, indicating, as Noble knew, that he was a QC—Queen's Counsel—evidencing a highly successful career at the bar. Noble saw him only in profile, but enough to see in the slightly wrinkled face the man he recalled from that encounter at Hedgely Farm.

He began, "M'Lords, I appear for the appellant, and my learned friend, Mr. Montague, appears for the Crown." It quickly became evident to Noble, from Cromlyn's presentation, that this was an appeal from a conviction for murder and that the main argument for overturning the conviction was that the trial judge had erroneously instructed the jury on a material point of law. The judges peppered Cromlyn with questions. The proceeding was more a conversation between judges and counsel than the kind of argument Noble was accustomed to seeing in American appellate courts. There was much discussion of two prior decisions of the Court. At one point, the judges lapsed into reading one of those cases, and all was silent for several minutes. While Noble knew nothing of the facts of this case or of the prior decisions, it all sounded familiar, and he felt that given a little time he could get up to speed on the case, such were the common roots of the Anglo-American legal systems.

At length, the presiding judge said, "Thank you, Mr. Cromlyn. Now we'll hear from the Crown."

Mr. Montague rose. He was a tall, thin man, younger than Cromlyn, likewise wearing a short gray wig, but his gown was not that of a QC. He was immediately met with a barrage of questions from the bench. He attempted to defend the trial judge's summarization of the case to the jury. After several minutes, the judge said, "Thank you Mr. Montague."

One of the judges on the flank came around and leaned over between the other two. A whispered conversation ensued. The barristers, solicitors, and spectators sat quietly in the pews.

The center judge then began summarizing the facts of the case and analyzing the question presented. He concluded that the trial judge had misdirected the jury, resulting in a miscarriage of justice. He wound up by saying, "The appeal is allowed, and the conviction quashed." He then announced that the court would be in recess. The judges left the bench, and there was a hubbub, as all arose and began departing.

Noble moved down the aisle to the front where Edward Cromlyn stood, gathering up papers. He said, "Mr. Cromlyn, you probably don't remember me, but I'm Noble Shepperson from the States."

Edward looked at him with that distant, cool aloofness that the English have mastered so well. Then in a disinterested tone, "Have we met?"

"Yes. At your house at Hedgely Farm in December 1943. I was stationed nearby and was having tea there when you arrived back from North Africa."

"Yes," Edward said, drawing out the word at greater length than its mere three letters would seem to allow. "I do recall."

"I shipped out on D-Day and haven't been back since. Here now for the thirtieth anniversary. I'm a lawyer myself and just dropped by to hear a case. It was quite a surprise to find you one of the counsel. How is your wife?"

"I suppose you mean Jennifer. I don't really know. We divorced years ago. She remarried. Nice chap named Grantham. But he died a few years back. No children. I haven't seen or heard of her since."

Noble saw no point in pursuing the inquiry. "Well," he said, "I must run along. Congratulations on winning your case."

"All in a day's work," Edward said, with complete disinterest.

Noble extended his hand to shake. "Good to see you again." Edward put out a limp hand, saying, "Enjoy your reunion."

Out on the Strand, walking toward the Savoy, Noble found Jennifer back in the forefront of his mind. Damn that encounter with Edward Cromlyn! Just when he had put all this away. What he now knew that he had not known was that she was alive at least a few years ago and was then unmarried with no children. But was she still alive? Had she possibly married again? And he had no clue as to her whereabouts. He should again forget her. But meeting Edward had excited his curiosity enough to cause him to consult the London telephone directory when he reached his room. He found no Grantham listed. Staying at the Savoy made forgetting Jennifer particularly difficult. Every time he passed through the lobby and took the lift up, he remembered that night thirty years ago.

At last the formal and official observances began. Their first was a reception in Guildhall hosted by high-ranking D-Day veterans of the British Army, the RAF, and the Royal Navy. Most were in uniform, resplendent with rows of multi-colored ribbons. Among them, here and there, Noble saw the Victoria Cross. A cacophony of English and American voices filled the medieval space. Champagne was being dispensed liberally. A musical group from a regimental band played songs from the wartime years. As Noble and Nan entered, the group was holding forth with "There'll be blue birds over the white cliffs of Dover … tomorrow … just you wait and see." Another reminder of Jennifer.

In the middle of the crowd they found Toby Kendrick. Except for gray hair and a slightly enlarged waistline, he looked much the same as when Noble last saw him in fatigues and steel helmet. Standing next to him was his wife, Marcie, whom they had not seen since their wedding. Well preserved, tall and willowy, she was the perfect General's wife, Nan later told Noble—attractive, smiling, and saying the right things to the right people.

Toby said, "The coach leaves at nine in the morning for our old stomping ground. I assume you're coming." Turning from Noble, he looked at Nan. "You too, Nan."

Nan said, "I wouldn't miss seeing where Noble was all those months, complaining of English weather."

They ran into Tim Jenkins and his wife, Barbara, whom they had never met. She was slightly less attractive than Marcie but still up to regular army wife standards. Maybe the difference between the two women was reflected in Toby's three stars compared with Tim's one. Noble thought to himself that Nan could hold her own with either of those wives. If he'd stayed in the army he and Nan might be right here, with him being addressed as General Shepperson. The three women fell into animated conversation, and Noble wandered over to speak to several Americans he knew from his division.

The gala affair was interrupted by a fanfare from the regimental musical group. "Ladies and Gentlemen," came a crisp English voice, "we conclude the evening with our national anthems."

There were hurried last swallows of champagne. The crowd fell into still and rapt attention as the band broke into "The Star Spangled Banner," followed by the somber strains of "God Save the Queen."

Shortly before noon, the coach pulled into the central square in Bramton. Toby Kendrick, in charge as usual, stood up in front and said, "We'll be here an hour and a half for lunch. There's a hotel dining room there," he pointed off to the side, "and there are several pubs within a block."

Noble stood in the square, looking around. There it all was—the county hall where the local officials and the ladies association had entertained him and his staff and where he had met Jennifer Cromlyn, the church where he had sat with Jennifer on that damp December evening to hear the children singing Christmas carols, and the monument to the Great War. He was beginning to think this outing was a mistake—everything here was inextricably tied up with Jennifer.

He was explaining the Ladies Association reception to Nan when she said, with what he thought was a slight note of suspicion, "How were the ladies here?"

"Middle-aged, warm and cheerful, but a little frumpy. They were good to us, though, so I shouldn't be critical."

They walked out to the monument. When Noble had seen it last there was only the roll of the lost in the Great War of 1914-18. Now the roster from 1939-45 had been added. It was lengthy but not nearly as long as that of the first war. "It's hard for us now," Noble said, "to comprehend the ghastly casualties in that first one."

"Wasn't it supposed to make the world safe for democracy?" Nan said.

"That's what Wilson said. Also the war to end wars. But it didn't work. Look at that second list of names."

They ducked into a pub and ate plaice and french fries; "chips" is what the waiter said. Plaice was a fish they never saw in the States. Then they were back on the bus at the appointed time.

As the driver was starting the motor, Toby, standing up front again, said, "Now we're going to swing out through our old area. I'm told a good bit has changed, so see if you can spot familiar places."

The coach moved out along a street Noble found familiar, but it was now lined with new shops, petrol stations, and, startlingly, a McDonalds. The street had lost its quaint charm. Beyond the edge of town, the coach slowed and turned. The road sign flashing by the window said, "Tiltham's Corner."

Noble's heartbeat quickened. Hedgely Farm was a half-mile down this road. Was it still there? More important, was she still there? To his disappointment, he saw that this was no longer open country. They passed several small manufacturing plants, a petrol station, and a warehouse. Twentieth century commercial blight had afflicted Bramton as much as Remberton. When they should have been at Hedgely Farm all he saw were several multi-story buildings that appeared to be apartment houses.

"What are those buildings?" Noble called to Toby.

Toby leaned over to consult the driver and then responded. "They call them council flats. It's public housing."

Then they were past, turning into another road. So Hedgely Farm had disappeared, removing Noble's last hope for a clue as to Jennifer's whereabouts. For the nth time, he resolved to put her out of mind and just enjoy this trip.

"There's your old headquarters, Noble," Toby called out, pointing to the manor house Noble had known so well. It still sat back from the road, but was now in the midst of various commercial enterprises.

"So that's where you were," Nan said. "Not bad lodging."

"You don't get the full picture. Think canvas army cots and unheated rooms. But you're right. As the army went, it was first class."

The coach continued on, with voices speaking up every minute or so.

"That was the supply dump."

"Here's where Divarty was."

"Out there, across that field, that was the 210th Engineers."

And so it went for another ten or fifteen minutes.

On the drive back to London Noble dozed most of the way. Nan, too, was quiet, perusing her guidebook, considering what she wanted to see in their remaining time. That evening they took in a performance of "A Ghost on Tiptoe," playing at the Savoy Theatre, just next to the hotel.

Bells in the towers of Westminster Abbey were sounding forth with their intermingled deep-throated booming. Noble and Nan followed the crowd into the nave. They came to the poppy-bordered inscription to the Unknown Soldier of the First World War, memorializing the many thousands forever missing along the western front, who gave their lives "for King and country." And then the memorial stone for Winston Churchill, placed there by Queen Elizabeth II. The thundering notes of the organ filled the soaring space as they moved along the aisle and took their seats. Lines from Gray's Elegy came to Noble: "Where down the long drawn aisle and fretted vault the pealing anthem swells its note of praise …

Several figures in elaborate clerical garb appeared in front and the service began. There were scripture readings and prayers for all those who had faced death and destruction, not for self or selfish gain, but to lift the dark night of tyranny from millions in Europe. A choir sang something unfamiliar to Noble. But his mind wandered. He saw again the ships loading at Southampton, the channel crossing, the landing on Utah Beach. Then the hedgerow country, the intense fighting there, and finally the breakout. He ticked off in his mind the names of those in his outfit who did not make it back.

The assemblage rose, carrying Noble and Nan to their feet, singing "O God Our Help in Ages Past." There were more prayers and then it was all over, the organ again thundering out its mighty tones. They filed out into the sunshine and blue sky of a perfect English day.

With two other couples they took a taxi back to the Savoy. As the group was standing in the lobby waiting for the lift, Nan said abruptly, with a note of concern, "What's the matter, Noble?"

Noble was staring across the lobby, his mouth slightly ajar, his face a mixture of shock and astonishment. He was absolutely certain that he was looking at Jennifer. She was walking toward the front entrance with two other women.

"Er …" he fumbled for words. "I thought I saw someone I knew. Nan, wait right here. I'll be back in a minute." He moved half running toward the front.

Out on the sidewalk he saw the woman he took to be Jennifer getting into a taxi with the other women. The taxi immediately pulled away. Noble ran up to a doorman. "In that taxi there. Do you know where they're going?"

"Sorry, sir. I don't."

He stood, teeth clenched in frustration, watching the taxi turn into the Strand and disappear. Maybe he was mistaken, he thought, in an effort to console himself. But he didn't really think so. She was slimmer, but the face and hair were unmistakable. He was overcome with a feeling of helplessness. So near and yet so out of reach. He composed himself and went back into the hotel.

"Who was it?" Nan asked.

"Nobody. I was mistaken. But it surely looked like a fellow I met during the war."

The next day was their last full day in England. Nan wanted to visit the Victoria and Albert Museum and some other galleries. Museum strolling was not particularly attractive to Noble. So he said he would probably explore a little more of legal London. They agreed to meet back in their room at the end of the day, with no special plans for the evening, other than to pack and get ready for the morrow's departure.

Noble spent a couple of hours wandering through the buildings of the Inner Temple and Middle Temple and in the Gardens down toward the river. He looked into the library and the Middle Temple's Great Hall, admiring the hammer beam roof and savoring the history of the place. Of the four Inns of Court, the Middle Temple had the closest link to America. Here numerous Americans had studied law before the Revolution, including several signers of the Declaration of Independence. He felt a close kinship with this place, viewing himself in an unbroken line of descent, living and practicing under the body of law born and developed right here and transplanted across the sea, surviving and flourishing in the New World, despite revolution and independence. When he stood before Judge McKnight seated high up on his bench in the Remberton courtroom, the language and procedure they employed had their roots in these Inns and Westminster Hall, a short way up the Thames, traces of that heritage still pronounced after nearly two hundred years.

He had lunch in the George, a nearby pub. He ordered that ubiquitous English meal—roast lamb, roasted potatoes, and brussel sprouts. He washed it down with lager, having decided it resembled American beer more than any other drink here.

He lingered at the George, having another lager, and thinking back over the trip. It had gone well. They had seen most of what they wanted to see and had enjoyable social outings with old army buddies and their wives. It had awakened long dormant memories of that great crusade of 1944-45. Best of all was the thrill and interest the trip had stirred in Nan. He had not seen her this happy about anything in years. Their marriage, he concluded, had been revived, and he felt closer to her than ever.

Back in the room for a nap, he was dozing off when the phone rang. Arousing himself, he said, "Hello."

A female voice said, "Noble?"

"Yes?" He thought it must be one of the wives they had met, but it sounded too English.

"I hope you remember me. This is Jennifer."

Chapter 12

▼

Stretched out on the bed, half asleep when the phone rang, Noble took a long second to react to the words he had just heard. Then they hit him like a dash of cold water in the face.

"Jennifer?" The word came out in half-whispered incredulousness.

Then in her charming English accent, "Do you remember me?"

Now he was sitting straight up on the bed, feet on the floor. "How could I forget? Where? … How …?"

She laughed. "I saw you in the lobby of the Savoy. At least I thought I did. I was stunned. I didn't come over to speak because I wasn't certain. And you were with a group. One was your wife, I assumed. Instead I went to the reception desk and found that a man named Noble Shepperson was registered."

"I can't believe this. I actually saw you in the Savoy, heading out the door and into a cab. I ran out, but you'd pulled away."

"Can we see each other?"

"Well, the situation is complicated."

"Could you possibly come out to tea? It's not a long tube ride from where you are."

Noble hesitated. He didn't know how to react to this extraordinary twist of events. "When did you have in mind?"

"What about this afternoon at four?"

He looked at his watch. Two o'clock. Could he have tea and be back by the time Nan returned? He had no idea when she might get back. They had no plans for the evening. All the alarm signals were sounding: no, no, no. But he was unable to say it.

His long hesitation prompted Jennifer to say, "Are you still there?"

"Yes. Just … er … just thinking over my schedule." Then, after another silence, he plunged recklessly ahead. "All right. Can you tell me how to get to your place?"

"Take the underground to South Kensington. My flat's only three blocks from the station." She gave him directions.

"I'll be there at four." He hung up and for a long while sat on the side of the bed, motionless, his mind in turmoil.

He reached her apartment a few minutes before four. It was on the second floor of a small apartment house on a quiet, cozy street in South Kensington. He paused for a minute, collecting himself, and then pushed the bell. His heart was thumping like that of a teenager on his first date.

The door opened and there stood Jennifer. For a fraction of time—it seemed longer—they looked at each other saying nothing. It was all as he remembered—those bright green eyes, wavy chestnut hair, creamy skin. When the rush of perfume hit him—that familiar, sharp sweet aroma—thirty years were wiped away.

Breaking into a big smile, she said, "Noble, do come in." She took both of his hands in hers and steered him through the door.

As the door clicked shut behind him, she said, "I do believe you haven't changed a bit."

He said, "I think you have—and for the better."

"It wasn't too good back then?"

"Oh, no. Just even better now." She was still in full figure, but a little thinner.

"Come over and have some tea," she said, leading him to a chair. Beside him was a teacart laden with scones, clotted cream, and a large pot of tea, along with sugar, lemon, and milk. She sat down and poured the tea. He wanted sugar and lemon.

They were silent during the pouring. Noble felt awkward and didn't know quite what to say. He looked around the room, a far cry from the floral stuffiness of the Edwardian sitting room at Hedgely Farm. It was done in what he assumed to be contemporary London high fashion—elegant sofa and chairs and draperies.

When they both had cups in hand, she said, "Well, how does one begin after thirty years?"

"Maybe I should begin by apologizing for not saying goodbye. There was no way."

"You had told me that, so I was prepared. Do you remember that last time we were together?" She glanced at him with a knowing smile.

Did he! It had lingered mentally for months thereafter in France and Germany. "It's stored away forever," he said, tapping his head.

"Those were quite some days," she murmured. "But tell me all about yourself since the war."

"Mostly back home in Remberton, practicing law, raising a couple of children, and generally trying to be a good citizen." He went on to tell her about the children, their families, and what they were doing. His nervousness caused him to keep talking to fill the time, so he rambled on about his life as a small town lawyer.

She poured more tea. "And what about your wife?"

"She spent the war with her parents in New York …"

"Yes, I recall."

"When I got back she came home and adjusted more or less to Remberton life. To make a long story short, she's been there ever since. Now tell me about yourself."

"It may not come as a surprise to hear that Edward and I divorced after the war."

"I know. I ran into Edward in court."

Surprise lit up her face. "You saw Edward?"

"By sheerest coincidence. I dropped in to hear an argument in the Court of Appeal, and there he was, one of the barristers."

"Did he have anything to say about me?"

"He told me you had divorced and that you then remarried a man named Grantham. I understand he died. Actually, I looked up that name in the London telephone directory and didn't come across it. So I gave up hope of finding you."

"After two husbands I took back my maiden name, Hedgely. My professional name, too. You remember Hedgely Farm, don't you?"

"Of course. But I never thought of the connection."

"Were you trying to find me?"

"As a matter of fact, yes."

"But your wife is with you, right?"

"Yes she is."

"Then why were you hoping to find me?"

Noble became more ill at ease. He resented her pressing him. "For old time's sake, I guess. A man doesn't forget somebody like you."

"It works the other way too. A woman doesn't easily forget a man like you."

After another awkward silence, Noble said, "But go on and tell me what you've been doing all these years besides having two husbands."

"I went back into the work I first did—journalistic work, writing for newspapers and magazines. I'm now freelancing, working right out of this flat. Let me show you my office."

He followed her down a short hallway and into a small room lined with overstuffed bookshelves. A window looked out on an interior courtyard shaded by trees. In front of the window was a large desk and chair. An electric typewriter sat on the desk, surrounded by file folders and notebooks.

"This is where I spend most of my days," she said. "It's quiet and peaceful." She talked about things she was writing on at the moment—the wife of a Member of Parliament, life on the London underground, construction of a new motorway, and so on.

He ran his eyes along the shelves. "I see you have a good many books on the RAF."

"My brother was a Spitfire pilot, in the Battle of Britain and later over the continent, and I've written some pieces about it."

"I recall your mentioning that."

Heading for the door, she said, "Let me show you the rest of my little nest."

They went into the hall. "Here's the dining room. Tiny, but adequate. And next is the kitchen, then the bath, and finally my room. This is just a one bedroom flat."

The room was obviously feminine—fluffy pillows on the bed, colorful pink and flowered bedspread and curtains. It looked out on the same courtyard as her office.

Standing by the bed, Noble felt the powerful pull of those days at Hedgely Farm, days he had resolved to put behind, to be locked away in memory. But now in her bedroom, seeing her in living, vibrant flesh, he felt that resolve eroding.

His detached and dreamy expression brought her over from the dressing table where she had been standing. She ran her arms around his waist, beneath his coat, her hands pressing against the back of his shirt. Nuzzling alongside his cheek, she whispered in his ear, "Noble, what are you thinking?"

He said nothing, remained motionless. He felt the full length of her body firmly against him. His thoughts were a confused jumble. Here was the powerful, sensual attraction he had known. It was all still there, maybe even more so. This was not the lonely young wife of a far away British officer, but an experienced woman of the world, sophisticated and aggressive. His fantasies over the years could be realized right here and now. But he was lacking the rationalization and justification of that long-ago dalliance—the wartime exemption from the normal standards of decent human behavior. This was not wartime, and Nan was not three thousand miles away but right here in London. He could think of no exemption now. He wanted to say he should leave.

Instead, he put his arms around her and said, "I'm not sure."

For a moment her large eyes bore into his. Then she pulled him forward and kissed him.

Mustering a weak resolve, he said, quietly, "Maybe I ought to be going. It's getting late."

"No, no, don't go. We've waited too long for this." She hugged him tightly, pressing her cheek against his. He felt the warm wetness of tears. He held her tightly, and neither said anything.

Then she backed up, pulling a tissue from her dress pocket and dabbing at tears. "I think we're both a bit edgy. Let's have a drink and relax."

Relieved, he mumbled, "Good idea."

So they went to the kitchen. She placed two glasses and a bottle on the counter.

"Help yourself," she said. "If you want it American style, there's ice in the fridge."

Noble poured half a glass of scotch. "Think I'll take it English style," he said. "May I help you?"

"Sure. I'll have the same."

He splashed scotch into her glass, handed it to her, leaned against the counter, and sipped the peat-smoked liquor. She sat down on a chair at a little table and crossed her shapely legs. She did indeed look every bit as good as she had thirty years ago—and maybe better to his sixty-five-year-old eyes.

With the warmth building up in his stomach, Noble began to feel more relaxed. But he had to think this situation through, not lose control. He didn't want to hurt Jennifer. And then there was Nan. She might be getting back to the hotel about now.

Jennifer said, "This is a little like old times, isn't it? Not as cozy as Hedgely Farm, but nice enough."

Noble nodded, said nothing, and sipped his drink. Another awkward silence ensued.

Then she got up, put her glass on the table, and stepped over to him. She took his face in her hands and said, "Noble, I have to tell you something." She stopped and hugged him around the neck.

He ran his arms around her waist and said, "What?"

"Here goes a real confession, a bearing of my soul." She paused, as though debating whether to proceed.

When she didn't continue, he said, "I'm listening."

"My second husband and I got along all right, but it was a marriage of convenience, no real love. And of course, there wasn't much with Edward. But you, you have never been out of my mind. Those weeks in the spring of '44 were the best of my life, an idyllic time. I've come to realize—you're the only man I've ever really loved."

He squeezed her more tightly, but made no response.

Looking at him intently, she said, "I've always thought you felt the same about me."

His embrace tightened, impulsively, not thinking—rational thought was diminishing—and they kissed and kissed again.

Then with all the deliberation he could summon, he said, "I did love you then. I can't say I don't still love you—but I'm a married man."

"You were married then."

"I know, but it was the war."

"But it was you and me, just like it's you and me here right now. Let's forget everything else for just a little while." She kissed him again. Then whispered, "Let's go back to my room."

Never in his life had he felt so torn, so caught in a painful tugging, so wrenched in a moment of critical choice. It was either the bedroom or the front door. Every primeval instinct in his body pulled him toward that room where they could relive those emotionally intense hours on the eve of the great drama of 1944. With the warm and cuddly Jennifer in his arms, her soft, scented hair pressing against his cheek, her suggestion seemed irresistible; whatever reluctance he had within him was melting. But like the drowning man in a last heroic effort to reach the surface, he summoned all his inner strength and said, weakly, "I can't do it. You know I want to, but I just can't."

She held on to him, tears flowing again. He said softly, "I'm sorry."

Dabbing her cheeks and sniffling, she said, "I thought it providential that I saw you in the Savoy—a miracle—something, if I can be a bit melodramatic, divinely engineered. But I guess I was wrong. We would be better off if I hadn't seen you."

"No. I don't think so. I've wanted to see you again for years, to know what happened to you, how you were getting along. I wouldn't take anything for this afternoon."

"It's odd. Back then, I was upset over not having a chance to say goodbye. Now I'm upset over actually having to say it. That's what it is, isn't it? We'll never see each other again."

Noble now did not want to prolong matters. He didn't want to hurt her feelings. He did love and respect her. But there was no good way to leave except to leave. He disengaged, took her hand, and began moving toward the front door. "I really must be going."

At the door, he turned, and they faced each other, their eyes meeting. There was a last intense embrace and kiss. He opened the door, stepped outside, and turned.

She said, "Last time I had no chance to say it. This time I won't say it." Then, in a whisper, "I think we'll meet again."

He smiled, said nothing, but raised his hand in a semblance of a farewell wave. Then he was gone.

By the time he got back to the Savoy, Noble had recomposed himself. The ride on the underground had given him time to come down from the emotional high with Jennifer and readjust his thoughts to Nan. When he reached the room, he found her packing.

"Well," she said, "I was beginning to get worried. You must have had a full day."

"Rambled through the Inner Temple and Middle Temple and did the gardens all the way down to the river. How about you?"

"Spent the whole day in the Victoria and Albert. Could spend several more. It's a fantastic place." Turning to an open suitcase on the bed, she said, "I'm just about packed."

"I can put my stuff together pretty quickly. I'll tell you what. We started our time here with roast beef at Simpson's. I suggest we end it with Dover sole at Simpson's."

"You won't get any objection from me."

"First, though," he said, "let's have a little shooter." He went to the dresser where he had a bottle of gin. He poured some into a pair of glasses and handed her one. "Ice will seem funny when we get home."

She took her glass, went to the window, and looked up the Thames. The scene was suffused with the last glow of a fading sunset. "Oh, Noble," she said, "this is the finest trip we've ever had. It's been nearly perfect, don't you think?"

He walked over to her, put his arms around her waist from behind, and gazed with her up the river, his cheek pressed against her soft brown hair. "Yes it has been."

Snuggled up to Nan, Noble felt more in love with her than he had at any time in recent years. But the afternoon had rekindled all his old emotions about Jennifer. Could a man be in love with two women at the same time? Could the mere thought of another woman make him an unfaithful husband? Maybe he was rationalizing, but he thought not. So long as he was a loving and attentive husband to Nan, he found it hard to condemn himself for his fantasies about Jennifer. After all, until that afternoon he hadn't seen her for thirty years and would never see her again. Nan would be a living flesh and blood love, with him every day, while Jennifer would be only a mental abstraction. He persuaded himself that he could live with that duality with no disrespect to Nan. He would go forward with her, having Jennifer as only a memory.

Chapter 13

Miss Alice, at her desk as usual, smiled broadly as Noble walked in. She said, "Welcome back! How did the trip go?"

"Fine. No glitches. It was everything we expected. I'll have to tell you more about it later. Anything important here?"

"Probably not. There's a whole stack of mail on your desk."

Noble went back to his office, sat down and surveyed the daunting piles of letters and other documents. He never enjoyed the first day back. Plowing through accumulated mail was a tedious task. Now he had also to return to the Grady investigation and negotiating the library deal.

"I hope I don't have any appointments today," he said to Miss Alice, who had followed him.

"No. I kept your calendar clear."

"Good. Now if you can just get me a cup of coffee, I'll start wading through this pile."

There were letters from clients, the state bar, law book publishers, and charities wanting money. Other lawyers had been busy—a motion to produce documents, a motion for summary judgment; also the circuit court's docket for July.

"How about telephone calls?" Noble said, when Miss Alice returned with the coffee.

"No messages of any importance. Most said they would call back."

"Call Melba Robinson and see if she can set up a meeting of the library board in the next few days—here in my office."

Summer had now descended on Remberton. Mid-afternoon temperatures were ninety degrees and above. The air-conditioners that had taken over the town were in high gear. No longer were neighbors sitting on porches in the late afternoon and evening or on lawn chairs outside. Everyone was sealed up inside, most of them looking at television. The combination of AC and TV had struck a powerful blow at community life. The quietness of summer evenings, with the rising and falling sounds of katydids in the trees, was seriously disturbed by the incessant humming of window units or monstrous boxed machinery supplying central systems.

On top of TV and air-conditioning had come the interstate highway, working still more far-reaching change in the Remberton Noble had known in the 1930s and forties. Back then, one could get his arms around the whole town, with its simpler institutional structure—one bank, one picture show, one business street, a train station. There were, of course, the divides between black and white, between the cotton mill and the rest. But within the world that Noble inhabited was one swimming pool, one grammar school, one high school, one Boy Scout troop, one country club, one church for each major denomination. All that had changed, giving way to a more fragmented and dispersed community, a loss of coherence. Of all the institutions, the law and the court through which it was administered endured most unchanged, the glue holding society together. They were symbolized by that somber Victorian edifice, its tall clock tower dominating the head of Center Street and sounding out the hours across the decades.

Another change was in the state of summer dress. Paradoxically, with air-conditioning chilling all interiors had come deterioration in business attire. Coats and ties were disappearing, in favor of the short-sleeved sport shirt. Noble realized that this trend was well advanced when Ben Harris arrived for the library board meeting tieless and in short sleeves. The bar and the bench were among the last holdouts. Noble and the Judge appeared in suit and tie.

Women too had not been immune from the deteriorating state of dress. More sleeveless sun-back dresses and shorter skirts were worn than ever before, and tank tops and cutoffs were common at the shopping center. Even Ann Simmons showed up for the board meeting in Bermuda shorts.

As the members assembled in Noble's conference room, they all took the same seats they had previously occupied, as though they had staked out a piece of personal turf. All were perspiring; the women's faces flushed pink.

Norma Armistead said, "It's another hot one. Those of us who grew up without air-conditioning ought to be used to it, but we've gotten soft."

Melba Robinson said, "Noble, this room is like a meat locker. I'm going to start carrying a sweater in the summer. Isn't that crazy?"

Noble went over to a wall thermostat and turned it up. "Tell me if that gets better."

They wanted to know about his trip, so he gave them a brief outline.

Finally Noble said they had better get down to the business at hand. "I gave a lot of thought to our library funding problem on the flight back," he said, "and I developed an idea I want to try out on you."

Miss Alice stuck her head in the door and asked whether anybody wanted coffee, but all declined. She was among the shrinking minority of women who maintained what Noble considered a proper state of dress. Looking like the 1950s, she increasingly stood out from the rest.

Noble continued. "I start with the fact that Lucille and Jesse have each proposed to give over two million dollars for the library building. My thought is that rather than have them compete over this, we get them together and coordinate their efforts. It's ambitious and maybe unrealistic, but here it is. We persuade each one to give two million dollars, thus giving us a total of four million." He spoke these last words slowly and deliberately.

"Noble, did the oxygen run low on your flight home?"

"I know it sounds crazy, but I think it's worth a try. I would propose to use that money in three ways. First, to build and equip the new building, giving us one of the best libraries in the country. Next, I would put some of the money into a permanent endowment, the income to be used for general maintenance and future book acquisitions. Then, finally, I would take whatever is left over and create a permanent scholarship fund, to provide financial aid for needy Rembert County residents who want to attend college."

They all looked at him intently, gripped by the unthinkable prospect of four million dollars.

Melba, sitting at the other end of the table, smiled and said, "Noble, that is indeed a creative idea. It's breathtaking. The only catch is that somebody has to talk those two into doing it."

Norma said, "How does the name thing figure into your idea?"

"A good point," Noble said. "It seems to me we'd have to stomach these names or have no deal—probably have to use both names, either Funchess-Rooter or Rooter-Funchess."

"Two illustrious and distinguished names in the history of Rembert County," Ben said, "inspirations for future generations." There were mild chuckles around the table, sounding more disgusted than amused.

"What order would those names be in?" asked Ann.

"I guess we'd just have to flip a coin," Noble said. "Maybe the winner would have the name first on the library, but have it the other way around on the endowment and scholarship funds.

Silence fell over the group, all meditating over this bold idea—four million dollars being more than anyone in Remberton had ever dreamed of—and the prospect of seeing those two names so prominently installed in the center of their town.

The Judge then spoke up. "We've never decided what we think about those names."

"They haven't exactly been greeted with enthusiasm," Norma said.

"You haven't decided anything," Noble said. "What I would like to get from this board is a decision on whether you would like me to pursue this idea with Lucille and Jesse. In other words, I need a green light before I do anything."

Ann said, "I like it. Four million would confer unimaginable benefits on this community. As for the names, neither is a criminal, as far as I know. They wouldn't be my first pick, but I can live with them for four million."

"If you found out that one of them had committed a crime, would that make a difference to you?" asked Norma.

"That's where I'd draw the line, but nobody's suggested any criminal activity," replied Ann. "So, just to get the matter formally before us, I move that the board accept Noble's idea and request him to proceed with it."

Judge McKnight said, "Leaving aside for the time being the question of the names?"

"Yes," said Ann.

Norma said, "There's a cynical old adage that everything is for sale—at a price."

"I'll second the motion," Melba said. "Now we can discuss it. Any further thoughts?"

"To be brutally frank," Ben said, "I can't stomach the idea of the Rooter and Funchess names on this library. But I see the handwriting on the wall, and I don't want to be an obstructionist. To be comfortable with my principles, I think I should abstain."

"Any more comments?" asked Melba. "This is the most important matter we've faced on this board in my time." She paused for a long moment, looking around the table. Then she said, "If no one has anything else to say, let's take a vote. All in favor of the motion raise hands."

After looking at each member, she said, "The motion is carried by a vote of four in favor, with one abstention. Noble, you have a green light."

Shortly after lunch a few days later, Noble was climbing the familiar steps of the Craighill house, a place he had visited many times over the years. Not to see Catherine, but because Dr. Lucius Craighill had been one of his clients as well as close friend and doctor, having brought his two children into this world and overseen the departure from it of his sister, Emily, and her husband, Edward Kirkman. Noble was here now in response to a call from Catherine saying she wanted to talk to him but preferred not to do so in his office. He assumed it was a follow-up to their conversation about a library contribution. He didn't want to abandon that possibility; the grandiose scheme to get millions from Lucille and Jesse might fall through.

Catherine greeted him at the front door and took him into the parlor. The central air-conditioning gave immediate relief from the humid midday heat. She was in her library work mode—hair pulled back in ponytail, plain dress, and comfortable shoes, presenting a much less glamorous appearance than when she was in party attire.

After asking about Nan and their English trip, she said, in her slightly husky voice, "I understand Jesse Rooter has offered to give two million dollars for a new library building."

"I never cease to marvel at the news-spreading capacity of this town."

"Is it true?"

"Partly. He might even give more. But his offer is conditional and by no means final."

"Conditioned on what?"

"On my Grady investigation. If I don't get to the bottom of the affair he might back off entirely."

"That's what I've heard and that's why I asked you to come over."

"Last time we talked you said you didn't have anything else to say."

"I wasn't altogether honest. I hope you'll forgive me. Now that I see all this money at stake, I'll swallow my pride and give you a tidbit that may or may not be helpful."

"By all means."

"Well," she hesitated, "Last time we talked didn't you say Jesse told you about Grady and me?"

"Yes, but he didn't say much."

"I guess he's too much of a gentleman. There was more to it than you know. It's terribly embarrassing. I hope you will keep this in absolute confidence."

"You can count on it."

She took a deep breath. "Well, here goes." She proceeded to describe how they came together while Grady was working at the house and eventually ended up in bed.

Noble was taken aback, although he shouldn't have been, in light of what he had heard about Grady's sexual prowess. But news that this cotton mill lowlife was in bed with the daughter of the revered Dr. Craighill in this very house was almost too much to absorb. He made an effort to conceal his reaction and simply said, "I suppose that's not surprising. He seems to have been quite a ladies' man."

"No telling what he was doing with some other girls. I have my suspicions. But anyway, my parents found out about it and were outraged, as you can imagine. I'd never seen my father so upset. They prohibited me from seeing him. Now I get to what may be of some help in your investigation. Do you mind if I smoke?"

"No, not at all."

She got up, went to the chest of drawers, and picked out an already open pack of cigarettes and a lighter. "I get all edgy when I think about that foolish escapade." She sat down, lit up, and crossed her legs. Noble could not avoid noticing their shapeliness.

"Now let me go on," she said. "I have to admit, as crazy and embarrassing as it is, I wanted to see him some more. One day he called me—fortunately when nobody was here—and we agreed he would pick me up the next night at 10:30 at the foot of the driveway. My parents always went to bed at ten." She paused, drew deeply on the cigarette, and exhaled. "When the next night came—and this was the night before they found him in the creek—I slipped out the back door and went around the house and started down the driveway. Then I saw his convertible pull up and stop. Before I could get down the driveway, a car pulled up and stopped in front of him. Two men got out and ran back and jumped in Grady's car. Then both cars took off."

"Did you know those two men? Could you recognize them if you saw them again?"

"No. It was too dark. We picked that spot for him to pick me up because there's no nearby street light. It was a dark night too. No moon."

"What kind of car were they in?"

"Couldn't tell. Just a standard-looking car."

"What did you do then?"

"I stood around for a little while, wondering what was going on and whether Grady might come back. Finally I slipped back in the house and went to bed. I was really disappointed."

"When did you first hear what happened to Grady?"

"The next afternoon Julia McKnight called and told me. Said her father had just told her. You remember he was the solicitor then. She was upset and crying. After we hung up, I cried too."

"And you never said anything to anybody about what you had seen?"

"That's right. I was afraid how my parents might react if they heard about it. Then, too, there didn't seem any point in mentioning it."

"Every piece of a puzzle is important. Put together with other pieces it might give us a picture. Anyway, I appreciate knowing about it."

"Well, that's all I have to say. I hope you won't think any less of me because of that juvenile fling. It's horribly embarrassing and I can't imagine telling anybody but you about it."

"We all have things in our past we wish weren't there." That thought lingered in the quiet air for a moment. "So don't worry about it. Your secret is safe with me." Then he added, in a lowered voice, "Let him who is without sin cast the first stone."

She smiled at the Biblical allusion. "Thank you," she said. "I'm glad to get it off my mind." She rose and snuffed out her cigarette. "I know you're busy, so I won't keep you."

At the door, she put her hand on his arm and said, "Do come back anytime."

Approaching his office the next morning, pondering what to do, Noble encountered Frank Brandon on the sidewalk. The June sun was already high in the cloudless blue sky. The never-dressy newspaper editor had adopted the summer style of most denizens of Center Street and was in short-sleeved sport shirt.

"Morning, Colonel," Frank said, "what's the news?" The military address for Noble was used by many of the younger set, partly out of respect and partly to play to his ego.

"I thought you were the one with the news."

"I have to get it from somewhere. I hear you're a good source for a couple of hot stories. Can we talk?"

"Sure. Come on in."

When they had seated themselves in Noble's office, Frank said, "Two rumors going around I'd like to check out with you."

"No telling what they are, but let me have them."

"One is that this mystery man from Chicago named Jesse Rooter is talking about giving two million dollars for a new library building. Any comment?"

"Am I right, Frank, in thinking that the *Progress* views as its mission the good of the town and county?"

"One of its missions. Another is to print the news—and talk about two million in this place is real news."

"If it were a done deal, yes. But at the talking stage I'd like to ask your cooperation in not undoing the possibility."

"Are you affirming or denying the rumor?"

"Neither. I'm asking your help in not derailing a possible bonanza for this place by not printing anything about it for the time being. There'll be time enough to run the story if anything comes of it."

"O.K. As usual, you've persuaded me. But I have another. Word is that you're investigating the 1946 death of a man named Grady Rooter, brother of mystery man Jesse. Is this true?"

"Now, that's something we can talk about," Noble said. "In fact, I was just considering asking you for help." Noble explained the whole situation. The town had a big stake in facilitating his investigation, he said, because it might affect what Jesse would do with his money. "We need to find somebody who knows something. Money might induce somebody to talk, and Jesse is prepared to put it up. Would you consider doing a story on this including the proposed rewards?"

"What kind of reward?"

"Up to $25,000."

Frank whistled. "That kind of money in Remberton ought to start tongues wagging."

"Can I talk you into a story?"

"You don't have to talk much. You've got it."

They discussed details, and Frank left saying he would do a draft and run it by Noble.

The next week's issue of *The Remberton Progress* carried this front-page item:

INVESTIGATION UNDERWAY IN 1946 ROOTER DEATH; SUBSTANTIAL REWARDS OFFERED

Grady Rooter, a Marine Corps veteran and employee of Denkens Construction Company, was found dead in Possum Creek on August 6, 1946. His red convertible automobile was parked nearby with empty beer cans and liquor bottles in it. Authorities ruled that death was the result of accidental drowning.

Now the deceased man's brother, Jesse Rooter of Chicago, has engaged attorney Noble Shepperson to investigate the event. The elder brother wants to find out whether the death was accidental or whether foul play was involved. Both Rooter brothers grew up in Remberton and are graduates of Remberton High School.

With the hope of inducing those who might have information related to Grady Rooter's death to come forward, Jesse Rooter is offering rewards up to $25,000. The exact amount of each reward will depend on how important the information is in shedding light on the death. Anyone with relevant information on this matter should see Colonel Shepperson in his office on Center Street or contact him by telephone.

Since returning from England Noble had been working longer than usual hours, catching up on matters accumulated during his absence and getting ready for a busy July. Judge McKnight, determined to eliminate his docket backlog, had set a full schedule for July. Noble was on the docket for three trials and several other hearings. A few decades ago, the sultry heat of mid-summer, turning the courtroom into something like a Turkish bath, would have made July trials a rarity. But the technological marvel of air-conditioning had made July as useable as October or any other month. Indeed, the whole South had been transformed into year-round life, much like the

North. So the Fourth of July came and went, and Noble was as busy throughout the rest of the month as he had ever been.

After the last library board meeting he had a couple of telephone conversations with Jesse Rooter and Lucille Brentson, laying before them the idea of a joint gift. Jesse did not like it but did not reject it out of hand. He maintained he wanted Noble to pursue the investigation further before making up his mind.

Lucille at first was irate. "What? Link Funchess with Rooter! It's ridiculous." But then she calmed down, as Noble explained the great benefit that could come to the community. In any case, nothing more could be done until Noble could satisfy Jesse with some investigative results. She agreed to withhold judgment.

One afternoon Noble came home slightly earlier than usual, pleased that one of his cases had just been settled, avoiding what would have been a difficult trial. He was anxious to tell Nan, but when he came in the kitchen she was not there.

He walked through the house and found her in the bedroom. She was in her standard around-the-house summer outfit—Bermuda shorts and T-shirt—rummaging around in a drawer. On the bed was an open suitcase.

"What's going on?" he said.

"Mama took a fall and broke her hip this morning. I just got a call a couple of hours ago. I've got to go."

"Sorry to hear this. Doesn't she have her usual help?"

"She does, but she needs me now. They don't know how long she'll be in the hospital or what the situation will be when she gets home."

"Hate to have you go, but I understand. When do you plan to leave?"

"There's a flight early tomorrow that will get me to Newburgh by mid-afternoon."

"How long do you think you'll be gone?"

"I just can't say." She seemed distraught. "Mama was doing so well and now this has to happen."

He gave her a hug. "Now don't get upset. I'm sure it'll all work out. She's got good doctors. Just stay as long as you think necessary. Nothing much is going on here."

"I've talked to Ruby. She'll come every day and fix your lunch and get something together for supper. Now I better get back to packing."

"Looks like you need a little pick-me-up."

"Do I ever! Gin on the rocks."

Noble was left alone in the house for the first time in years, with time in the quietness of the evenings to reflect over Nan and the last few weeks. The English trip had been a mountaintop experience. From that high, which Noble at the time thought might be artificially inflated, she had fallen back into one of her moody periods. He couldn't figure out why. Part of it may have been the long hours he had been working, with correspondingly less time to be with her. Maybe, as always, it was Remberton. Whatever the reason, she once again seemed distant and aloof. He resolved to be more attentive when she returned, maybe take her down on the Gulf Coast for a little while.

Word got around quickly that Nan was gone, and he began to get invitations to dinner or for drinks. Everyone had, of course, seen the newspaper article about his investigation and the astronomical rewards Jesse Rooter was offering. In fact, Jesse Rooter, son of a tenant farmer and cotton mill worker, was now the fashionable topic of conversation in the best houses in town.

A few days after Nan left, Noble was in his office when the buzzer sounded. Miss Alice said, "There's a woman on the phone, with an English accent, who says her name is Jennifer Hedgley."

Noble said nothing. What he had just heard was so out of context, so far removed from where it should be, so startling and unexpected that he was thrown mentally off balance.

Miss Alice said, "Are you there?"

"Oh, er, yes." His voice was low and tentative. Then, recovering a bit, he added, "Yes, put her on."

He heard the phone click, signaling that Miss Alice was off and the caller was on. "Hello, Jennifer?"

"Noble, how are you?"

"Surprised out of my mind. Where are you?"

"Washington. *The Manchester Guardian* sent me over here to do a series of stories on the British Ambassador and his staff. It's a great assignment."

"Extraordinary to find you in the States. Where are you staying?"

"At the Statler Hilton. But my days are so busy that I'm rarely here except to sleep."

"How long are you staying?"

"Probably another couple of weeks. Which brings me to one of the reasons I'm calling. There's a big reception coming up at the British Embassy next week, the last social function before things shut down for the summer. Any chance you could come up?"

Still struggling to regain mental equilibrium, he said, "Just a minute. Let me look at my calendar." His mind went into a whir. He flipped through his appointment book. With the settlement of his big case, he had no more trials scheduled until fall. He saw two appointments with clients that could be rescheduled. Nan had said she would be gone at least another week. So the deck appeared to be clear. But he needed time to think.

"Jennifer, I'll have to call you back. I would have to rearrange some things."

"I understand. The best time to reach me here today and tomorrow is between five and six." She gave him the telephone number. "You remember in London we didn't say goodbye."

After they hung up, Noble sat immobile for several minutes. It had been less than two months since he had put her away. Why did she have to resurface? He was irritated—mildly angry—at her reappearance, yet also excited. His internal warning system seemed to fail. With Nan gone indefinitely, his resistance to that lilting English voice crumbled.

Chapter 14

They stood in the receiving line in the great hall of the British Embassy. Throngs had preceded them and many were coming in after. It was a social occasion that brought out everybody who was anybody in Washington.

Noble had arrived late the night before and checked into the Statler Hilton. He and Jennifer had met in the lobby shortly before the reception. "This is unreal," she had said, as they embraced lightly. "I knew we shouldn't have said goodbye." They had taken a taxi to the imposing establishment on Massachusetts Avenue.

On the way, she was bubbling over with accounts of her experiences in Washington in the last few days. Noble said little, mesmerized by her glamorous presence and marveling over the unlikelihood of the whole situation. Seeing her twice in seven weeks after a thirty-year absence! Having commended himself on his resistance on that last meeting, he was now wondering whether it could be sustained. He already felt himself being drawn in, like a fly in a spider's web, by her soft English accent, the pungent sweetness of her perfume, a scent he remembered so well, and those large, bright eyes.

The line was edging closer to the Ambassador. Over the hubbub of the crowd, sounds of a distant string quartet could be heard.

Noble said, "This is pretty fancy business for a small town Alabama lawyer."

Jennifer said, "That young man standing just this side of the Ambassador is his aide, Nicholas Cottingham. He's been a great help to me. He'll present us to the Ambassador."

The tall, thin man she pointed to appeared to be in his late twenties. Above his sharp, fox-like face was a thick clump of sandy blond hair. Noble thought him rather handsome.

As the line brought them forward, the young man said in a buoyant voice, "Jennifer! You're looking marvelous."

"Thank you, Nicky," she said. "This is Mr. Shepperson, an old friend and a lawyer from Alabama."

"Delighted to have you with us," Nicky said. Turning to the Ambassador, he said, "You remember Jennifer Hedgely."

"Of course," the Ambassador boomed. He had the red-sunburned face of a yachtsman, topped by a full head of white hair. "You're going to tell all about us in *The Guardian*."

"I doubt it will be all," she said.

"Well, do make us look as good as you can."

Nicky said, "This is Mr. Shepperson, a friend of Jennifer from Alabama."

"Welcome to the Embassy," the Ambassador said. "I remember the *Alabama Claims* from English history."

"Those were Northern claims," Noble said, with a big smile.

"So they were," the Ambassador said, with a laugh. "We did give your side a rather good ship."

"None better in that war," Noble said.

The line moved on. A white-coated waiter handed each of them a glass of champagne. They emerged into a garden. Summer was not prime time for Washington garden parties, but they were lucky today. The temperature had taken a drop and the sun was behind clouds. Jennifer encountered a couple of Embassy staff members she had met and they chatted. Otherwise, they saw no one they knew.

"Let's sit over here," she said, pointing to an empty table under an open-sided tent. A breeze had sprung up, making the afternoon quite pleasant.

They had been talking awhile about what Noble had been doing since getting back home when Nicky Cottingham approached. "Mind if I join you for a moment?" he said. "The line has finally dissolved."

"Do sit down," Jennifer said, just as a waiter appeared and refilled their glasses.

Noble said, "How does a young man like you get such a choice assignment?"

Nicky laughed. "A bit of luck. I hadn't been with the Foreign Office long, actually just a couple of years out of Oxford, when one day I was asked if I would like to be posted to Washington. You may imagine my delight. One never knows how these things happen."

"I should tell you, Noble," Jennifer said, "Nicky's father was a life peer—Lord Cottingham. He died a few years back. The family has a grand country place in Hampshire."

"It is nice," Nicky said, "but unfortunately I'm not able to get there much these days. When I do get back, Jennifer, you'll have to come down for a weekend. Bring Mr. Shepperson, too."

"That's very generous," Noble said, "but I don't expect to be back in England for quite a while. I don't suppose you've ever been to Alabama."

"No. I've been to only a handful of states—nothing south of Virginia—but would like to do more before I leave."

"Well," Noble said, "if you're ever in the mood to see Alabama please let me know. I'd be happy to have you as a guest and show you around." He handed Nicky his business card.

"Thank you very much," Nicky said. "Now I'm afraid I must move on to speak to some of our other guests. Jennifer, I imagine I'll be seeing more of you."

"You certainly will, but I'll try not to make a nuisance of myself."

When Nicky had gone, Jennifer said, "He's really made my job easier, introducing me all around and talking with me about what goes on here. His father was a real bibliophile and Nicky inherited a wonderful library. Cottingham Hall is a grand place, judging from what I've heard about it. Wouldn't it be nice if we could have a weekend there?" She smiled suggestively.

"Another one of those fantasy trips," Noble said quietly.

"It wouldn't have to be fantasy. It could be real."

Noble said nothing, but sipped champagne, looking out over the crowd, apprehensively wondering how this evening might go. Then he said, "Would it suit you to leave and go on to dinner?"

"Let's do."

In the Statler-Hilton dining room they both ate salmon, accompanied by a bottle of California Chardonnay. The noisy room was filled with men and a scattering of women—businessmen and lobbyists from all over the country—mixed with Washington politicians and bureaucrats, dispensers of federal largess, either of money or of favorable regulatory treatment.

The room was alive with talk about Watergate, speculation over whether President Nixon would be impeached or would resign.

Midway through the meal Jennifer said, "Noble, going back for a minute to Nicky." She hesitated. "Perhaps I shouldn't say this, but I think you should have the full picture. Of course, I say this in complete confidence." She paused and took a sip of wine.

When, after a few seconds, she didn't continue, he said, "Well, what is it?"

"With all the charm you saw Nicky exuding, there is another side to him. I get this from some of his father's friends in London. For one thing, Nicky is a big spender, living beyond his means. His father left a good-size debt and Nicky has added to it. He's tried to lean on family friends for financial help, in a way they think is overbearing and rather unpleasant. One of them said he's downright deceitful. Since I've gotten to know him on this trip, I can see signs of deviousness. I'm reluctant to say all this, because he's been a real help, and I do like him personally."

"You know," Noble said, slowly, "there's more than one side to most people. It's good to perceive something like this before you get drawn in. With all that, I'm surprised the Ambassador has him on his staff."

"It's hard to believe he doesn't know about some of it. My guess is he keeps him on despite this because Nicky is so charming and good at his job."

"Well, anyway," Noble said, "it's doubtful my path and his will ever cross again. Can't see how they would."

After Noble paid their check, he said, "How about a nightcap in the bar?"

"It would be more comfortable in my room. *The Guardian* has set me up with spacious accommodations, and I do have a bottle of scotch."

Noble hesitated, torn as he had been in her London apartment. But now alone with her in Washington, with his eyes locked on hers, he felt powerless to do what his rational faculties told him to do.

The words came quietly and surprisingly, as though spoken by someone else. "All right."

They went to the front desk in the lobby to pick up their room keys. The attendant, handing the keys over the counter, said, "Here's a message, Mr. Shepperson."

Noble tore open the small envelope and read, "Please call your wife as soon as possible."

He looked at Jennifer and said, "I need to put in a quick phone call. I'll make it from my room and be on up shortly."

Fifteen minutes later, Noble knocked on Jennifer's door. She opened it and he stepped in. She closed the door, but her smile instantly vanished.

"What's the matter?" she said, with concern, seeing from his expression that something was wrong.

"Nan's mother died this afternoon. I've got to go right away. I called the airline. There's an eleven o'clock flight I can just make if I hurry."

Her face was a mask of disappointment. Her bright eyes dulled. She stepped forward and ran her arms around his neck and hugged him tightly. He put his arms around her, but neither spoke. They kissed, and then she nuzzled up against his ear.

"Noble," she whispered, "why does fate tantalize us, torture us, this way—bringing us together and then tearing us apart?"

He pulled her more tightly against him, his hands rubbing the soft warmth of her back. "Jennifer … Jennifer," he sighed. "I do love you, but nothing can come of this. There's the Atlantic Ocean between us, not to mention my wife."

"Worse obstacles have been overcome. You've said yourself that you think you're bored. Your children are grown and married. Why not start a new life? I'd move to the States in a heartbeat. Or you might like England."

"It's an enticing dream, almost irresistible. But it can't be. I can't leave Nan. Not now anyway."

"Never say never."

"I really must run."

"We didn't say goodbye last time, so let's not say it now."

Noble could think of nothing else to say. He had to catch a plane. He squeezed her to him and kissed her again, then quickly disengaged and slipped out the door.

A week later Noble was back in Remberton. He had helped Nan with arrangements for her mother's funeral and stayed around for a few days. But then he had to get home to attend to client matters and Judge McKnight's docket. Nan was staying on in Newburgh to close out her mother's apartment. When her father died several years earlier her mother had sold the house and disposed of much furniture and other accumulated artifacts, so Nan had less to deal with now.

On this Sunday afternoon Noble was sitting on his porch reading the *Birmingham News*. The paper, like television and radio, was filled with news of President Nixon's resignation, ending the long nightmare of Watergate. Although it was a sultry August day, the dense shade and the steadily clicking ceiling fan made the porch livable. He much preferred fresh air to air-conditioning unless the heat and humidity were too great for the fan to overcome.

With Nan away, he had played hooky from church in order to relax and go through backed-up mail and newspapers. He needed some quiet too, time to come down from the emotional rollercoaster of the Washington evening and the Newburgh funeral. He was emotionally conflicted over the appearance of Jennifer. While he had again been entranced, he resented her reopening what he had put behind. He didn't trust himself in her magnetic presence. What would have happened if he hadn't had the call about his mother-in-law's death? Once again, he resolved to put Jennifer away. Nan had taken her mother's death hard, and he determined to give her all the support he could muster.

The telephone began to ring. He put down the paper and went to the den and answered.

"Is that Colonel Shepperson?" said an unfamiliar male voice.

"Yes."

"I hear tell you're willing to pay money for information about Grady Rooter."

Noble was snapped out of his summer afternoon lethargy. "It's possible. Do you have something?"

"Yes, sir. How much will you pay for it?"

"Depends on how valuable and credible it is."

"Couldn't get more valuable than what I've got to say."

Noble tried to identify the accent. It was country, but didn't sound familiar.

Noble said, "Can you tell me who you are and where you are?"

"Not anywhere near you. But I want to hear about this reward."

"Let me ask you a few questions," Noble said. "Can you tell me something specific about how Grady Rooter died?"

"Yes, sir."

"Does your information show he did not accidentally drown?"

"Yes, sir."

Now Noble put the big question. "Does the information you have show he was murdered?"

"I think you'd have to say that."

Noble made an effort to sound matter-of-fact despite his inner excitement. "Are you prepared to name names—to identify who was involved?"

"If I know what you'll pay for it."

"Can you meet with me here in Remberton?"

"I've got to know what you'll pay."

Noble was caught in a circle. This man might have the key to the mystery, but without hearing from him in detail, with an opportunity for probing examination, Noble couldn't tell whether what he had to say was credible or worth paying for. But if he didn't promise to pay the man something, he apparently wouldn't talk at all. After considering for a moment, Noble said, "Are you a long way from here?"

"I'm in Texas."

"I'll cover your expenses to fly here. Then we can talk about it. How much reward you get depends on what you say."

"I need to know more than that."

Noble hesitated. "O.K … I'll guarantee you $5,000 just to come here and talk to me. Then if you can give me specific information such as you say—naming names and factual details—and I find it credible, I'll pay a total of $25,000."

"You gonna send me a ticket and give me $5,000 as soon as I get there? Cash, no check."

"Yes, but now I've got to have your name and address."

The man identified himself as Henry Watkins, with a mailing address in Tyler, Texas.

"There's another thing," the man said "I don't want nobody to know I'm in Remberton. Can you keep it secret?"

"I'll get a room at the Holiday Inn in my name and we'll meet there. Nobody will know you're here."

Noble drove out to the Holiday Inn and checked into a room. The motel was just a year old. It was part of a burst of construction in and around the shopping center that had sprung up just off the interstate exit. Only a decade ago, all of this land had been pastures, dotted by two or three farmhouses. A two-lane road had led through it going on up to the northern part of the county. Now he could be on the edge of any one of hundreds of American towns, a dot on the nationwide network of interstate highways and shopping centers, fed by an endless stream of cars and trucks. A hometown Rip van Winkle brought back from thirty years ago would have no idea he was near Remberton. It had often occurred to Noble that all of this was the result of the happenstance in the location of the interstate. If the highway had been routed 15 or more miles to the west there would be none of this; Remberton would have remained pristine. In the late twentieth century, the coming of the interstate highway to a town was like the coming of the railroad to a nineteenth century town.

Noble checked in a half an hour before Henry Watkins' plane was scheduled to land in Montgomery. He settled into a chair to collect his thoughts about his upcoming conversation with Watkins. Behind him was the humming window air-conditioner, struggling to defeat the ninety-five degree heat outside. They had agreed that Watkins would rent a car at the airport and drive down but would telephone first to get the room number so he could avoid the front desk.

The call came, and forty-five minutes later there was a knock on the door. Noble opened it and saw standing there a stocky middle-aged man with thinning gray hair. His weathered face suggested long years in the out-of-doors. He wore a short-sleeved denim shirt and heavy-duty khaki pants. He could have come straight from work as a filling station attendant.

Noble closed the door and said, "You're Henry Watkins?"

"Yes, sir." The man extended a ham-like leathery hand and they shook.

Noble, sensing this was not an occasion for small talk, said, "I think we should get right down to business." He motioned Watkins to a chair beside a round table. Noble sat down in a chair on the other side. In between them was a tape recorder.

"First thing," Watkins said, "is my $5,000."

Noble smiled faintly. "I thought that might be on your mind." He reached in his brief case on the floor beside him and pulled out a fat envelope. "Here it is, in cash. You better count it."

Watkins commenced counting out the hundred dollar bills on the table, one by one, with fingers not accustomed to the task. It took him a couple of minutes. Finally he said, "Looks like it's there." He put the bills back in the envelope and stuffed it in his pants pocket.

"All right," Noble said, "let's get started. I'm going to ask you a lot of questions, and I want you to answer as specifically and in as much detail as you can. I'm recording this so I won't have to rely on my memory or notes. Is this agreeable?"

"When do I find out how much money I get?"

"As I explained, when I know what you have to say. Until then I can't tell how useful it is."

"You said $25,000."

"I said I could go up to that figure if what you tell me is as pertinent as you say it is. So let's go." Noble turned on the tape recorder.

Watkins shifted nervously in his chair. "I don't like that machine, but for twenty-five grand I guess I can live with it."

"Let's start at the beginning. Tell me where you grew up and your connection with Remberton."

Watkins said he grew up in the country near here, son of a sawmill worker. He dropped out of school near the end of the Second World War and joined the army. He was discharged in 1946 after never getting any farther than Fort Bliss, Texas. He came back to Remberton and got a job at the same sawmill where his father had worked. By then both his father and mother had died. Prodded by questions, he went on to say that the sawmill laid him off, and there weren't other jobs around. So he got hold of an army buddy who lived in Tyler. He said come on out, plenty of jobs there. He worked first at a filling station and then went with an auto parts company and was still there.

Noble asked, "Did you know Grady Rooter?"

"No. Never saw him."

"Tell me what you know about his death."

Watkins, ill at ease, shifted position in his chair and began slowly. "I used to run around with this fellow named Bert Trimble. We'd go up the road to the beer joint every now and then and sometimes get pretty drunk. One night he was mixing whiskey and beer and got really slopped up. I'd been going pretty light on just beer. He started mumbling about a lot of things. Then I heard him saying he'd done something he felt bad about, said he ought'n to have done it. So I asked him what it was. He said him and a couple of other fellows had been hired to get rid of Grady Rooter. I'd never heard of Grady Rooter, so I asked him who he was and why somebody wanted to get rid of him."

Noble interrupted. "Where was this conversation taking place?"

"In a booth in the beer joint. The jukebox was going and a lot of noise. Couldn't nobody else hear him."

"When was this?"

"About early September. Maybe three or four weeks after they found Rooter drowned."

"Go on. What did Trimble say next?"

"He didn't answer me about Grady Rooter. Just mumbled on that one of his buddies, fellow named Tommy Lukens, come to him one day and said he had a proposition, something that could make them a lot of money. Bert was getting drunker all the time and I didn't know whether he could keep talking—but he did. Said Tommy told him a man with a pot full of money had come to him and said he'd give him $10,000 if he'd take care of Grady Rooter. The man said he'd pay the same to a couple of other guys if necessary. Bert said Tommy asked him to help out, said he'd get ten thousand."

Watkins stopped and said, "Mind if I get a drink of water?"

"Help yourself in the bathroom."

He returned in a moment with a plastic cup of water. He took a long swallow. Noble noticed his hands shaking slightly.

"So Trimble was authorized to hire some others to help with the job?"

"That's what it sounded like. Anyway, Lukens signed on. Then Bert said they got another man named Joe Kinston to go along."

Noble blurted out, "Joe Kinston? Do you know him?"

"No. Don't know Lukens either. Never saw 'em."

"Where did they work?"

"Bert was a section hand on the railroad. Don't know about the others. He didn't say."

"So what did those three men do?"

"By the time he got to that point, Bert was pretty sloppy, half crying, hard to understand. But from what I could get I think he said they got Grady Rooter late at night in his car and drove him to Possum Creek. They held him underwater until he was dead."

Noble sat motionless, saying nothing, letting sink in the startling tale he had just heard—facts he had been seeking for months and expecting never to find, facts validating Jesse's darkest suspicions. But could this story be believed? He had been watching Watkins' face intently for signs that he was fabricating or outright lying. He saw none. The story had credibility because it fit in with Catherine Craighill's account of the late night pick-up of Grady in front of her house, and with Amos Brewer's story. The pieces were beginning to fall into place.

After an interval, with the air-conditioner humming on and Watkins drinking water, Noble said, "Where is Bert Trimble now?"

"Died a few years ago with a heart attack."

"What about Tommy Lukens?"

"I asked about him soon after Bert told me this story, and somebody said he'd gone to California and been killed in a car wreck out there. Don't know anything more."

"What do you know about Joe Kinston?"

"Nothing."

"Do you have any idea who the man was who paid them for this job?"

"All Bert said was he had a pot full of money."

"You don't know where he lived or why he wanted to get rid of Grady?"

"No, sir. I've told you everything I know. It ought to be worth twenty-five grand. I don't think Bert was making this up. No reason why he would."

Noble remembered Jesse's words: money is not a problem, pay whatever it takes to get the facts. So he said, "O.K., I'll mail you a check."

"I'd rather have cash."

"I don't walk around with that kind of money."

"Ain't there a bank here?"

Noble looked at his watch. Half an hour until closing time. "You drive a hard bargain. But wait here. I'll be back."

When Noble returned he found Watkins asleep on the bed. He nudged him awake. "All right, here it is. I'm giving you this with the understanding I may want to get back in touch and talk some more. If your story turns out to be phony you'll be hearing from me. Is that understood?"

Watkins nodded and counted out the thousand dollar bills. Then he stood up and walked out, not bothering to close the door. A gush of hot, humid air flowed in, along with throbbing sounds of interstate traffic.

Noble shut the door and sat back down under the cooling breeze from the window unit. He stayed there a long time, lost in thought, pondering what he had heard.

Chapter 15

▼

Far from the sweltering Alabama heat, Jesse Rooter sat on his tree-shaded terrace overlooking Lake Michigan, which on this late afternoon in August was dotted with a multitude of sailboats. The North Shore temperature, combined with a light breeze from the lake, provided natural air-conditioning. High overhead, on the flight pattern into O'Hare, jets were whining downward every few minutes. In another hour most of the evening flights would be in, and tranquility would return. Just as a 747 passed out of sound over the house, the extension telephone on the table beside him began to ring.

He answered. It was Noble Shepperson—the tone of his voice suggesting he had news of more than usual import. Noble told him about Watkins.

When he finished, Jesse said quietly, "So now we know."

"Only if Watkins' story is true," Noble said. "But my instinct tells me it is."

"It doesn't really surprise me to hear about Joe Kinston. From what I saw of him, I'd say he was a pretty rough character. But where did that money come from? That's the big question now. And why?"

"A lot of money back then," Noble said." Probably not more than a half dozen men around Remberton could have come up with $30,000 in cash."

"What could possibly have been the motive?"

"A big question. Looks like my next step is to go see Kinston. He may not talk and even if he does he may not know anything about the money."

Jesse said, "He would have had a personal motive because of his sister, so they came to the right man."

Noble went on to say that although this appeared to be a major breakthrough they might never be able to get any further. Anyway, he would keep at it and keep in touch.

Jesse put down the phone and gazed thoughtfully out to the lake. At least he now knew that Grady's death was not accidental. But his question about that was replaced with equally troubling questions: why would anyone want to murder Grady—and, most important, who put up the money?

The rattle of ice in a glass from just across a low table brought him back. He looked over to where Lucille Brentson was sitting. She said, "What was that all about?"

Jesse stood up and said, "It was Noble Shepperson. Let me freshen your drink and I'll tell you what he said."

He took her glass and went over to the small cart that Mrs. Schneider had rolled out earlier. It held gin, vodka, tonic, sliced limes, and an ice bucket. She was drinking vodka, he gin. He replenished their glasses, put a fresh napkin on hers, and handed it back.

A week earlier Jesse had been startled to receive a telephone call from Lucille. Their only previous contact had been the frosty encounter at the wedding reception. She said she had been giving a lot of thought to the Remberton library situation and had decided it was foolish for them to be engaged in this competition. She would like to talk to him about Noble's proposed joint gift. Besides, she said, she wanted to get better acquainted with a Rooter who had gone so far and done so well. She wound up, rather bluntly, Jesse thought, by asking if she could come up for a brief visit.

Jesse was stunned by her brashness. Here was the daughter of Sam Funchess wanting to come all the way up to Chicago to see him. He doubted that she knew of the relationship her father had had with the Rooters and his deep-seated resentment. He had no desire to spend time with her. But he felt on the spot, no good way to say no. He ended up inviting her to stay at his house.

So here she was. He had arranged for her to be met at O'Hare by a driver and brought to his place. When she arrived, Mrs. Schneider had shown her to her room where she had changed into a light summer dress, fine for August in Alabama but too cool for a North Shore evening.

She came onto the terrace raving over his house and the view, exclaiming several times that it was incredible that Jesse Rooter could find himself set up in such a situation. When he noticed her shivering after a few minutes he sent Mrs. Schneider upstairs to get a sweater.

He sensed that her chatter about the lake and the splendors of the place was a nervous cover-up for the awkwardness they both felt. He had been saying to himself in anticipation of her arrival that perhaps the sins of the father should not be visited on the daughter, but he had not convinced himself. In any case, the gentlemanly manners drilled into him by his late wife required him to attempt to be a cordial host.

He had invited her to sit down, then fixed her a drink. He said, "Why is it any more remarkable for a Rooter to be living here than it is for a Funchess to be living as you do?"

She seemed flustered. "Well ... why ... er ... I guess it isn't, now that I think of it."

"You know, don't you," Jesse said, "that Funchess and Rooter have the same background?"

"I really don't know anything about background. I'm not one of those women who run around looking into genealogy."

It was at this point that Noble Shepperson's call came.

Sitting down now with fresh drink in hand, Jesse repeated to her what Noble had said. She listened with stunned incredulity. When he finished, she said, in a tone of disbelief, "You're telling me Grady was murdered?"

"I'm telling you what Noble says someone told him. If that's all true, we've got murder."

She said nothing, and he looked absently at the sailboats heading for their marinas in the waning afternoon sunlight.

Then he asked, "Do you know who Joe Kinston is?"

"There're some Kinstons around Remberton, but I don't know any."

"Right now he looks like the only link to what happened."

"And he's a murderer! What are they going to do about it? Shouldn't he be arrested and prosecuted?" Her voice was agitated. She had a sharp, unpleasant accent, unlike Catherine Craighill's soft, husky tones.

"I doubt he could be convicted on this second-hand report. Looks like he was hired to do the job. So the question now is who hired him and why."

"If somebody did hire him, he would still be guilty of murder, wouldn't he?"

"I would think so," Jesse said.

"So we end up," she said with rising irritation, "with a murderer walking around Remberton and never prosecuted?"

"It does seem shocking, or unjust," Jesse said with an air of resignation. "Maybe there's some wrongdoing in this world the law can't reach."

"That's a sad commentary," she added. "If the law can't handle it, maybe somebody else should."

Jesse let another 747 pass overhead and then said, "Noble told me that Grady was working on a construction job at your house in that summer of '46. You must have seen him around then."

"Yes."

"When you heard of his drowning did it occur to you that it might be murder?"

"Not at all."

"Me neither. But I began to wonder about it when I was in Remberton. So that's why I got Noble to look into it."

"He's the only man I really trust."

"You can trust me."

"Not if you're like Grady," Lucille said.

"What do you mean?"

"I mean I didn't trust him."

"But why?"

She took a long sip from her drink and then said, "Well, O.K., I'll give you a shorthand version of the story. Grady was really handsome, a sort of debonair type. I was home from that all girls' college and in the mood for a little romantic adventure. There weren't many boys around town that summer. He began hanging back after work in the afternoon. There was a vacant room over the garage. Well, things got pretty hot and heavy, to put it mildly." She stopped and took a drink.

Jesse thought he was hearing a replay of Catherine Craighill's story. He waited for the next step, but she just sat there, looking out at the lake.

So he said, "Then what?"

"I was probably in love with him, definitely infatuated. I don't know why I'm telling you this. Never told anybody else."

"You said you didn't trust him. Why was that?"

"From things I heard here and there I got the impression he was running around with some other girls—friends of mine too."

"Did you know who they were?"

"I suspected Catherine Craighill and Julia McKnight. Amanda Harris too, although she didn't look like the type. One day I confronted him and we had a knock down drag out."

"Was that the end of it?"

"No. I let it blow over. What ended it was that my father learned about us. He went into a rage. And when Daddy was in a rage it was something. He told Mr. Denkens he ought to fire Grady."

Jesse asked, "Did you ever see him again?"

"No. Two weeks later I heard he drowned."

"What was your reaction?"

"I was pretty upset."

Jesse heard the ice rattling in her glass. "I think all the news of this afternoon calls for another drink." He refilled her glass along with his.

She sipped the fresh drink and said, "As time passed I became disgusted with myself and wanted to forget the whole episode, wanted to put the name of Rooter out of mind forever."

"Did you?"

"Not entirely, but for most of the time. It would crop up all along in my dreams and thoughts—a love-hate memory. And then, damn it, you showed up at—of all places—my daughter's wedding reception. It was like seeing a ghost."

"I'm sorry, that was Catherine Craighill's doing."

Twilight was coming on. The jet flights had diminished. Stars appeared faintly in the cloudless sky. The sailboats had disappeared. Quietness enveloped Jesse and Lucille.

Lucille said, "Enough of this ancient history. The library situation is what I came here to talk about. I believe in being frank. Some people think I'm too abrupt, but that's just my style."

"I hadn't noticed."

"To get to the point," Lucille said, "my understanding is that you've offered to give two million, or more, to the library, on condition that the building be named for your mother."

"That's more or less correct, but my offer is not final."

"As I'm sure Noble told you, I had a reaction when I heard that, and on the spur of the moment offered to top it."

"What was that reaction?"

"I hope you won't be offended, but it was the idea of a big prominent building named for a Rooter."

"That episode you had with Grady must have really gotten to you."

"It damn sure did."

"But I heard you say you were in love with Grady. Why such a change?

She was quiet for a moment, taking a sip. "In light of all the things that happened. In a sick kind of way I sometimes think I'm still in love with him. But then I dismiss that as disgusting."

"In the spirit of frankness, I have to tell you the name Funchess has a pretty bad place in my mind."

"Why?"

Jesse told her of the unforgettable moment when her father ordered his family off the land and how he prevented them from getting a loan at the bank.

"That was a long time ago. It should make no difference now. You're eight hundred miles from Remberton."

"Those roots are hard to cut, memories hard to erase. What most people don't know or don't remember is that your father and my father came out of exactly the same circumstances—dirt poor, down-and-out white trash from the piney woods."

"That's putting it pretty strong," she said, obviously irritated.

"The only difference is that your father struck it rich and my father hardly had a dime to his name." Gin had loosened his tongue, and he felt the old anger rising up inside. "To put it frankly, your father had the reputation of being ruthless, of walking over people."

"I'm aware of that. Life is odd. You and I may have started out under radically different conditions, but, boy, you've made up for it. Look at this place. There's nothing in Remberton to compare with it. As for my father, I saw none of what you experienced. I have to say I adored him. I was pretty much of a tomboy and I think he enjoyed that since he didn't have a son. He would take me out to one of his places in the country and teach me to shoot a pistol and a shotgun. He thought every woman should be able to protect herself. I still have all his guns."

Twilight had turned into deep dusk, and the evening chill was beginning to penetrate. Jesse's smoldering hatred of Sam Funchess was tempered by his sense that Lucille herself might not be some sort of she-devil. It was strange indeed, he thought, that with their mutual antipathy—she apparently despising Rooter as much as he despised Funchess—they could be sitting here in civilized fashion.

He said, "Let's move on to dinner. I'm taking you to the club. We'll eat in the grill. It's casual. You don't need to change. We can talk some more there about the library."

"Good morning, Jeanie," Noble Shepperson said to the woman behind the reception counter in the front lobby of the Craighill Memorial Hospital. On the wall behind her hung an oil portrait of the revered Dr. Loosh. "Is Gladys Houston around?"

"Just down the hall, I think."

Noble went through a pair of swinging doors into a long hallway. Antiseptic, medicinal, unmistakable hospital odors instantly struck his nostrils. He passed patient rooms, their doors half open. IV tubes and other medical contraptions surrounded some beds. In some rooms, the patients were sitting up, chatting with visitors. In others they were prone and motionless. Over the years he had known someone in every room of this hospital—some recovering from surgery, some for a short-run malady, others there to die. He had known so many of the latter that he had come to think of the place as a point of exit from this world as much as a place for healing.

At the nurses' station he came up to a middle-aged woman in a nurse's uniform, bent over, intently scrutinizing some papers. "Gladys," he said.

She looked up. "Oh, hey Colonel."

"Could I talk with you privately for just a few minutes?"

"Sure." She turned to an aide. "I'll be back."

She led him two doors down the hall into a vacant treatment room and closed the door.

"You've probably seen in the paper," Noble said, "that I'm investigating Grady Rooter's death. I know Jesse Rooter talked to you a few months ago and I know what you told him. You had a terrible experience with Grady, and I can't say how sorry I am to hear about it."

"It was pretty bad. But you have to put things like that behind and go on with life."

"You've certainly done a good job of that—you are one of the mainstays in the hospital."

"Thanks. But what do you want to see me about?"

"I now have evidence that Grady's death was not accidental, that he was actually murdered."

She sucked in her breath. "Oh, my Lord. Earl Scroggins always suspected that, so I guess it's not a big surprise."

"When you have a murder there is usually a reason for it. Someone has a motive to kill. Who would have a motive to kill Grady? In looking around for possibilities—I hate to say this—but your father and brother, Joe, come to mind. I gather they were plenty upset with Grady, understandably, about your pregnancy."

She nodded, but said nothing.

"Men have been known to kill in such circumstances. Now I know you don't want to incriminate your father and brother, but I'm wondering if there's anything you can recall that might shed any light on who killed Grady."

Her sad, compassionate face was impassive. Then she said, slowly, "Don't know that I do. Daddy's dead so I don't see any point in dragging him into this. Joe's still around but we don't see much of each other."

"The night Grady came to your house and there was that big fight with your father. Did you hear Joe say he would kill Grady?"

"I did, but Daddy told him not to do that, that he would get in a heap of trouble. You don't think either of them did it, do you?"

"I don't know what to think," Noble said. "I have to look into all possibilities."

"You know, Grady was running around with some other women. It wasn't just me. Have you checked that out?"

"Do you know who any of them were?"

"I heard rumors but I didn't believe them or didn't want to believe them."

"What were the rumors?"

"I don't know whether I ought to say, but if you'll keep it confidential, I'll tell you what I heard."

"You can rely on me to keep it under my hat."

She hesitated, then said, "Well, there were three names—Lucille Funchess, Catherine Craighill, and Julia McKnight. I couldn't believe any of those girls would give Grady the time of day—you know, him coming from the cotton mill and all that."

"I appreciate your frankness. It must be painful to have to think back on that bad time."

"I hadn't thought about it for a long time until Jesse showed up. That news about my pregnancy is something I had never told anybody. I hope you'll keep it to yourself. No point now in getting that out."

"It won't go beyond me. The reason I'm here is at Jesse's request. He wants to give you something to try to make up for what Grady did, at least a little bit." He handed her an envelope.

She opened it. "My God!" She gasped. "Thousand dollar bills! I've never seen any." She counted out twenty-five. "Jesse doesn't have to do that."

"No, he doesn't, but he wants to. Money can't really compensate you for what happened, but it's at least an indication of Jesse's regret for what his brother did."

Noble stood on the small front porch of Joe Kinston's unpainted house on this last street on the southern edge of town before plunging into Liberty Hill. Moments after he knocked on the sagging screened door, a frowzy looking woman in a loose-fitting cotton house dress and bedroom slippers appeared.

"Hello," Noble said, "Is Joe here?"

"Ain't you Colonel Shepperson?"

"Yes, ma'am. How're you doing today?"

"Pretty well, considering the heat. You want to see Joe?"

"If he's around and not too busy."

"He's out back. I'll see if I can get him." She turned and disappeared into the gloom of the house.

It was Saturday afternoon, picked by Noble as a likely time to catch Joe Kinston at home. He pulled a handkerchief from his pocket and pressed it to his perspiring forehead, at the same time waving away flies. Somewhere in the weeds beside the porch unknown insects buzzed away. Being out of the office and not wanting to appear too formidable to Kinston—and to cope with the heat—Noble had dispensed with the usual suit and tie and put on a sport shirt.

He was looking up the street at some workmen unloading lumber from a pick-up truck in the clean-swept yard of an Assembly of God Church. He heard the screened door open behind him.

Joe Kinston stepped out. He wore a dirty white, sweat-soaked T-shirt and blue jeans. He said, "You want to see me?" His attitude was surly.

"Yes, if you can spare a few minutes." Noble stuck out his hand, and they shook—Noble wondering whether he was grasping the hand of a cold-blooded murderer. "Could we sit down over there?" He looked toward a couple of wooden chairs.

"It's about the coolest spot," Joe said, "but ain't nowhere cool today."

When they were seated, Noble said, "I knew your father. A good man. Where're you working now?"

"Out at the Fowler Lumber Yard."

"I know Oscar Fowler. Is he O.K. to work for?"

"He's all right." Noble sensed that this was not a voluble talker. He looked sullen, and his small, close-set eyes stared at Noble suspiciously.

"I don't want to take up much of your time, so let me get to the point. I want to ask you about Grady Rooter and some things that went on in August of 1946. If you give me some answers I'll make it worth your while." Noble pulled an envelope from his pocket. Opening the flap, he edged out a thick clump of hundred dollar bills, just far enough for Joe to see what they were. Fingering them lightly to convey the thickness of the stack, he said, "This can be yours if I get the right information."

Joe's eyes widened and fixed on the clump of bills. "What do you want to know?"

"Did you know Grady Rooter?"

"Knew who he was but didn't know him."

"Do you know what happened to him?"

"Heard he drowned."

"How did he drown?"

"Just heard he drowned in Possum Creek."

"I happen to know that Grady was picked up by three men that night and driven out to the creek. Then they drowned him. What do you have to say about that?"

"Look, Colonel, I don't know what this is all about, whether you're trying to trick me into something."

"I'm not trying to trick you. I'm trying to find out what happened to Grady Rooter. Suppose I told you that I have evidence that you were one of those men and that you held Grady underwater until he died."

"It would be a lie."

"Then what's the truth?" Noble said, riffling the hundred dollar bills through his fingers.

Joe stared at the money, then at Noble. "How do I know you ain't gonna get me in trouble?"

"I'm just here to help Grady's brother find out what happened. He's willing to spend some money, and here's some of it—five thousand, to be exact. It could be yours."

They sat in the heavy, humid air, sweating, the insects buzzing away beside the porch. Then Joe said slowly, "I didn't have nothing to do with no drowning. I was in the car."

"Why were you there?"

"They come to me and said would I like to go along on a ride, drive a car, play a little joke on Grady."

"Who is 'they'?"

"Two guys I knew—Tommy Lukens and Bert Trimble."

"Did you get any money?"

"What difference does that make?"

"I want to know where the money came from."

"I don't know where it come from."

"Who gave it to you?"

"I ain't saying I got no money."

"Well," Noble said, sliding the bills back into the envelope, "if you want to walk away from five thousand dollars that's your business."

"You ain't gonna turn me over to the law, are you?"

"I told you I'm just trying to find out what happened so I can tell Grady's brother."

"I don't know where the money come from. All I know is who give it to me."

"Who was that?"

"Bert."

"Didn't you think it was a little funny to give you all that money just to go on a joke ride?"

"I didn't think much about it. It was a lot of money and I wasn't gonna argue."

"When Tommy and Bert came back from the creek without Grady, what did they say?"

"They said Grady had gone and got hisself drowned."

"What did you think about that? What did you say?"

"I didn't say nothing. Bert said to turn the car around and get out of there. So that's what I did."

"Didn't it occur to you that the sheriff might investigate?"

"On the way back Bert said to keep our mouths shut and we wouldn't get in no trouble. Said he knowed the law wasn't gonna bother us."

"How did he know that?"

"I don't know. He just said it, like he knowed what he was talking about."

Noble paused for a moment and then said, "You knew about Grady and your sister, didn't you?"

"You been talking to her?"

"I know she was pregnant, and I know your father and Grady got into a big argument. You were there, weren't you?"

"I was standing off to the side."

"Didn't you say you would kill Grady if he didn't marry your sister?"

Joe wiped his face on the sleeve of his T-shirt and shifted in his chair. "I don't remember. That's a long time ago."

Noble pulled his handkerchief out and mopped his forehead. On this Saturday afternoon the street was quiet and deserted. The men unloading lumber at the Assembly of God Church had gone.

Noble said, "There's one more thing. I want to know where Bert got the money. Who gave it to him? Now think hard about that."

Joe, looking at the bills Noble was holding, said, "You want just the name of the man? You ain't gonna ask me anything else?"

"That's all. Just the man's name."

"How do I know this ain't some kind of trick?"

"I've told you I'm not a law officer. If you don't want this five thousand, I'll just run along."

Again a long hesitation. "The name you're probably looking for is Billy Morton."

"How do I know you're not just making up that name?"

"You can ask him."

"Where is he?"

"I don't know. Been gone a long time."

"If it turns out this name is phony, I'll be back for the money, and then I may have the law with me."

Noble stood up, handed the envelope to Kinston, and left.

As he drove away, he turned the name Morton over in his mind. It had a vaguely familiar ring. He thought he remembered some folks with that name who lived out in the county years ago, but he couldn't quite place any. As Nan would say, they were hardly among the county's first families. There was the possibility that Joe had made up the name, but it was all he had to go on. He was puzzled because he thought he knew all the men in these parts with $30,000 in 1946—and able to spend it on a nefarious job of this sort—and Billy Morton was not one of them. Each question answered in unraveling this mystery raised another.

Catherine Craighill sat across the desk from Noble. She had made an appointment to see him about her alimony. Her ex-husband was four months behind in his payments, and she could get no response from letters and telephone calls. She wanted Noble to do something about it.

She had a deep late summer suntan that Noble could not avoid noticing, especially her long, brown legs. She had grown up in that generation of girls whose major objective was to acquire and maintain a tan. Despite warnings in more recent years about skin cancer, she had kept it up. The results were often the subject of admiring comments.

"Since it's doubtful we can get jurisdiction over him in Alabama," Noble said, "we'll have to proceed in a court in Atlanta. You told me you didn't like the last lawyer you had."

"That's right. He didn't do anything."

"I'll call a friend of mine in a firm there and get him to recommend somebody good."

"Here's the court order on alimony." She pushed the papers toward Noble. "I suspect his new wife is draining him dry. She looks like a high maintenance type."

"Not like you?" There was a smile in his voice.

"In no way!" she said with disgust.

"O.K., I'll get right on it."

Changing the subject abruptly and recrossing her legs, she said, "Did you know Lucille went up to Chicago to visit Jesse Rooter?"

"No," he said, with surprise. "How did that come about?"

"When I got wind of it I finally got him on the phone. He said she invited herself—called him up and said she wanted to come up and talk about the library. Have you ever heard of anything more nervy?"

"It's hard to believe in light of the way she reacted to naming the library for a Rooter."

"My guess is that the library was just an excuse. Lucille has always been attracted by money. Once she got to thinking about Jesse's millions, I suspect she warmed up to him. We all know she's man-hungry. No telling what scheme she has in mind. Next thing we know she'll have her hooks in him. He'd better watch out."

"I expect Jesse can take care of himself."

"I wouldn't be too sure. I got to know Jesse some when he was here. He's a pretty nice fellow—a chip on his shoulder—but attractive in some ways. I just hate to see him fall into Lucille's clutches."

She picked her purse up off the floor, as though preparing to leave, and said, "I don't want to take up any more of your time, but let me ask you a personal question. I hope you won't mind."

He smiled and said, "You can ask me anything, but I don't promise to answer."

"Well, this is rather delicate. You and Daddy were close, and that's always given me a sense of closeness with you, even though we haven't seen much of each other." She paused, as though hesitating over whether to continue. Then she added in a lowered voice, "Close enough to ask this question. Is there something wrong between you and Nan?"

Noble was caught completely off guard. He resented the question, was irritated at her for asking. His first instinct was to say that it was none of her business, but he refrained. Instead, he said, "What makes you ask?"

"Well, it's been a month since her mother died and she's not back yet. Also, as you might know, there's been a lot of talk over the last couple of years that things are not the happiest."

"You don't believe all the talk you hear, do you?"

"No, but I've got my own eyes and ears."

Noble weighed his words. Catherine was the type of woman that made men want to confide in her. Now her caring expression and sympathetic tone led him to consider letting down his guard. But he simply said, "I'd really rather not talk about it."

"I just want to let you know that if you ever feel the need to talk to somebody I'm available. I've had a little experience in marriage, as you well know, so I think I can understand these situations better than some people."

For a long moment they looked at each other. And then she said, "And I know something about loneliness."

Chapter 16

When Catherine had gone, Noble sat back down, recalling a telephone conversation with Nan the day before. Didn't she think she had been there long enough, he wanted to know, had time enough to wind up her mother's affairs?

"Seems there's always something else to do," she had said.

"When do you think you might be coming home?"

"I just can't say. I don't feel well."

"All the more reason to come on back. Exactly how do you feel?"

"It's hard to say. England was glorious. But when I got back to Remberton I ... I ... just went into some kind of slump. Then when Mama died that really threw me for a loop. These old friends of mine here are a great comfort."

Noble considered flying up to Newburgh to see whether he could bring her back with him. Something inside told him he should go. But he decided he would give it a little more time to work itself out. In light of what happened later, he would profoundly regret not following his instinct.

Miss Alice came in and dropped off some letters for him to sign. As she turned to leave, she said, "Incidentally, and this may sound catty, I think Catherine Craighill is trying to make herself look younger. Have you noticed?"

Reaching over to pull a volume of the *Alabama Code* off the adjoining bookshelf, Noble said, "Can't say that I have. She does seem to have quite a suntan."

"And that short skirt and new hair-do!"

Eight miles north of town, Noble turned his car off the black top road into a gravel drive leading straight ahead to the front portico of Mathews Hall, the residence of Judge Andrew McKnight. For the last mile he had driven along extensive pastures, seeing a herd of Hereford cattle grazing in the distance. Lush Johnson grass bordered the road on both sides. Forty years ago cotton would have been here, as far as the eye could see. Now cotton had gone west, cattle come east.

The house was a large two-story frame structure with four square columns rising to full height across the front, typical of plantation houses built in those parts in antebellum times. It had been the home of the Judge's wife's family from the beginning. He and his wife had lived there all their married life. When she died, he inherited it, along with two thousand acres which he leased to cattle growers.

Passing between rows of aged cedar trees, Noble pulled up in front and got out. The Judge's rotund figure filled the doorway.

"Come on in, Noble," the Judge boomed as Noble mounted the front steps and crossed the veranda. Shaking hands, he said, "Let's sit on the back porch. It's real pleasant out there today."

They walked through the spacious center hall. On one side a broad staircase led up to the second floor. The house had changed little in over a hundred years. Its builder, Captain Edgar Mathews, had been killed at the Battle of Shiloh, commanding the Rembert Rifles, a company he had raised in the county. He stared out from his portrait over the mantelpiece in the front parlor, a stern, gray-clad figure with hand on sword hilt. Some of the furniture was original; much of the rest was late Victorian. The dim interior and perpetual mustiness accentuated the sense of time gone. Here Noble felt the past pressing in on him more than any spot in the county.

The Judge's daughter, Julia, would eventually inherit the place. There was speculation as to whether she and her husband, Dr. Jimmy Goodson, would ever want to move out here from their comfortable house in town.

On the porch they sat down in wooden rockers. The judge's two hunting dogs—a Pointer and a Setter—stretched out asleep at the bottom of the steps. Venerable live oaks shaded the rear of the house, beyond which, in a distant patch of sunlight, was a scuppernong arbor filled at this season with ripening brown grapes. Only the far-off cooing of doves broke the silence of the Sunday afternoon. The air was pleasantly warm but not hot, giving the first faint hint of approaching fall.

Noble told the judge he had come out to bring him up to date on his Grady Rooter investigation. He related what Henry Watkins had told him and how he had then gone to see Joe Kinston.

After summarizing what Kinston told him, Noble said, "I must say I was surprised to hear him admit he was at the creek, but just as the driver. There's no way, of course, to confirm or refute his version. He's the only living witness. But at least we now have some direct evidence that Grady was murdered."

The Judge spoke for the first time. "Did you get any indication of a motive?"

"Seems it was done for money, just as Watkins said. So the big question is—who put up the money—and why? This fellow, Billy Morton, may have been just a middleman. Ever heard of anybody named Billy Morton?"

Rocking gently back and forth, looking off into the distance, the Judge said, "I don't think so. Looks like you're at a dead end."

"Maybe and maybe not. My biggest concern is with Jesse's library gift. He's obsessed with his brother's murder, and he may not come through with the money unless I can get to the bottom of the whole thing. I have to say that I'm getting obsessive myself. Having gone this far—and I wish I'd never heard of Grady Rooter—I'd have a hard time resting without tying down this last loose end."

"If Jesse is satisfied with what you've got now, wouldn't you be willing to let it go?"

"Well, there's Joe Kinston that's nagging me. On his own testimony, he's an accessory to murder. But he's walking around a free man, and I don't see any way to get him. Watkins' account of what Bert Trimble told him would be inadmissible, and, of course, we can't force Kinston to testify against himself. I do now have a confession from him, but I doubt any prosecutor would go on that alone, without corroboration. Anyway, he might deny it later."

"I've seen situations like this before—saw several when I was prosecutor—cases where there's every reason to believe a man is guilty but can't prove it under the law. The law is a human construct, and it's not perfect. You know as well as I, there're some things it just can't reach. Justice can't always be done. Looks like we'll have to leave Joe Kinston to a higher court."

"Sometimes when the law can't handle a situation we get vigilante action."

At the foot of the steps, the two dogs rose slowly together, as though acting in concert, stretched, and sauntered lazily off to the side, out of sight. Crows squawked in the distance. From high overhead came the sound of a small plane, its single engine throttling down, as it descended toward the Remberton Airport several miles away, an asphalt strip beside a windsock and small hangar.

The two men, rocking in their chairs, sat quietly for a few moments, each lost in his own thoughts. Then Noble said, "There's another aspect I wonder about. Did you ever have any reason to think that the sheriff—Norman Tucker then—was on the take?"

"If he was, I never saw any indication of it. I thought I could accept his word that this was an accident."

Noble detected, as he had before, a defensive note—as though the Judge was apprehensive that his responsibility as prosecutor be questioned. To put him at ease, Noble said, "I think you acted perfectly reasonably at the time. The burden was really on the sheriff. But what was the source of the assurance those three men got that the law would not come after them?"

"Another of those unanswerable questions," the Judge said. "Too much time gone. Too many people dead." He paused, collecting his thoughts. "Look, Noble, I really think you ought to give up this phantom chase. You've done a grand job, answered the central question. So I hope you'll tell Jesse this is it and then persuade him to give the money."

Noble did not respond, but in a moment said, "Well, Judge, on this fine Sunday afternoon I wont' tie you up any longer." The two stood up and started toward the hall.

To part on a lighter note, Noble said, "I hope Willie May's taking good care of you."

"Couldn't do without her. But she's getting on, like me. You know, my term ends in two years and then I'll hang it up."

"It'll be hard to see the courthouse without you."

"I'd like to see this library deal sealed in my time. So think about it. There's not much point in looking for things that make no difference now."

Noble paused at the front door and turned to face the Judge. "I want to see this library project move ahead as much as you do. But I've got to stay with the game one more round, got to try to find this Billy Morton."

Noble's visit to Mathews Hall, where the past hung so heavily, put him in a nostalgic mood. His thoughts turned back to his grandfather, Adrian Shepperson, who had died when Noble was thirteen. He had little recollection of his grandmother who had died several years earlier, but he remembered Adrian Shepperson—a formidable figure, standing well over six feet, with a huge shock of gray hair and walrus-like mustache. Eleven years old when the Civil War ended, he grew up during Reconstruction, an experience that had imprinted in him the firm conviction that the United States should never loose a war and had given him a hostile attitude toward government from Washington. For college, his family had sent him off to the University of South Carolina where one of his forebears had graduated. The Sheppersons had migrated from South Carolina, and the family wanted to keep a connection with the state. Coming back home as Reconstruction was ending, Adrian took hold of his family's 3,000 acre plantation. He later established a cotton gin and wholesale grocery. He was chairman of the board of directors of the bank. After his death in 1920 the family's fortunes declined. The plantation was lost in the Great Depression of the nineteen thirties, but Noble's father continued operating the gin and wholesale grocery until they closed some years later.

This burst of nostalgia, overcoming Noble as he drove back from Mathews Hall, moved him to swing through parts of town he rarely saw these days because they were not on the way between his house and office. Coming into town at the rear of the courthouse, he turned off on a side street. A block after the jail he came to what had been the Shepperson Cotton Gin. Closed and idle now for over two decades when cotton gave way to cattle, it had been a thriving business in ginning season. Noble remembered every year, from late summer into fall, the long line of high-sided cotton wagons, each pulled by a pair of mules and waiting its turn. The driver would then yell the mules forward, until the huge suction pipe would be lowered into the cotton, gradually drawing it all up. Eventually, through a roaring and clanking of machinery, the cotton, now devoid of seed, would miraculously appear on a platform in a tightly compacted, five hundred pound bale, bound in burlap and metal straps. As a boy, he loved to hang out there on Saturdays, watching the men weighing the cotton, maneuvering the suction pipe, and manhandling the bales. The place now had an abandoned look; the ground around it was filled with weeds and underbrush; spider webs hung in the openings. There were no buyers for defunct gins in a land where cotton was no longer grown.

Swinging around toward downtown, Noble passed Remberton's original cemetery covering half a block. It was deeply shaded by live oaks and surrounded by an iron rail fence. It had long ago ceased to be used. To Noble's young eyes, it had seemed a ghostly place where he would not want to be after dark. The first generation of Sheppersons was buried there. Through the iron railings Noble could see his ancestors' moss-covered gravestones. The only activity he could remember taking place there when he was a boy was on Confederate Memorial Day when the UDC placed wreaths on the graves of Confederate veterans, accompanied by a handful of still-living, aged soldiers of the Lost Cause.

Now he came to his grandfather's wholesale grocery. It was next to the railroad station. He pulled in beside it, a two-story dark brick structure with a wooden platform at its rear, backing up to a railroad siding. He often had wandered through its dimly lit and cavernous storage room. He could still smell its pleasantly mixed aroma of flour, meal, and all sorts of packaged food. Like the gin, the building had long stood empty and unused. Wholesale groceries had seen their day.

On impulse, Noble got out of his car and walked over to the railroad station. One end of the building was still used part-time by a freight agent; otherwise it was empty.

He stood on the concrete platform for a while, looking up and down the tracks, recalling the countless times he had met and seen off friends and relatives. Far off in his memory he heard the hissing of steam and metallic screeching of brakes as those trains ground to a stop. Then came the long series of whistle blasts signaling departure and reminding the entire town that Remberton was connected to the world beyond, a world accessible to anyone with enough money to buy a ticket from Mr. Andy Ratford, the station agent, standing behind his grill enclosed window in the depot waiting room.

Especially vivid in his mind was that day forty-five years ago when he left from this platform for West Point, feeling green as new spring leaves and not knowing what to expect, much less any inkling that this was a step that would eventually take him to England and Europe.

This now deserted platform was a busy place in those days, a stop for several passenger trains going north and south daily, all gone now, like the stagecoach, a casualty of the internal combustion engine and interstate highway.

Back in his car, as he drove toward home, he found himself passing the house where he grew up. Built by his grandfather at the turn of the century, it was a large one-story frame house with a broad front porch. It had passed out of his family some years earlier after his sister, Emily, and her husband, Ed Kirkman, died.

Noble slowed his car to take it all in, pleased to see that the new owners were keeping it up in good style. This was where he had spent his childhood and teen-age years, the house from which he had departed on that momentous journey to West Point. He remembered every room in it and the spacious tree-shaded backyard where he had played on long summer afternoons. He was jarred by the sight of a large metal box standing at the side rear, evidencing the recent installation of central air conditioning. There were still rocking chairs on the front porch, but he doubted they were used anymore.

Some of Noble's fondest memories were of his rocking away on that porch with his grandfather. There he followed the First World War—he was nine when the United States entered the conflict in 1917—through talk with his grandfather as he perused the daily newspaper. It was then that the army and West Point had been planted in his youthful mind. The military was reinforced in him by his grandfather's tales of the Civil War that he had learned from his own father, Noble's great grandfather, a lieutenant in the 5th Alabama Infantry, wounded at Malvern Hill.

Adrian Shepperson had a strong sense of public service, having represented Rembert County for three terms in the legislature where he was a leading backer of the program to establish at least one public high school in every county. This spirit, too, young Noble had absorbed. He also considered himself an inheritor of his grandfather's sense of humor and his raucous laughter, though not his touch of flamboyance. A memorable instance of that flamboyance was on Armistice Day, November 11, 1918, when Adrian Shepperson put Noble up behind him on his horse and led the parade down Center Street.

Those were the yesteryears of Remberton. His experiences then and the people he had known had burned the place into his very soul. As he learned at West Point and later during the war, not everybody felt that way about his hometown. For some, the connection was only tenuous and memories much more casual with little abiding significance. But that time, now two generations back, had attached the town to him like his skin, was what had brought him back.

The generation ahead of him, which he had known so well while growing up, had now almost entirely gone, leaving him and his contemporaries as the elders.

Reflecting on that change in Remberton's life brought home to him that collectively the changes that had been wrought were quite profound—the stores he knew replaced by supermarkets and discount houses, Center Street replaced by the shopping center, the railroad replaced by the interstate, a private school in addition to the public school. In short, the Remberton he knew, the Remberton ingrained in his very soul, no longer existed.

One thing, however, remained—the courthouse, the tall brick building standing at the head of Center Street, not just the physical structure but what it symbolized—the law, the glue holding society together. He, like all lawyers, was part of it, one of its ministers who kept the system alive and moving. However much the town may have changed, the law remained, not unchanging but evolving slowly, continuity with the past being unavoidable. It was what gave Noble a sense of stability, something to hold on to as the world changed around him.

For several days after talking with Judge McKnight, Noble seriously considered the Judge's suggestion and was on the brink of picking up the telephone to tell Jesse the investigation was at a dead end. But he couldn't rest easily with the knowledge that somebody had spent $30,000 to kill Grady Rooter. He had to know who.

So it was that Owen Nichols now sat in Noble's office facing him across his perpetually cluttered desk. Nichols was a lean, athletically built man in his forties. During the Korean War he had served in the Army CID and had come to be known as the best private investigator in the state. His military style crew cut and no-nonsense demeanor reminded Noble of regular army officers he had known. They had talked for an hour, Noble telling him everything he knew about Grady Rooter and the circumstances of his death.

Winding up, Noble said, "The point is to find who put up the money. Also, what was the source of the assurance that the law would not intervene, if there was such assurance."

"There had to be a substantial motive," Nichols said. "Nobody puts up that kind of money just for kicks, especially in '46."

"That's the way I see it," Noble said.

"We're talking twenty-seven years ago. It won't be easy."

"That's why I've got you," Noble said. "Let me stress again: spare no expense. Find the man."

After Nichols left, Noble called Judge McKnight to tell him what he was doing. The Judge's only response was to say, "I was hoping you'd be getting back to Jesse on the library. I still hope you'll do that."

Noble next got Jesse on the telephone and described his conversation with Joe Kinston.

"So Kinston is a confessed murderer!" Jesse blurted out.

"An accessory to murder, if we believe what he says."

"Still guilty, isn't he?"

"Yes, but not of first degree murder."

"He could be lying," Jesse said. "He might have been right in the creek with the others."

"Of course. But we have no way of knowing. He's the only one left."

Jesse was increasingly agitated. "Well, what are you going to do about it?"

"Don't see anything to do, except to try to find who paid the money." Noble explained that he had engaged Owen Nichols, an experienced private detective, to do just that.

"What's the district attorney for?"

"To prosecute where he has legally admissible evidence the person has committed a crime."

"And we don't have that here?"

"His confession to me is all we have, and I doubt the DA would proceed on that alone."

"Can't a court order Kinston to appear and testify?"

"No. He's got an absolute ..."

"I know ... privilege against self incrimination! How in hell did we ever let that get in the system to block bringing a man like this to justice?"

Noble thought of the rack and screw, but decided not to go into the centuries-long history that lay behind the privilege. Instead he said, "It's pretty fundamental. But it does have the unfortunate result of letting some guilty persons get off."

"This is the kind of situation that leads people to take the law in their own hands. If the law won't deal with it somebody has got to deal with it."

"I don't recommend it," Noble said. Wanting to get Jesse off this subject, he quickly added, "Incidentally, I heard you had a visit from Lucille. Quite an event—you two together at your place. How did it go?"

Jesse calmed down. "Cool but civil. No conclusion on the library. I'm still waiting."

The telephone call bringing news that was to change Noble's life came just before noon the next day. It was from one of Nan's friends in Newburgh. Nan had suffered a stroke, she reported, and was in a coma in the hospital.

At mid-afternoon Noble was on a plane flying out of Montgomery. Settling back in his seat, he had his first chance to think about Nan since his telephone call to her. He cursed himself for not having gone up to Newburgh. Not that it would have prevented the stroke, but it would have given him an opportunity to talk with her, to bring her home. Now he may never have it again. Their past life together played out in his mind, all of his shortcomings as a husband being underlined, highlighted, and pressed upon him. How could he at times have been so uncaring, so inattentive? If only he could have a second chance. People did recover from strokes, at least partly. Maybe she would have a paralyzed arm or leg or maybe she would be completely functional. It didn't matter. As he planned to ease up in his law practice, he would be in better position to be a good husband than he had ever been. He talked himself into being optimistic, imagining a future they could have together.

By the time he reached Nan's bedside she had come out of the coma. Her eyes were open, but she was not talking. Her arms and legs were limp.

Noble held her hand. "Nan, Nan," he said over and over, desperately hoping to get through to her. But there was no response, no sign of recognition, no change of expression. He couldn't tell whether she heard or understood him.

In the hall just outside her room, Noble finally had a chance to speak to her doctor. "What's the situation?" he asked.

The doctor sighed. "Sorry to tell you this, but the arteriogram shows extensive brain damage."

"What's her outlook?"

"Not good. This is hard to say, but I don't want to mislead you or create false hope. To be frank about it, with this amount of brain damage there's virtually no chance of recovery."

Noble was silent for a long moment. "There's nothing that can be done?" He felt tears welling up in his eyes.

"In the current state of medical science all we can do is keep her comfortable and feed her intravenously."

Kirk and Martha arrived, having been summoned by Noble. Martha, the younger, had her mother's eyes and hair, but in the rest of her features she had hints of her father. Kirk, on the other hand, was a carbon copy of his father—same height, build, and features. Nan and Noble had been relieved at getting them through the hazards of the sixties, relatively unscathed, and pleased that they had both married what they considered suitable spouses. Kirk had been particularly close to his mother, frequently talking with her on the phone after he moved to Mobile. On entering her room, he immediately grasped her hand—Martha took the other—and said repeatedly, "Mom, Mom," but her expression did not change.

Not wanting to leave Nan alone, the three took turns sitting by her bedside. They talked to her intermittently, hoping constantly for some sign of recognition, but none came. Noble was despondent, also angry and frustrated over the inability of the medical world to do anything.

After several days, Martha said, "Why don't we get her home? They're not doing anything here."

Noble agreed. He saw no point in Nan's remaining in Newburgh, simply being housed. He wanted her back home. The doctor saw no medical reason why she couldn't be transferred to the hospital in Remberton. So Noble chartered a plane to fly all of them back, with an ambulance meeting them at the Montgomery airport.

Nan thus came under the care of Dr. Bartow Simmons at the Craighill Memorial Hospital. In his mid-forties, he was now, since the death of Dr. Loosh, head physician at the hospital. He had also succeeded Dr. Loosh as Noble's family doctor. Noble had come to know his wife, Ann, through her work on the library board.

Kirk and Martha had to go back to their families and jobs but promised to return often. Noble dropped by the hospital every day to see Nan. Nothing changed. She was always propped up in bed; eyes wide open, saying nothing.

After a week, Noble said to Bartow, "I want to get her home. She can be as comfortable there as here, maybe more so."

"Normally we would keep a patient like this here," Bartow said. "But you have a point. We can't really do anything for her. If you'll provide twenty-four hour nursing assistance, I don't see any reason not to let her go."

Noble installed a hospital bed in the guest room in their house and engaged round-the-clock nursing attendants. Bartow helped set up the room with an IV and other necessary equipment. He would be by at least every-other-day, he said.

Noble refused to accept the proposition that medicine could do nothing for Nan. So he engaged a specialist to come down from the Medical School in Birmingham. He was a gray-haired, unsmiling man in his fifties, cool and aloof, with more of a professorial air than that of a bedside physician. He spent an hour with Bartow Simmons examining Nan and going over her history. To Noble's disappointment, he added nothing to what had already been said. The upshot was that normal functioning could not be restored, and it was not possible to say how long this condition would last.

Friends and neighbors dropped by in a constant stream, hugging the inert Nan and holding her hand—many of them more on Noble's account than on close friendship with Nan.

Noble found it difficult to leave her. Those big eyes looking vacantly into space broke his heart. He did, though, force himself to get to his office part of every day to try to keep up.

A few days later Noble was just finishing breakfast when Miss Alice rang him on the phone. "There's shocking news. Judge McKnight died last night."

"How? Where?"

"Died during the night, at home in bed."

"Good Lord," Noble said, emotionally rocked, trying to assimilate the fact that the Judge was gone. "He looked in good health when I saw him recently."

"Apparently a heart problem. I'm told that the time for the service hasn't been set."

Noble hung up and stood by the phone, not quite believing what he had heard. Judge McKnight gone, he repeated. He would leave a void at the courthouse and in the town and county.

After hurriedly dressing, Noble drove out to Mathews Hall. Julia was there in the kitchen, directing Willie May to prepare as much coffee as possible in anticipation of the onslaught of visitors. She gave Noble a hug, pressing her wet cheek against his.

"I can't believe it," she said. "Daddy seemed in such good health."

"He did," Noble said. "He's a big loss all right. One of my best friends, as well as a fine judge. Now, what can I do to help?"

They sat down in the parlor. Noble took out his notebook and pen. He agreed to draft the obituary and see that it got in the newspapers. He would notify the chief justice and invite him to make some remarks at the service. Julia had already talked to the preacher at St. James Church, and they had set the service for 3 p.m. day after tomorrow. She would meet with the people at the funeral home later today after lunch. She especially wanted Noble to participate in the service by offering some thoughts about the Judge's life.

They heard the front door open and then shut. Catherine Craighill came in, trailed by her cook carrying an armload of large containers. She directed the cook to the kitchen and then gave Julia a long hug.

"I'm so sorry," Catherine whispered. "It's really shocking."

"It truly is," Julia said. She took a handkerchief from a dress pocket and wiped her eyes. "It's sweet of you to come out."

"I've brought along something for the folks to snack on during the day."

"Wonderful," Julia said. "There's not much in the house here."

Catherine turned to Noble who was standing just off to the side. "Hello, Noble," she murmured and then gave him a hug. "I know the Judge was a great friend of yours."

"He was, and I'll miss him."

At that moment they heard car doors slamming out in the drive, as people began to arrive. Catherine hurried back to the kitchen, and Julia went to the front door to greet the callers. The stream kept up all day, life-long friends and others from all over the town and county—courthouse employees, lawyers, businessmen, farmers, wives, and Julia's friends. Noble left to take care of what he needed to do for Julia.

The fall afternoon was somber and gray, heavily overcast, with rain threatening. As the hour of the service approached, every seat in St. James Episcopal Church was taken. Dozens stood along the side walls. The bronze-colored casket rested in front just below the pulpit, covered with a massive spray of gladiolas. Noble and five other members of the bar served as pallbearers. The chief justice and four other members of the state supreme court had come down from Montgomery. On hand also were a half-dozen members of the legislature who had served with the judge when he was in the senate.

The organ ceased, and the booming voice of the Rector came from the rear. He led a procession of family and relatives. "I am the resurrection and the life. He that believeth in me though he were dead yet shall he live." The Rector was the Reverend Henry Edmonds who had arrived only a month earlier and thus did not really know the Judge. But, as Noble had often observed, the set-piece ritual in the Episcopal Church made the service almost preacher-proof; by following the script he couldn't go wrong. After the group reached the front and was seated, the Rector read familiar passages reciting the sure and certain hope of the resurrection. A male soloist, in a high, plaintive voice, sang "Shall We Gather at the River," one of the Judge's favorite hymns. The Chief Justice and Noble spoke in turn, each lauding the Judge as an able public servant, legislator, and judge, a man of great integrity and honesty, a good citizen. After more readings and prayers, the service concluded with the singing of another of the Judge's favorites:

> Our God our help in ages past
> Our hope for years to come,
> A refuge from the stormy blast
> And our eternal home.

When Noble reached home from the cemetery, a chill rain had begun. He went to Nan's room and found her, as usual, propped up in bed, eyes open but apparently seeing nothing. The room had developed the sickening aroma of a nursing home—medicinal odors mingled with a hint of urine. He gave her a hug and kiss. The aide had dabbed her with a familiar perfume which at close range overcame the less pleasant odor of the room.

Noble went to the den and sat down. Rain now came in sheets, setting up a steady drumming on the roof. Throughout the funeral service, with its reminders of human mortality, his thoughts had never been far from Nan. Now, again seeing her here, speechless and helpless, his pent-up emotions were unleashed. He broke down, as he had not done since childhood—crying for Nan, crying over the good times they had had together but now gone forever, crying over all he had not done but should have done, over the many times he had neglected her, had cooled in their relationship. If only he could do it all again! He saw her now as a good wife, a good mother, one who had stood by him, kept him functioning—and in a town she never felt comfortable in. He owed her much, but he now saw himself as a poor, unappreciative husband. It was too late now—too late … too late. He sat for a long while listening to the rain pounding on the roof and splashing down the gutters, reliving those forty years.

When Bartow Simmons came by the next afternoon to check on Nan, he asked Noble to step in the den. The two sat down in chairs flanking the fireplace. A log fire helped to ward off the chill.

"This is strictly confidential," Bartow said. "Probably shouldn't be mentioning it." He hesitated and then said, "It's a question I thought you might be able to shed some light on."

"I'll do my best," Noble said.

Lowering his voice into a secretive tone, Bartow said, "Do you know any reason why Judge McKnight might have been led to commit suicide?"

"That's a startling thought. Why do you ask?"

"He came to me a few days ago—two days before his death—complaining he couldn't sleep. Wanted me to give him a prescription for sleeping pills. That's a common problem, so I didn't think anything about it. I talked with him a little bit and then wrote out a prescription. When Willie May called me early in the morning saying the Judge wouldn't wake up, I went right out. It took me only a moment to see he was dead. He had had heart disease for several years so I suspected heart attack. When I pulled the cover back to examine him I found an empty bottle. Willie May was not in the room. The label showed it was the prescription I had just given him. Ingesting that entire bottle at once, as he must have done, could cause death. I sat there for a minute, pondering what to do. I decided, rightly or wrongly, to enter the cause of death as heart attack, a not implausible diagnosis. I saw no good reason to raise the suicide question. There was no autopsy. But I'm just curious about what might have driven him to this."

Noble sat reflectively for a long moment, looking into the fire. Then he said slowly, "Last time I saw him he seemed in good spirits. He was a little lonely, living out there all by himself, but hardly suicidal. I'm really shocked by this thought."

"O.K. Let's keep this between us. The case is closed as far as I'm concerned."

Chapter 17

Autumn was moving on, darkness coming earlier and earlier. As days passed and nothing changed with Nan, Noble decided life had to go on, his life, though Nan's would not. He saw there was nothing he could do for her except to see that she was kept comfortable. So he had resumed going regularly to his office, working long hours to catch up.

He felt himself in a peculiar limbo. For the first time he sensed what it was like to be a widower, with no one around the house to talk to or to go with him to dinner or parties. But biologically and legally he was not a widower. His wife, however, was nothing more than a physical shell of who she had been. With heart and lungs functioning, she was not dead, but hardly alive. Here was something that was neither life nor death, but something in between, a sort of twilight zone. Real death lay ahead, but real life was behind. And the worst of it, he thought, was that this could go on for years.

One day a call came from Jesse Rooter. He and Noble had not talked since Nan's stroke. Aside from being preoccupied with Nan, Noble had not called him because he had not yet received Owen Nichols' report and had no other news. After telling Jesse about Nan and hearing his condolences, Noble said, "What's on your mind?"

"I want to talk to the private eye."

"Fine with me, but you might wait a little while. He says he hopes to have a final report before long. His office is in Montgomery." Noble gave Jesse the address and telephone number.

"I hope he's caught some bigger fish than Joe Kinston," Jesse said. "Unfortunately Kinston may be the only living survivor of the whole episode. If that's the way it turns out, we'll have to decide what to do."

"When I told Lucille what you'd learned from Henry Watkins," Jesse said, "she got upset over the idea that Kinston might go around as a free man. Upset is an understatement. She got red-faced and livid. I'm surprised she hasn't gone to the DA. She wants something done."

"Lucille's temper is about as hot as Sam Funchess'," Noble said. "I have to say, though, that I'm pretty frustrated myself over Joe,—him walking around untouched. But try to stay cool. Anyway, I'll talk to you after we get Nichols' report."

More days passed. Then in the small hours of the morning Noble was suddenly aroused from sleep by someone shaking his shoulder. "Colonel Shepperson," the nurse's aide said, urgency in her voice cutting through the darkness. "Something's going on. You'd better come."

He was at Nan's bedside instantly. She was making sounds he had not heard before. Without hesitating, he picked up the phone and called Bartow Simmons.

Within fifteen minutes Bartow was there. Standing beside her bed, he had his stethoscope on her chest, then his hand on her pulse, then on her forehead, then repeating it all. Nan was quiet now, eyes closed. Noble and the aide stood by silently, as Bartow continued checking blood pressure and heart. Minutes ticked by. In the silence of that pre-dawn hour, the only sound was the rustling of Bartow's movements as he continued his monitoring. Noble looked at the inert Nan, face at peace, reminding himself that this was once a vibrant, living woman, his wife of forty years. After what seemed an interminable time, Bartow straightened up, emitted a long sigh, his face sadder than Noble had ever seen it, and half whispered those words of ultimate finality, "She's gone."

With the coming of daylight, word swept over town. Friends began to stream by. By late afternoon Kirk and Martha and their children had arrived.

Catherine Craighill called to say she and her cook would be over with a complete supper for all; Noble and family were not to do a thing. He protested only mildly. At sunset she appeared with cook in tow and enough fried chicken, potato salad, baked beans, rolls, and apple pie, to feed a platoon. Not only did she bring the entire meal but she and the cook served it and then cleaned up the dishes afterward.

For the second time this fall the town gathered for a farewell, filling the Presbyterian Church to capacity. Nan's close personal friends were not all that numerous. Many were there out of respect for Noble. The family sat in the front pew—Noble, Kirk, Martha, and their spouses, the two grandchildren nestled beside their parents. Cousins, close and distant, filled the next pew.

Noble stared fixedly at the cream-colored casket, topped with a profusion of red roses and ferns. Because he had in practical effect lost Nan on the day of her stroke, and had been living in a half-life limbo ever since, the impact of her death was not quite what it would normally have been. Still, death brought finality, an awareness that he would not again see her on this earth, not hear her voice, not feel the warmth of her body. He felt tightness in his stomach. He sought to ameliorate the overwhelming sadness by reminding himself this was a blessing, that the kind of existence she had been experiencing was not life, that death was a release—if the preacher's words he now heard were to be believed—a release into the joys of eternal life.

Words floated in and out of Noble's consciousness, but he paid little attention to the service, being preoccupied with recollections of Nan and regrets over what he had done and not done.

The service over, the family went quickly out a side door into waiting limousines. With the hearse in the lead, the procession moved along Center Street and out to the cemetery. The afternoon was dull and gray, filled with autumnal chill. As they assembled around the open grave in the Shepperson plot, Noble surveyed the other graves and the names on the weathering granite headstones. The most recent was Robert Edward Kirkman, his sister Emily's husband and his law partner. Emily lay beside him, now over fifteen years gone. Then there were his parents and grandparents. Beside Nan's fresh grave was a vacant space that would one day be claimed for him. Again the preacher recited familiar reassurances—that we bring nothing into this world and we take nothing out, that in our father's house are many rooms, and we go in the sure and certain hope of the resurrection.

At the conclusion, friends pressed in from all sides—members of Nan's book club and garden club, the younger crowd who had grown up with Kirk and Martha, and a multitude of long-time Remberton residents.

Lucille Brentson had insisted that Noble and the entire family come to her house for supper. And so they did. She explained to Kirk and Martha, as they munched away on roast beef sandwiches, how much help their father had been to her father and to her too and how sad it was that he was left all alone.

The children and grandchildren left the next day and Noble was indeed alone. He didn't want to see anybody for several days. He was in the office only part-time for the next week. Gradually, though, he realized he had to take hold of himself and that life had to go on.

Two weeks after Nan's death, Jesse Rooter stood at Catherine Craighill's front door in the late afternoon and rang the bell. Catherine opened the door and exclaimed, "Jesse Rooter! The return of the native! I can't believe it's you."

"May I come in?" He was dressed in dark suit and tie but looked weary and harried and was breathing heavily.

"Of course." She stood aside as he walked into the hall. "I'm afraid you've caught me in a rather bedraggled shape. I've been working around the house all day. Come on in and have a seat while I run and change."

As they walked into the parlor, she said, "Is something wrong? You look tired."

"Just a long day. A little stressful too."

Although only shortly past six o' clock, it was already dark. She switched on a lamp at the end of the sofa. "You might be interested in this: *A Pictorial History of Remberton.* Just came out."

Catherine left and Jesse wearily slumped on the sofa. He began paging through the book. The first section focused on antebellum houses, some grandiose, some modest. Captions under three of them stated they had been torn down to make way for commercial enterprises. Then he came to a picture of three men standing at a gate leading to what appeared to be a lumberyard and a large building. The caption revealed them to be the Mayor of Remberton, State Senator Andrew McKnight, and Sam Funchess, at the opening of Funchess' new saw mill, the largest in the county. It went on to praise the men as among the county's most distinguished citizens who had contributed much to life in the region.

Disgusted with those words, Jesse looked long and hard at Sam Funchess. He had never seen the man himself or any photograph of him. What he saw now was an ordinary looking man, but in the close-set eyes behind a large nose he thought he saw pure evil. What he had learned this afternoon intensified his smoldering anger. His inability to reach Sam Funchess now, to follow him beyond the grave, was maddening. And standing there was also Andrew McKnight who became the much respected judge. Whoever would have thought those two, of such differing backgrounds, could have been linked together, as they now were in Owen Nichols' report.

He was still fixated on Sam Funchess when Catherine appeared from the hall. She was an entirely different person now, all scrubbed with khaki skirt and blue blouse. "Now," she said, "can I get you something to drink?"

"Do you still have martinis?"

"Sure do."

"I think I need one."

"Come on back to the kitchen."

He followed her along the hall. She switched on the light. The windows were black against the night. She put the martini shaker on the counter and pulled gin and vermouth from a cabinet. He leaned against a counter, watching her. He felt tired, very tired, and wondered about his heart. He pulled out a chair and sat down at the table.

As she mixed the drinks, she said, "Would you like the guest room for the night? Remember I said you have a standing invitation."

"Thanks, but I'm already checked in at the Holiday Inn."

"May I ask to what I owe the honor of this visit?"

"I had some business in Montgomery so decided to run on down."

She handed him an oversized martini glass filled to the brim. "Cheers," she said, lifting her glass. "Welcome back to Remberton."

After a long sip, he said, "That hits the spot. Just what I needed." Then after a moment: "it was sad about Noble's wife."

"Yes, it was. But it's really a blessing. She would never have recovered. Would you like to go up front and sit down?"

"Just let me sit here and relax for a few minutes."

She said, with a slight smirk, "How are you and Lucille hitting it off?"

Hitting it off is not the way I would put it."

"How would you put it?"

"Not sure I would put it at all. We've had one telephone conversation since she came to see me."

"You did have her as a guest in your house."

Jesse sighed. "At her request, as I told you, not at my invitation."

"Lucille is interested in two things—men and money. To put it bluntly, you are both."

"So?"

"So you'd better watch out."

"Look, my only connection with Lucille is with the library funding …" He hesitated. "Well that's not quite all. There's her father."

"He really bugs you, doesn't he?"

"Bugs me is not strong enough. What do you remember about him?"

"When I was growing up I would see him sometimes around the house when I was there with Lucille. That's about it."

"What was his relationship with your father?"

"I don't recall any. They were certainly not big buddies. He may have been one of his patients."

Just finishing a sip of martini, Jesse said, "Tell me about your father."

"He practiced medicine here for nearly fifty years. Much beloved."

"When news came Grady had drowned, did he say anything?"

"All I recall is that he said something to the effect that a man living like he did was bound to come to a bad end."

"Did your father have any connection with Judge McKnight?"

"Again," she said, "I don't recall anything particular. You have to keep in mind this place is small. Everybody knows everybody else, have known each other all their lives."

She took the shaker and refilled their glasses, then said, "Let's go up front and sit down. I want you to tell me what you remember about any of the scenes in that book."

When Noble walked into his office the next morning, Miss Alice was sitting at her desk, hands on keyboard, typing away—the sight Noble had encountered on arriving every day for more than twenty-five years. He rarely beat her there.

She looked up and said, "Some startling news this morning."

"What's that?"

"We had a murder last night. First in five years, they say."

"Who was it?"

"One of those Kinstons. Joe Kinston."

Noble stopped abruptly. "Joe Kinston! What do you know about it?"

"I was just over at the drug store and they say he was shot in his driveway late yesterday afternoon. No suspects."

Noble was immediately on the telephone to the police station. The chief was out investigating the case. There was nothing else they could say right now.

Who could possibly have done this? Maybe one of his fellow mill workers or somebody he got in a fight with up at the beer joint. Noble had an eerie feeling about it. Was this justice unwittingly inflicted on Joe Kinston—justice the law could not impose?

Noble was finally able to get the police chief on the phone. He said Joe's wife, when she got home at about six, found him lying on the ground by the open door of his pickup, shot through the heart.

"Seems to have been dead less than an hour," the chief said. "We found the bullet, from a .38 revolver. One of the neighbors—the only one at home around that time—says she heard a gun shot but didn't think anything about it. Nobody saw anything. You know it gets dark now by 5:30."

"Any theory about who might have done it?"

"No. I talked with the men he works with at the mill. Can't find anything suspicious there. His wife's no help. Doesn't know why anybody would have it in for Joe."

"How about the crowd up the road at the beer joint?"

"Haven't had a chance to check them out yet. But I'll keep you posted."

Noble telephoned Jesse to give him the news. Mrs. Schneider answered.

"He's not here," she said.

"Do you know where I can reach him or when he'll be back?"

"He left a couple of days ago, said he was going to Montgomery. I think he's coming back sometime tomorrow."

Jesse called Noble the next evening. "I understand you tried to reach me."

"Right, I wanted to give you some startling news." He proceeded to tell him of Joe Kinston's murder and what he knew and didn't know about it.

When he finished, there was a pause before Jesse spoke. "Joe Kinston dead! And they have no idea who did it?"

"Not a clue."

"At least we can say justice has been done—been done when the law couldn't."

"That's one way to look at it."

"Now all three of those murderers at the creek have gone to their reward," Jesse said, "whatever that may be. Listen, I was going to call you anyway to tell you I went to see Owen Nichols."

"Mrs. Schneider said you had gone to Montgomery. I'm surprised you didn't let me know."

"It was a quick, spur-of-the-moment trip. He went over everything with me. Said he'd talked with you the day before. So you and I both know what he's found. It's pretty shocking."

Noble sighed. "At long last the full story, and I wish I never heard it. I feel sick at my stomach when I think about it. In a way it's not a huge surprise to know that Sam Funchess put up the money. It's consistent with his temperament. And he was one of the few with that kind of money. But Judge McKnight! My God! Who would have ever thought it?"

"Didn't we want to know the truth?"

"Well, at least you did. But what can we do about it?" Noble said. "They're all dead."

"I'm not dead," Jesse said.

Noble paused and then said, "But we don't want to do anything rash. And we don't want to hurt the innocent living."

"I'm not through with it yet," Jesse said. "I'll be talking to you again."

When they hung up, Jesse sat for a long while, thinking over the situation. And he thought about it all the next day—a sullen late fall day—looking out of his library windows at the increasingly wintry scene. There had already been one snow, the trees were now bare, and the lake was beginning to freeze at the edges. It would not be long before winter was upon him in full force.

He concluded that Noble would do nothing—was too concerned over those still living. But something had to be done. He could not let it rest, knowing what he now knew. But what could it be? The justice done to Joe Kinston had removed the last living participant. But there remained the chief villain, Sam Funchess. Jesse resolved not to permit death to provide an escape. But how to do justice in this case? He would have to think it through carefully. There was time, but it was not unlimited. His health was no better.

He would also need to think more about the library. He was inclined to think that Remberton didn't deserve his largess. Maybe his idea of charitable revenge would have to give way to pure revenge.

Christmas was approaching. Center Street was adorned with strings of colored lights. A massive decorated tree stood on the City Hall lawn. Carols sounded everywhere—on the radio, the TV, in the stores. Noble approached the day with dread. Not since the war had he been without Nan at Christmas.

Catherine Craighill called, saying she was having a small group for Christmas dinner and she would love to include him. He thanked her but explained he would be with Martha and her family in Nashville.

She said, "Just wanted to let you know I'm thinking about you. Incidentally, I assume you saw Jesse Rooter when he was here."

"Jesse here in Remberton? When?"

"Last Thursday night. Didn't you see him or hear from him?"

"No, I didn't. It seems strange. Why was he here?"

"He told me he had some business in Montgomery and just ran down here."

"Did you say last Thursday?"

"Yes."

"What time did you see him and where?"

"He came by the house a little after six. Why are you asking?"

"Just curious why I didn't hear from him."

Home from Christmas with Martha—the occasion as pleasant as it could be under the circumstances—Noble was back in his office in early January. The buzzer sounded and Miss Alice said, "A man with a British accent wants to speak with you. Says his name is Nicholas Cottingham."

Noble's mind took a moment to click into gear and fix on the name. Then it came back. "Put him on."

"This is Nicky Cottingham," came the strong English voice. "We met at the British Embassy last summer."

"Yes. I remember it well. How are you?"

"Doing splendidly. And you?"

Noble told him about Nan. After an elaborate expression of sympathy, Nicky said, "Something unusual has come up, and I would very much like to talk with you about it. I could fly down to see you there."

"Is it something we could discuss over the phone and save you a trip?"

"I'm afraid not. It's frightfully important. I feel it essential to see you in person."

Noble couldn't imagine what would lead Nicky to him, a small town lawyer in Alabama, given the access he would have from the British Embassy to all manner of persons in the United States. For a second there flicked through Noble's mind what Jennifer had said. Could this be some devious scheme, possibly having to do with his financial difficulties? But there was a tone of sincere urgency in Nicky's voice. So, overcoming his hesitancy, Noble said, with artificial cheerfulness, "Oh, please do so. And plan to stay at my house. With children and wife gone I have plenty of room."

They agreed Nicky would fly to Montgomery and Noble would meet him at the airport.

Chapter 18

▼

Nicky's plane was late and darkness was setting in when he arrived. Noble met him at the gate, retrieved his bag, and they were off down the interstate to Remberton. Noble proposed they stop at Spiffy's, a relatively new restaurant right off the exit. "A bit of Americana from the heartland," he said. "Nothing fancy, but not bad."

All the way down from the airport and during dinner Noble had talked steadily on the nature of Remberton and the history of the region, interrupted by an occasional question from Nicky. So it was not until they reached Noble's house and Nicky had settled in his room that they finally got down to business.

In the den, Noble lit a log fire. He fetched two glasses of brandy and they sat down. He said, "Now you can tell me what's important enough to bring you all the way to the middle of Alabama."

"It's a truly extraordinary story. I would say that it could not be believed without the documentary evidence. What makes it so extraordinary is that by sheer coincidence I met you at the Embassy and you gave me your card. Were it not for that I would not be here and wouldn't know what to do. Our meeting was a great bit of luck—providential, I would say."

"We had a preacher here once who said there's no such thing as coincidences."

"Whatever you call it let me get right to the point. I am an adopted child. This is little known in England. It really didn't make any difference because my father was only a life peer, so there was no sticky question about my inheriting a title. They told me about the adoption when I was in my teens. Since then I've had what I suppose is a natural curiosity to know who my real parents were. Adoption records in England are well protected in the office of the Registrar General. No ordinary inquiry is likely to produce any information."

"It's been my impression that adoption information is pretty well sealed up everywhere," Noble said.

"It normally is. But I engaged a top-flight investigator. Some how or other he got the facts. His methods would probably not bear close scrutiny—most likely he violated some ethical rules, not to mention statutes. But I don't want to know about that. The fact is he produced results. He ascertained I was born on March 17, 1947 at St. Jude's Hospital in London. But here's the truly startling fact: my mother listed her residence as Remberton, Alabama."

In the momentary silence, Noble's eyes half closed squinting at Nicky, then opened wide. His voice dripped with incredulity. "Are you telling me your mother—your real mother—came from right here in Remberton?"

"That's what the record shows."

Noble nearly exploded. "My God! This is too much. Do you have her name?"

"It's listed as Lucille Funchess."

It was as though a 500-pound bomb had plunged through the roof and exploded in the room. The shock, falling debris, and sound had to wear off. After a while, looking intently at Nicky, Noble said, "Let me be sure I have this straight. You are telling me you are the son of Lucille Funchess?"

"According to the official record, yes. But what about her? Do you know her?"

Noble's face was that of a man lost in troubled thought. "Do I know her?" He paused. "I should say so." Another pause. "It's taking me a minute to absorb this. What was that birth date?"

"March 17, 1947."

Once again Noble thought of Jennifer's words. Was this some devious gambit? "Tell me again your source."

"Papers on file in the Registrar General's office. Here, I brought a copy." From his inside coat pocket, Nicky pulled out a couple of folded sheets and handed them to Noble.

Noble studied them carefully. They looked official and authentic, reciting the facts as Nicky had stated. He half mumbled, "Lucille in London? So that's it."

"What's that?" Nicky asked.

"Lucille and her mother left here in late summer of 1946 for Europe, saying they would be gone for several months. They described it as the Grand Tour, an educational venture for Lucille."

"So she had to be pregnant before she left here?"

"That's a reasonable inference," Noble said. He was still turning over in his mind the incredible facts. "I suppose it's possible she got pregnant along the way, but that would have made for quite a premature baby."

"The father is the remaining mystery," Nicky said. "The record doesn't show his name. But tell me about Lucille."

After Noble gave an abridged version of Lucille's life, Nicky said, "So I don't come from a long line of Southern aristocracy?" Noble thought he detected a slight note of disappointment.

"That's a fair statement. But this is typical of the South these days. Lucille has established herself in the top social circles. Money does it. But some of the old-timers look down on her. They're put off by the fact that she doesn't have an ancestor who was an officer in the Army of Northern Virginia."

"Would it be possible to meet her?"

Noble stood up. "This news calls for another brandy before I can think about anything else." He reached out and took Nicky's glass. Noble's instinct was to protect Lucille from this potentially embarrassing or even devastating information. At the same time, he thought Lucille might eventually want to know.

Coming back with the two refilled glasses, he sat down and said, "I have an idea. There's a lot of interest here in our public library. It badly needs a new building. I gather you have a fine library yourself. I could invite Lucille—who may be a prospect for a gift—and our library board here for drinks to meet you, a distinguished English visitor very much interested in libraries. How does that sound?"

"I can't improve on it. Did you say that Lucille might make a financial contribution to the library?"

Wishing he had not mentioned it, Noble said, "Well, that's just something being talked about."

"Then I take it," Nicky said, "she's well off financially?"

"I think we could say she's comfortably fixed."

The next day Noble drove Nicky all over town, pointing out the antebellum houses left and giving him the history of each.

"This is a beautiful town," Nicky said.

"Not as much as it used to be. Look at that new building," Noble said, pointing to a squat brick structure beside an asphalt parking lot. "It's a dentist's office. One of our prettiest old houses stood there—a two-story Greek revival with trees in front and azaleas all around. Progress is the way they describe this. I call it criminal."

The dentist's office was one of the twentieth century commercial intrusions that had begun to invade the oldest part of town. It was the section that had been laid out when the town was being settled, Which, as he explained to Nicky, was why the streets were named for the presidents of that time—Jackson, Polk, Tyler, and so on.

When Noble pointed out the library in its cramped frame house, Nicky exclaimed, "That's a library?"

"You can see the need for a new building. You'll get to meet one of the librarians tonight."

They parked at the courthouse, the town's dominant architectural feature. Noble took Nicky inside and upstairs to the courtroom. With court not in session, the high-ceilinged room was quiet and deserted.

They walked down the center aisle and passed through the bar rail. Noble said, "Here's where I've spent a large part of my adult life, sitting at one of these counsel tables or standing in front of the witness stand. Witness box, I believe you say." Smiling, he added, "We allow our witnesses to sit down."

Nicky was an interested tourist, listening intently to all Noble was saying and looking at everything as though he were visiting some exotic colonial outpost.

Standing just below the bench, Noble felt the presence of Judge McKnight, sitting there for many years but sitting there no more, having taken with him to the grave the dark secret known now only to Noble and Jesse. But, so it was said, corruption shall put on incorruption. Looking now at the empty bench, Noble's troubled thought surged up. He couldn't get it out of his mind that he was responsible for the Judge's death. If he hadn't engaged Owen Nichols, the judge would still be alive. But Noble would never have known what he now knew.

His thoughts were interrupted by Nicky. "I suppose being a trial lawyer puts you in the midst of all sorts of conflicts, some pretty nasty."

"That's right," Noble said. "In the middle of the whole range of human conflict."

Back in the car, they drove the length of Center Street and on out to the cemetery. "Here is the Funchess plot," Noble said, as he parked in a lane bordered by a line of camellias, with graves on both sides. The camellias at the height of their season were covered with red, white, and pink blooms, and blossoms of variegated colors. Around them on the ground were fallen petals. Nicky marveled over seeing so many colorful flowers in the middle of winter.

Noble said, "This section was added to the cemetery in the late thirties. Sam Funchess immediately acquired this choice plot in the most prominent part."

They got out and stood at the edge of the graves. The single word "Funchess" was inscribed in large letters on a thick vertical slab of white marble, seven feet long and five feet high. No other marker in the surrounding plots equaled it in size. There were only three graves—those of Samuel Funchess, his wife, Margo, and Robert Brentson, Lucille's late husband. Each was covered by full-length white marble. Graves in all the other plots were marked by gray granite. Funchess alone stood in resplendent white marble. And it alone had a marble bench, where presumably one could sit and contemplate. And it alone was bordered by marble curbing.

"As you can see," Noble said, "Sam Funchess did things in a big way. No half measures."

Looking dreamily at the graves, Nicky said softly, "If the record is right, those are my grandparents."

Noble shook his head and said, "I still can't grasp it."

As they got back in the car, Noble said, "Over there in the old part is my family's plot. Two generations of Sheppersons are there. That's where Nan is buried."

"This must have been a terribly sad time for you," Nicky said.

"It hasn't been easy. But the human capacity to adjust is enormous."

What remained on the Remberton tour was Lucille's house. Noble had saved it for last. He drove by slowly, almost stopping, to let Nicky get a good look.

Nicky exclaimed, "I say, this must be the largest house here!"

"You've got it. That's the way Sam Funchess wanted it."

"Do you have any idea how much Lucille is worth?"

The question again made Noble uncomfortable. "I really don't know."

"But her husband is deceased and she has only one child?"

"That's right."

January being a slack social time, Noble found all members of the library board available, along with Lucille and Catherine. He stimulated an irresistible curiosity when he said he had an unexpected visitor who was an English bibliophile; heightening interest even more by saying he was the son of an English Lord. In Remberton, foreign visitors were rare. A special cachet attached to Englishmen in this land where Anglophilia ran deep. He and Nicky had agreed they would explain his unlikely presence by saying they had met in London the previous spring when Noble was there for the D-Day celebration and that Nicky was now attached to the British Embassy and was on vacation traveling through the South.

They were gathered in Noble's living room, drinks in hand, standing around talking, with Nicky the central attraction. He cut a handsome figure in a blue blazer. The bar in the adjoining den was manned by Zeke, Noble's long-time yardman, trained by Noble to do rudimentary bartending, who had put on a white coat for the occasion. A faint, pleasant hint of wood smoke was in the air, coming from the log fire simmering in the fireplace.

Noble had learned that an English accent would carry a man a long way in the States, especially in the South. So entrancing was its effect that an Englishman, if so disposed, could get away with something bordering on fraud. But to Nicky's credit, he did not represent himself to be more than he was. Noble had told the group that Nicky's father had been Lord Cottingham, an active member of the House of Lords. Nicky made it clear, however, that his father was only a life peer and that he would have no inherited title. But to the assembled group this made no difference. As far as they were concerned, Nicky was an English Lord.

He fascinated them with his description of Cottingham Hall, his ancestral home in Hampshire. Everyone had been to England, at least briefly as a tourist. But only Norma and Catherine had been to Hampshire, other than Noble who had passed through it during the war.

Norma was giving Nicky her impressions of Winchester, while Ben was trying to get particulars on Nicky's eight thousand-volume library.

Noble was interested above all else in the interaction of Lucille and Nicky and especially in Nicky's reaction to her. She had arrived late, after most of the other guests. Noble had met her at the front door and taken her coat. He thought she looked better than he had ever seen her. She sported a new, stylish hair-do and wore a bright red, form-fitting dress, touched off by a necklace of gold and multi-colored stones. "Come on in and meet the guest," he said.

Noble led her into the living room toward Nicky. "Lucille," he said, "this is Nicky Cottingham."

For a moment Nicky's face was a frozen mask, his eyes unnaturally riveted on Lucille, mother and son facing each other for the first time, a relationship known only to the son. But then he broke into a smile—a nervous smile, Noble thought. He took her hand in his, his eyes never leaving hers. "Lucille, this is a great pleasure. Noble has spoken to me about you."

She smiled and said, "I hope you didn't hear too much of my bad side."

Noble said, "Today I gave Nicky the grand tour of Remberton. Lucille, you can probably guess what he said when he saw your house."

"What?"

"That looks like an oversize Mount Vernon." They all laughed.

"That's what Daddy had in mind," Lucille said, in her brusk manner.

Zeke appeared and handed Lucille a scotch and water. He asked whether anyone wanted another drink. Catherine and Ben surrendered their glasses for a refill.

Noble studied the faces of Nicky and Lucille, struggling to identify any physical resemblance. There was a little, he thought, although he could be imagining it. The nose and the mouth were not unalike.

Nicky said to Lucille, "I understand you have a daughter who was married recently."

"Yes. Last April. Are you married?"

"No. I haven't found any woman who'll put up with me. When were you in England?"

"Way back when I was in college. My mother and I went there as part of a European tour."

"What year were you there?"

"Let me see," she said, hesitating, "It was 1947."

"I suppose signs of the war were still around."

"Oh, yes. I remember seeing rubble in London."

"That's the year I was born, so I don't have any personal recollection. But I've heard plenty about it."

"If you're going to be around tomorrow I'd love to have you and Noble come by for a drink. I can show you the inside of Mount Vernon."

"Thanks, but I need to press on."

Catherine moved up. "In your tour today, did Noble show you our little library?"

"He did and he told me there's an effort to get a new building."

"I imagine you could see why we need it."

"Your quarters do seem a bit small."

Zeke was at his elbow. Nicky said, "Another whiskey, please."

"Sir," Zeke asked, a little puzzled, "Scotch or bourbon?"

"Oh, I forgot. Our only whiskey is what you call scotch. That's it," he said to Zeke, "scotch."

After the crowd had gone Noble and Nicky sat down in the living room, but not before Noble had put another log on the fire and punched it up.

"A charming group," Nicky said. "All keen over the library. You have a good town."

"We think so. But now, what do you think about Lucille?"

"She's a strong woman, I would say. Knows her own mind. Attractive too, but perhaps a bit brusque. How long has her husband been dead?"

"Six or seven years."

"Any remarriage prospects?"

"She's had overtures. She turned them all down. Thinks they're after her money."

"Now that Catherine strikes me as a charmer, a bit warmer, and I love her melodious accent."

"Look," Noble said, changing the direction of the conversation, "what do you think now about telling Lucille?"

"What I think is I want to think some more. I need to fly back tomorrow for a function at the Embassy, but I'll be in touch."

A couple of days later Noble and Lucille sat in her den. Outside, the sky was leaden, the day gray and soggy, damp and chilly, a typical depressing mid-winter day in Remberton. He had come in response to a phone call saying she wished to talk to him about the library.

Before she could get on that subject, he said, "What did you think of Nicky Cottingham?"

"Typical Englishman. Full of fancy talk. But, an attractive young man. A lot of mothers might like to see their daughters get interested in him."

"He enjoyed talking with you. Was impressed you had spent time in England. How long were you there?"

"It's hard to remember now. Maybe a few weeks. I didn't enjoy it as much as I should have. I was ready to come home."

Noble scrutinized her face as he never had before, looking for traces of Nicky. "Did your stay not go well?"

"Oh, it went as well as it could have under the circumstances. But look, I called you to come here to talk about the library situation. I don't understand Jesse Rooter. We talked on the phone soon after my visit but I haven't heard from him since."

Noble found it hard to concentrate on Jesse Rooter and the library, burdened as he was with an explosive secret—no, two explosive secrets—one about her father and one about her. He alone knew them both. It was a terrible burden to bear. He was feeling the emotional strain of containing them within himself. Sooner or later, he thought, they would have to come out. For now he simply said, "What's your view of the matter?"

"Jesse ought to fish or cut bait. Either he puts up his money or he drops the idea."

"He's said he was waiting to see what the investigation turns up."

"Well, what has it turned up?"

"The latest twist is the murder of Joe Kinston."

"The law couldn't get to him, but justice did. I can't shed any tears over it."

"The police have almost no clues. So far it seems to be the perfect crime."

"Do they know what killed him?"

"A single shot from a .38 revolver."

"Don't they have ways of tracing bullets?"

"Only if they have something to trace it to. They haven't found a gun. Apparently there were some footprints. They've made casts so they can be matched with shoes. It's particularly baffling because the police can't find a motive. Anyway, what do you want me to do about Jesse?"

"I want you to pin him down. I don't see what more he needs. We know the three men who took Grady to the creek. All three are now dead. What more does he want?"

"There's the question of who paid them."

"What difference does that make now? Whoever did is probably dead."

"For Jesse it seems to make a lot of difference. He's got a bee in his bonnet to find out. But what will you do about the library?"

"Depends on what he does or doesn't do. I don't know right now."

Noble stood up. "I've got to run along. I'll talk with Jesse."

Walking up the hall with him, she said, "How much longer do you think the investigation will take?"

"It may be about over now."

"And what have you found we didn't already know?"

"At the moment I'm not at liberty to say."

A week later, a call came from Nicky. "Noble," he said, "I have a splendid idea."

"I'm all ears."

"I'm not ready to blurt out this news to Lucille. So I've come up with a plan for the next step. It may sound implausible, but here it is. I would like to invite the Remberton library board, plus Lucille and Catherine, to visit me for a weekend at my place in England. The stated reason would be to see my library. They expressed a lot of interest in it. The main reason, of course, would be for me to let Lucille get to know me better, and vice versa, and to get comfortable with me in my native habitat. Does this strike you as too far-fetched?"

Noble half laughed. "Words that come to mind are ridiculous, generous, exciting."

"Oh, I overlooked saying that, of course, you are invited."

"Seeing this crowd in Cottingham Hall is something I wouldn't want to miss—not to mention seeing the place myself."

But after they hung up Noble had second thoughts. The trip really didn't make sense. Why would a sophisticated Englishman like Nicky want this group from a remote, small town in Alabama to be his weekend guests in far-off England? Especially if he was having financial difficulties, as Jennifer had intimated? There were surely other, simpler ways for him and Lucille to become acquainted.

He was uneasy over the prospect, wishing he hadn't so readily agreed

Chapter 19

As it turned out, Ben Harris was the only library board member who could make the trip. Melba Robinson felt obliged to stay with her daughter who had just had a baby. Norma Armistead said overseas travel was now too much for her. Ann Simmons thought it not feasible to leave her three young children for that length of time. Jesse Rooter was added to the invitation list after Noble explained to Nicky the potential financial bonanza he represented. Lucille and Catherine jumped at the opportunity. Noble, as self-appointed leader of the group, coordinated travel arrangements.

The prospect of England immediately brought to Noble's mind thoughts of Jennifer Hedgely. The gloom enveloping him since Nan's death was beginning to lift. He noticed a faint but perceptible revival of interest in attractive women. Now as he planned the upcoming trip, images of Jennifer flooded his mind. At last, after all these years, with the restraint of marriage now gone, he could relish being with her—could give rein to his lustful feelings—without a sense of guilt. He visualized himself in her South Kensington apartment with the delicious, soft, fragrant, and loving Jennifer, just the two of them, alone with nowhere to go and no time constraints.

Eager though he was to see her, he decided not to contact her in advance but to call her from Cottingham Hall and arrange to meet her in London after the others left. He could linger for several days in an idyllic interlude. Where they would go from there he did not know and, for the moment, did not care.

Soft twilight settled over the Hampshire countryside as they assembled for sherry in the library at Cottingham Hall. Together in the same room for the first time were the three principals in this intertwined Remberton drama, ironically transferred to the heart of England: Jesse, Lucille, and Nicky. Each knew something the others did not know which if exposed in Remberton would have unpredictable and possibly shattering consequences. Noble alone knew all those secrets—and suspected another. They would all be better off, he was thinking, if these could be put away forever and forgotten. Men in the past had lived out their years without disclosing devastating facts. But he thought it unlikely here. These matters were too emotion-laden, too intimately intertwined with life itself. But when and how and with what impact would they surface?

Sherry glasses and a filled decanter stood on a side table. Catherine Craighill was pouring. She handed Noble a glass. "This is like a dream. I haven't been to England since just after college. I'd forgotten how beautiful it is."

She and Noble stood together aside from the group, looking out a tall window down a two-hundred yard gentle slope to a small lake. The expanse of lawn was still vividly green in the dusk, reminding Noble of the same English green in the spring of '44, and along with it, Jennifer.

Catherine said in a whispered voice, "I can't get over Nicky's hospitality. Don't you think it's strange of him to have this crowd from little old Remberton all the way over here? I don't understand it."

"He was taken with Remberton—had never seen an American small town before—seemed to be surprised it was not inhabited by barbarians. He was especially interested in our library project."

From across the room came the voice of Ben Harris. He had detached himself from the group and was running his eyes along the book-filled shelves. "Can you believe it?" he exclaimed. "Here's a first edition of *Great Expectations*." He was turning the pages of a worn volume. In his tortoiseshell eyeglasses and thinning hair he looked like an aging and retired schoolmaster.

"My father was big on Dickens," Nicky said. "He liked the Victorians generally. He had most of Trollop." He pointed to a section of shelves beside the fireplace. "And here's Tennyson and Thackeray. He also was fond of Kipling. Actually, a large part of his library was inherited from his father and grandfather and some even earlier."

Out of his black-suited Embassy clothes, Nicky was dressed informally in a tweed jacket. He was slightly shorter than Noble and had a lankier build. He was, of course, the center of attention.

He moved to a table on which stood several framed photographs. "Some of you have asked about my father. He was in the First World War, a pilot in the Royal Flying Corps.

Because of his young age he came into the war late, in 1918. Here he's standing in front of his Sopwith Camel. He shot down two German planes. He was hit himself, but managed to get back over Allied lines and make a crash landing. I have the propeller of his plane downstairs—an old style wooden propeller."

"What did he do after the war?" Noble asked.

"He went into business, mainly railroads and coal mining. During the second war he was with the Transport Ministry. He was knighted by George VI and took a seat in the House of Lords. Here he is with my mother around that time." He pointed to a photograph of a middle-aged couple—an attractive though plumpish woman and a tall, moderately handsome man.

Noble noted that there was little or no resemblance to Nicky.

As they stood admiring the photographs and other artifacts from several generations of Cottinghams, Catherine said, "Nicky, would you like another glass of sherry?"

"That would be nice, thank you."

The group drifted toward the sherry. Lucille pulled Jesse off to the side. She spoke in a low voice. "Why haven't I heard from you?"

"I've been thinking," Jesse said, looking somber.

"How long does it take you to think?" She was obviously irritated.

"We need to talk. Tomorrow."

Nicky came up. He and Jesse had been introduced but had not talked to each other. "I understand," Nicky said, "you're a Remberton native son who went away and made good."

"I suppose that's one way to put it," Jesse said.

"They seem to think you might do something really fine for the library."

"I'm giving it some thought." Jesse was proving not to be especially sociable or talkative. He was unsmiling as usual.

Nicky had been keeping Lucille constantly in view. Speaking directly to her, he said, "I'd love to hear more about your trip to England. Where did you and your mother stay?"

"Since we wanted to be there for a while, we rented a flat. I forget the address. It was near Grosvenor Square."

"What did you like most about London?"

"Oh, I guess the plays and the shops."

"I think you said you were here in '47, the year I was born."

"That makes you twenty-eight. You've certainly done well for a man so young."

"I've had some lucky breaks. How old is your daughter?"

"Twenty-four."

"Does she resemble her mother?" As he had done in Remberton, Nicky examined her every feature—eyes, nose, mouth, hair—searching for any trace of himself.

Lucille said, "A little bit. Fortunately, she's better looking. Her hair is the color of yours."

"Is she your only child?"

"Yes."

Ben's voice rose above the conversation. He stood on a short ladder enabling him to reach the upper shelves. "I can't get over it. Here's a first edition of Gibbon's *Decline and Fall*."

"Actually," Nicky said, turning toward him, "most of the nineteenth century literature here is first edition."

A white-coated butler appeared at the door and announced dinner was ready. They accompanied Nicky along a hallway, passing from the heated library into the chill of a huge hall with no central heating, into a heated dining room. Heavy draperies were drawn across the tall windows. It was dark now and a chandelier gave off a soft light. The table in the center of the room, covered with a white cloth, was set for six.

When they were seated, Nicky said, "I thought it appropriate to start off your visit with a classic English dinner—lamb, roasted potatoes, and brussel sprouts."

As they ate, Nicky gave them a history of Cottingham Hall. It was built in the late eighteenth century and came into possession of his family in the 1820s. His grandfather improved the grounds, adding the lake, gardens, and walking paths. Winchester was only a half hour's drive away, he said, and he would be glad to show them around if they would like.

Catherine said, "I remember going there on my tour years ago. What I recall most is the cathedral."

"That's its main claim to fame," Nicky said. "Every cathedral in England has some unique feature. Winchester's is the longest nave."

Noble found himself not paying close attention to the conversation, which was droning on about Winchester and Hampshire. Jennifer was on his mind. He wondered when and how he could get in touch with her. Several glasses of wine, on top of the sherry, had made him drowsy. It took two cups of black coffee to get himself alert for what he had to do.

Ben's voice cut into his consciousness. "Nicky, this is all grand, but I've had a long day and think I'll excuse myself." That seemed to be a signal for all to rise, saying they would do the same.

Nicky said, "Breakfast will be available anytime after seven. Come on down whenever you'd like and order what you want."

Noble was sitting next to Lucille. As they rose from the table, he said quietly, "I need to talk to you."

She looked puzzled. "When?"

"Right now."

"Where?"

"How about your room? It's just two down from mine. I'll be by in a few minutes."

Conveying copious thanks to Nicky, they drifted into the hall and upstairs to their rooms. Nicky came over to Noble who was the last to leave.

"I invited Jennifer Hedgely to come down, but she said unfortunately she was facing a tight deadline and simply could not get away for the weekend."

Surprised that she had been invited, Noble said, "That's too bad. It would have been nice to see her." He felt a flush of disappointment. Did this mean she might not be available later?

"She sent a note down for you." Nicky handed Noble a small sealed envelope. He jammed it in his coat pocket and they said goodnight.

As Noble closed the door behind him in Lucille's room, she said, "This is an unexpected pleasure, having Noble Shepperson pay a late night visit to my bedroom."

"I'm afraid it may not be a pleasant social call. May we sit down?"

The room was high ceilinged and spacious with an Edwardian flavor. The curtains were drawn, and a single lamp was lit on a table flanked by two chairs. An electric fire glowed in the fireplace, creating a small circle of warmth amidst the chill of the room.

As they sat down, Noble said, "There's something we need to talk about. First, let me ask you if you've had any conversation with Jesse Rooter about Joe Kinston."

"Jesse hasn't said much on the whole trip, but he did bring that up this afternoon. Said Joe got what he deserved."

Noble saw no reason to dance around the point. "This question may shock you, but do you have any reason to suspect Jesse did it?"

"What makes you ask that?"

"I happen to know Jesse was in Remberton the evening Kinston was shot. He had as much motive as anybody."

"Are you telling me Jesse Rooter has been back in Remberton?"

"Yes. I didn't see him, but I have proof it was that very night."

"Are you doing anything about it?"

"Not yet. I'm uncertain. Jesse seems like a decent fellow." Noble looked around the room. "You don't happen to have anything to drink, do you?"

"Do you think we were a little short on wine?"

"No, but I feel the need for some reinforcement for what I've got to say."

Well, Nicky seems to think of everything. Over here is a flask of brandy."

"I'll have a good-sized shot," Noble said. "You better have one too."

She walked over to a corner table and poured brandy into two glasses, gave him one and sat down with the other, saying, "All right, what is it?"

"After we found out what happened to Grady at the creek—the three men who did him in—the big question, as you know, was who paid them to do the job. I thought we were at a dead end, but at Jesse's insistence I hired a private investigator. He finally got the facts." He sipped the brandy, felt the warmth moving down toward his stomach. "Only Jesse and I know what he's uncovered. It's not a pretty picture—actually shocking. I wish to God I'd never known. Jesse says he's going to tell you about it tomorrow, but I decided it's better if you hear it first from me." He sipped more brandy, feeling the need to fortify himself.

"Well, what is it?"

"You better take a deep swallow of that brandy." He shifted in his chair so he could look more directly at her. "I would give anything not to have to say this, but Jesse's going to tell you, so here goes. To put it bluntly, your father put up the money. Paid $30,000 to the three men who drowned Grady."

Watching her face closely, Noble saw a wincing of her features and a slight drop of her jaw. Her eyes were directed at him, but they were blank, unseeing. The room was silent, except for the faint hissing of the electric fire, then Lucille's breath coming in small gasps. Her bosom heaved.

When she finally spoke, her voice was shrill and agitated. "I don't believe it! Do you know what you're saying? What evidence do you have?"

"Owen Nichols has the evidence. I wouldn't be telling you this if I weren't satisfied it's true."

Tears welled up in her eyes. "Damn Jesse Rooter for ever coming back to Remberton. This is all his doing." Her voice grew ever louder. "Why in hell did he have to show up after all these years? When I saw him at the wedding reception I had a feeling he was bad news. Damn him! Damn him! Damn him!"

"I know this is a hard thing to take. I would have let it remain buried, except I know Jesse is determined to tell you. He's pretty upset. You have to remember what he thought of your father. He never forgot being put off the land when they were destitute. Now this latest news has just about put him over the edge. I have some apprehension as to what he might do."

She calmed down. Her face was a picture of dejection. After a moment, she said quietly, "Now I see it. It actually makes sense."

They sat in silence for a long minute. When she didn't continue, Noble said, "What do you mean?"

"This seems to be a night for surprising revelations, so I might as well get it all out."

"You know I'll treat it with appropriate discretion."

"Well, here goes." She took a deep breath and exhaled. "I told you Grady was playing up to me in that summer of '46. What I didn't tell you is … is I got pregnant." She stopped, as though uttering that statement had sucked all the energy out of her.

Noble cleared his throat, searching for the right words.

He muttered, "It's not too surprising in light of what you've already told me."

Ignoring that statement, apparently not even having heard it, she continued. "Daddy found out about it. You knew him so you know how he didn't react well to things he didn't like, to put it mildly. Some say he was ruthless, always got his way. Anybody who crossed him had better beware."

"That's a fair description."

"He was plenty mad with Grady; enraged would be a better word. He raised holy hell. So I guess I have to say—but I hate to say it—what you tell me fits in."

"What happened to you?"

"My mother and I took off on our extended trip to Europe. To make a long and painful story short, we ended up here in London, where I gave birth. It was a boy and I put him up for adoption immediately. That was the end of that, and we went home."

They both fell silent. He took a long swallow.

She erupted again. "All this was buried forever. I had done a pretty good job of putting it out of mind. Now here comes Jesse Rooter and gets it all opened up again. Damn him and everything Rooter! That name has meant nothing but trouble, a bunch of no-goods from nowhere." Tears ran down her cheeks. "But I have to admit it—I was in love with Grady Rooter."

"Well," Noble said slowly, "that is quite a story. I assume nobody in Remberton knows about the child."

"Oh, God, no. You and I are the only living persons. My father and mother were the only ones beside me who ever knew. I see no reason now for anyone else to know. Do you agree?"

"Yes. At least not without your consent."

"I can't imagine ever wanting to let it get out. Think of its impact on Ellen, not to mention my own reputation, whatever that may be. Wouldn't that be a choice piece of gossip for those old biddies around town?"

"Have you ever thought of trying to find out what happened to the child?"

"Oh, once in a blue moon. But I've quickly dismissed the thought. It's so long ago. Why try to reopen it now?"

Noble shook his head. "I can't quite take it in. Unless he's died, you have a grown son somewhere in England, son of Grady Rooter, nephew of Jesse Rooter. Now there's a real Funchess-Rooter connection."

"Don't mention those two names together! I don't want to hear it again."

Noble drained the last of the brandy from his glass. "This has been quite a session. I dreaded telling you about your father. But now you've hit me with a bombshell. This Rooter-Funchess entanglement gets ever stranger."

He stood up to go and she stepped over and took his hand. "Noble, I've always counted on you. So I have to believe you now, even though my instinct is not to believe what you say about my father. But another part of me says it's true, knowing him and his temperament. What do you propose to do?"

"Nothing. We can't reach beyond the grave. I don't know what Jesse might do. You might have a stormy session with him tomorrow."

He walked to the door with her hand still holding on to his. When he paused, she put her arms around his neck and said, "I hate what you've told me, but I can't do without you." Then he was out of the door.

Back in his room—smaller and cozier than Lucille's—Noble sat down in front of the electric fire. Through a state of alcoholic fuzziness loomed the shocking fact: Grady Rooter was the father of Nicholas Cottingham. Though he had suspected it, hearing Lucille confess it hit him like a physical blow.

As though having to convince himself it was true, he mentally repeated several times: the ancestry of Nicky Cottingham, their host in this very Hampshire house, lay in two sets of down-and-out Rembert County tenant farm rednecks.

Gladys Houston popped into his mind. Two Remberton pregnancies at the hands of Grady. Then there was Catherine's revelation of her encounters. No mention of a pregnancy there. But then, he remembered the newspaper item reporting the Craighills' Chicago trip soon after Grady's drowning. And he wondered. And there were the suspicions about Julia McKnight, indirectly verified by what Judge McKnight had done. Grady Rooter was nothing but a Remberton tomcat. To his unscrupulous credit, though, Grady was egalitarian, unconcerned with class distinctions.

Lucille seemed to have forgotten, or conveniently put out of mind, the common origin of Sam Funchess and the Rooters. He had been tempted to remind her but had resisted. He foresaw an explosive confrontation with Jesse next morning.

His hand encountered Jennifer's note in his coat pocket. Tearing open the envelope, he extracted a cream-colored sheet of notepaper. In handwriting he still recognized, he read:

> Dear Noble,
>
> What a surprise to find you and your Remberton friends in England. Nicky's hospitality never ceases to amaze me, especially considering his straightened financial condition.

I was saddened to learn from him of your wife's death. This must have been a difficult time for you, but I hope you are able to go on with your life and find happiness in the future.

It was thoughtful of Nicky to invite me to join you. I told him I regretted I would be unable to do so because of a pressing deadline. But the truth, my dear Noble, is that I am engaged to be married. Several months ago, I met a wonderful man who is an executive with BBC. We are planning to marry next month.

This is a strange turn of events, is it not? Just as you have become free I find myself out of the picture. At any time over the past thirty years I would have jumped at the chance to see you——indeed, as I told you, would have gladly come to the States. But, alas, it is too late. Maybe somehow it is for the best. After all, as you often said, there is the Atlantic Ocean between us.

It goes without saying that I have many fond memories of you, and these will not fade. To have known you has meant much to me——especially in those war-time years, now so long ago.

Lots of love,

Jennifer

Noble felt as though the floor had opened up under him and he was in free fall with nothing to grab onto and no bottom. Too late ... yes, too late. All his hopes and fantasies undone by her short note. What a cruel twist of fate. Why, just at this time, after all these years ... His eyes watered with tears.

He did not know how long he had been sitting, Jennifer's note in hand—it could have been five minutes or half an hour—when he thought he heard a soft knock at his door. Then it came a second time. He roused himself, crammed the note into his pocket, and said weakly, "Come in."

Catherine Craighill slipped in, quietly closing the door behind her. She wore a blue dressing gown, belted around the waist. Her fluffy blond hair fell just below her ears. "I'm glad you're still up." She stopped abruptly and said, "Noble, you look so sad. I guess you've been thinking about Nan—how nice it would be to have her on this trip." She gave him a sympathetic hug.

"I'm sorry. Just musing over old times."

"May I sit down for a minute?"

"Certainly," Noble said, pointing her to a chair. He was struck with the contrast between her and Lucille. Although one could see in Catherine's face traces of some rough passages, still her expression was soft and warm, even loving—and definitely feminine. "Would you like some brandy?"

"No thanks. It's a little late. This house is creepy," she said, crossing her legs and wrapping the dressing gown over her knees. "These long, dark halls, and cold too, floors creaking. I see why they talk about ghosts in old English houses. Something funny's going on. Something I don't understand. Jesse is morose and has hardly said a word all evening—looks at Lucille in a strange way. Nicky's looking at her too. His having us here all the way from Remberton just doesn't figure. Do you suppose he has some nefarious scheme up his sleeve?"

Noble was struck with the parallel to his own question, but he thought it prudent not to pursue the point. "I don't know what that could be. The best thing to do is just relax and enjoy it all."

"I guess so."

"You know, Catherine, it just occurred to me that I've seen more of you in the last ten months than in the rest of your life. I saw a lot of your father, went by your house many times, but you were nearly always away, either at college or in Atlanta. I'm happy to say that I've enjoyed getting to know you better."

She smiled and said, "I'm happy about it, too. I didn't realize that lawyers could be such good company."

Their eyes met for a moment. Then she stood up. "It's late. I should go. Sorry to have bothered you, but I couldn't sleep and just needed to talk to somebody."

Standing up, Noble said, "You cheered me up."

She stepped forward, put her arms around his neck, and kissed him on the cheek.

He pulled her firmly against himself. Her soft hair was against his cheek; he caught a faint scent of perfume. He had not held a woman this way since Nan's death. Suddenly he realized what he was doing and released her.

She said in a half whisper, "You remember I told you once if you want somebody to talk to, I'm here."

She backed away, said "Goodnight," and slipped out the door.

Noble went back and sat down in a chair, the emotional turmoil of the evening swirling in his mind.

The next morning, having slept fitfully, Noble sat in the library with a cup of black coffee beside him. He had begun perusing the *London Times* but couldn't concentrate. He put the paper down and picked up the coffee. Beyond the windows the world was pale and gray. Early morning fog obscured the lake.

Nicky burst in, excitedly. "Noble, an extraordinary development. Lucille has gone."

"Gone? Gone where?"

"Apparently to the States."

Noble sat for a second in disbelief. "How could this happen?"

"My manager tells me he was out by the stable about 6:30 when Lucille comes out carrying her case and asks him to drive her to the station so she can take the morning train to London. He didn't see any reason not to, so he took her. They found the next train was due in twenty minutes, so he left her there. She gave him a note for me. I'll read it."

Dear Nicky,

You are a grand host. Your hospitality and generosity this weekend have been overwhelming. I do appreciate being included.

Unfortunately, for urgent personal reasons I must return home immediately. Please excuse my abrupt departure. I regret not seeing you again. Please know I have enjoyed meeting you and being a guest in this wonderful place.

Fondly,

Lucille Brentson

Chapter 20

▼

Nicky had lost his cool sophistication. "Did something go wrong? Did I unknowingly offend her?"

"Certainly not," Noble said. "I heard her commenting on what great hospitality this was. You shouldn't let it trouble you."

Nicky stuffed the note in his pocket and sat down. "This does upset me a bit. I have been thinking I would tell her about me while she is here. It's awkward to be around her knowing she's my mother but having to keep it secret."

"Well, the awkwardness should be relieved for the moment now that she's gone."

"It's just put off. I studied her closely yesterday. If I didn't have an official piece of paper from the Registrar General, I wouldn't believe she's my mother."

"You're not unlike physically. If you could see her daughter, Ellen, I think you'd notice a resemblance."

Up to now Noble had been examining Nicky's face for Funchess traces. Now he looked hard for signs of Rooter. He thought he saw some in the hair and chin, maybe the ears. In a baggy woolen sweater Nicky looked more boyish than when he was in his usual coat and tie. That he was a flesh and blood combination of Funchess and Rooter functioning in upper class English society was something Noble was having trouble assimilating.

Nicky said, "I'm back to square one. I don't know where to go from here."

"Last night Lucille and I had a long talk, a peculiar confessional session. I won't rehash it all. But along the way she suddenly was telling me she gave birth to a baby boy here in England. If you hadn't already shown me that birth record I would have been bowled over."

Nicky perked up. "How did that come up?"

"We got to talking about her family problems in the past—I represented her father sometimes—and she just came out with it."

"What else did she say?"

"Only that she put the baby up for adoption immediately and then left for home. She said she had never attempted to find the boy and would just as soon not know anything about him."

"Does that mean it would be better if she never knew about me?"

"Not necessarily. But I'm coming to the crucial revelation."

"What's that?"

"Your father."

Nicky sat up straight. "She told you that?"

"Yes."

"Well, my God, who is it?"

"Hold on to your seat. This is hard to believe." Noble paused, searching for the best way to put it. "Your father was Jesse Rooter's brother."

"Jesse Rooter's brother? The brother of Jesse who is right here in this house? Who is he? Where is he?"

"His name was Grady Rooter, but he's long dead. Let me give you the whole story."

Noble described the background, how Jesse and Grady were the sons of a tenant farmer named Lem Rooter, later grew up in the cotton mill village, and then came back from the war—Jesse to Chicago and Grady to Remberton. Then how Grady and Lucille got involved and she became pregnant. Grady, he said, died shortly after in a mysterious drowning accident. To avoid embarrassment and scandal, Lucille and her mother went to Europe and wound up in England where he, Nicky, was born.

"Didn't you tell me Lucille's father was the son of a tenant farmer?"

"Yes he was."

"Then Lucille and these two Rooter boys had similar backgrounds?"

"Identical. To put it bluntly, Lem Rooter and Sam Funchess both came out of what that part of the world disparagingly called po' white trash. The only difference is Sam Funchess moved to town and made a fortune by hook or crook. Lem Rooter eked out a bare living as a farmer and then as a mill worker."

"Hardly what you could call landed gentry."

"No plantations. No slaves. But then look at the next generation. Lucille with the biggest house in Remberton and Jesse in a mansion on the North Shore of Chicago." Noble was instantly sorry he had suggested their affluent status, suspicious as he was of Nicky's intentions.

Nicky had settled back in his chair looking thoughtfully in the distance. "So Jesse is my uncle. This is going to take time to get used to. Does Jesse know anything about it?"

"Nothing. Lucille knows only that Grady is the father of the child to whom she gave birth. You and I are the only two human beings who have the full picture." But not really the full picture, Noble realized as soon as he spoke. Nicky knew nothing of Grady's murder and of Sam Funchess' part in it. But at least for now, Noble thought, he didn't need to know more.

Nicky said, "Sooner or later, I want Lucille to know about me—and possibly Jesse too."

Before Noble could say anything, Ben Harris came in. "Good morning, folks. I've just had a grand walk." His face was flushed. "Some beautiful pathways. A little damp and chilly but I saw patches of blue sky."

Nicky immediately recovered his affable stance. "We're supposed to have a fine day. Despite the chill, spring is not far off. We benefit from the Gulf Stream."

Ben said, "I see from the map we're not far from Middle Wallop. You probably know that's one of the Battle of Britain air fields."

"Right you are," Nicky said. "We could drive by there on the way to Winchester, if you would like. But there's really nothing to see."

Ben said, "What time are we leaving?"

Nicky looked at his watch. "In about forty-five minutes. Catherine wants to go but Jesse says he'll stay here. Noble, would you like to come along?"

"Thanks, but I think I'll just relax here and do a little reading and thinking."

"The place is at your disposal," Nicky said. "We'll all gather here at tea time."

An hour later Noble and Jesse sat together on a bench at the lake's edge. The fog had lifted and the day had indeed turned fair but still held the damp English chill. High white clouds in all shapes and sizes passed swiftly overhead moving from west to east, just as Noble remembered from days of maneuvers on Salisbury Plain. From somewhere in the distance came the quacking of ducks. Otherwise, the silence was profound.

Noble had just finished explaining that he had told Lucille what they knew about her father. He told her, he said, because he thought it would be better if she heard it first from him.

Jesse was in a somber and angry mood. "And what did she say?"

"At first she was upset, got almost physically violet, denied it could be true. Then she pulled herself together and acknowledged that it could have happened."

"Did she have any thoughts about why he did it?"

The shroud of confidentiality clamped down over Noble. He felt that he should not tell quite the whole story to Jesse, at least at this time. "It seems Grady lived up to his reputation as a womanizer while he was on the Funchess construction job. The short of it is—he and Lucille got in bed, if I may put it that way. Sam Funchess found out about it and was hopping mad, ordered Grady never to come around again. That's apparently what moved Sam to the drastic step. It's consistent with his reputation for ruthlessness."

"And you tell me he's going to get away with murder? That we can't do anything about it?"

"The law hasn't figured out a way to follow a man beyond the grave."

"Damn the law! It's not the only way to handle something."

"If you know how to reach a man who's passed to the other side," Noble said, "I wish you'd tell me."

"The man himself is dead, but his reputation is not. His family is not. His assets are still here."

"Well, so what? What do you plan to do?"

"I don't know yet. I wanted to confront Lucille today, put it right to her. But she's cheated me out of that." Jesse was agitated, his face flushed. "This isn't good for my heart."

They both sat without speaking for a few moments, looking absently across the lake at a gazebo on the other side.

Then Jesse said, "Did you say anything about Judge McKnight?"

"No."

"Do you plan to tell Julia?"

"No. What would be the point? You know, Jesse, there are things that happened long ago that make no difference now. Maybe all this about Grady is one of them."

"How can you just dismiss murder? You, a man of the law!"

"I don't dismiss it. I just recognize there are some things in this world the law can't reach, that none of us can reach. Isn't it more important to think of the living rather than the dead? We have to consider the feelings of Lucille and Julia."

"It's not just murder. Look at Sam Funchess' whole life. Walking over people, interested only in himself and making money." His voice rose angrily. "And he doesn't have to pay for it, never suffers any consequences. Builds himself a big house, arranges a fancy grave in the center of the cemetery. You'd think he was one of Remberton's most respected and honorable citizens."

Noble didn't know what to say. He was becoming concerned at Jesse's outrage, what Noble thought was bordering on irrationality, and worried over what he might do.

Jesse continued his outburst, "And, can you imagine Rooter and Funchess being linked? On the front of a building or anywhere else?"

Noble resisted saying they were already linked in the most intimate way. Instead, he said, "You've made a magnificent offer for the library and I don't want you to give up on it. Just keep thinking about it and we'll talk some more." He stood up. "I'm getting chilly. Let's walk up to the house."

Jesse went back to his room. He turned on the electric fire and sat down. The main reason he had come on this trip was to confront Lucille. Now, damn her, she had cheated him out of the opportunity. He told himself he had to calm down, to think through the possibilities. Sam, of course, was gone. As Noble said, there was no way to get at him. But there was his money, his house, his reputation, and his daughter.

Jesse felt sick. Maybe his heart. But there was no chest pain, no numbness. He just felt bad. The best thing to do now was to try to relax, enjoy the rest of this trip, and then figure all this out after he got home.

Of one thing, though, he was sure: he would not let it go. There had to be some accountability, some consequence, some payment for Sam Funchess' murderous action, on top of retribution for the way he treated the Rooter family.

In the late afternoon through the windows of the library they saw a light rain falling. "I thought the day was supposed to be fair," said Ben.

"It's a rare day without some rain," said Nicky. "It'll probably be over in a few minutes."

A loaded teacart stood at one side of the room. A maid in white apron poured. There was much talk about the day's outing—the cathedral, castle, Winchester College, where Nicky had gone to school.

Nicky managed to pull Noble off to the side. "All day I've been thinking about what to do about Lucille. I thought this was the ideal place to sit down and get it all out. I do want to tell her."

"Let me see her when I get back home and find out why she left."

"I've been looking at Jesse, trying to grasp the fact that he's my uncle. Do you see any physical resemblance?"

"There may be something about the hair and chin."

"Is there any way I might get a photograph of Grady?"

"There's probably one in the Remberton High School yearbook in the library. I'll check."

They rejoined the group and chatted for a while. Then they all dispersed to rest for dinner.

They stayed another day and night at Cottingham Hall. They spent that day touring Stonehenge and Salisbury, comparing its cathedral with the one at Winchester. The next morning Nicky rode with them on the train to London, saying he had to report to the Foreign Office. They said their farewells in Waterloo Station. Ben urged Nicky to revisit Remberton some day.

At Heathrow, Jesse, solemn and untalkative throughout, left for Chicago. Noble, Catherine, and Ben perused the duty free shop, had a cup of coffee, and finally answered their boarding call.

Catherine and Noble had side-by-side seat assignments. Ben was across the aisle. As the jet engines roared to full thrust and the huge plane lunged forward down the runway, Catherine grasped Noble's hand and leaned her head against his shoulder. "Take-offs make me nervous," she said, gripping his hand ever tighter. With the plane airborne and gaining altitude, she relaxed her grip and kissed him on the cheek.

"What's that for?"

"For you."

He looked at her impish smile and smiled back. Then he reclined his seat and lost himself in thought.

Far below was the receding English landscape. Memories tumbled through his mind: 1944, Jennifer, D-Day. Then only nine months ago with Nan and her enthusiastic enjoyment of their trip. How his world had changed, with Nan now four months gone. Strangely, he loved her more in death than he had in life. Guilt still plagued him.

He felt Catherine's warmth next to him. Over the past few days he had caught himself taking note of her, taking note, for the first time since Nan's passing, with what might be described as masculine interest.

But now his mind focused on Jennifer. It was hard to believe he was leaving England without seeing her, without a word with her. His dream of days in London still haunted him. But the finality of her note could not be denied. He must accept closure of that fantasy for the third time within the past year. He closed his eyes and slept.

Miss Alice had cleared Noble's desk of the volumes of Alabama Reports and the Code and arranged all the incoming mail into four neat piles. Never had his desktop been so well organized. In one pile were documents received from other lawyers and the courts. In another were first class letters. In still another were notices and other items that might be of interest. And, finally, a pile of junk mail. Noble spent his entire first day back in the office going through it all and discussing with Miss Alice what had gone on in his absence.

The next morning, after returning telephone calls, he called Lucille Brentson. He recognized the answering voice to be that of her maid, Bonita Thomas.

"May I speak to Miss Lucille?" Noble said.

"Is that you, Mr. Noble?"

"Yes. Is Miss Lucille there?"

"No sir. She ain't back yet."

"Not back? Not back from England?"

"Yes, sir. She called and say she be there a little longer."

"Let me be sure I've got this straight. You say she called from England and said she'd be staying a while longer?"

"That's right. She say she'll call me when she's ready to come home."

"Did she say where she's staying?"

"No sir."

Noble asked her to let him know if she heard anything else and then hung up.

He leaned back in his chair, puzzled. What in the devil was going on? Had she left just to get away from Jesse? It had been almost a week since her abrupt departure. What could she be doing in England?

He had been brooding over the bizarre Cottingham-Funchess-Rooter tangle, wishing Jesse Rooter had never come back to Remberton and he had never heard of Nicholas Cottingham, when Catherine Craighill called.

"Well," she said in a huskier than usual voice, "have you recovered from jet lag?"

"Pretty much. How about you?"

"I think so. I've done a lot of sleeping. Listen, I've made up a batch of lasagna. How about coming over for supper? Just put in a fresh stock of Jack Daniels too."

Noble hesitated. He wasn't sure why, but he sensed one of those internal warning signals alerting him he might be moving along a path from which it might be hard to turn back. At the same time, he envisioned all those lonely nights ahead, at home alone. After a second or two he said, "Sounds good. What time?"

"Is 6:30 O.K.?"

"I'll be there."

The days were longer now. Spring was in the air. Daffodils had come and gone. Bridal wreath was in full bloom. The last of the camellia blossoms were fading, their petals dropping. But evenings were still a bit cool for the porch.

Two days after his evening with Catherine, Noble had a call from Bonita. She said that Miss Lucille had telephoned and said she would be home the next day. Noble decided to give her a couple of days to get resettled before going to see her. Then he had to go down to Mobile on a client's business and didn't get back until the following Monday.

Late in the afternoon, he was in his kitchen fixing himself a bourbon and water, reflecting on that evening with Catherine. It had been simple and informal, the two of them sitting at the kitchen table eating tossed green salad and lasagna, sipping cabernet sauvignon. They talked about the English trip, their children, and laughed over the peculiarities of some of the town's more bizarre citizens. There was nothing particularly memorable about it. Still … still his mind kept coming back to it.

The telephone rang. It was an officer at the county jail. "We've got a man in custody who says he needs a lawyer and wants to see you."

"Who is it?"

"He gives his name as Jesse Rooter."

Noble was momentarily speechless. "Jesse Rooter! What's he doing in custody?"

"Tentatively charged with assault with intent to kill."

Stunned though he was, Noble retained his lawyerly cool. "Who was assaulted?"

"Mrs. Lucille Brentson."

Noble let out a groan. "Where is she? What's her condition?"

"In the hospital. Seems to be in critical condition."

"All right. I'll be right down."

Noble immediately rang the hospital and spoke to Gladys Houston, who happened to be on duty. She gave a terse report. "A gunshot wound in the abdomen. Pretty serious. She's in the operating room now."

"O.K., I'll check later."

The jail was a fifty-year-old, two-story square brick structure set behind a chain link fence on a side street a block from the courthouse. The small yard around it was weedy, and the building was shabby from lack of maintenance. Rusting iron bars adorned all windows. Noble had been there many times to see clients, mostly accused of knifings, shootings, drunken fights, and assorted petty crimes. When he arrived, the air was heavy with the greasy aroma left over from the evening meal. A deputy led him to one of the three ground floor cells. He selected a key from a huge bunch on a ring and unlocked the barred door.

In the overheated cell, Jesse sat on a narrow bunk, his coat lying beside him, collar unbuttoned and tie loosened. His hair was disheveled and he looked distraught. His face was damp with perspiration and he was breathing audibly.

The iron-barred door clanged shut. "What in God's name is this all about?" Noble said, sitting down on the bunk beside Jesse.

"I can't believe it and you won't believe it either."

"I didn't even know you were in town. Tell me what happened."

"I went to Lucille's house. Had to get off my chest the business about Sam Funchess. It's been eating at me ever since we got back from England. Everything's all jumbled in my mind. We got into a hot argument. Then some sort of tussle and the pistol went off. She slumped to the floor. I'm too confused to talk about it. Tired too … very tired." He exhaled heavily.

Noble let out a long sigh. "A hell of a mess! What about Lucille?"

"I don't know. The maid got down on the floor trying to help her. The police and an ambulance came."

"O.K., now listen," Noble said. "I'm going to leave to see about Lucille. Don't talk to anybody about this except me. Do you understand?"

"Yes. I'm too sick to talk."

"I'll look into bail to get you out of here but that'll have to wait 'til tomorrow. You'll have to be a guest of the county tonight. Now lie down and get some rest."

The Craighill Memorial Hospital was on the edge of one of the town's better residential sections. It had been founded by Dr. Lucius Craighill and two other physicians in the 1920s, not far from the Craighill residence. Over the years, the sprawling one-story structure had been expanded and the building now contained forty beds, a modern operating room, and some up-to-date medical equipment. Noble's family had a long and intimate connection with the place. Several of his forebears had died there, his children had been born there, and he himself had been a patient on a couple of occasions. The founders had all passed on and the hospital was now in the hands of a new generation of doctors—Dr. Bartow Simmons and three others.

Noble hurried down the corridor to the nurse's station where he found Gladys Houston.

"How's Lucille?" Noble asked, slightly out of breath.

"Not good. The bullet tore through her abdomen and damaged her liver and pancreas."

"Where is she?"

"In the operating room. Probably be in there two or three more hours. It's pretty complicated."

"Look," Noble said, pondering, "have somebody call me if things don't work out. Otherwise I'll be back to see her in the morning. Is there a phone nearby I could use for a quick call?"

"Just step in the business office—nobody's there."

Three doors up the hall, Noble went in the darkened room, found a phone, and dialed.

When Catherine Craighill answered, he said, "Is any Jack Daniels left?"

"You sound like you need some. I've just heard the news. God, it's terrible. I can't believe Jesse shot Lucille. What's the situation?"

"I'll be there in five minutes and tell you then."

When Noble went in Lucille's room the next morning he found Gladys Houston standing by her bed. Lucille was pale and appeared to be asleep.

Gladys said, "Mrs. Brentson, here's Colonel Shepperson."

Noble took her hand and said, "Lucille, it's Noble."

She opened her eyes and said in a voice not much louder than a whisper, "Noble … I'm so glad to see you … Looks like I'm pretty torn up."

"Don't try to talk." Looking at Gladys he said, "Has Ellen gotten here?"

"Been here all night. She's just gone to the house to get some rest. I'll leave you now. If you need anything, I'm just outside the door."

Noble was suddenly struck with the realization that these two women fate had brought together for the first time in this hospital room shared a powerful common experience—a pregnancy at the hands of Grady Rooter, a fact neither knew about the other. And this twist of fate putting them together as nurse and patient was the action of Grady's brother, Jesse. In a weird way, Rooter had struck again.

"There's something I've got to tell you," Lucille mumbled hoarsely. "I was going to call you. Just got back."

"I understand you stayed on in England. We thought you had gone home."

She closed her eyes and lay still for a moment. Then she said softly, "I left because I didn't want to face Jesse. But on the train to London I was gripped with the idea of finding that baby boy. Didn't think I'd ever want to, but suddenly I did. I guess being in England …" Her voice trailed off. She breathed deeply several times. "I went to see a solicitor in London. He said he'd put an investigator on it. If I'd stay around for a few days he might have some results." For an instant, her face contorted from a flash of pain. Noble braced himself for what was coming.

In a moment she continued. "What he found was so shocking I spent two days in my hotel room trying to figure out what to do."

Gladys stuck her head in the door and said, "Is everything all right?"

"I think so," Noble said. "I'll call you if we need help."

Lucille went on. "Noble, you won't believe what he found. I still can't believe it. That baby is Nicholas Cottingham."

Noble squeezed her hand. "Lucille, I know. Nicky knows. He intended to tell you while we were there, but you left before he could get to it."

Her voice strengthened a little. "You mean Nicky knew all the time? How?"

"He had recently launched an investigation just like you did. He told me and was uncertain whether you would want to know, but had finally decided to tell you."

"How about Jesse? Does he know Nicky is Grady's son?"

"No. The only persons on earth who know are you, me, and Nicky. I told Nicky that Grady was his father."

She lay still for an interval, eyes closed. Noble continued to hold her hand. Then, in a whisper, "I think that's the way I want to keep it."

"Should I tell Jesse?"

"I don't know. I may not make it out of here. If I don't, I leave it to you. But I'd rather Ellen not know, at least not now." Her voice was barely audible. "Really remarkable, isn't it, that Funchess and Rooter blood is combined way over there in England. He seems a fine young man—not bad from Rembert County country stock." A faint smile parted her lips. Then very slowly, "you know, Noble, I guess I always had a love-hate memory of Grady—growing hot and cold over the years."

"You'd better rest now," Noble said. "I'll be back later."

She squeezed his hand. "Listen, Noble, there's something else—what you told me about my father and Grady. Let him rest in peace. Keep it to yourself."

"I will. Now you'd better sleep some. Remember, we're all pulling for you." He gave her hand a final squeeze and said, "I'll have the nurse step in."

Outside her door, Noble took a long breath and tried to collect himself. Up the hall, he saw Bartow talking to a nurse. He walked up and said, "What's her outlook?"

Bartow, in a white coat with stethoscope around his neck, turned, "Touch and go. We took out the bullet and patched her up as best we could. Some bleeding might develop that we can't do much about."

"If there's any change for the worse, I'd appreciate your letting me know."

"Sure."

No new judge had yet been appointed to take Judge Andrew McKnight's place. In the meantime, the chief justice had assigned Judge Dabney Williams from an adjoining county to preside temporarily in Remberton. Noble had tried many cases before him and knew his style well. He was considered to be of the old school—courteous, painstakingly careful, and fair. With a portly build, thick white hair, and a face that had seen all the sorrows of the human condition, he looked the part. He now sat behind the desk in the high-backed chair once occupied by Judge McKnight.

There still hung on the wall the deceased judge's law school diploma, bar admission certificate, and commission as circuit judge. Noble still felt the old judge's presence, having met with him in this room so many times over so many years. But Owen Nichols' report had forever skewed his memory of the man. He was deeply perplexed. How judge a man? How weigh a single, reprehensible, immoral act against years of useful contributions? And what to do about it, if anything, the judge having passed beyond earthly reach?

He sat now with the district attorney, David Strothers, facing Judge Williams across the desk. The DA was a tall lean man in his late thirties who had grown up in Remberton, son of a moderately prosperous merchant. He had spent three years in the Army JAG during the Vietnam War and still affected a military style haircut. Two years after coming home he was elected district attorney. As was often the case with these prosecutors, he had obvious political ambitions and viewed his position as a stepping-stone to something else. Noble thought him reasonably competent and easy to deal with.

They had assembled in the Judge's chambers at 2 p.m. for a bail hearing. The DA presented the sketchy facts as they were then known and explained Jesse was being held on a charge of attempted murder. The key fact, he said, in relation to bail was that Mr. Rooter was a non-resident of the state with no local connections.

"Noble, what do you have to say?" the Judge asked.

"Your honor, as of course you know, the concern here is to insure the attendance of the accused at trial. Bail should be denied only if there's a substantial risk of flight. I know Jesse Rooter personally and I can assure you he can be relied on to be here when his case is called."

There was a knock on the door. The Judge, looking slightly irritated, said, "Come in."

The secretary walked in, saying, "Please excuse the interruption, but here's a message I think you'll want right away."

The Judge took the note from her and read. After a moment he looked up solemnly and said, "Gentlemen, I regret to inform you that Mrs. Lucille Brentson died at 1:40 this afternoon."

Chapter 21

▼

The announcement of Lucille's death laid a pall over the room. No one spoke; no one knew what to say. Noble felt a lump in his throat, his eyes moistened, his hands gripped the arms of the chair. He uncontrollably muttered, "My God!"

Finally, David Strothers said quietly, "Your Honor?" He waited to get the Judge's attention.

"Yes?"

Strothers measured his words carefully. "Your Honor, this development leaves the state no choice but to upgrade the charge to homicide."

The Judge said, "What degree?"

"Tentatively, based on what we now know, it would be first degree murder."

The word "murder" left the room again in silence.

Judge Dabney Williams sat impassively, the human drama of the moment reflected in his face. Noble thought it wise to say nothing.

Then Judge Williams said, "This changes the equation. We now have a capital felony. As I'm sure you're aware, Noble, the practice in this circuit has been to deny bail in such cases where the accused is a non-resident."

"Yes, sir. That's the presumption. But I would argue for an exception in this case because of the high degree of reliability that the accused will appear. We're prepared to put up bond in whatever amount the court thinks appropriate."

"I can appreciate your position and have a good deal of sympathy for it." Turning to the DA, the Judge said, "David, do you intend to submit this to a grand jury? If so, when?"

"It so happens, Judge, a grand jury convenes here next week. I'll put it before them then."

"Very well. I feel that prudence requires me to stick with established practice and deny bail at this time. I might say now, David, if the grand jury indicts, I would continue to deny bail only on the condition that the accused is brought to trial expeditiously, say within thirty days."

"I understand and the state will act accordingly."

"Noble," the Judge said, "I'm denying bail now without prejudice to your renewing the application later in light of whatever circumstances may then prevail."

"Thank you, your Honor."

Noble knew he should break the news of Lucille to Nicky Cottingham. Yet he was reluctant to call him. He had mixed feelings about this young man. Nicky could hardly appear more friendly and personable. His hospitality in England had been overwhelming. But Noble had a sense of unease about him in light of what Jennifer had said. Looking for hints of the dark side of his personality, Noble had noted Nicky's interest in Lucille's financial situation. He would have preferred that Nicky simply go his way and they not have any more contact. He realized, though, he must tell him what had happened. He put it off another day and then called the British Embassy in Washington.

After a brief exchange of pleasantries, Noble said, "Nicky, I've got some sad and shocking news."

Nicky's jauntiness suddenly turned serious. "What is it?"

"I don't know any way to put this except to say it. Lucille is dead. Died of a gunshot wound."

Nicky gasped. "How can this be? It's too much to believe."

Noble described what had happened, characterizing it as an accidental shooting. Nevertheless, he explained, the prosecutor was indicting Jesse for murder.

Nicky listened without interrupting. With a long sigh, he said, "This is terrible. If only we'd had a chance to talk in England. And I was hoping to visit her sometime soon."

"I saw her in the hospital. She was in a lot of pain but entirely rational."

"Did she say anything?"

"She knew about you. Had just found out."

"Impossible!" Nicky blurted out. "How could she?"

"The same way you did. When she left us at your place she went to London and engaged a solicitor and investigator."

"The system must not be as air-tight as I thought."

"I took the liberty of telling her you knew. She was as startled as you are now."

Nicky said nothing for a long moment. "So we both knew," he murmured as though to himself. "But never communicated. Never had a chance for what would have been an extraordinary reunion ... if that's the right word."

"I asked her if I should tell Jesse and she left it up to me. Incidentally, I've agreed to represent him at trial. I want you to know this implies no hostility to Lucille. I do think he's got a defense of accident. With my knowledge of the circumstances and background I think I'm in a better position than any other lawyer to represent him. And also to treat Lucille with appropriate dignity."

"I understand. You should do what you think right. Isn't Ellen likely to inherit all of Lucille's estate?"

"I would imagine so, but I don't know what her will says. A Montgomery lawyer handled it."

"I hope one day I can meet Ellen. After all—I have to remind myself—she is my half sister. Blood is thicker than water, they say."

Noble said nothing to encourage such a meeting but simply said he would keep him informed about Jesse's situation.

The tower clock was booming nine as Noble walked into the courthouse. Inside, he went up the broad steps to a landing and then up another flight. The office of the district attorney was on the second floor a short way along the hall from the courtroom.

The secretary waved him through her room into David Strouther's inner office. Its walls were adorned with the usual law school diploma and bar admission certificate and with several plaques and tributes from worthy organizations—Jaycees, Boy Scout Council and so on—letting the world know here was a civic-minded, public-spirited citizen, all important to a future political career. Papers, files, and books were everywhere; no flat surface was left uncovered. David removed a stack of files from a chair saying, "Here, Noble, have a seat."

Although a generation older, Noble had known David since he was a child, had often seen him running around his father's store, which used to stock the best men's clothes in town.

He and Noble dealt with each other in the relaxed and polite style of Remberton law practice. Occasionally when a city lawyer came in to try a case—some supposedly great trial lawyer from Birmingham or Montgomery or Mobile—did things get a little raw-edged. But among the half dozen members of the Remberton bar, there was none of that.

David began. "Noble, I can tell you right off I'm prepared to settle this case on what I consider very generous terms: a plea of guilty to manslaughter, with my recommendation for a suspended sentence of two years."

"Well, I'd have to agree that's a pretty generous offer, but at the moment Jesse is in no mood to settle on any terms. He wants to say his piece in open court. That could change, of course."

"What is that 'piece'?"

"He hasn't told me. I have an idea, but I don't think it appropriate to guess at it."

"All right. Let me outline the state's case. A key witness is Mrs. Brentson's maid, Bonita Thomas. She overheard a loud argument between the accused and the deceased for several minutes before she heard the shot. To be perfectly candid, her description of what she heard has varied. I don't want to try to tell you exactly what she'll say on the stand. We'll not know for sure until we hear her testimony. I can tell you, though, I expect it to show Mr. Rooter was threatening Mrs. Brentson in some way. I don't want to say any more than that because I may turn out to be wrong."

"Do you have a written statement?"

"Just the police report. Here's a copy." He handed Noble a two-page document. "As you can see, it doesn't give you anything we don't already know."

"Do you plan to get a written statement from her?"

"It's hard. She's not the most articulate person you'll meet. If I do get something in writing, you'll get a copy."

"O.K ... What else do you have?"

"The usual forensic evidence, testimony as to the cause of death. Rooter's fingerprints on the pistol."

"Where's the premeditation?"

"He came to her house on his own. She didn't ask him to come. Then we have the threats."

"Whose pistol?"

"It belonged to her father. He had quite a gun collection, as you probably know."

"So your case is that Jesse arrives at her house intending to commit murder but without any weapon?"

"I didn't say Jesse arrived with an intent. Premeditation can be formed in short order."

"I know the law. This is a factual question, and you'll have to convince the jury."

"We're both in the hands of the jury."

"This may be one of those rare cases where I can persuade the judge to hold the evidence insufficient to go to the jury."

"It doesn't take much to get to the jury, as you well know."

"Listen, David, here's something I'd like you to think about. As you know, the law gives you a lot of discretion to prosecute or not to prosecute. When you back up and look at all these circumstances, it's hard to say that we've got anything more than an accidental shooting. The fats are muddled. There was a heated argument, some apparent tussling, and then a gunshot. It seems to me that justice and the public interest would be served by your exercising your discretion not to prosecute."

"I've thought about that," David said, slowly. "My view is that in a close case the public is better served by letting a jury decide it. What you have here is a prominent local citizen—whatever people might think of Lucille personally—shot and killed, at least for the sake of argument, by a man from Chicago, thirty years gone from here. My guess is that most local folks would like to see this case prosecuted."

"But it's your discretion and responsibility, not theirs."

"I understand that, but I think public sentiment is a relevant factor—if there's enough evidence to put it to a jury."

"Well," Noble said, "it's your call. I just wanted to be sure you'd given it some thought."

"If I change my mind, you'll be the first to know. Now, there's something else I want to tell you, nothing to do with this prosecution."

"O.K., shoot," Noble said, as he began to stuff the police report into his briefcase.

"You were interested in the Joe Kinston murder, weren't you?"

"Yes. I knew him."

"We recovered the bullet that killed Lucille Brentson and sent it off for analysis. We just got the results the other day. Curiously enough, the bullet that killed Lucille Brentson and the bullet that killed Joe Kinston came from the same .38 caliber revolver."

Noble narrowed his eyelids, looking out the window toward the jail. He said slowly, not knowing quite what to say. "Remarkable. Really extraordinary. The pistol that killed Lucille belonged to Sam Funchess. You never had any report, did you, that it had been stolen?"

"No. But if it had been stolen, wouldn't it be extremely unlikely the thief would have returned it to the Brentson house?" After a pause, he added, "Unless, of course, the thief was Jesse Rooter."

They were both quiet. Noble thought of Jesse's mysterious visit to Remberton the evening Kinston was shot. He almost mentioned it but then decided against it. He broke the silence and said slowly, "Does that leave us with the conclusion ...?" His voice trailed off as though he couldn't bring himself to complete the thought.

"The only conclusion I'm prepared to reach at the moment is that somebody using that pistol shot Joe Kinston."

"What do you intend to do?"

"We have casts of shoeprints from the spot where Kinston was shot. You can guess where this is leading."

"I can guess one place, but I don't like to think about it."

"I feel sorry for Ellen," David said. "This is potentially embarrassing—way more than that, scandalous. But I feel obligated to pursue any leads we have, to try to bring the Kinston case to closure."

"Suppose you determine the unthinkable to be the fact. What would you do?"

"Quietly close the case. I see no need for any public announcement. We can't pursue a defendant across the river. Of course, some of Kinston's family may eventually want to know what's happened. Frank Brandon could get nosey. The case is, after all, a matter of public record, so it may be hard to keep it under wraps forever."

"Do you propose to get a search warrant?"

"Rather not. I'll just ask Ellen permission to look around the house as part of wrapping up the investigation of her mother's death. No point in dragging her into this Kinston affair, if we can avoid it."

Noble nodded approvingly. They rose and shook hands. David said, "See if you can't bring Rooter around. Settlement makes a lot of sense."

Through the ever-present aroma of stale food, the deputy led Noble back to Jesse's cell. When the door clanged shut, he sat down on the bunk.

"Look what I've got," Jesse said, holding up a tin cake box. "Cookies from Catherine."

"She's always thoughtful," Noble said. "How are you feeling?"

"As well as can be expected in the county's accommodations. Here I am, after more than thirty years, back at the level where I started. Forget all the time on the North Shore, forget those black tie balls, forget all my wife's money. In Remberton it's all the same as it was. Back down at the bottom of the heap. I imagine folks out there saying they're not surprised, what can you expect from a Rooter. Why in living hell did I ever set foot back here again? I swore I never would."

Noble shook his head. "It is remarkable when you think about it."

"The deputies and prisoners all talk like I used to talk," Jesse said, looking despondent. "I'm even beginning to talk like them—tell 'em I ain't had no breakfast. It wouldn't take long to regress to my beginning. It shows how thin the veneer is."

"Listen, I came to tell you now that the grand jury has indicted, the DA has set your case at the top of the criminal docket when the spring term opens in two weeks. So it won't be long now. He asked me to tell you his offer of settlement is still open."

"Can't settle. I want a chance to tell my story, tell it to everybody in Remberton."

"When are you going to tell me your story?"

"Not sure yet what I'll say. I'll decide by the time I take the stand."

"That will be too late for me to be of any help."

Noble was frustrated. Without more from Jesse he couldn't know how to proceed. "You've got a lot at stake. This is no traffic violation. You'd better think about going over it all with me beforehand. You've got to be truthful, of course, but there're some things you may want to say that aren't necessary and can only get you in trouble."

"Here's my only chance to tell the true story of Sam Funchess, to keep him from escaping justice."

"That's the kind of thing I'm worried about. It may not help your defense. The judge will probably give you a lot of latitude to say what you want to say, but you've got to think about whether it hurts or helps you. Now I have two specific questions, and I want straightforward, truthful answers, If I'm going to represent you."

"O.K., what are they?"

"Did you go to Lucille's house with an intention to shoot her or assault her in some way?"

"No, sir."

"Once you were in there with her, did you decide to shoot her?"

"No. I never thought about it. It just happened."

"All right," Noble said, "I'm relying on that."

"What about Judge McKnight?" Jesse asked.

Noble ignored the question. "Are you so determined to get it all out that you're willing to risk your neck and years in the penitentiary?"

Jesse was quiet for a moment, looking at the floor. "I'll think about it."

After chatting for a few more minutes, mainly consumed with Jesse's description of the sorry state of jailhouse food, Noble stood up and said, "I'll be back to talk some more. In the meantime, make yourself at home."

"I've been trying. It don't work."

Ben Harris had called Noble to suggest they have dinner together at the country club. "I've been hoping to catch up with you since we got back," Ben said. "A lot to talk about now."

The dining room had been created by walling in a portion of a porch when the club underwent a general refurbishing several years before. They sat at a table on the edge of the small space, the only diners there. Business was light on mid-week nights.

Susie, the waitress, a thirty-year-old buxom divorcee with bleached blond hair—Noble had represented her in the divorce—came up and handed them menus. She radiated a heavy, sweet perfume. As usual, she wore a tight low-cut blouse and mini-skirt. "Honey, we got fresh snapper from the Gulf tonight."

"That sounds good," Noble said, "but I think I'll stick with a New York strip." That was said to be the club's specialty, if indeed it had one.

"That'll do for me too," Ben said.

Wine was a recent addition to the club's offerings, adopted in the spirit of the county's having gone wet. The list was not extensive: two reds and two whites, all California. Noble and Ben each ordered a glass of Merlot.

They chatted about the weather—it had been raining off and on for a couple of days—until interrupted by Susie. "Here you are, Sweetie," she said, placing a glass of wine in front of Noble and then one in front of Ben. She followed up with a tossed salad for each.

After munching on salad for a bit, Ben said, "I can't get over the shock of this homicide. It must be the biggest news around here since V-J Day. And to think, we were together with them in England just days beforehand. I must say I thought Jesse looked morose, almost sinister. I couldn't get anything out of him."

"Jesse is always morose," Noble said. "I've rarely seen him smile."

They had been talking a while about what this turn of events might do to Jesse's possible gift to the library, when Susie appeared and laid in front of each a plate bearing a thick, juicy slab of beef. "Two strips, medium rare," she announced, her perfume wafting over the table like an almost visible cloud. In the middle of the table, she set a bowl overflowing with french fries, enough to feed a party of four.

After Noble had sliced into his strip with a steak knife and chewed a piece of the succulent meat, he said, "I'll have to give them credit. They do about as good a job on a steak as you can find."

Ignoring the comment about the steak, Ben, who had been in a reflective mood while they were being served, said, "My father used to talk about the bottom rail getting on top. What we've got here is two bottom rails on top and then crashing down together. As far as you know, Noble, did Lem Rooter and Sam Funchess ever meet face to face?"

"I don't think so. To the Rooters Sam was a distant abstraction of evil. Jesse never saw Sam either, but in his mind, Sam represented all the forces that made the Rooters' life miserable. And what made it worse was Sam was basically one of them, genetically speaking." Ben had suspended eating his steak for a moment in order to sip some Merlot.

The local optometrist and his wife entered and seated themselves at a table across the room. Glancing toward Noble and Ben, he nodded a greeting with a slight wave. They nodded back. They were acquainted, of course, but neither would have considered themselves social friends. Ben was not comfortable with some of the newer members, convinced the club was lowering its standards in the interest of increased revenue.

Placing more fries on his plate, Noble said, "Incidentally, what did you think of Nicholas Cottingham?"

"A polished young man. A superb library. For me, that was worth the trip. His hospitality could hardly be faulted. As I look back on it, it seems an extraordinary thing for him to have us over there. It was very curious, and I don't know why he did it. He bears out my theory that good genes, good breeding, shows, unlike, I might add, what you see in this Funchess-Rooter scandal—a white trash fight if I may put it so indelicately. Nicky's the kind of charming Englishman who overawes Americans. Once, during my student days, an Oxford don came to Sewanee. The way the faculty, particularly their wives, fawned over him you would have thought he was a personal representative of the Almighty."

Dr. Jimmy Goodson walked in the dining room accompanied by a stranger. He paused at their table. "How are things with you folks tonight?" He spoke with exaggerated joviality, placing his hand on Noble's shoulder.

"Fine," Noble said, holding in abeyance a forkful of steak. "How about you?"

"Still treating the sick. No lack of business there. I want you to meet an old med school buddy of mine, Dr. Mel Gleason."

Mel shook hands. He was a stocky man with longer than usual hair. Noble would never have taken him for a physician. Unlike the other men, who were in coats and ties, he wore an open-collared plaid shirt and a jacket that looked like a cross between a sport coat and a cardigan sweater.

Dr. Jimmy said, "Mel's throwing in the towel. Wants to take to life on a boat."

"Will you stay tied up somewhere or be on the move?" Ben asked, obviously puzzled over such a drastic career change.

"Always on the go, I hope. Destin's theoretically my home port, but I don't expect to be there much."

Noble said, "How's Julia?"

Dr. Jimmy said, "Still working our way through probate of the Judge's estate. We go back and forth on whether to move out to the house in the country. She's thinking about establishing some sort of memorial to the Judge—maybe a scholarship fund or a room in a new library building, if one ever gets built."

"That's a fine idea," Ben said. "The library needs all the help it can get."

"Well, we better get some dinner," Dr. Jimmy said. "Glad to see you." They moved over to another table and sat down.

The thought of a memorial to Judge McKnight gave Noble an unpleasant mental twitch. It was one thing to let the Judge rest in peace and to save Julia from a scandalous revelation. It was another to honor him affirmatively. He was uncomfortable in recalling how he had lauded the Judge at his funeral, in light of what he now knew. He thought of it now as retrospective hypocrisy. But then, too, all fall short. What about himself in England in '44?

"Y'all doing all right?" Susie asked, pausing on her way to deliver menus to the new arrivals.

"Just fine," Noble said. She moved on, leaving a perfumed wake.

Ben said, "Mention of Judge McKnight brings to mind something I was thinking about the other day. And it's this. When a man dies he doesn't altogether die. He lives on in the memory of those who knew him. That will give him a kind of after life for another generation or two. But when those following generations are gone, the man is gone."

Noble was nodding his head, pausing in his eating. "In other words, you're saying that a man is not really dead as long as there are those living who remember him."

"That's the way it seems. We have our time on this earth; we strut our stuff and then are gone. Shakespeare said it much better."

That's right. For example, I remember my grandfather very well and often think of him and things he said and did. I've told my children much of that, so they know it. But it's unlikely that it will all be passed to their children."

"It will diminish with each generation and eventually be gone. Then that man will be gone, swallowed up by time. Unless, of course, he was a notorious figure of some sort or president of the United States."

"In other words, in another two generations you and I will be forgotten, faded from history as though we never existed."

"Each generation does its bit, for better or worse. Here we are in the twentieth century. In Remberton our names may carry into the early twenty-first century, but then that will be it."

"I hadn't much thought of it that way. It means that my mother and father and sister and all those family and friends I knew but who've gone on are still alive at least in my mind."

"And when you're gone," Ben said, "they'll be gone."

That somber thought held them in silence for a moment. They could hear the jukebox out on the dance floor playing some unknown piece. Then Noble took a sip of wine and said more quietly, "Ben, you've been alone nearly six years now. How does it feel?"

"Pretty lonesome at times. But you get used to it. It's hard at first."

"I'm wondering whether I'll get adjusted to it. Nan's been gone five months now—actually seven. In her last two months she might as well not have been here. There's emptiness about the place, a void, especially on nights and weekends. I feel like something's been drained out of life."

"I know what you mean. All I can say is time should ameliorate that. Some men get interested in other women. I've never been attracted in that direction. Maybe your comb will get red again."

"Well, I don't know."

"If I may venture an observation, Catherine Craighill seemed to be looking your way an awful lot when we were in England."

Noble prolonged his chewing of a piece of steak. He tried to be casually non-committal. "Catherine's an interesting woman. But I'm not ready for any new ventures right now."

Noble and Ben finished what remained of their steaks. Coming up to the table and seeing the empty plates, Susie said, "How about some apple pie? It's mighty good tonight."

They both declined. Noble said, "Ben, let me put this one on me."

Susie gave Noble the ticket. He signed, added a generous gratuity, and gave it back to her.

"Gee, thanks, Colonel. Ya'll come back real soon."

Chapter 22

Jury selection took all morning. Prosecution counsel Strothers and defense counsel Shepperson alternated in questioning prospective jurors. In the end, some were eliminated for cause—too closely connected with persons involved in the case or having formed an opinion—while others were peremptorily struck. Of the twelve jurors left in the box, seven were men and five were women. Three were black. Trying cases before juries that included women and blacks was still somewhat novel for Remberton lawyers. Until recently, their entire professional experience had been with juries of twelve white men.

When Judge Dabney Williams gaveled the courtroom to order after the luncheon recess and called the case of State against Rooter, the place was packed. Not a seat remained. Standing spectators lined the side walls and filled the back. The case had all the drama of a soap opera, fueled by an article in the *Remberton Progress*. It was the kind of article the former editor, Herbert Winston, would never have written. But his son-in-law, Frank Brandon, did not share his father-in-law's reticence about reporting the less savory aspects of Remberton life.

He had done some investigative reporting; interviewing everybody he could find who had known Sam Funchess and any of the Rooters. The article sketched the hard bitten growing-up time of Jesse and Grady, their high school years as boys from the mill, Grady's unusual drowning death, and Jesse's miraculous rise to wealth in Chicago. It told the Funchess side of the story too, describing Sam Funchess' emergence as a nobody from the piney woods, his extensive financial holdings, and his treatment of the Rooters. After the newspaper's exposure of all that, the trial became an irresistible attraction. Crowds had been streaming into the courthouse since early morning. There was not a parking space within three blocks.

Inside the bar rail the key figures in this judicial drama were assembled. Behind the dark wooden elevated bench, Judge Dabney Williams sat in a black robe flanked by the U.S. and Alabama flags hanging limp on their tall staffs. Here, Jesse was to have his day in court in accordance with "the law of the land,"—presumed innocent until proved guilty beyond reasonable doubt by legally admissible evidence presented under established procedure.

For Jesse this scene represented no such high purpose. Here he was in the heart of the courthouse he had never entered in his earlier Remberton life, this forbidding structure standing at the head of Center Street, seat of the power that backed up Sam Funchess in throwing them off the land and backed up his denial of money in their desperate plight. What could a man with nothing do against the combined power of courthouse and bank? And now he was caught up in the toils of this very system, convinced that Remberton had laid a curse on the Rooters, a curse from which there was no escape, not even for a millionaire Rooter long gone to Chicago. The combined power of the law and money having murdered his brother, the system was now set to condemn him also. But it would not do so without hearing from him, hearing what nobody in Remberton knew. Along with Jesse Rooter, Sam Funchess would at last have his day in court.

On behalf of the State of Alabama, District Attorney Strothers proceeded to introduce evidence in support of the indictment. He had the burden of convincing the jury that Jesse Rooter was guilty as charged. Defense counsel Shepperson, now at the defense table with the accused, did not, as a matter of law, have to prove lack of guilt. But as a practical matter, in order to persuade the jury not to convict, he had to create at least a reasonable doubt that the accused did what he was charged with doing or to show what he did was legally justified.

The jail authorities, at Noble's insistence, had allowed Jesse to put on a suit and tie. He was dressed like a North Shore businessman boarding a commuter train for the Loop. The attire was designed to make it difficult for anyone—more particularly, a juror—to believe such a man could be guilty of murder. But Jesse was not helped by his sullen, almost antagonistic look. His sunken eyes were fixed vacantly on the witness stand, the empty chair between the bench and jury box, awaiting those who's testimony, one way or the other, would determine his fate.

DA Strothers spoke crisply, emphasizing his words. It was the "Southern emphatic" accent, which he had picked up in court-martial work, often heard among important, or self-important, officials in the South. Proceeding in that style, he put in evidence the facts that the cause of death was a wound from a .38 caliber revolver and that the revolver from which the bullet came bore the fingerprints of both the deceased and the accused. The revolver itself was introduced in evidence. A police officer took the stand and testified that when he arrived at the Brentson house, in response to an urgent call, he found Lucille lying on the floor of the den with blood oozing from her abdomen and Jesse sitting in a nearby chair. The pistol was on the floor beside him. Thus the stage was set for the prosecution's main witness.

Strothers, tall and lean, in his dark, going-to-court suit, called to the stand Bonita Boshung Thomas. She lumbered heavily forward—a fat, middle-aged woman the color of strong coffee without cream—and took her seat on the witness stand, twisting a handkerchief nervously with both hands.

After urging her to relax and just answer his questions truthfully and as fully as possible, Strothers had her explain that she had worked for Mrs. Lucille Brentson for twenty-five years, that she was in the house on the afternoon of the shooting, that Mr. Rooter arrived unexpectedly, and that he and Mrs. Brentson went into the den. She testified that she remained in the hall polishing furniture and that she could hear them talking but couldn't hear everything they said.

At the defense table, Noble sat apprehensively, not knowing what this witness would say. But neither did Strothers. Since she didn't see anything, the words she overheard could be crucial, either condemning or exonerating Jesse.

DA: Now, Bonita, would you please tell the court what you heard Mrs. Brentson and Mr. Rooter saying to each other.

Bonita: Well, for a while I couldn't hear nothing. They was talking too quiet. Then they get louder. I hear Miss Lucille say you can't talk that way 'bout my father. Then Mr. Rooter say these Funchesses done got away with too much. (She paused, twisting the handkerchief with increased animation.)

DA: What else did Mr. Rooter say, if anything?

Bonita: They was talking back and forth and I couldn't make out all they was saying.

DA: Your Honor, I request permission to refresh this witness's recollection by some leading questions.

Judge: (Looking at Noble) Mr. Shepperson?

Shepperson: No objection.

DA: Now, Bonita, do you recall telling me when we talked about all this a while back that Mr. Rooter said something to the effect that Miss Lucille's father had thrown the Rooter family off the land and had denied them credit at the bank?

Bonita: He might'a said something like that.

DA: And do you recall telling me Mr. Rooter said he had had enough of Funchess, the last straw was when he found out Sam Funchess had his brother Grady killed?

Bonita: Yessir, I remember that last straw.

DA: Do you remember Mr. Rooter's saying Sam Funchess had killed his brother?

She twisted the handkerchief but said nothing. A murmur swept the courtroom like a far-off rising wind. Strothers hesitated, letting it die down.

DA: Do you recall telling me that?

Bonita: Yessir, I guess I do, if you say so.

DA: Then what did you hear next?

Bonita: Well, Miss Lucille say you can't come in this house and say that 'bout my father. I done heard her already say that before. She say she don't want him saying anything like that around town.

DA: What did you hear next?

Bonita: Mr. Rooter say Funchess got to reckon with it, he got to let the world know what Funchess done.

DA: Did Miss Lucille say anything then?

Bonita: Miss Lucille real mad now. She say, "Damn you Jesse Rooter. You lint head ain't got no business coming back to Remberton and disgracing my family." (She squirmed in the chair and pulled at her handkerchief.)

DA: What was said next, if anything?

Bonita: Mr. Rooter say this family done disgraced itself. It ain't right for a man to get away with murder. Then he raise his voice and say murder! There was a little bit of quiet. Then he say you got to face it. Sam Funchess is guilty of murder, murder of Grady Rooter.

Strothers stood motionless in front of the witness, hearing a murmur again welling up across the courtroom, this time louder, prompting the Judge to rap twice with his gavel.

So there it was, Noble thought, out in the open, the secret he had assumed would remain forever with Sam Funchess in his grave, the secret he had promised Lucille he would never reveal. At least he had been faithful to his word. But the genie out of the bottle could not be put back. It was just as well Lucille was not here to face public disclosure. But there was Ellen, sitting in the front row just outside the bar rail, behind the prosecution table. She was patting her wet cheeks with a small handkerchief. Noble felt sorry for her. His inclination was to go over and say something to her, but, of course, he couldn't.

DA: What did you hear next, if anything?

Bonita: Some kind of moving around. Then Miss Lucille say you get out of town and don't say nothing 'bout this and don't come back.

DA: Then what?

Bonita: He say Sam Funchess run us off the land. You ain't gonna run me out of town. Then nobody say nothing.

DA: What did you hear next, if anything?

Bonita: Some sort of commotion. They saying something, both of 'em talking loud at once, but I can't tell what they saying. Then I hear a shot.

DA: What did you do?

Bonita: I run in the room and see Miss Lucille on the floor. I say to myself oh Lord Jesus what's going on?

DA: What was Mr. Rooter doing?

Bonita: Just standing there holding the pistol.

DA: You say that Mr. Rooter was holding the pistol in his hand?

Bonita: That's right.

DA: Then what happened?

Bonita: Our yard man Buster come running in. Mr. Rooter say call an ambulance. Call the police.

DA: Did Mr. Rooter do or say anything else?

Bonita: No, sir. He just stood there 'til the ambulance come. Then the police come and take him away.

Strothers said, "Bonita, that's all the questions I have right now but the defense counsel may have some." Turning to Noble, he said, "Your witness."

Noble stood and came from around the defense table and walked toward the witness stand. He too wore the standard dark courtroom suit.

Before he could speak, Bonita said, "Mr. Noble, is you 'bout to ax me some questions?" The room broke out in laughter.

Noble smiled and said, "Just a few. When Mr. Rooter came to the house that afternoon, did you let him in at the front door?"

"Yes, sir."

"Did he have a pistol with him?"

"I ain't seen none."

"What was he wearing?"

"A suit. Looked like he look now."

"Did you see anything bulging in his pocket, anything that might have been a pistol?"

"No sir."

"This pistol you mentioned, had you seen it before this time?"

"Yes, sir. It used to stay in a cabinet. But she got it out one day and say she going in the country and do some target shooting."

"When was that?"

"It won't right recent. Maybe a few weeks ago."

"Did you hear Mr. Rooter say he would kill Miss Lucille?"

"No, sir."

"Did you hear him threaten her in any way?"

"No, sir. 'Cept he say he would tell everybody 'bout Mr. Sam Funchess."

"Before this day had you ever seen Mr. Rooter?"

"No, sir, but I knowed there was a Rooter."

"What do you mean?"

"Miss Lucille sent me to the florist shop to get some flowers and take 'em to a Rooter grave."

Noble was genuinely puzzled. He now violated a basic rule of witness examination: never ask a question to which you do not know the answer. "What grave was that?"

"Grave of Grady Rooter down at Shiloh Church."

"When did you do that?"

"Easter last year, but I done it once before that."

"Do you know why she sent flowers to that grave?"

"No, sir."

"No further questions."

Bonita Thomas lumbered back up the aisle and took her seat.

Strothers rose and said, "The state rests."

The Judge said, "The court will be in recess for fifteen minutes." He banged the gavel and left the bench.

A loud hubbub erupted all over the courtroom, the crowd rising as one, stretching and talking. Noble said to Jesse, "Come on. Let's step back in the conference room."

The deputy accompanied them and stood by the door as they went in. Noble closed the door and said, "Now, as we discussed, I'm going to lead you through the background—how you grew up and how you got where you are. Then we get to your description of what happened. That's what you've never told me."

"I haven't been sure myself."

"Good God man! I can't help you if I don't know what you're going to say. The state's case is weak. I may be able to persuade the judge to charge the jury that they can find you guilty of nothing greater than manslaughter. But you could blow it on the stand."

"I've got to get it off my chest."

"You could end up supplying some critical elements for the prosecution."

Jesse said nothing. He was sweating and looked intensely preoccupied.

"Are you all right?" Noble said, concerned over his appearance.

He murmured, "Remberton. Why in hell did I ever come back to this place?"

"It's a little late to worry about that now. Come on. It's time to go."

Judge Williams gaveled the courtroom to order. Outside the tall windows the sky was darkening. Faint, distant rumbling signaled an approaching thunderstorm. The Judge announced, "The defense may proceed."

Noble stood and said, "The defense calls Mr. Jesse Rooter."

Jesse, looking like a man who had never smiled and never would, walked forward and took his seat with an attitude bordering on defiance. As usual when a defendant takes the stand in a criminal case, the jurors perked up.

In response to Noble's questions, Jesse described his impoverished growing up years—in gritty, unpleasant detail—how Sam Funchess had put them off his land, how he and his brother Grady were nobody, how Grady came home from the Marines, worked for a construction company, died in a mysterious drowning. Noble was sure there were at least a few on the jury who would identify powerfully with that story. Jesse went on to tell of his getting the GI Bill and going to a university, getting a job with a stockbroker and his miraculous luck in marrying a wealthy woman. For over half an hour he held the jury's attention with this biographical tale of a poverty-struck local boy made good. His leathery face was expressionless throughout.

Noble let him go on without interruption. When he reached what seemed to be a stopping point, Noble moved on to the key event.

"Before you arrived at the Brentson house that day had you ever met Lucille Brentson?"

"Yes. I met her on a brief visit to Remberton a year ago and I've seen her a couple of times since."

"Did you ever meet her father, Sam Funchess?"

"No, but we knew his name. As I just explained, he was a mortal enemy of my family."

"Now, Mr. Rooter, you heard the testimony of Bonita Thomas, what she said she heard you and Lucille Brentson saying. Please describe for the jury exactly what actually happened after you arrived at the Brentson house."

Jesse took a deep breath and exhaled. The thunder had grown louder, the sky darker. The tower clock boomed the hour of four. "I went in the den," Jesse began. "She came in. I was at the end of my rope on this Sam Funchess thing. It was bad enough before I learned what he did to Grady." He stopped, breathing heavily. Then he said, "What I learned is that Sam Funchess paid $30,000 to three men to kill Grady."

The blunt statement of murder by hire had a stunning effect. For a moment, the audience was silent. Then a loud babble erupted. Among those seated on the courtroom benches mixed reactions could be heard: This can't be true. How does he know? I wouldn't put anything beyond Sam Funchess. The gavel banged down. "Quiet, please," said the Judge.

When the crowd settled down, Noble resumed. "What did you intend to do about it?"

"All I thought I could do about it was to tell the world, and I told her that's what I was going to do."

"What then?"

"She took on that arrogance I associated with everything Sam Funchess got away with, including murder, and here she was going to see to it he kept on getting away with it. From somewhere she come up with a pistol. She told me to keep quiet about her father and even had the gall to tell me to get out of town and never come back. She said if I didn't think she meant business I ought to remember what happened to Joe Kinston."

"Who is or was Joe Kinston?"

"He was one of the men paid by her father to kill Grady. Everybody here knows, I guess, he was murdered last fall."

"Did you take that as a death threat?"

"I did. Anyway, she was standing there, eyes blazing. She had always struck me as a tough character so I took the pistol pretty seriously. There was just one thought in my mind—here was a Funchess again lording it over a Rooter, was not going to let a Rooter expose Sam Funchess for what he really was, was going to preserve this ruthless fellow with his millions, big house, marble gravestones. So the world would never know and she could go on in her grand style. All that was rushing through my mind." He paused, breathing heavily and perspiring. Noble was about to say something when Jesse resumed.

"I was overcome by an impulse. Here a Rooter would draw the line. Funchess won't going again to squash a Rooter. I grabbed the pistol. She hung on. Finally I was able to wrench it from her. And then … then the pistol went off." A crash of thunder almost drowned out Jesse's voice. Rain drove hard against the windows, illuminated by intermittent lightning flashes. The day had grown prematurely dark.

The Judge motioned Noble to hold up while the worst of the thunder passed. After a few moments, Noble asked, "Why did you grab the pistol from her?"

"To keep her from shooting me."

"Did you go to Lucille's house that afternoon with the intent to kill her?"

"No, and I don't think I intended to kill her when the pistol went off. There was no intent of any sort. I was just acting—acting on blind, emotional impulse."

Noble turned to Strothers. "Your witness." Thunder was moving off to the East; the storm was passing.

The DA walked over in front of the witness stand and said, "Mr. Rooter, would it be accurate to say that when Lucille Brentson held a pistol on you and told you not to say anything about her father and to get out of town you felt enraged?"

"I don't know nothing about enraged."

"But you were angry and resentful, weren't you?"

"Yes."

"And you wanted to get revenge on her, to settle old scores with the Funchess family. Isn't that right?"

"I wasn't thinking. You might say I was acting involuntarily, like some outside force was controlling my actions. I wanted to keep from being shot."

"But you know now, don't you, that you took the pistol from Mrs. Brentson and fired it at her?"

"As I just explained, the pistol done went off."

"Went off while you were holding it?"

"Yes."

"And when the pistol went off, as you put it, when the pistol fired, it was pointed at Mrs. Brentson, wasn't it?"

"It must have been because she was hit."

"No further questions."

Noble stood up and said, "No further questions." Jesse resumed his seat at counsel table.

Then Noble said, "Your Honor, I have here three affidavits from persons who have known and worked with Jesse Rooter for over twenty-five years, testifying to his good character and integrity. I've shown them to the district attorney, and he has no objection to their being admitted into evidence, so I offer them as Defendant's Exhibits A, B, and C."

The Judge said, "Without objection, they are admitted."

Jesse's unanticipated mention of the Joe Kinston affair had placed Noble in a painful dilemma. Should he attempt to introduce evidence that Lucille was the murderer? It would badly besmirch Lucille's memory and be extraordinarily embarrassing to Ellen. But as defense counsel he owed an undivided obligation to his client, to present all arguably relevant evidence in his behalf. He owed no ethical or legal duty to protect Lucille. Yet he didn't want to harm her or Ellen if it could be avoided. Maybe he was caught in an impermissible conflict of interest. If there were a conflict, he should withdraw as defense counsel. Thinking fast on the spot, he resolved the dilemma, at least for the moment, by asking Judge Williams for a brief conference in chambers.

When David Strothers and Noble were seated across the desk from the judge, alone in his inner sanctum, Noble said, "Judge, David and I know something is not generally known, maybe not by anybody else, and it is that Lucille Brentson murdered Joe Kinston. This was not discovered until after her death. As you know, one of my theories is self-defense. Showing she had previously killed a man would go to show that Jesse's apprehension over the prospect of serious bodily harm or death was justified. But this evidence would be so embarrassing for Lucille and her family I didn't want to bring it up in open court without getting a ruling on its admissibility."

The Judge said, "Did Jesse know Lucille had shot Kinston?"

"There's no evidence he did. In fact, it's certain he did not."

"What do you say, David?" the Judge asked.

"I think that last point answers the admissibility question. If Jesse didn't know Lucille shot Kinston then that fact could not have any bearing on the degree of his apprehensiveness."

"What do you say to that, Noble?"

"It's hard to argue with it."

"Then," the Judge said, thoughtfully, "I'll rule inadmissible any evidence that Lucille shot and killed Joe Kinston."

"I appreciate the ruling," Noble said. "I brought it up because I didn't want anyone later saying I had been remiss in not presenting it in Jesse's defense."

When the Judge reconvened court, Noble said, "The defense rests."

The Judge said, "Mr. Strothers, does the prosecution have anything further to present?"

"No sir, your Honor. The state rests."

The Judge summoned counsel to the bench and informed them that given the lateness of the hour he proposed to adjourn and hear closing arguments the next morning. With that, he proclaimed to the audience that court would reconvene at nine a.m. He brought the gavel down and all rose.

At the defense table, Jesse slumped in his chair. His face was red and damp with perspiration.

"Are you not feeling well?" said Noble.

"Not too hot."

Noble told the deputy standing by to get Jesse back to the jail. "He needs to get some rest. Get him to bed right away. If he turns out to be sick let me know and call a doctor."

The storm had passed, but lightning still played off and on against the now darkened windows, and diminishing thunder could still be heard.

Noble was assembling his papers when a secretary from the clerk's office handed him a note. He tore open the envelope and read: "Drinks are ready at my house when court adjourns. Catherine"

Chapter 23

Before eleven the next morning Noble was back in his office. He and David Strothers had made their closing arguments; the judge had denied Noble's motion for acquittal and had instructed the jury, and the jury had retired to deliberate. Now began one of the most tension-filled times for a litigating lawyer—that time between the retirement of the jury and the moment when it sends out word it is ready to announce the verdict. Noble had seen juries come back in less than an hour and he had seen them take two days and more. There was no way to predict. All he could do was try to occupy himself with something else to help the time pass.

His hope for a favorable outcome was bolstered a bit by what he thought was a lackluster performance by David Strothers. His examination of Bonita and his cross-examination of Jesse were not as vigorous and probing as they might have been, and his closing argument to the jury was not up to his usual level. Noble concluded that Strothers' heart had not been in it, that he probably wished he was not prosecuting this case.

Noble felt deeply about Ellen. It must be tough, he thought, to hear your grandfather, whom you had been taught to respect, described as a murderer. Tough to hear of your mother's threatening with a pistol. But at least they managed to get through the proceeding without getting into the Kinston affair, although there was a close call.

Then there was Ellen's illegitimate half brother, of whom she knew nothing. Should he tell her? In all of Rembert County, in all of the United States, he alone knew of this. Indeed, in all the world only he and Nicholas Cottingham knew, except for the investigators in London. He felt himself a peculiar custodian of this potentially explosive piece of information. Bearing such a secret alone is a heavy burden, but Noble had learned long ago that bearing such burdens is the fate of lawyers.

He was concerned over what Ellen's attitude toward him might now be. He would not be surprised if she looked on him antagonistically as attacking her grandfather and mother, a claim he would stoutly deny. From the outset, he had been concerned about unnecessarily defaming any member of the Funchess family and had tried to avoid doing so. He particularly didn't want Ellen to think of him as betraying Lucille's friendship. He did not think defending Jesse in the circumstances of this case caused him to do so. If he had thought that, he would not have undertaken the defense. He didn't want lingering bad feelings. Ellen was an admirable young woman—warm and sincere, as far as he had seen, without her mother's hard edges and concern with social status.

It was late afternoon when the telephone call came from the clerk's office. The jury was ready to report. By the time judge and company reassembled in the courtroom the clock was striking six.

Judge Williams said, "Members of the jury, are you ready to announce your verdict?"

The foreman stood up. He was a farmer from out in the county, a generally well-regarded citizen. Noble had known him for years. He said, "Your Honor, the members of the jury are unable to agree on a verdict."

The effect was almost as stunning as the revelation about Sam Funchess. After a momentary silence when no one spoke or moved, a low wave of murmuring rose out of the audience, now smaller than it had been earlier. The judge rapped for order.

"You may be seated," the Judge said to the foreman. Then he proceeded to give the lecture judges give to a jury when it claims to be unable to agree. He explained that this case had been fully tried at considerable investment of time and expense to the taxpayers as well as to the parties and witnesses, that it was unlikely it would be tried any differently if tried over again, and that no future jury would be in any better position to decide the case than this jury.

Then he said, "Mr. Foreman, do you think with further deliberation, in a spirit of genuine collegiality, the members might reach an agreement?"

The foreman rose again. "No sir, your Honor. We have discussed everything about the case back and forth, from A to Z. There's nothing more to be said. Views are too far apart. I don't think any minds will change no matter how long we talk." The jurors nodded agreement.

The Judge's face registered disappointment. He sat impassively for a few moments as if considering what to do. Then, with a barely audible sigh, he said, "If you are certain, I thank you for your service. You are discharged."

The Judge turned to face the DA and Noble. "Gentlemen, I hereby declare a mistrial. The case will be set for retrial at the next term of court, subject, of course, to the discretion of the state not to re-prosecute. Court stands adjourned." The gavel banged.

Jesse said to Noble, "Does this mean we've got to go through it all again?"

"I regret to say it does, unless Strothers decides not to pursue it further."

"So the way it stands now, I haven't been either convicted or cleared?"

"That's it; we have a hung jury," Noble said, looking quizzically at Jesse, whose face had broken out in perspiration. "Are you feeling all right?"

"Not good. Afraid the old pain is coming back."

"What pain?"

"In the chest ... arm too."

Noble stood up. "Come on," he said to the deputy, "let's get him to the hospital."

"It's a pretty serious heart attack," Dr. Bartow Simmons told Noble three hours later, after Jesse had been admitted, examined, and medicated. "We don't know how it will go. He could have another soon, which could take him out. Or he might pull through and be back up and around. The next three or four days will be critical."

"Would it be all right for me to talk to him?"

"Yes, but I wouldn't stay very long."

Jesse was lying in bed, slightly propped up, in a dimly lit room. His eyes were open and he was alert.

"Another weird chapter in this crazy chain of events," he said. "Here I am, laid up in the Craighill Hospital just a few miles from where it all started over fifty years ago. Except I never saw the inside of this place. The great Dr. Craighill never treated my family. We didn't have no doctors and medical care."

"Well, you're in good hands now," Noble said.

"I'm realistic enough to know I may not make it this time. A man can have only so many heart attacks and keep going. So just in case, let me say I want to be buried in the cemetery on the North Shore beside my wife. For God's sake not down here in the country. Remberton did me in at the beginning and has done me in again here at the end. I can at least escape it in death. Another thing. Whatever arrangements need to be made, expenses involved and so on, you should contact my attorney in Chicago. He's my financial advisor and executor."

Noble pulled out a pen and pocket notebook and wrote down the name and telephone number.

He debated with himself for a moment, then said, "Jesse, there's something I want to tell you. I hope it's not too much for your heart."

"I can't imagine what it is, but go ahead."

"A lot of Grady's womanizing in his last summer involved Lucille."

"We've talked about it."

"To get to the point, she got pregnant."

Jesse sucked in his breath. "Good Lord!"

"Listen," Noble said, with concern, "take it easy. We don't want to do in your heart."

"I'm all right. What happened?"

"Well, for one thing, it explains what Sam Funchess did."

"So there's the motive."

"Yes. But what I really want to get to is this. Lucille gave birth to a baby boy."

"That's incredible. How could that be, right here in Remberton without everybody knowing about it?"

"It wasn't here. It took place in London."

"London? How ...?"

Noble explained the trip Lucille and her mother took through Europe, winding up in England. Nobody in Remberton had any inkling of what was really going on.

"Well, I'll be damned. Does anybody know anything about what happened to the boy?"

"Yes, but it was discovered only in recent months." Noble looked closely at Jesse. "How are you feeling?"

"Not too bad. I can take whatever you've got to say."

"O.K., just relax." Noble hesitated, wondering if it were wise to continue, but he couldn't back off now. "If you were standing up I would tell you to sit down."

"Is it that bad?"

"Not bad, just startling. Here it is. A real bombshell. The boy is Nicholas Cottingham."

Jesse closed his eyes and sucked in his breath. Noble thought he might have fainted. He was reassured to see him breathing regularly. Jesse opened his eyes and said, "Good God! I think my heart done took a jump. But you jarred my mind even more. I want to say you're kidding. This must be a joke."

"I can assure you it's not. We have the official record."

"It takes a while for this to soak in. Who knew this? Did Lucille know? Does Nicky know?"

"Yes, both knew. But they never confronted each other. Nicky knew before Lucille, and he was going to tell her while we were there at his place. But, as you may remember, she left suddenly so they never talked."

"I wondered why he had us there. It didn't make sense."

"Now you know. And you have to realize you are Nicky's uncle."

A second or two passed before Jesse spoke. His voice was getting weaker. "My Lord. I can't take it in. Nicky, Grady's son!" He paused, eyes shut, brow furrowed.

Then he said, "Look's like Grady made good on those high school threats. He figured out some way to get at those bitches."

"It's really something to realize that Funchess and Rooter are joined in living flesh. Whether we like it or not Funchess and Rooter blood run together in Nicky Cottingham and will run together in his descendants for all time."

"It's too much to believe. Are you absolutely sure?"

"There's no doubt about it."

"Thinking of a Rooter-Funchess combination almost makes me gag, even throw up. And I've never thought much of the English." He paused, as though letting himself regain energy.

"What Funchess and Rooter can produce jointly may be better than anything they can do separately. And maybe this younger generation will be purged of all the old ruthlessness and bitterness. But I'm not sure I want to keep in contact with Nicky. He would always remind me of the Funchess connection."

"Listen," Noble said, "this is enough for the time being. You've got to rest. I'll be back in the morning." He took Jesse's hand.

Jesse said, quietly, tiring now, "I want to thank you for all you've done. As I told you when we first met, you're the only man in Remberton who's ever done anything good for a Rooter. And that's still true. I have to say, though, Catherine could not have been more hospitable. She's an attractive woman. If I were ten years younger and in good health, I could get interested. You know, Noble," he said, after a reflective pause, "having been thrown back down like a common criminal, put in jail, tried in court, has, I think, done cause me to revert to talking like I used to. I can't help it. It just comes out. Have you noticed? I'm embarrassed. Folks are probably saying, 'you can't take the country out of the man.'"

Noble squeezed his hand and smiled. "I have noticed a few times when there was some slight slippage, but you surely don't have to worry about it. You get some sleep now. I'll be back."

In the hall he encountered Gladys Houston. "Colonel, can I see you for a minute?"

They stepped into a vacant room and she said, "Can you believe this? Here I am, nearly thirty years later, taking care of Grady Rooter's brother. He would have been the uncle of my child."

"One of life's strange twists."

"I was at the trial and heard mention of my brother, Joe. Do you know any more about that case?"

"The district attorney and police have never announced any suspects."

"I heard you went to see Joe. What did he say?"

Noble was in a quandary. If he weren't going to tell her who shot Joe, should he tell her what Joe did? He wouldn't feel good whatever he said.

"Well, I'd rather not tell you this, but since he's your brother and is now gone I guess it doesn't make much difference."

"I wish you'd tell me whatever it is."

"At the trial you probably heard that Sam Funchess paid money to have Grady killed." She nodded. "To get right to the point, Joe was one of the men he paid. There were two others."

Her jaw dropped. "Oh, Jesus. I knew Joe was pretty rough but I never thought he'd do anything like that."

"According to him, he didn't have anything to do with the drowning. He only drove the car, and he said he didn't know what the other two men were going to do."

"But why would old man Sam Funchess want to kill Grady?"

Noble hesitated. Here, he thought, is where he must draw the line on disclosure out of respect for Lucille and, more important, Ellen. "Looks like that's one of those things that will remain a mystery."

"Having Jesse here is upsetting. When I stand by his bed and look at him I can't help thinking of Grady. He resembles Grady, except more serious. And when I think of Grady I think of heartache. Jesse has brought it all back. It'll never leave me, I'm afraid. By the way, what was this business at the trial about flowers on Grady's grave?"

"Bonita said Lucille had her take them there."

"But why?"

"That's another part of the mystery we face."

"Sounds like there was something going on between her and Grady, like the rumor I heard."

"Maybe so, but she's gone, Grady's long gone, and Jesse may be gone. The best thing to do, I think, is try to put all this behind us and just move on."

"I guess you're right. The Lord does move in mysterious ways." She sighed. "Now I better get back and check on Jesse."

The balmy night air was filled with the scent of honeysuckle. It was clear and mild, the sky spangled with stars. As he walked out of the hospital to his car, Noble looked at his watch. Ten-fifteen. A little late, but maybe not too late.

He drove away. Shortly he turned the corner and in a block slowed in front of the Craighill house. Through the trees he saw lights still on. No cars in the driveway. He pulled in far enough to be out of sight from the street.

Frank Brandon, his hair even more tousled than usual, sat across the desk from Noble. "There's no way to avoid running another story about this case," he said.

"Even Herbert would probably agree. It's the nearest thing we've had around here to a soap opera. Hope I can have your help in filling out the details."

Noble, looking across the usual clutter of books and papers, said, "You would serve the community well and satisfy your journalistic responsibilities if you simply reported on what occurred at trial, the facts that came out there."

"My vibes tell me there's a lot more than what we heard in court. For example, the story behind the claim that Sam Funchess paid to have Grady killed. Why? Who did he pay? Then there was a reference to Joe Kinston, a murder never solved. What's that all about? And that business of sending flowers to Grady's grave. Very strange."

"Frank, I admire your zeal in wanting to get facts and reporting on what's really going on. But there are limits. Not everything has to appear in print, especially if it makes no difference now."

"Do you mean to say local murders are not legitimate news?"

Noble rotated his chair and gazed reflectively out the window at the courthouse tower. For no particular reason he noted the clock's hands stood at 3:40. Frank had a good point. What could he say?

He turned and said, "I hope you'll trust me when I say you ought to leave it alone. Jesse Rooter's return has already worked enough damage and heartache. Why cause any more? But whatever you decide to do, I can't be any help."

"I've always respected your judgment, and I'll think about it. I must say, though, what you've said deepens the mystery. It gets my journalistic juices flowing. But I won't do anything rash."

Catherine continued to be upset over Lucille's death. She had been really shaken by that sudden event, crying on Noble's shoulder and telling him: "I know she was abrasive, rubbed some people the wrong way, but I really liked her. We grew up together so I was used to all that stuff. I didn't pay any attention to it. It never occurred to me I'd miss her as much as I do."

"I'll miss her, too," Noble said. "I liked her a lot. I didn't mind all her tough talk. Having known Sam Funchess, I could understand her."

"The way she died!" Catherine said. "It's terrible—she and Jesse having that fight. I believe it was an accident. But you could argue it was the ultimate Rooter revenge on Funchess, unintended as it was."

"That's one way of looking at it," Noble said. "It's truly bizarre."

Then when Catherine got word of Jesse's heart attack she broke down again. "It's strange how fond of him I got. I felt sorry for him, even with all his millions. He had such a tough life early on. It's just too bad he ever came back—gave Remberton one last chance to get at him."

"And there's a good chance he won't make it." Noble held her in a consoling fashion, "we have to remember that death is a part of life, like birth." Then, remembering his conversation with Ben, he said, "They will live on with us. Like all those we've known—Dr. Loosh, your mother, the grandparents we remember—they will live on as long as we live. We can call them up at any time. It's only when we're gone that they'll be gone."

Noble, too, took Lucille's death hard, along with Jessie's precarious condition. They intensified his sense of guilt. If he had never agreed to investigate Grady's death, Judge McKnight and Lucille would still be alive, and Jessie would not be at death's door. Likewise, if he had ended the investigation after discovering the three men involved. But the moving hand had writ. He reconciled himself to carrying that burden for the rest of his days. He had not altogether emerged from grieving over Nan. These deaths on top of that put him into a low state.

Noble waited a week after the trial to telephone Ellen. "I know you're probably upset with me over what happened in court," he said, after announcing himself.

Her voice had a bitter edge. "Upset doesn't begin to get it. I had thought you were Mama's friend."

"I was. I was very fond of her. Also I represented your grandfather at one time. I want to explain the situation so there'll be no hard feelings." He went on to say how he considered the shooting an accident and felt obliged to represent Jesse, how he did his best to prevent the Funchess name from being defamed, how any other attorney might not have been so solicitous, and how neither he nor the DA knew what the evidence would be until Bonita and Jesse took the stand. What the two of them said in court was beyond his control. "Now you think about all that and let's get together when you come down again. Out of respect for your mother I don't want us to be estranged."

Her voice was calmer. "Well, I'll think it over. Anyway, it's all behind us. Nothing now we can do about what's happened."

"That's right. So please give me a ring when you're in town."

They were about to hang up when she said, "Oh, I want to ask you something. A while back, Mr. Strothers called me and asked permission to look around the house in connection with their investigation. I said all right. I didn't want to interfere with their work. Bonita tells me they went to Mama's closet and pulled out all her shoes. Why would they do that? I don't see any connection."

"I suppose they're just being thorough, leaving no stone unturned, if I may coin a phrase."

"I guess so, but it sounds strange."

Jesse held on. He mostly slept through the next three days. Normally a guard would have been stationed at the room of a prisoner like Jesse, but Noble persuaded the sheriff that this would be pointless. Jesse wasn't going anywhere.

On the fourth day Bartow Simmons told Noble, "He's past the critical time. I think he's likely to make it. But we need to keep him here for at least another week."

Noble came by every day. Jesse was sitting up more and more and beginning to take walks along the hospital corridor on the arm of Gladys Houston. "Got to get my strength back," he said, "got to get out of here as soon as possible."

"You realize, don't you," Noble said, "that getting out of here takes you back to the jail. This room looks better to me than that cell. So I wouldn't be in a hurry."

"You mean they still won't let me go?"

"Your status hasn't changed. You're still under indictment for murder awaiting trial and not out on bail."

"God! This misery will never end."

"It might, sooner than you think. My instincts tell me that David Strothers is hesitant about trying this case again."

And that is indeed what happened. A couple of days later, Strothers called Noble. "I've decided to have this indictment dismissed."

"Better late than never," Noble said.

"I thought I had to go to trial once, even though the case was shaky. But now I don't see any point in pursuing it further."

"You did what a reasonable prosecutor would do—put the case to a jury. Now you're doing the right thing." Noble could hardly wait to get to Jesse. "You're a free man! That is, as soon as they'll let you out of this place."

Jessie was happier than he had been since his father bought him his first ice cream cone at the age of ten. "I'm heading north—never to return. Remberton has seen the last of me."

"What about your idea of a benevolent revenge?"

"To hell with it. If I was going to do anything it would be pure revenge. Forget the benevolent business. I don't want any more connection with this damnable place. Actually, Grady has worked enough revenge on Remberton to take care of both of us."

"Does this mean that the library idea is dead-the Sadie May Rooter Library?"

Jesse let out a long sigh. "I think it does. I thought that was a pretty clever idea, but in light of all that has happened I just want to get back to the North Shore and forget Remberton."

A week later Jesse was gone, not bothering to say good-bye to Gladys Houston or Catherine Craighill or anybody else. Noble drove him to the airport and put him on first class to Chicago. Mrs. Schneider had him met by a driver at O'Hare and delivered back to the place he swore to himself he should never have left.

Brooding over the events of the past year kept Noble in a slump. The tragic twist of fate—the ultimate collision of Funchess and Rooter—had united Lucille and Jesse in a bizarre way and also deprived the library of an unbelievable financial benefit that would have made it the envy of the country.

He telephoned Melba Robinson to commiserate. "Looks like the grand dream is over."

"It always seemed too good to be true," Melba said. "Is there a possibility Lucille might have put something about the library in a will?"

"Afraid not. I've checked with her executor. There's nothing."

"Well, this puts us back to square one—trying to raise money around here."

"And without the big kick-off gift we'd hoped to get from Lucille."

"Why can't we still hope to get something from Jesse?"

"He's more embittered than ever. Says he doesn't want anything more to do with Remberton. If Jesse had just stayed away from Lucille everything would be different."

"I'll let the dust settle," Melba said, "and then get the board together to discuss it."

When he hung up, Noble thought more about Jesse Rooter. He may have left Remberton as a nobody, but he surely came back as somebody. To say he had had an impact on the place would be a gross understatement. Indeed, it would not be unfair to describe his return as catastrophic—a revenge far beyond what could have been imagined. In its wake, and as a direct consequence, three persons had died: Judge Andrew McKnight, Joe Kinston, and Lucille Funchess Brentson. And there was now no offsetting benefit in the way of a huge library gift.

Catherine Craighill was on the phone. "Frank Brandon came to see me and was asking what I knew about Lucille and Grady Rooter. What's this all about?"

"He's trying to act like an investigative reporter. Since Watergate a lot of them are into that. What did you tell him?"

"Very little. I don't have much to tell, except I remember Grady was working on a job that summer at the Funchess house. Then he asked me what I knew about Lucille's trip to England."

"England? How did he ...? What did you say?"

"I knew she and her mother went to Europe for several months. Everybody thought it was unusual. They said it would be more educational than the same amount of time at college."

"Did he ask you anything else?"

"No. That was it. How are you doing?"

"Busy getting caught up on what I neglected during the Rooter-Funchess affair."

"Can you find time to run by for supper some night?"

"I imagine so. Let me give you a ring when I see where I am."

After they hung up, Noble leaned back to meditate. He had to give this Catherine situation some thought. He sensed he was coming closer and closer to a critical line, possibly a point of no return. Far back in his mind was a nagging question: had she told him everything about her relationship with Grady Rooter? There was that item in the newspaper reporting her trip to Chicago with her parents two weeks after Grady's death. He recalled noting, when he reviewed those 1946 issues, the unusual circumstance that there were three trips within a month of Grady's death—Julia, Catherine, and Lucille, all with their parents to distant places. He, of course, knew of two pregnancies—Gladys Houston and Lucille. It seemed not unlikely that there were others. But he argued to himself that he should not let this shadow over Catherine's youthful dalliances bother him. It was so long ago now, and his suspicion might not be well founded.

But now if he weren't careful, things might run out of control. Did he really want to continue? There was a lot of charm there, not to mention sensuality. She was good company and seemed genuinely interested in him. He thought of all those lonely nights stretching over the months and years ahead. Maybe he should relax and let events take him where they would.

Before he could get around to calling her back she called again. This time she proposed they go down for the weekend to her condo at Destin. "Honey, its warm enough now and there're no crowds yet."

He saw the sunny beach, the sugar white sand, the aqua water, good seafood. All so enticing. And the prospect of those nights with Catherine, just the two of them alone with no interruptions, nothing to rush around for—in the dark with the windows open, the mild Gulf breeze and the rising and falling and murmuring and pounding of the surf. He needed time to think.

"I'll have to check my calendar to see what's ahead for the week," he said. "I'll call you back this afternoon."

What should he do? After what he had been through in recent weeks, he could use a break. Then, too, he was feeling the accumulated strain of a whole year of deaths, the saddest of course, being Nan's. But it was one thing to go by Catherine's house for drinks and supper. It was another to go away for a whole weekend at the coast. Destin might truly be a point of no return. But what the hell? He was sixty-six, getting no younger. He was caught in a pulling and hauling between the emotional and the rational. It was a close contest.

At the end of the afternoon, he telephoned her. Summoning all his will power, and with a good deal of regret, he said, "I'm afraid there's just too much ahead for me to get away. I'm terribly sorry. But is dinner available tomorrow night?"

Jessie sat alone in his library, looking across the lawn to sailboat-studded Lake Michigan. It was a bright sunny day, and boating enthusiasts were taking advantage of it. He had now been back home in Winnetka for nearly a week, gradually regaining strength. He found pleasure in again reading the *Chicago Tribune* and the *Wall Street Journal*, but he had not yet ridded himself of his dark Remberton memories.

Mrs. Schneider came in and closed the door behind her. "Mr. Rooter, there's a young man, English I think, at the front door asking to see you."

Jessie turned from the window, surprised. "What's his name?"

"Says its Nicholas Cottingham."

Feeling suddenly weak in the knees, Jesse sat down.

His face still exhibited hospital pallor. Mrs. Schneider quickly walked over. "Are you feeling all right?"

"Just a little weak." He paused and took a deep breath. "I don't see how this can be. How did he know where I am? Will Remberton never leave me alone?"

"Would you like me to tell him you can't see him? I don't think you should strain yourself."

"No," Jesse said slowly and despondently. "I better see him."

In a moment, Mrs. Schneider returned with Nicky. He was in his buoyant style. "Hello, Jesse. I'm delighted to find you back from your ordeal, legally and medically." Jesse, who had risen to shake hands, sat down and motioned Nicky to a chair. "How in the world did you find me?"

"I called Noble Shepperson to get up to date on you, and he gave me your address."

Noble should have had more sense, Jesse thought. He had decided that he had no desire ever to see Nicky again, indeed strongly preferred not to. Now that Nicky was right here he would attempt to be pleasant but not to prolong the occasion. He felt a slight sense of obligation from Nicky's hospitality in England. But this was the first time he was looking at Nicky with awareness that he was Grady's son. Seeing him in this light gave Jesse a creepy sensation.

"What a magnificent view," Nicky said, looking out of the window toward the lake. He ran his eyes around the room. "And what a splendid place this is! I see what they mean when they say you've come a long way from Remberton."

Ignoring the comments about the setting, Jesse said, "Come a long way and don't expect to go back. In recent weeks, I've had a tough time. But it looks to be over."

"Let's hope so. Remberton has certainly gone through a lot since I was there."

"I'm really sick about Lucille. A ghastly accident. The most startling thing is to find out that Grady is your father. Still can't quite believe it."

"Yes and Lucille's my mother. It means you're my uncle."

Jesse inwardly winced at the reminder. Rooter and Funchess linked here in this flesh and blood form sitting in front of him. He could only mumble a cliché, "Life is stranger than fiction."

"I must say that I'm proud to have the relationship," Nicky said.

Jesse's heart fluttered, but he kept his composure. "Have you met Lucille's daughter, Ellen?"

"No, but I hope to do so soon." Nicky hesitated, his expression growing serious. "Look, I have only a short time here. I just flew in from Washington and need to fly right back for an Embassy event. So if I may I'd like to take up a little matter of business."

Jesse braced himself. He didn't want any involvement with Nicky in any way, shape, or form. He simply said, "Yes?"

"You saw Cottingham Hall and what a grand place it is. Well, I'm in real danger of loosing it. For reasons I won't get into, my father left a lot of debt when he died, and I regret it's increased since then. Creditors are putting on the pressure. I have no other assets, only my Embassy salary. Unless some payments are made they are likely to have the court seize Cottingham Hall."

Jessie knew about being ejected. But being kicked off a tenant farm in Rembert County and being ejected from Cottingham Hall in Hampshire were hardly in the same league. He sensed a growing resentment of Nicky, this product of his brother's outrageous behavior that had brought so much misery. After a few seconds, he said, "So what do you propose to do?"

Nicky was uncharacteristically flustered. "Well, frankly, I am hoping that you might be able to help me a bit, that it might not be an imposition on you. I gather you have no other family to support."

Jesse didn't know what to say. His resentment against Nicky surged. The gall of this upstart Englishman! This fusion of Rooter and Funchess! His heartbeat had quickened. He must not get excited. Stay calm and don't do anything rash.

Finally, Jesse said, slowly and quietly, "Well, Nicky, this is out of the blue. It will take some thought. I can't give you an answer today."

"This is urgent. If I don't get the money within the next two or three months, I'm doomed."

"How much money are you talking about?"

"At least $500,000 and maybe more."

"That's not chicken feed."

"But I heard that you offered two million to the Remberton Library."

"We just talked about it. That was a special situation."

"Listen, unfortunately I've got to run to catch my plane. I left a taxi out front. Please give this some thought right away—a lifeline for a beleaguered nephew."

He took Jesse's limp hand and shook it. "I'll call you in a few days." Then he was gone.

It was mid-morning when Noble had just finished talking with a client, gotten a second cup of coffee, and settled back in his chair to read the complaint just filed against one of his clients. Miss Alice announced over the intercom that a Mrs. Schneider wanted to speak to him.

"Hello," Noble said, "I hope things are going well with you and Jesse."

"I'm afraid I have bad news. Mr. Rooter died last night. A massive heart attack."

Noble was stunned. He had felt good about Jesse's condition when he left town and had assumed he was well on his way to full recovery. "That's terrible. How did it happen?"

"My view is that it was caused by the visit he had two days ago from Nicky Cottingham."

"Nicky was there? This is news to me."

"He arrived here unexpectedly but didn't stay long. Mr. Rooter told me he asked him for a lot of money to pay off his debts. I could tell this visit was upsetting. Mr. Rooter looked despondent and was saying he didn't feel well. I was going to take him to see his doctor today. It's all a great shock."

They chatted a few more minutes and then hung up. Noble felt sick at heart. It was his fault for giving Jesse's address to Nicky when he had called to ask about Jesse. At that moment it would have been awkward not to respond to Nicky's request, and it seemed innocent enough. Now he could see that there was something to Jennifer's warning. He should have suspected that Jesse was a prime target for Nicky.

Noble felt a great sense of personal loss. Although he had known Jesse for only a short time, he had developed affection for him and regret over the way the town had treated his family. But Jesse had unwittingly inflicted a revenge on the place that could not have been imagined when he first walked into Noble's office. And after all that, there would be no big library building.

But as to the library, a thought occurred to Noble as he sat brooding over Jesse's death. He was not ready to abandon that project.

Two weeks later, the library board assembled in Noble's conference room. They all sat in their usual positions—Melba Robinson at the head of the table, with Norma Armisted on her left, Ben Harris on her right, and beyond him Ann Simmons. Next to Norma was the empty seat formerly occupied by Judge McKnight.

Melba opened the meeting by reciting the sad and dramatic events that had occurred since they had last gathered, noting especially the loss of their esteemed member, Judge McKnight. Then she said, "Noble asked me to convene this meeting, so I'm going to turn it over to him."

"Thank you, Melba," Noble said. "It's sad to realize that two of our group together on our trip to England—Lucille and Jesse—are no longer with us. As you can imagine, their demise destroyed all our lavish funding hopes. It is indeed remarkable that those two potentially magnanimous funding sources left us within weeks of each other—tragically intertwined, I might say. At first, I thought it was over for the library. But I decided not to abandon all possibilities. And I now have some unbelievably good news."

Noble proceeded to explain that he had contacted Jesse's executor in Chicago. Under Jesse's will, the executor had broad discretion to make charitable contributions from the estate. The executor said Jesse had spoken to him several times about his interest in the Remberton library and his idea of a substantial contribution for a new building. In light of that, the executor told Noble he was prepared to authorize a contribution of one million dollars from the estate with the understanding that the building would bear the Rooter name.

"So we've come down from two million to one," said Norma.

"Look at it this way," Noble said, "we've come up from zero to one million."

Noble would never reveal the supreme irony in this situation. If Jesse had lived, the library would have gotten nothing; he had firmly resolved to abandon the whole idea. But his executor was unaware of this, not having talked to Jesse since his return from Remberton. Noble felt no twinge of conscience in leaving the executor's mind undisturbed. It was in the interest of a good cause. It would enable Jesse unwittingly to implement his benevolent revenge.

Noble went on. "But this is not the end of the story. Hang on until you hear the rest."

He then explained that he had had discussions with Ellen. She said she and her mother had talked about the library and the possibility her mother might want to make a big contribution. She didn't quite understand the hold-up or what the complications were, but she thought her mother was committed to the idea, provided the building would carry the Funchess name. The upshot was, Noble said, he had persuaded Ellen to contribute one million dollars from her inheritance.

After a moment in which no one spoke, Melba said, "Well, I declare. Noble, it looks like you've pulled a rabbit out of a hat."

"More like bringing Lazarus back," Norma said. We're certainly grateful to you, Noble, but what about the naming? We've got two conflicting conditions—one saying Rooter and one saying Funchess."

Noble said, "You remember Jesse didn't want his name linked with Funchess. I'm concerned about doing something in death he wouldn't have agreed to in life. I might add, though, Rooter and Funchess are, in a sense, forever linked now." For an instant there flashed through his mind the linkage more intimate and powerful than anyone around the table could imagine

Noble went on. "But I had an idea how to get around the problem. I put it to Ellen that she should make her contribution in memory of her mother and therefore the name on the building should be Brentson. Then she and Jesse's executor agreed on the joint name."

Ben said, "An inspired idea, Gets away from Sam Funchess. At least there's no allegation his daughter committed any crime."

Noble's ethical antenna was instantly alert. Could he remain silent and let the board act on an erroneous factual premise? He alone knew Ben's statement to be untrue. A debate roiled in his mind for a few seconds. Then he let the point pass. After all, what harm would there be to any living person if Lucille's crime remained undisclosed?

Melba said, "But we do have the charge that Jesse committed homicide."

Noble quickly added, "He's not been convicted and would never be convicted even if he had lived. The prosecution has been dismissed."

"The whole thing is bizarre," Ben said.

"No doubt," Melba said. "The question is whether we can put up with the oddity for two million dollars."

"One way to view that sad event," Noble said, "is to consider the parties equally at fault. If Lucille had never pulled out the pistol she would be alive today. So if there's mutual fault it's not as though we are using the names of a murderer and his victim. In any case, I view the shooting as accidental. When Ellen balked at having her mother's name joined with that of her killer, as she put it, I made this argument and finally persuaded her."

"Noble, I admire your creative thinking and diplomatic skill," Norma said. "I hate to be crass—but for two million I can live with that theory."

"What about the order of the names?" asked Ann.

"Since Jesse started this whole thing," Noble said, "I suggest you name the building the Rooter-Brentson Library."

"As you know, Melba," Ben said, addressing the chairman, "I've had trouble with these names from the beginning. I abstained when we voted some time back so as not to stand in the way of what the board obviously wanted. So in order to remain consistent with my principle I will abstain again."

"Thank you, Ben," Melba said. "Now do we have any discussion of Noble's suggestion?"

Ann said, "We have to recognize the social conditions of our time. A dollar is a dollar, whether it is old or new. It may be regrettable we don't have more distinguished names for the library, but those distinguished names unfortunately don't have the money. Or if they do, they don't part with it. So I go for Noble's proposal."

"Well," said Melba, "are we ready to vote?"

Heads nodded. "All right, those in favor of the Rooter-Brentson name, please raise hands."

"Three for and one abstention. The proposal is accepted. Noble, where do we go from here?"

"We get the money actually in hand," Noble said, "and then buy the land."

Then Melba said, "O.K. Once we have the land and have engaged an architect I think it would be in order to have a public celebration of some sort. After all, this is a hugely important development for Remberton."

"I agree," Norma said.

"You know," Ben said, "I suddenly have a wild idea. How about inviting Nicholas Cottingham? It would add glitter to the occasion having a representative from the British Embassy. He's a real bibliophile and could make a few appropriate remarks. We owe some return hospitality anyway."

Noble was immediately uneasy. Given what Jennifer had told him and Nicky's call on Jesse, he was convinced that Nicky was potentially bad news. He thought it unwise to do anything to continue his Remberton connection. But all he said was that he thought the idea a little far-fetched.

Melba said, "Let's take it under advisement. We have plenty of time yet."

With both money and land—two choice acres behind city hall—the library board moved to engage an architect. No town of this size in the state would have a library half as fine. They also set a date for a big kick-off party and agreed to invite Nicky Cottingham, despite subtle efforts by Noble to discourage the idea. Ben Harris was asked to draft the letter of invitation.

Noble had fallen into a pattern of going to Catherine's house once or twice a week for dinner. One night as he was leaving, she ran her arms around his neck and kissed him, as she always did. She hugged him more tightly than usual and said in her most mellifluous voice, "Honey, why do we have to keep on saying goodnight? I hate to see you always leaving. It's not necessary." She kissed him again. "Let's just get married. You know I love you."

He had an easy way to avoid an immediate commitment. "It's customary for a man not to remarry until at least a year after his wife's death."

Nuzzling into his neck, she said, "You do love me, don't you Sweetie?"

With her soft body pressed against him and her perfume filling his nostrils, he could only say in a quiet voice lacking enthusiasm, "Yes." It was not altogether false.

A couple of days later Noble was walking across the street to Abbott Drug Store as the courthouse clock above him was striking ten. The morning coffee crowd would be gathering inside. Noble needed toothpaste but he also wanted to check on the latest gossip. As he approached the door, he encountered Julia Goodson.

"Haven't seen you in a spell," he said. "How are things going?"

"Still clearing up daddy's affairs. I'm glad to run into you. I have a question."

"O.K., shoot."

"I want to set up something in Daddy's memory. A man like him—a public servant of integrity—ought to be remembered as an example to our young people."

"What do you have in mind?"

"I understand the big library project is about to get off the ground."

"That's right. It's looking good now."

"You may recall Daddy was fond of history. There are a couple of hundred books out at the house. I would like to give them to the library to form the nucleus of a collection on local and state history. We would make a financial contribution to create a special room for the collection, called the McKnight Room. Who should I see about this?"

Her words, "a public servant of integrity," circulated in Noble's mind, jangling with what he knew and spinning off a huge irony. He and the library board had cleverly sidestepped the Funchess name. What about McKnight? The Judge hadn't been publicly accused as had Sam Funchess. But can facts be ignored because they are unknown? Noble fished around for something non-committal to say. "The right procedure would be for you to present it to the board."

They chatted for another couple of minutes and said goodbye. He went in the drugstore where he was loudly greeted as usual with, "Come on in, Noble," from the bombastic Jim Abbott standing behind the prescription counter.

Planning moved forward for the big occasion. Nicky Cottingham enthusiastically accepted the invitation. Librarians from the University of Alabama and Auburn agreed to appear. Ellen would speak on behalf of her mother. As there were no Rooters around—one of Jesse's sisters had died and the other was too ill to attend—Noble agreed to represent Jesse. The unprecedented magnitude of the project, for a town of Remberton's size, attracted statewide press attention.

Noble had made his conference room available to the board as headquarters for the event, as there was no room in the library. Melba Robinson was on hand part of every day, writing letters and talking on the phone.

There was much to be done. The program was to take place on the site purchased for the library. Underbrush had to be cleared and the place generally spruced up. Food and beverage service had to be arranged, a platform for speakers constructed, invitations issued to appropriate dignitaries and motel rooms reserved for them. Noble invited Nicky to stay at his house, despite his resentment over his visit with Jesse and lack of enthusiasm over his coming back.

At Melba's request, Frank Brandon dropped in to talk with her about news coverage. She had all the information spread out on the table. After they finished talking, Frank waited in the reception room until Noble finished meeting with a client. Then he was ushered in.

"This thing is taking off in a big way," Frank said. "We'll give it all the news attention it can bear."

"I thought it would never come to pass," Noble said. "It actually died with Lucille and Jesse, or so we thought. But Lazarus-like, it was revived."

"In the meantime, I've been exploring other matters not altogether unrelated I might say."

"I'm not surprised."

"And I don't think you'll be surprised at what I've found."

"Probably not. You have the instincts and drive of a ferret."

"For a newspaper reporter that's a compliment. Anyway, this relates to Joe Kinston. You remember I mentioned him to you right after the trial."

"I do." Noble braced himself for what he was certain was coming.

"Bonita Thomas' testimony that Lucille threatened Jesse with the same fate as Joe Kinston now makes sense in light of what I've discovered."

Noble listened with a poker face, saying nothing, and Frank continued.

"I've breathed not a word of this to anybody. It is startling, no, I would say, shocking. What we have here is the inescapable conclusion that Lucille Brentson shot and killed Joe Kinston."

"I thought you'd get there. It was just a matter of time. Now what?"

"That's what I'm here to discuss. The normal news reporter's instinct would be to publish this story if he were in Chicago or Washington or New York. But this is Remberton."

"Glad you appreciate that distinction."

"The information about this case is in the district attorney's office—in public documents. It's not as though I've found some deep dark secret no one could otherwise know."

"All true. The question is whether the benefit, if any, you would bestow on the community by publishing the story outweighs the harm—the pain and embarrassment it would cause."

"I'm not sure I agree with that formulation, but I'll surprise you by telling you I've decided not to run the story."

"A surprise I'm happy to have."

"So putting that aside, my journalistic nose tells me there's a lot more here I don't know but I suspect you do. For example, what was Lucille's motive in shooting Joe Kinston? What about sending those flowers to Grady Rooter's grave? We know that in the weeks before his death Grady was working on a job at the Funchess house, as well as at houses of other local big shots. My gut feeling is that somehow Grady Rooter is the root—pardon the pun—of everything that's gone on. Or at least some kind of connecting link."

For months Noble had brooded over the ethical question of what to disclose to whom and whether there are circumstances where he should lie outright. Lucille's discovery of Nicky had relieved Noble's mind as far as she was concerned. Then, he felt he owed it to Jesse to tell him. As for Ellen, it was obvious that Lucille had not told her about Nicky before she died, and he now felt uncomfortable hiding this explosive secret from her. He was uneasy not telling Gladys Houston about the fate of her brother, Joe, and the Lucille-Grady relationship that lay behind it. Was there not a difference between non-disclosure and lying? Could there be lies of omission?

Now, with Frank Brandon sitting in front of him, Noble felt no obligation to reveal the facts. It was not as though he was concealing a critical piece of information that would aid law enforcement authorities in apprehending a dangerous criminal. In his view, Frank's being a newspaper publisher gave him no special right to know, and where there was no right to know, there was no corresponding duty to disclose.

Realizing Frank was waiting for some response, Noble said, "There are some mysteries in life destined never to be solved."

"May I quote you on that? Look, Noble, consider the year since Jesse Rooter reappeared. We've had a string of deaths related in one way or another to the library or to the Rooters. It's beginning to look like a curse was put on the place."

"That's a little melodramatic, isn't it?" Then hesitating, he said, wistfully, "It has been quite a year. Of course, for me, the worst of it was Nan's misfortune."

"That was especially sad. We've thought about you a lot since then." After a momentary pause, he added, in a lighter tone, "I hear Catherine Craighill's been taking good care of you."

Noble didn't appreciate the slight, knowing smile. He said, matter-of-factly, "She's been thoughtful."

"Well," Frank said, standing up, "I'm looking forward to the big event. Melba says we've got a star-studded cast, including an Englishman—a pretty fancy, cosmopolitan touch for Remberton."

So there must be rumors around town about Catherine and him, Noble reflected, as Frank left. It would have been surprising if there weren't. Despite his efforts to be discrete, there was no way to hide something in this place. Catherine was indeed more and more on his mind. She had become the one bright spot in his life, the only thing lifting the gloom that had enveloped him. In the face of her undeniable attractions, attractions he was finding it hard to resist, why was he reluctant to take the big step? Especially since he increasingly felt a need to be with her.

The courthouse clock announced the hour of four. Noble looked at his desk. Nothing pressing. He walked out through the reception room, saying to Miss Alice, without pausing or looking at her, "I've got to attend to some things. See you in the morning."

As had become his practice, he pulled his car all the way around to the rear of the Craighill house, out of sight of nosey neighbors and passers by. It was an unseasonably hot early October afternoon. The dark green foliage of late summer, beginning to turn brown and drift to the ground, still provided a shaded parking spot.

He had walked out of his office, gotten in his car, and driven here in an almost sleepwalking state, not thinking, oblivious to his surroundings, his mind fixated on Catherine. It was as though he was under her hypnotic control.

He stepped out of the car, took off his coat and tie, and laid them on the seat. The only sound was the distant cooing of doves. He shut the car door and immediately heard Catherine's voice from overhead.

"Noble, what a nice surprise. Has the law run out of problems?"

Her voice pulled him back toward reality. He looked up and saw her leaning over the rail of the porch roof deck. "Not at all, but they can wait. Is this a bad time for a visit?"

"There's no bad time."

"What are you doing up there?"

"Taking advantage of the last-of-season sun. The back door's open. Come on up."

As Noble came to the upstairs window opening on to the roof, Catherine, having been sunbathing in the nude, was slipping on a short cotton wrapper. She walked toward him and said, "Honey, I hate for you to see me this way. I must look like a piece of greased meat baked in the oven."

He had never seen her like this—covered with oil and glistening with perspiration from head to foot—face, neck, arms and all the way down the loose wrapper to her long shapely legs. Her deep summer tan had not faded. For an instant, he thought of one of those exotic women in the South Sea Islands.

Taking in the scene and smiling, he said, "I'm happy to see you any way you are, but I'm not sure I want to get mixed up with that oil."

She stepped through the window into the hall. "Let me run take a quick shower. Make yourself at home. There're a couple of new books from the library." He went in and sat down in the small upstairs sitting room.

In fifteen minutes she was back, scrubbed clean and wearing a simple blue cotton dress. Her feet were in a pair of sandals. She leaned over, tilted his head and kissed him, emitting a fresh fragrance he found especially alluring. Then she sat down on the sofa beside him.

"It's nice to have you here at this hour. You'll have to do it more often."

"I couldn't get you off my mind. I had to come over and talk."

She snuggled up against him and took his hand in hers. "I'm listening."

He looked into her eyes and spoke slowly. "On this thing about marriage. I might have seemed a little standoffish or reluctant."

She gave a small laugh. "That's an understatement if I ever heard one."

"It doesn't have anything to do with you personally."

"I don't see anybody else around."

"What I mean is I have a built-in notion that a man needs to wait a respectable time after his wife dies before remarrying. I've mentioned this before."

"How long is respectable?"

"Longer than right now."

"How much longer?"

"Just a little more time. I wouldn't be coming around if I didn't find you enormously appealing, a lot of fun, and mighty good company—not to mention your other strong points."

She squeezed his hand, looked into his eyes and said, "I love you. But do you love me?"

Suddenly Noble felt himself being swept out beyond his depth, his resistance gone. He kissed her. Then whispered, "I do."

She put her arm around his neck and kissed him back.

He ran his hand through her fluffy, just-washed hair, stroking it gently. It had the texture of corn silk.

They remained there for some seconds, neither saying anything, he wondering what to say or do next.

Then she pulled slightly back and said, "What would you think of getting somewhere more comfortable?"

"Where would that be?"

She stood up, grabbed him by the hand, and said," Come on."

The long-awaited day was now only a week away. Having come home from the office late, Noble was in the kitchen and had just fixed a bourbon and water when the phone rang.

It was Nicky Cottingham, calling from Washington, effusive over the prospect of his visit to Remberton. Then he said, "Somebody here wants to speak to you."

After a momentary interval, the familiar English voice said, "Noble, this is Jennifer."

He could not have been more stunned if the Queen of England had been on the line. "Jennifer? What are you doing in Washington?"

"I came over to do another story. Nicky has been telling me about the library celebration in Remberton. It sounds truly exciting."

"It should be quite an occasion for this small town. Are you getting settled into married life?" His voice was flat, matter-of-fact.

"It didn't happen."

"What do you mean?" His voice came to life.

"We both decided it probably wouldn't work. He was a nice man in some respects, but in the end, I saw that we didn't really click. Anyway, I'm still an unmarried freelancer."

Noble didn't know what to say. Since his stay at Cottingham Hall and his big disappointment there he had been successful in putting Jennifer behind him. Catherine's attraction had helped. Now Jennifer was back, resurrected from what he had assumed was a married state, single, here in the United States.

"Noble, are you there?"

"Er, yes. Go ahead."

"Nicky has suggested I come with him to Remberton. Would it be too much of an intrusion if I tagged along?"

Noble's mind was awash with ambivalence. Six months ago, nothing would have excited him more—the prospect of Jennifer right here in Remberton, the two of them for the first time unencumbered by marriage, his dream of last winter in England to be realized here. But now …? Now the picture was complicated. There was, however, only one polite response he could make.

"No, not at all. We'd love to have you."

"You know I've always wanted to see the place I've heard so much about—and, of course, to see you."

"It's grand of Nicky to suggest this." Noble was thinking fast. As Nicky would be staying at his house, he thought it would be inhospitable not to include her. "Nicky will be my guest and I would like for you to be also. I have plenty of room and it would give us more opportunity to have a good visit."

"Noble, darling, that is so thoughtful. I won't hesitate in accepting."

Noble asked for Nicky to get back on the phone so they could discuss arrangements.

When he hung up, he took a long swallow of bourbon and sat down in the den. Jennifer Hedgely coming to Remberton and staying with him in this very house! He closed his eyes and thought about her, thought about her all the way back to the beginning, back across thirty-two years, to the cozy farmhouse in the English countryside, to that memorable night at the Savoy, to their recent meetings when he was saved from the brink, once by will power, once by his mother-in-law's death. All of her charms filled his mind. He remembered his keen anticipation over their getting together in London last winter, frustrated by her startling announcement of an impending marriage. How would he react when he was once again in her magnetic presence? In the past his respect for Nan had held him back. Now he was free to give rein to his emotions, to enjoy himself with Jennifer as he had often fantasized. Now, though, there was Catherine. Why couldn't life be simple, uncomplicated? If she had only come here six months ago!

He fixed another bourbon and water. What would be Jennifer's expectations? Twice in recent times she had bared her soul, professing her love. Now that she knew Nan was gone, he could expect no less. Otherwise, why would she be coming to Remberton? Would his feelings for her be the same? He now had to face the ultimate truth. Did he love Jennifer? Did he want to spend the rest of his life with her? How did Catherine fit into the picture? He finished the drink and went to bed, his hunger having vanished. But he slept only fitfully.

Noble dropped by his conference room, as he had been doing from time-to-time, to chat with Melba Robinson, to see how plans were developing. The large table was covered with file folders and piles of letters and newspaper clippings. She had the concerned look of a high school teacher whose students had just written bad exam papers.

"There's a lot to worry about," she said, "rain, for example."

"Think positively," Noble said. "The prediction is for good weather."

"Look at all these clippings. I can't get over the press coverage from all over the state. The board met yesterday to go over final arrangements. All seems to be in order, but I've got my fingers crossed. You know it's only three days off."

The board accepted Ellen's offer to hold a reception at her house the night before. Ellen had decided to move back to her mother's house. "It's too nice a place to let go," she told Noble. Her husband would be only forty minutes from his office in Montgomery. She had hesitated, she explained, because of the scandalous revelation about her grandfather. "But what the hell," she said, "life has to go on. That was two generations ago. This is now."

Miss Alice stuck her head in the door and said, "Catherine wants you to call her when you get a chance."

Melba gave a knowing smile to Noble as he left.

"Noble," Catherine said, when he rang her up a few minutes later, "where have you been? Is everything all right?"

"Everything's fine. I've been tied up helping Melba and cleaning up some matters before the big day."

"Well, I'd begun to wonder what's going on. This is the longest stretch we've been. But it's probably just as well. I haven't been feeling good for the last day or two. I still think a lot about Lucille and Jesse. Can't get over what happened. Maybe that's what's got me down."

"I think about it a lot too. All very sad. We just have to live with it and eventually get over it. Do you have an invitation to Ellen's reception?"

"Yes. She seems to be following in her mother's footsteps. I'll have to give her credit—a lot of nerve moving back here, with old man Funchess exposed, the family disgraced."

"She does seem to be exhibiting some of Lucille's gutsy traits."

"Are you all set for Nicky?"

"Think so."

"Is there anything I can help you with?"

"Thanks but I think everything is all set. I'm tied up between now and the time he gets here, so I'll see you at Ellen's."

When they hung up, Noble felt ashamed of himself for not having mentioned Jennifer. Why hadn't he? Catherine would, of course, know sooner or later. Then how would he explain an attractive woman in his house?

Frank Brandon was again seated across the desk from Noble. He was not exactly a welcome sight. Noble was apprehensive over what his probing might unearth.

Frank said, "I know we're all busy, so let me get right to the point. The bare bone facts we all know are these: Grady Rooter died on August 6, 1946. On September 10, 1946, Lucille and her mother left for Europe. They wound up in England for several weeks and returned to Remberton in April 1947. The *Progress* reported all that."

Noble nodded but said nothing.

Frank's owlish expression took on the air of a boxer about to deliver a knockout punch. "Now here is the crucial fact unknown in Remberton—unless you know it." He observed a dramatic pause. "When Lucille left for Europe she was pregnant."

Noble was stunned. How could he possibly know? But he remained outwardly unperturbed. With a lawyerly calm, he said, "What's the source for that?"

"An old black woman living out on Liberty Hill, whose name I won't disclose. She worked in the Funchess household in the forties. We tend not to be aware of how much our hired help observes and how much they overhear."

"So now what?"

"There are three possibilities. Either she had an abortion or a miscarriage or she gave birth while away."

"I can't think of any others."

"When the chase is on and I've got a scent, I don't quit easily," Frank said, leaning forward on the desk. "So, pursuing the birth hypothesis, I engaged a private eye in London. Some of them over there are really good. I asked him to do what he could to examine records of the major London hospitals functioning from late February to early April 1947. What he found startled me as much as you must have been when you learned it."

"You keep assuming I am all-knowing," Noble said.

"So far I haven't been wrong, have I?"

"I'm waiting to hear the rest."

"O.K., if you want to be non-committal. But here it is. On March 7, 1947, Lucille gave birth to a baby boy in St. Jude's Hospital, London."

The noose is tightening, Noble thought. There are only two more facts to be known. He waited.

"That's heady stuff," Frank said. "A first class scandal. It doesn't get more explosive than that around here. Any advice or comment?"

"We've had this conversation before. What do you intend to do?"

"Nothing at the moment. You will be pleased to hear that I see no redeeming value in publicizing this information. But I must say my curiosity is whetted. One of the missing facts can be readily inferred: Grady Rooter was the father. Wouldn't you agree? It's the business of lawyers to draw inferences from evidence."

"Assuming the facts to be as you have stated and from what we know from other evidence, it does seem a plausible inference."

"Damn it. You lawyers are obsessively cautious. I don't see any other possibility. The only question left is the fate of the child. Unless it died at birth, and there's no evidence of that, it had to be put up for adoption. That means somewhere in England today there's a twenty-eight-year-old man who is the son of Grady Rooter and Lucille Funchess—a half-brother, I might add, of Ellen. Also a nephew of Jesse Rooter. Don't you find this just too fantastic?"

"It is that." Noble was thinking if Nicky and Lucille had each learned the identity of that adopted child through some clever sleuthing, it was likely Frank could do so if he really wanted to.

Frank said, "Hearing that Sam Funchess paid to have Grady murdered was scandalous enough. But this raises the scandal level to new heights. And you and I are the only human beings who know it. Am I right?"

Again for Noble the old ethical question, the distinction between lying and non-disclosure. Leaving Nicky to be discovered by Frank, Noble simply said, "All those involved in it are dead. Let the dead bury the dead."

Frank rose to go. "Right now we've got to deal with the big library event. So I'm putting it on the back burner for a while."

"That's a good place for it."

"Ellen has invited me to her reception, so I'll be there with photographer in tow. We want to do the news coverage up right."

Noble's heartbeat quickened when he saw Jennifer coming off the plane and into the gate area, Nicky right behind her. He thought she looked stunning, more glamorous than he had ever seen her. Although she was in her early sixties, she could pass for ten years younger, with the figure of a thirty-year-old.

She walked briskly toward Noble, smiling broadly. Dropping a small carry-on bag at her feet, she hugged him tightly, kissing him on the cheek, breathily saying, "Darling, I cannot believe I'm really here." He kept one arm around her waist as he shook hands with Nicky.

It was dark when they reached Remberton and pulled into Noble's drive. Because he knew it would be late when they arrived, he had planned a quiet dinner at home for just the three of them. He had Zeke standing by in white coat to serve drinks and help Ruby in the kitchen. He showed Jennifer to the guest room and Nicky to what had been son Kirk's room.

During drinks in the den and dinner in the dining room, they chatted about the upcoming events and the town and its history, Noble answering questions, mainly from Jennifer, Nicky having heard much of it on his previous visit.

Noble was excited by Jennifer's presence. He was especially glad to have her there, as she relieved him of having to deal with Nicky. The visit to Jesse of this flesh-and-blood Rooter-Funchess incarnation had left Noble with a heightened sense of disquiet, a premonition that his return to Remberton bode no good. He would play the role of a polite host, but with no enthusiasm.

When they rose from the meal, Nicky asked to be excused, saying he had had an unusually busy stretch at the Embassy and wished to get a good night's rest

Chapter 24

Left alone with Jennifer, Noble was as nervous as a schoolboy called to the principal's office. In the den, she accepted a glass of port and they sat down. For a few minutes they chatted about her work in recent months. Her English accent melted in his ears. The charms that had so gripped him in the past began to have their effect again, like brandy-induced warmth building up in the stomach.

When she paused in her rambling about one of her projects, Noble said, "If I may change the subject, I never responded to the note you sent me at Cottingham Hall because ... well, because it didn't seem to call for a response."

"We needn't talk about it now. That's all over. We can be back where we were, can't we?"

"Where were we?" Noble was uncertain about where he wanted this conversation to go.

"We were in the Statler-Hilton in Washington. You left abruptly because of your mother-in-law's death."

"A lot has happened since then."

"I know this has been a difficult year for you and I've thought of you many times. I've been on a bit of an emotional rollercoaster myself. But, as I say, all that is over now. I must say, you look fit and well."

"You're looking mighty good yourself. Time improves you, I think."

"That's something many a woman would like to hear."

There was an awkward silence as each sipped port. Noble's mind was in turmoil. In front of him was the living Jennifer, in all of her sensuality, reviving the full range of his dormant emotions. But also in his mind was Catherine toward whom he had been more and more drawn, even to the point of confessing his love.

Breaking the silence, Jennifer said, "Noble, for the first time since I met you all those years ago, you and I are free of involvement with any other person. The restraints that understandably held you back are gone."

Not so, not so, his inner voice shouted. There's Catherine. But he said nothing. He simply nodded, looking at her, eyes half closed. He felt himself slipping, as though he were on a wet, muddy slope with nothing to grab onto. The combination of English voice, bright green eyes, well-filled-out body had an hypnotic effect.

She stood up impulsively, stepped forward, and knelt on the floor beside his chair. She took his hand in hers and looked penetratingly into his eyes. "You know what this means, don't you?"

He ran his other hand through her thick chestnut hair, but again said nothing, only nodding.

"Listen, darling," she said, now taking both of his hands in hers, "I want you to come to London for a week or two so we can really renew our acquaintance. We could have such a grand time, going to the theatres, sampling the new restaurants, and just relaxing. You could stay in my flat. Doesn't that sound exciting?"

Noble now faced a daunting fork in the road. One way led to Catherine, the other to Jennifer. Why must he always be conflicted over two women?

Their faces were almost touching. She kissed him lightly on the cheek. He caught the scent of her familiar perfume. Days with her in London, all he had fantasized last winter, could actually come to pass. He couldn't say no, but he couldn't quite bring himself to say yes. He still had a tenuous hold on rationality.

Slowly he said, "It sounds like what I've dreamed of. I just can't say yes at the moment. You understand, don't you?"

"Of course. But do see what you can work out." She got to her feet. "I better retire now, to be fresh for my great Remberton experience. You better get some rest too."

Noble stood up, wrapped his arms around her waist, pulled her body hard against his, and kissed her—a prolonged kiss.

In a moment she came up for air, smiling. "Honey, that was like old times. But we had best go to bed now. She lowered her voice and smiled slyly. "In separate rooms. With Nicky right here, we can't do much else."

At six the next afternoon, Noble, Nicky, and Jennifer arrived at Ellen's house, Nicky carrying the powerful secret that he was entering the home of his mother and his half-sister. Ben Harris had taken Nicky in hand during the day, doing lunch at the Country Club and showing him the insides of some of the town's most impressive antebellum houses.

Noble had given Jennifer the Remberton tour—the old houses, the courthouse, the Confederate monument, and the cemetery.

Along the way, he asked, "Have you heard any more about Nicky's problems?"

"Things aren't any better," she said. "From what I hear, he seems to have a way of ingratiating himself with people and then putting pressure on them for money."

"You probably don't know that Nicky went to see Jesse and asked him for money."

"No, but that's not surprising. He's always alert for opportunities. He'll likely be looking around in Remberton."

Now they were at the Funchess house for the kick-off reception.

Noble, alone among Remberton residents who knew the biological truth, watched as Ellen came forward to greet them. He introduced her to Nicky and Jennifer. Nicky grasped her hand warmly, holding it in both of his.

She said, "I heard Mama talk about her visit with you in England. Your hospitality made quite an impression."

"She was an interesting person," he said, as he subjected her face to microscopic examination. "I'm so glad I had a chance to meet her, and I was terribly saddened over what happened."

Ellen turned and spoke to Jennifer and introduced her husband, Jack Palmer. He was of slight build, an unimpressive fellow, wearing black rim glasses, not a good crowd mixer. This deficiency in personality was overcome, however, by his distinction—carrying considerable weight in Remberton—of being from a Montgomery family that was both old and wealthy. Other guests began arriving, and Ellen moved off to greet them.

Nicky renewed his acquaintance with the other members of the library board. A waiter was taking drink orders.

Frank Brandon appeared with his photographer. "We've got to have some pictures before the evening gets too far gone," he said, after being introduced to Nicky and Jennifer. He arranged several groupings: Nicky and Ellen, Nicky and the board members, Nicky and Jennifer, and so on.

Suddenly there was Catherine Craighill at Noble's side. "Well," she said, "I'm certainly glad to see you. It seems like forever. Let me speak to our old friend, Nicky."

Noble took her over to where Nicky and Jennifer were talking to Ben Harris. "Excuse me," he said, "Nicky, you remember Catherine."

"Absolutely. Delighted to see you again. This is my friend, Jennifer Hedgely. She's a London journalist in Washington at the moment."

"Welcome to Remberton," Catherine said, extending her hand.

"Thank you," Jennifer said. "I'm enjoying it thoroughly. Noble is a superb host."

"Where are you staying?" Catherine asked.

"Nicky and I are both Noble's guests."

"I see," Catherine said, in a flat voice. "I hope you enjoy the rest of your visit." She turned to accept a drink tendered by the waiter.

A few minutes later she found Noble on the edge of the group. "You never said anything about Jennifer Hedgely. How does she happen to be at your house?"

"It's Nicky's doing. He called at the last minute and asked whether he could bring her. Naturally I couldn't say anything but yes."

"She's a pretty flashy model. How old do you think she is?"

"I would guess around sixty."

She looked at him imploringly. "I hope we can get together before too long. Right now I'm going home—I'm tired." She squeezed his hand. "I'll see you tomorrow."

It was a golden autumn afternoon. The sky formed a cloudless blue canopy. The temperature hovered around seventy. A light breeze faintly stirred the leaves remaining on the oaks.

The site for the new library building had been cleared of underbrush. The speaker's platform was draped in red, white, and blue bunting. Over two hundred chairs had been placed in its front with plenty of standing room in the rear.

For the half hour before the program began, the Remberton High School band had been playing its way through a litany of familiar pieces—stirring marches from John Philip Sousa, nostalgic strains from Stephen Foster, and, of course, "Dixie," bringing many of the over sixty crowd to their feet, yelling and clapping.

The band fell silent. From several blocks to the east came the sound of the courthouse clock tolling the hour. The program began with the singing of "America the Beautiful." Seated on the platform were the entire library board, the mayor, Ellen Funchess Brentson Palmer, Noble Shepperson, and Nicholas Cottingham. As board chairman, Melba Robinson presided.

When the crowd finished singing of spacious skies, brotherhood from sea to shining sea, and alabaster cities, the Reverend Henry Edmonds, rector of St. James Episcopal Church, came to the podium. He had been a compromise choice for this assignment, to relieve an impasse among the Baptists, Methodists, and Presbyterians, each of whom wanted the honor of delivering the invocation. Also, somebody had suggested that with Nicholas Cottingham present it would be nice to have an Anglican touch.

The Rector was a large man with a flushed face. Noble had first encountered him at Judge McKnight's funeral. In his short time in Remberton he had become well liked, despite word that he had been defrocked a decade earlier as the result of an entanglement with the bottle and a female choir member in his North Alabama church. He had been reinstated but had been relegated by the Bishop to what was considered in high clerical circles to be an ecclesiastical backwater. He stood there now, black suited in white clerical collar, and invoked the blessing of the Almighty on the great depository of learning to be built here, books being the preservers and transmitters of civilization, and reminding the audience of Him who was the source of all knowledge, the Alpha and Omega, from everlasting to everlasting. He sat down amidst the intermittent dropping of acorns from overhanging oak branches, each hitting the wooden platform with a tiny thump.

After opening remarks in which she described the magnificent gift and plans for the grand library of the future, Melba Robinson read a message from the Governor sending his best wishes and congratulations.

She then introduced the mayor. He was a short, stocky man in his forties, the local booster type, former president of the Jaycees and owner of a dry cleaning business, the mayor's job being only part time. He made appropriate remarks about the great benefit to the town of this grand new library. Applause followed, as it did every speaker.

Noble looked out over the crowd. All seats were taken, and a sizeable clump of attendees stood in the back. To a limited extent the assemblage cut across class lines. The self-considered upper echelon predominated, but there were others—good, solid citizens, he thought, sincerely interested in the life of the place.

In the front row was Jennifer Hedgely, seated beside Frank Brandon, who was directing his photographer. Far in the rear was Gladys Houston. Near the front were the other Grady-connected women—Catherine Craighill and Julia McKnight Goodson.

Not a Rooter was present, and none had lived in Remberton for nearly thirty years, but the Rooters weighed heavily on Noble's mind—the offspring sitting next to him on the platform, the series of catastrophes Jesse's return set in train, and his weird idea of benevolent revenge that had brought all of them to this moment. The idea had worked far beyond anyone's imagining.

Catherine was seated three rows directly behind Jennifer. She caught Noble's eye, smiled and lifted her hand slightly in a discreet wave. He smiled back. Moments earlier he and Jennifer had exchanged smiles. He had both of these women in his line of sight, could look at them at the same time, comparing them, and torturing himself over the painful dilemma they posed. In one light, he thought, a man must surely be blessed to be loved by two such attractive women. But the situation subjected him to a torment from which he devoutly wished to be rescued. How to choose? Did he love them both? He thought so. But equally? Was that possible? If not, which one did he love more and why?

Ellen came to the podium. With sun-lit sandy blond hair, she made a striking appearance. Noble wondered whether anyone noticed the resemblance between her and Nicky. Recently she had taken on more of Lucille's toughness and aggressiveness.

She spoke for her mother, who, she said, through a happenstance of fate was no longer with us. Going out of her way to flaunt Sam Funchess, ignoring the murder charge, she unabashedly praised her grandfather for achieving the American dream and providing the assets which made possible this gift to the library, praising also the life of her mother whose memory would be preserved with this building. Her remarks were brief, the applause tepid. As she resumed her seat, a fresh breeze caused a small shower of acorns to descend, one landing on Noble's lap.

Her words set up a twitching in Ben Harris as though she had directed an electric charge at him. He whispered to Norma Armistead, sitting beside him, "The world has turned upside down."

She whispered back, with a sly smile, "The old order changeth."

Now it was Noble's turn. Figuring out what to say on behalf of a man charged with murder and not acquitted was not easy, especially for the man who had shot and killed the woman whose daughter was right here on the platform. He began by saying it was Jesse Rooter who was responsible for their being gathered here today. Whatever we think of the Rooters, he said, we must never forget that.

"In Remberton, the Rooters were down and out and ignored. Jesse had no reason to look back on Remberton with anything but bitterness. To his credit, he put that behind him and pursued a highly successful business career in Chicago. In the end he came home. I talked to him many times and I think he would not object to my telling you he had in his heart a peculiar combination of revenge and a desire to do something good for this place. The result was his proposal to give an unprecedented amount of money for the library. Unfortunately, death intervened. We are grateful to his executor for making good on Jesse's intention. So his name will be emblazoned on this superb building in the midst of the town that spurned him and his family."

Noble now came to a particularly ticklish point. He wanted to skirt the tangled relationship of the Rooter and Funchess families. An acorn bounced off his forehead, but he continued, undistracted. "Here Jesse Rooter's name will be forever linked with that of Lucille Funchess Brentson. It is appropriate that this be so. The Rooter-Brentson Library will serve generations to come and will serve as an institution that will help educate and improve the lives of all our people."

Noble concluded, as the irregular staccato of falling acorns on the wooden planking continued, by saying he was honored to stand in for Jesse Rooter and to join with Ellen, all of whose family he had known, in kicking off this historic project. He returned to his chair, amidst the heaviest applause of the day.

"Splendidly put," Nicky leaned over and said, as the applause continued.

Having been presented by Melba Robinson as a "special treat" and as "a real bibliophile," Nicky began by expressing his great pleasure at being there and his admiration for "this grand little town of yours." He brought special greetings from the

British Ambassador in Washington, reading a short note from him congratulating the citizens of Remberton on such a singular development in their cultural life. The accent, the clipped phrases, mesmerized the crowd. No Englishman had ever before spoken in Remberton. Noble again wondered whether anyone noticed the physical resemblance to Ellen.

Nicky extolled the importance of books, describing briefly the library he had inherited and what reading had meant to him. He came then to the sensitive territory that Noble had so gingerly negotiated.

"It was my pleasure and good fortune briefly to know Lucille Brentson and Jesse Rooter. Both were guests in my house. I developed a genuine affection for each. I had a special fondness for Lucille and am delighted to become acquainted with her daughter, Ellen. I felt a keen sense of personal loss over the deaths of these two benefactors. I like to think their spirits are looking down on us today."

He wound up by expressing appreciation for the Remberton hospitality and wishing them well as they moved forward with the creation of this library.

Melba Robinson recognized the presence in the audience of representatives from several of the state's major libraries. Then she called on the mayor to unveil a four by six foot preliminary architect's drawing of the new building's facade. It was on a large easel beside the speakers' platform. The program, she announced, would be concluded by the singing of "God Bless America."

When the mayor pulled the cloth aside, an approving murmur rose from the crowd. The three-story structure featured a Greek revival portico, insisted on by the traditionalists, and two fountains in the forecourt. Displayed alongside was a draft of the memorial plaque to be placed at the main entrance. It read:

> THE ROOTER-BRENTSON LIBRARY
> This building was made possible
> by the generosity of two Remberton natives
> in whose memory the library is named.
>
> Jesse Rooter
> 1922–1975
> Lucille Funchess Brentson
> 1926–1975

The audience sang its way lustily from the mountains, to the prairie, to the oceans white with foam, ending with those long, lingering words, "My home ... sweet ... home." The crowd began to disperse, amidst a buzz of talk and laughter. Ellen gave Nicky a hug. "Thank you so much for being with us and for what you said."

"It's my honor," Nicky said. "Perhaps we should not say goodbye. I'd like to think we'll meet again."

"Let's hope so," she said, brushing away a tear.

As the group came down off the platform, Gladys Houston approached Noble and said, "Colonel, I can't get over it. Nobody here knew a Rooter better than I did and who'd ever thought that name would be on something like this. Jesse must be off somewhere smiling, maybe laughing. Grady too. It's like a joke on the town."

Everyone was shaking hands with everyone else. The air was filled with mutual congratulations.

Nicky and Jennifer had planned to remain overnight with Noble and fly out the next morning. However, just before they left the house for the ceremony Nicky received a message from the Embassy that the Ambassador wanted him back as soon as possible. So Ben Harris had offered to drive him to the airport. After a quick round of goodbyes, they were off.

Jennifer accepted Noble's invitation to stay over, with his assurance that he would see that she got to the airport tomorrow morning.

Chapter 25

Noble and Jennifer went to dinner at the country club. When they entered the dining room they found a half dozen other diners seated at scattered tables. They were among the newer club members. Noble, of course, knew them, but they were not close friends and he felt no obligation to introduce Jennifer. They took a table at the edge of the room.

"This is not exactly up to the London clubs you're accustomed to," Noble said.

"It's charming in its own way."

Susie came over with menus. "How y'all tonight?" She was in her usual low-cut blouse and short skirt.

"Fine," Noble said. "Susie, this is Mrs. Hedgely from England. Jennifer this is Susie. She runs this place."

Susie smiled and said, "The Colonel says things he don't always mean. You from England? We don't get many from there." Jennifer smiled and nodded. Then Susie said, "Special for tonight is fried oysters and hush puppies. Oysters just come in this afternoon."

Jennifer said, "Noble, I leave the selection up to you."

"Let's have the oysters," he said. "Get a sample of some good Gulf coast eating."

"French fries or coleslaw?" Susie said.

They both said coleslaw. He added a bottle of white wine.

They talked about the day's ceremony. Jennifer said, "This is really quite a wonderful town. Who would ever have thought there was a place like this way down in the middle of Alabama?"

"That's a backhanded compliment."

"Oh, I didn't mean it that way. It really is a nice place."

Noble thought about all that had gone on—murder, illicit love affairs—wondering how "nice" the place really was. But he let it go, saying, "Nicky was in top form, putting on his maximum charm."

"He was indeed. He's very good at that. Seeing him that way, it's hard to believe there's another side. I've seen him in moments around the Embassy when he gets abusive with the staff. Then there's all the financial manipulation. He's sort of a Jekyll and Hyde figure."

"It's a damn shame," Noble said, "considering all he has going for him. It's probably just as well for us here if this ends our contact with him, as pleasant as this has been."

"With all respect to Remberton, I can't imagine what would bring him back here."

Susie arrived with the wine. Pouring some into Noble's glass, she said, "Honey, you want to taste it?"

Noble took a sip and pronounced it acceptable. She filled both their glasses and left the bottle on the table.

"I'll say this about Nicky," Noble said. "He did seem to genuinely enjoy himself."

"That he did."

In a few minutes Susie was back with tossed salads. "Oh, I didn't expect this," Jennifer said.

"It comes with dinner," Susie said. "We've got French dressing, thousand island, and bleu cheese." Both requested bleu cheese.

They talked some more about the day's events and then drifted into talking about what Jennifer was doing this time in Washington and her perception of the American political scene.

Susie brought platters filled with fried oysters, hush puppies, and slaw. Noble refilled their glasses.

When they finished dinner they drove back to Noble's house. In the den, they sat down side-by-side on the sofa, each with a glass of cognac.

"This reminds me," she said, dreamily, after a silent interlude, "of those days at Hedgely Farm, sitting in front of the electric fire. God! That was a long time ago."

"Thirty-one and a half years, to be exact."

"Yes. Those days before D-Day. There'll never be another time like it. We were living with no tomorrow. Now, though, the future's ours ... if we want it. Neither one of us has any encumbrance." She leaned over and kissed his cheek.

Noble had never been able to think straight in her presence. The touch of her lips, the warmth of her body, the soft English voice, the sensuous perfume—gripped his heart and mind. So when she said, in a whisper, "You will come to London, won't you?" he could do nothing but nod.

Suddenly the kitchen door slammed, followed by the pounding of footsteps on the linoleum tile. Startled, Noble sat up straight. "Who can that be?" He often left the door from the kitchen to the garage unlocked, but no one except Nan and himself ever came in that way.

He rose and started toward the kitchen. He had taken only a couple of steps when Catherine Craighill suddenly appeared in the doorway, her blond hair wind-blown and her face flushed. She stopped abruptly when she saw Jennifer.

She looked straight at Noble, her eyes blazing. "Well! Isn't this cozy! No wonder I haven't seen you lately. Where's Nicky?"

"He had to return unexpectedly to Washington," Noble said.

"How convenient." Her voice dripped sarcasm.

"Won't you have a seat?" Noble said.

"I wouldn't think of intruding."

Noble advanced toward her. In a low voice, he said, "I would offer you a drink but I think you've had enough." Anger flashed in her eyes. He had never seen her like this.

He took her arm and guided her toward the kitchen. "What are you doing?" she mumbled. "Where are we going?"

"Home is where you need to be."

"All right. Get rid of me."

They went through the door and out to her Cadillac. "Do you feel up to driving?" Noble said. She carried a strong odor of bourbon.

"Perfectly all right. How long will that English bitch be here?"

"Just until tomorrow."

She burst into tears. Through sobs she gasped, "Noble, how can you do this?"

He put his arms around her waist. He was in an excruciating dilemma. Only a minute earlier he had been mesmerized by Jennifer, by the prospect of an idyllic time with her in London. Now he was holding in his arms the woman to whom he had professed love just days ago. Was he about to betray her? Was he being deceitful with Jennifer?

They held on to each other for some seconds. He didn't know what to say or do. Then he whispered, "I'll call you."

He opened the car door and guided her onto the driver's seat. He kissed her on the cheek and said, "Please drive carefully." He stood there until she pulled away and disappeared out of sight. Then he went back inside.

Jennifer was still sitting on the sofa. "That was a dramatic little scene. Is there something going on between you two?"

Noble sat, stalling for time, trying to decide what to say. Finally, he said, "Ever since Nan died, she's been attentive, very helpful."

"I'm guessing there's more than a friendly concern there. But nothing that a week in London won't cure, I hope."

"A week in London can do a lot," he said. Catherine's sudden appearance had unnerved him, had dampened his mounting ardor for Jennifer. It was as though a bucket of ice water had been thrown over him.

She stood up and placed her glass on a table. "It's been a wonderful day—and a wonderful trip in every way."

He stood and faced her and they embraced. Nuzzling up to his ear, she whispered, "And it's not over yet."

His diminished desire for Jennifer left him feeling awkward. Beyond the emotional encounter with Catherine, Nan had flickered into his mind.

He forced himself to say, "A grand visit, I agree. But I think, now, though, we should just retire and save all the rest for London. I'll be more relaxed then."

She pulled back a bit and said, "That doesn't sound like the Noble I used to know."

"It's the same old Noble, just in a moment of fatigue. Maybe it's this room, where Nan and I spent so much time."

Her face showed disappointment. "Well, darling, If that's the way you want it, I can wait. But don't forget: we've been waiting a long time."

The day after Jennifer left, Noble telephoned Catherine. He did so with trepidation, uncertain what sort of reception he would get.

When she answered, he affected a light air. "Catherine, I'm free at last. Trying to get caught up. Hope all is well there."

"Still thinking about the other night. I'm afraid I made a fool of myself. But things did look mighty cozy there."

"I was just trying to be a good host."

"There's a limit to that."

"We didn't exceed it. Anyhow, she's gone. How are you doing?"

"So-so. I'd love to have you come by this evening, but I wouldn't be any fun. Been tired and now have a headache. Think I'll go in for a check-up."

"Is there anything I can do?"

"Not really. Just remember I love you."

When they hung up, Noble had a sickening sensation in his stomach. He felt guilty of deceit. It came to him that what he was doing was not fair or honorable. How much longer could he go on with this three-way relationship?

Melba Robinson was busy wrapping up the library board's business. Noble had told her she could continue to use his conference room until she was done. Frank

Brandon had brought in a copy of all the photographs he had taken. She and Noble sat there perusing several dozen.

"That English woman is a real beauty," Melba said, as she looked at a half dozen shots in which Jennifer appeared. She certainly is, Noble agreed to himself, as his pulse quickened a bit at the sight of the pictures and thoughts of a London trip.

"Here's something I hadn't noticed," Melba said, looking at a picture of Ellen and Nicky standing side-by-side. "There's quite a resemblance, don't you think?"

Noble looked at the two. Same sandy blond hair, sharp features, overall good looks. He said, "There does seem to be some."

In considering London, Noble had two problems. One was to find the time in this busy litigating season. The other was Catherine. How could he explain such a trip to her? He could invent a fictional cover, for example, saying he had to go to New York on business. But he was uncomfortable with deception. The fundamental question he was finally up against, and was reluctant to face, was whether he wanted Jennifer or Catherine. He had once before had the question whether a man could love two women simultaneously. He thought so, but he knew he couldn't have both indefinitely. Rationally, he knew he should go to London only if he wanted to cast his lot with Jennifer. That trip would probably be a point of no return. But if that's what he wanted, better to be forthright with Catherine and not rock along in festering ambiguity.

Some external force seemed to be pushing him step-by-step toward London. He couldn't spare an entire week away, so he blocked out five days, using a weekend. The next thing he knew he was booking an airline reservation, for a date three weeks ahead.

Jennifer was ecstatic but disappointed at the duration. "Darling, that's so short. It means we'll have to make every minute count."

Hearing from Jennifer again prompted Noble to contemplate, more seriously than he had, the practical, day-to-day aspects of what his life would be like in England if he decided to make the big move. Of course, Jennifer had said that she would move to Remberton. But he did not consider that a realistic option; it would not work in the long run.

So he had to face it head-on: the move would mean nothing less than a complete and final break with the law.

He could not see himself going through the years of study it would take to be admitted to the English bar. The only American lawyer he could recall who had done that was Judah Benjamin, former U. S. Senator and Confederate Secretary of State—an exceptional situation. Noble could, of course, have library privileges in the Middle

Temple which had the best collection of American law in London. But he could not imagine carrying on an American practice from over there.

So what were the offsetting advantages he would have in place of the law? Britain and Europe would be at his disposal—travel, museums, theatres, libraries, perhaps enrollment in courses of various types—an intellectual feast beyond anything that he had previously been offered. And in addition to all that, there was life with Jennifer. Considered in its totality, it was the enticement of a wholly new experience, a clean break with forty years of plowing the same fields.

The other choice was a continuation of life in Remberton, with or without law practice as he may choose, a new life increasingly enjoyable with Catherine—life in the only place on earth he could truly call home

So there it was—two quite different roads stretching out before him. He could take either, but not both. What tore at his heart was the realization that he could make neither choice without hurting one of the women he loved—or thought he loved.

Catherine was on the phone. "Noble, Maria came down yesterday. She wants to take me back to Atlanta for a while, and I think I'll go. I can get some rest there and maybe get over what ails me."

Noble had seen Maria a few times when she was visiting her mother, but he scarcely knew her. She had grown up in Atlanta before Catherine moved back to Remberton. From hearing Catherine talk about her, he understood she had married a CPA a couple of years ago and that they had a house in Chastain Park.

Surprised, Noble said nothing, and she continued. "I need a break from Remberton and a chance to think things over." Her voice was cool, detached, not quite like the Catherine he had come to know.

"What things?"

"Oh, my life in general, where I'm going, what I should do."

He had not heard her talk like this before, and he was uncertain how to react. "Well, we all need to take stock every now and then. How long will you be gone?"

"I don't know. A week or so, I guess. Maybe we can get together when I'm back. It seems forever since you've been here."

"Of course."

"All right. I'll call you."

"Give my love to Maria. Relax and get to feeling better."

Noble sat there, puzzled. This was a strange conversation. Cool, not the usual Catherine. Did she suspect something? Feminine instinct, he had learned, was uncanny. He was unsettled by the thought that she might possibly drift away from him. But why should that matter if he were going to London?

Autumn was moving along, the days getting shorter. He had come home from the office and turned on the evening TV news when the phone rang.

It was Ellen, speaking in a distraught voice. "Mr. Noble, I've got to see you as soon as possible. Can you come over right now?"

"Can it wait until tomorrow?"

"No!" She almost shouted. "I need to talk to you now." Her words were on the edge of sobs. Something told him that this was no ordinary call for help.

Fifteen minutes later, he walked into the Mt. Vernon-like house built by Sam Funchess, now the residence of Ellen and Jack Palmer. But Jack, she said, was staying in Montgomery tonight. She led Noble into the den.

She wore navy blue slacks and a pale blue turtleneck blouse. Her hair was disheveled, her eyes red, her cheeks tear-dampened. "The help has gone," she said, "So we don't have to worry about being overheard."

"What in the world is the matter?" Noble said, as the two sat down in chairs facing each other.

"I've just been through the most shocking experience of my life. Still shaking. So stunned I can hardly talk."

"Tell me what it is."

She dabbed fresh tears with a handkerchief. Her hands trembled. "You won't believe this, but Nicky Cottingham was here this afternoon."

"What?" Noble blurted out. "Nicky here today?"

"Yes. And here's what he told me. If I hadn't been sitting down I think I would have collapsed. I felt faint and still do." She drew in a couple of deep breaths. "What he said is—now get this—what he said is that my mother was also his mother. Can you imagine that, out of the blue? When I was able to speak, I said I didn't believe him. It was just ridiculous. But then he handed me some papers showing his birth and adoption. He said you knew."

Noble said slowly and quietly, "Yes, I did. But I only found out earlier this year, and I've debated with myself many times whether you should be told. I thought it was up to Nicky. You should know that your mother learned who Nicky was just days before she died. I guess she didn't have time to tell you."

"How could this be? It just can't be true."

"First, you need to understand that when your mother and her mother left for their European tour, she was pregnant. The baby was born in London. When she went to England with us to visit Nicky she decided to investigate the adoption and she discovered it was Nicky. She was even more shocked than you are now. But she and Nicky never discussed it. Neither one knew the other knew. I found out about this when I talked to her the morning of the day she died."

"This is just all too much. But I'm not through. After he told me this, he said all sorts of nice things about having me as a half sister. That made me a little sick. After that sweet talk, he explained he was in deep financial trouble, that he might lose his home in England unless he could get half a million dollars right away. He asked me for it."

"My worst suspicions about Nicky."

"I hadn't gotten over the first shock when I was hit with this. It was bad enough for him to ask me for money—but the amount! When I balked, he tried to argue with me. He was begging for help, almost persuading me. But I kept saying I just didn't think I could do it. His entire personality changed. You know how gracious and warm he had been. He suddenly became angry, said that if I didn't let him have the money he would tell people in Remberton that he was the illegitimate child of my mother."

"It's all inconsistent with Nicky's outward personality."

"I had the same reaction. All that charm was gone. He was a different person, mean and threatening. Looking back on it, I think all that geniality was just to set the stage to get some money out of mama and now me. What an underhanded character!"

"He did seem to be quite interested in Lucille's financial situation. I've learned recently that he does in fact have serious money problems. What did you tell him?"

"I said I needed time to think."

"This is appalling. It's nothing short of blackmail."

"How much is it worth to me to keep this secret?"

"I'm afraid that only you can decide that. You have to remember that a blackmailer rarely stops with the first demand. If you paid him now he would probably be back later for more."

"It occurs to me there's a way I can beat him at his own game. I could make known the secret myself."

"True. The cost would be whatever embarrassment it would inflict on you."

"I've already got a grandfather exposed in a murder for hire scheme, so why not add a bastard? What the hell! I know what a lot of folks around here think of my family. When they hear this they'll probably say what can you expect?"

"You're sounding more and more like your mother."

"I admire the way she could take it and dish it out. There's one point Nicky didn't mention and that's his father. Do you know who he was?"

"I might as well get the whole story out," Noble said. He proceeded to describe Grady Rooter's work at this house during the summer of '46, his dalliance over the garage with Lucille, and then his murder. "You can imagine the rest."

There was a momentary silence. Then she burst out, "My God! You mean Grady Rooter is Nicky's father?"

"Yes."

"This is too much!" Her voice rose again.

"It throws a lot on you in one day."

"It's so far-fetched. Unbelievable. If what you say is true, Nicky's father is the brother of the man who shot and killed my mother right here in this room. And ... he's my half brother. How in God's name did these Funchess and Rooter families get so mixed up together?"

"If it weren't true I wouldn't be telling you. We have to face it. Nicky is a flesh-and-blood incarnation of Rooter and Funchess. He's the one living combination of the two. Maybe his portrait should be hung in the new library reading room."

"That's not funny. It's disgusting."

"I'm sorry. I don't mean to make light of it. When did Nicky say he wanted an answer?"

"In a week."

"Well, you think about it and I will too."

They stood up and he gave her a hug. "We'll work it out somehow. Give me a call in the next day or two when you want to talk again. Now you get in bed with a hot toddy and see if you can get a good night's sleep."

Noble drove back to his house—dark, chilly, and empty. In by-gone days Nan would have been there, sometimes cheerful, sometimes less so, but always ready to give him a late supper. How cheerless, quiet, and lonesome it was now.

He found himself missing Catherine. Her absence intensified his loneliness. Remberton without Catherine was not the same.

In the day's mail, which he had not gotten around to opening, he found a London-posted envelope. Inside was a clipping from the *Times* giving a favorable review of a new play just opening in the West End. At the top was a scribbled note: "Darling, I've already reserved tickets for us. Love, J."

Chapter 26

All the next day Noble was tied up in court, trying a non-jury case before Judge Dabney Williams, still serving temporarily.

When court adjourned and he emerged onto the courthouse portico in the twilight of the fall day he was stopped short by the sight of the western sky. It was aflame with red, pink, and purple hues, shifting as he watched. Center Street, now largely deserted, was bathed in a surreal sunset glow. The distant trees lining the residential stretch were obscured in the gathering dusk.

The day was dying and with it, he wondered, was his time in Remberton. He had done his bit, served the people of his native patch of earth for forty years. After four generations he was the last Shepperson. His children would not be coming back. But there was Catherine … And far across the sea, Jennifer. Maybe she was a providential answer to the restlessness long besetting him.

He stood lost in his musings until the light faded altogether, day passing into night.

Miss Alice had gone but she had left a note propped up in the middle of his desk: "Call Ellen Palmer as soon as possible." He dialed her immediately.

"I've decided to get it all out," she announced, "tell the whole world the story of the Funchess bastard—a Rooter bastard too. I'd like to ask you to come here tomorrow morning and bring Frank Brandon with you. I don't want this news to seep out around town in gossipy drips and drabs. The newspaper is the way to go."

So the next morning the three of them sat in Ellen's den. She was now composed, in command of the situation. She told Frank the story of Nicky Cottingham's birth, with Noble adding details. She did not mention Nicky's demand for money.

"The cliché is right. Truth is indeed stranger than fiction," Frank said, shaking his head. "I knew there was one more piece to this picture, but in my wildest imagination I would never have thought of Cottingham. I have to say, though, now that I think about it, the two of you do resemble each other."

Turning to Noble, he said, "Now that we've filled out this story, what do you think about the Joe Kinston episode?"

"Well," Noble said thoughtfully, "as long as all this dirty linen is being washed in public I suppose we might as well go all the way. Ellen takes after her mother. I imagine she can handle it."

Ellen erupted. "What are you talking about? I can take whatever it is."

"Let me explain it," Noble said. He then described how Lucille was upset when she heard of Joe Kinston's part in Grady's murder, disturbed that the law couldn't or wouldn't get at him. But it wasn't until after her death that the police made a startling discovery: the bullet that killed Kinston came from her pistol. Then the matching of the footprints with her shoes clinched the matter. "It was a shocking conclusion, but we can't deny the evidence."

Ellen listened, stony-faced. Then spit out, "My God, how much more dirt is there? There must be a curse on this family. Grandfather financing murder, mother actually committing murder, giving birth to an illegitimate child then getting killed herself. Good God Almighty! It all goes back to Rooter—a Rooter fathering her child, a Rooter shooting her. Damn them all!" She burst into sobs.

Noble knelt beside her chair and took her hand. "This is a heavy load to have dumped on you." He put his hand on her shoulder, reassuringly.

Her sobbing subsided and she dried her eyes with her handkerchief. "Whenever I look at that new library building, with those names on it, this is what I'll think of."

Frank asked, "Do you want the Kinston business included in the story?"

"Might as well get it all out, every last nasty bit. Give the town something really juicy to talk about. The juiciest piece of gossip they have ever had."

"You're probably right about that," Noble said.

"But whatever the gossips say, when I invite them to a big party they'll all be here."

Frank reviewed some details of what he would write and said he would run a draft by her before going to press.

They stood up to go and Noble said, "You know my long connections with your family. So remember, if there's any way I can help you anytime, just let me know."

Ellen telephoned him the next day to say that she had called Nicky and told him no on the money and that she was releasing word about him, so he could forget his blackmail scheme. She also told him he would not be welcome back in Remberton and that she had no desire to maintain contact with him.

"Well," Noble said, "I guess that closes out the short chapter in the life of Nicky Cottingham and the town of Remberton."

"Let's hope so."

"It's sad," Noble said. "He was such a personable fellow."

"Now we know it was all a front, a deceitful scheme all along to get money. Even though he's my half brother—I almost gag when I say it—I never want to see him again."

"I guess there won't be any more flowers on Grady's grave."

"No. That's part of this closed chapter."

The *Remberton Progress* story hit the town like a nuclear explosion. For days nothing else was talked about. Ellen went to Montgomery to stay until things quieted down.

Two days after the story appeared, the library board met in Noble's conference room to review architectural drawings. Noble stuck his head in the door. "Can I get you anything?"

"Come in and join us," Melba Robinson said.

When he took a seat at the end of the table, she said, "We're just sitting here not knowing what to say about Nicky Cottingham."

"One thing that can be said," Ben Harris chimed in, "is that a combination of Funchess and Rooter blood apparently produces something better than either could produce alone."

It was all that Noble could do to hold his tongue, to refrain from saying that in fact this combination of Rooter-Funchess blood didn't really turn out any better. The blackmail threat would remain secret as far as he was concerned.

Norma Armistead said, "It seems almost providential that he was here for this event, for a building bearing the names of his mother and uncle, and nobody had any inkling of it."

"I still find myself denying it's true," Ann Simmons said.

Melba asked, "Do you think he'll be coming back to visit Ellen from time-to-time?"

Noble said, "The article didn't say this, but she's made it pretty clear to me that she's not interested in maintaining contact."

"That's too bad," Melba said. "He seemed to be quite charming."

Once again Noble yearned to disabuse them of this false image of the genial, charming Englishman.

"One thing the newspaper story tells us," Norma said, "is that we are doing something here one of us, I forget who, said we'd never do—name the building for someone who committed a crime."

No one seemed to know what to say. In a moment, Ann spoke up. "Maybe this just equalizes the names. We know that Rooter killed Brentson, although it was not necessarily a crime. Now we know that there was a killing on the Brentson side. It's too complicated to unravel. And too late in the day."

Again, silence. And then Melba saying quietly, "I think so—too late. We've taken the money, had a big public ceremony."

Not knowing what else to say and having to accept what had earlier been regarded as unacceptable, the members said nothing more but drifted into discussing the drawings spread out on the table. Noble went back to his office.

When the board adjourned, Melba came in to report that they had agreed to the plans, with a few minor suggestions.

"We also agreed," she said, "to accept Julia Goodson's offer of Judge McKnight's book collection, along with $25,000, to establish a small reading room to be known as the McKnight Room. It will house his books—about two hundred works of history and biography—and will concentrate on building a collection of local and state history."

"Did anybody think it was not a good idea?"

"No. I can't see why anybody would. In fact, there was some comment to the effect that it was nice to have at least one name in the building untainted by homicide."

"That's an interesting thought," Noble said, immensely uncomfortable over the nondisclosure of facts that would put the Judge in the same boat with the others. "By the way, when does construction start?"

"It's going out for bids next week. We hope to break ground in a couple of months."

"Telephone call from London," Miss Alice said over the intercom. "This place is just getting too cosmopolitan."

Noble's departure was five days away. He had never before been in such a state of mental anguish. He took a long, deep breath before picking up the receiver.

"Noble, this is Jennifer. I hope all systems are go. Excuse the astronaut lingo."

"At the moment, yes. Has something come up?"

"Nothing to do with your trip. It's about Nicky. I thought you might want to know right away."

"What is it?"

"His creditors have moved in and had Cottingham Hall put in receivership. I don't know what will eventually happen to it. His doings finally caught up with him, and the Ambassador had him shipped home. I think it's likely he'll be sacked by the Foreign Office."

"He really has turned out to be a Jekyll and Hyde." He felt no need to tell her of Nicky's encounter with Ellen.

"It's terribly sad," Jennifer said. "I really liked him and he was immensely helpful." Before hanging up, she outlined the best way for him to get from Heathrow to her place in South Kensington.

Walking back from the courthouse the next morning, Noble met Frank Brandon, hair uncombed and shirttail bulging over his belt. "Come on and join me for a cup of coffee," the editor said.

As they opened the door to the drugstore, they were met by the usual overbearing voice from the rear. "Howya Noble! Come on in, Frank!"

They picked up cups of coffee at the counter and sat down in a booth.

Frank said, "Melba sent me a statement from the library board—it would be called a press release if we had such in Remberton—announcing Julia Goodson's gift to the library in memory of her father." He paused and looked around to the booth behind him. No one was there or in the booth on the other side. He leaned forward and lowered his voice. "I've learned more since we last talked. I strongly suspect you know what it is. You've always been several steps ahead of me."

"I thought your blockbuster article finally wound all of this up, told all there is to tell."

"It turns out not quite. But you can relax. I'm not going to print anything more. Just let me put it this way between us. All three persons to be memorialized in this two million dollar library have participated in homicide, one way or another. Sam himself is not there but the Funchess name is on the plaque. The names also include the mother of an illegitimate child and brother of that bastard's father. The addition of a McKnight Room rounds out this entangled cast of characters. But unlike the others, the Judge comes in under the radar."

Noble, who had been leaning forward to hear Frank, sat back and shook his head. "It would be hard to summarize it more succinctly."

"For a nobody family, as Jesse liked to put it, the Rooters have probably had a greater impact on this town than any other family in the last hundred years. Is that too strong a statement?"

"Probably not," Noble said, "considering all the ramifications. Think how different things would be if Jesse had never come back. How much we know now we wouldn't have ever known. How many people would still be alive? If I had had any idea of what lay ahead that day Jesse first walked in my office I would have told him to get back to Chicago and forget Remberton."

"But we wouldn't have that new huge library building."

Noble looked vacantly beyond Frank toward shelves of over-the-counter drugs. "True ... Benevolent revenge. A curious concept. Jesse got more out of the revenge side of the equation than he reckoned. But Grady's no slacker on revenge."

They both drained the last of their coffee. Putting down his cup, Frank said, "Adding it all together, it might better be called the Rooter curse."

"Think how time will mellow it all," Noble said. "Future generations will see those two names on that bronze plaque and think of them only as public-spirited philanthropists and the McKnight Room as honoring one of Remberton's most respected public servants."

"Maybe that's the way we ought to leave it," Frank said, rising to go. "The last word on this mixed tragedy."

As they walked out, Frank asked, "How's Catherine? Haven't seen her lately."

"She's visiting her daughter in Atlanta."

With a sly, knowing smile, Frank said, "I'm guessing you'll be glad when she's home."

Noble was already moving away. "Good to see you," he called out, with a half wave, as he stepped off the curb to cross the street.

Catherine had been gone nearly two weeks, and he had heard nothing from her. He was worried, but he asked himself why he should be, in light of his imminent departure for London. Maybe it was better if she didn't come back before he left. He wouldn't have to face her. But is that what he wanted? The agonizing conflict was becoming almost unbearable.

When he walked into his reception room, Miss Alice looked up from her typewriter and said, "We've just had a telephone call you don't get every day. It's the Governor. He wants you to call him."

Noble had last heard from the Governor shortly after his inauguration nearly two years earlier. The Governor had been a well-known lawyer and he and Noble had once served together on a State Bar committee. Noble had a generally favorable impression of him.

"Governor, it's good to hear from you again," Noble said after the two were connected.

"I'm mighty glad to have this chance to speak to you. It's been too long." They shared some reminiscences from pre-gubernatorial days and then the Governor said, "Can you spare another couple of minutes?"

"Certainly. What's on your mind?"

"I've been concerned about the vacancy on the circuit bench created by Judge McKnight's death. Some political jockeying has delayed filling it. I won't go into that. The point of this call is to say I want to appoint you."

Noble was speechless. It had never occurred to him that at 66 he would be tapped for this place. There were younger, politically ambitious lawyers with an eye on it.

The Governor continued. "I hope very much you'll accept. The state's judiciary badly needs men like you. You've got it all—solid legal experience, professional integrity, and above all, judgment. You know, Noble, that is the most important quality a judge can have—good, common sense judgment. That goes for lawyers too."

Finally Noble was able to speak. "Well, Governor, this is the proverbial bolt out of the blue. It's a great honor to be considered. I need a little time to absorb the idea."

"Naturally. Take your time, but don't take too much. The circuit needs a judge."

For the rest of the day, Noble had difficulty concentrating on the work at hand. He dealt with a client who came in to talk about his will, and he handled several telephone calls. But in between, he just sat, leaning back in his chair lost in thought. Why had fate added the complication of this judgeship into his turmoil over Jennifer and Catherine? He wished he had never heard from the Governor.

As the afternoon was drawing to a close, Miss Alice reminded him of the pleading he needed to file with the circuit clerk before closing time. So he picked up the document and headed out.

He walked toward the courthouse, seeing it in the waning light of the shortened autumn day, the clock tower standing out against the evening sky, but seeing it now as he had not seen it before, seeing it as a possible future home, where he would preside as its dominant figure, capping off his professional career. Is that what he wanted? More important, is that what he should do? Had destiny marked him for this one last service to his people?

He concluded his business in the clerk's office and went back into the main corridor. On impulse, he started up the broad stairs to the second floor.

He entered the courtroom, deserted and silent in the deepening twilight. He walked down the aisle through the bar rail and stopped in front of the bench. On this spot he had stood through four decades as advocate for all manner of causes and people, from the poorest to the richest, ranging over all the travails of mankind. From his earliest days in law school he had been told that the law is a jealous mistress, that he who would win her must woo her persistently. He believed it and had lived accordingly, perhaps at times to the detriment of his family. This mistress had a powerful hold on him. Could he now give her up?

He stepped up on the platform, went around behind the bench, and sat down in the tall leather chair. Here the perspective was different, the vantage point unique. A judge sitting here was above the fray but in control of the fray—an officer specially ordained by the state to exercise an awesome array of power over the lives and well-being of his fellow citizens.

He leaned back in the huge chair, closed his eyes and let his mind run over those long years he had spent right here and in other courts, state and federal. Justice Holmes' memorable words came back: that a man may live greatly in the law as well as elsewhere, that there as well as elsewhere he may wreak himself upon life and wear his heart out after the unattainable.

High overhead the clock boomed six, bringing him back to earth. He speculated on his day-to-day life sitting in this chair. It would be confining, limiting his associations and activities, requiring him always to be an objective symbol of the law. Again the troubling questions: was this what he wanted? Was it where he belonged, the spot where he should spend his remaining years? Or had the time come to strike out in an entirely new direction, free of the heavy burdens the judiciary would impose? Hard as these questions were, they were complicated beyond measure by the two women who lived in his heart.

That night Noble did not sleep, did not even go to bed. He made himself a ham sandwich, drank a glass of milk, and ate a piece of leftover pie. He looked into the guest room where he was in the process of packing for London. His open suitcase lay on the bed, half filled with the warm clothes he had selected, having in mind the penetrating chill of the late English autumn. He had put in a pound of shelled pecans—unbroken halves—anticipating they would be an unusual item for the cocktail hour in South Kensington. His trench coat was laid out on the bed, along with shirts he intended to pack, his airline ticket, and guide book that he and Nan had used.

He went into the den and lit the already-laid fire. Then he sat down, mesmerized by the dancing flames. The logs blazed and crackled brightly for a long while and then began slowly to die out. But Noble did not move to replenish them. They gradually became glowing embers. Still Noble sat unmoved. He felt himself utterly alone in the throes of the darkest, most conflicted night of his life. The judgeship, Jennifer, Catherine, and his future were all intertwined. He had grown up being taught that his life, like that of everyone else, was part of God's plan—inscrutable though it be. What was in that plan for him now?

When he next became conscious of his surroundings day was breaking, a gray, cold, depressing dawn. Still he did not move. Only when the first rays of sunlight hit the windowpanes did he rise. With the chaos of the night continuing to roil in his mind, he went to the kitchen, put on a pot of coffee, then headed for the shower.

During the morning, he met with three clients, a blessing as they diverted his mind to other people's problems. He received a call from the airline advising him that the departure time for his flight from Washington-Dulles to London had been changed from 5:30 p.m. to 5:48.

Shortly past noon a telephone call came from Maria. "Mr. Noble, Mom and I just got in from Atlanta a little while ago. She asked me to call and say that we'd love to see you later this afternoon if you can drop by."

Startled by this sudden reappearance of Catherine, Noble said, "This is a surprise. How is she?"

"Fine. Good as new. Hope we can see you."

Noble looked at his watch and ran his eyes over his crowded desk. He was uncertain how Maria's presence might figure in his reunion with Catherine. Why hadn't she called him herself? For better or worse, he realized he had reached the long-feared moment of decision; the life-changing step could no longer be avoided. "Well," he said, after hesitating, "How about around 4:00 or 4:30?"

When he came out of his office he looked at the courthouse and thought of the words of Robert E. Lee, "Duty is the sublimest word in the English language." But had he not discharged his duty? How much can be expected of one man?

Getting in his car, he drove slowly away, circling the courthouse and heading back down Center Street, then passing along the streets of his boyhood, passing houses whose occupants he had known since infancy—those occupants gone now, the houses in the hands of a new generation and, in some cases, strangers. So much had changed that it shouldn't be hard to leave.

He stopped in front of the house built by his grandfather, the house where he had grown up, inherited by his sister, Emily, then her son, Rob Kirkman, now passed out of the family. A light was burning in the front parlor, a room he knew intimately. He thought of those long-ago days when he would come home at this hour, home from a touch football game or a Scout troop meeting, going into that very room. What would those who had gone before think he should do now? But should the dead determine the course of the living?

He sat there, lost in thought. A gust of cold wind stirred up the fallen leaves in the street, rattling them alongside the car. He felt a momentary shiver, felt a presence hovering by him, the almost physical presence of something or someone. His hands gripped the steering wheel, motor idling all the while. Reluctantly he pulled away, slowly, moving toward the decisive encounter, torn over whether he was doing the right thing.

He turned into the long-familiar Craighill driveway. The trees were bereft of leaves now, their bare branches standing out starkly against the sullen sky.

Maria answered the door. She was a junior version of Catherine—short blond hair, slightly sensual face, good figure. "Mr. Noble, wonderful to see you. Mom's in the front parlor."

Noble, nervous, not knowing what to expect, turned from the hall into the room and saw her sitting in a wing chair. He moved toward her, and she stood up, her face illuminated by a big smile. She wore a plaid skirt and pale blue blouse.

He automatically moved into an embrace. Feeling her warmth, he wanted to hug her tightly and kiss her, but in the presence of Maria, he felt restrained.

"It's certainly been a while," she whispered in his ear.

"You took off," he said, smiling and backing slightly away. "We couldn't very well get together while you in Atlanta."

"Well I'm back now, happy to be my old self again. The break from Remberton did me good in more ways than one."

"I like that new hair-do," he said. It was short and stylishly cut.

"Courtesy of my old Atlanta hairdresser."

Looking her up and down, he said, "Isn't this a new outfit?" Overall, he thought she looked better than ever.

"Yes. I did the whole Atlanta scene. Got it at my old dress shop."

She sat back down and crossed her legs in a familiar move. He seated himself on a chair next to her.

Maria said, "We were just about to have a cup of tea. Would you join us?" He agreed and she left the room.

Noble said, "I'm glad to see you looking so good. How do you feel?"

"Fine. Maria took me to the Emory Medical School and got them to put me through a bunch of tests. They didn't find anything but a low thyroid, thought that was causing my fatigue and low energy. So they gave me a prescription, and that seems to have done the trick. How about you?"

"Rocking along as usual. Very busy."

"I just can't get over this thing about Lucille and Nicky. Julia sent me the article from the paper. I wanted to call you, but I was so shocked I couldn't bring myself to pick up the phone."

Noble filled her in on some background, describing what was not in the paper—Nicky's blackmailing call on Ellen and his visit with Jesse. They talked about the sad turn of events for Jesse, just when he seemed at last free of his Remberton problems.

"The story bears out my suspicions about Grady," she said. "I thought he was up to something over there. What I don't understand is why Lucille went to Europe for all those months. With her father's money she could have handled the pregnancy in this country. There were places you could go."

Again his old unease about Catherine. What did she know about such places? But he didn't want to dwell on the point. He simply said, "Grady may have wreaked more havoc around here than will ever be known." He thought of Gladys Houston, her secret safe with him. And there was Julia, a highly likely possibility, given what Judge McKnight did.

Maria came in with the tea. She joined them, and Noble got her to talk about life in Atlanta—her husband's job and her work as a paralegal in a downtown law firm.

When the tea was gone, Catherine said, "This occasion calls for something stronger. What do you think, Noble?"

"Suits me."

"Maria, would you be good enough to fix us a martini?"

She left and Catherine said, "Henry Edmunds was here a little while ago. Came by to welcome me home and talk about some Altar Guild business. I really like him. You ought to come hear him some Sunday. His checkered past doesn't bother me. He talks a lot about forgiveness, and he ought to know."

"He gave a good invocation at the library ceremony."

Maria returned with Catherine's oversized martini glasses filled to the brim. Then she said, "Mom, if you don't mind, I'll run to the store and pick up a few things. I won't be long." Catherine nodded, and Maria left.

Noble's eye caught the portrait of Walter Craighill hanging over the mantel. It reminded him that the Craighills and the Sheppersons had a long history together in this place, the families having arrived the same time from South Carolina. That was four generations ago. But now the two of them sitting here were the last, the sole remaining survivors. It would not be a great many years before there would be no Shepperson or Craighill in Remberton. Why remain and be the last leaf on the tree?

When the hall clock finished striking five, she broke the silence by telling him about some of her old friends she saw in Atlanta. But he wasn't listening. He was preoccupied with what he was going to say. Then her voice cut in. "Noble, if you'll excuse me, I need to step aside to the powder room for just a minute."

Noble commenced pacing. His thinking had been thrown back into turmoil. He was beginning to doubt whether he had one of the essential qualities a judge must have: decisiveness—the ability to reach a decision and to move on without reliving it. Again he saw Walter Craighill looking down on him. The roots here may be more powerful than even he had realized.

His pacing took him back to the bookshelf in a corner, and his eye fell on a shelf of old books. He pulled out the Rembert County history that Catherine had once shown him. He paged into the book. There was the parade of his ancestors: Archibald Shepperson, the pioneer who had arrived in this unsettled territory in the 1830s and created a sizeable cotton plantation; then came his son, Courtney, a young lieutenant in the 5th Alabama Infantry, badly wounded at Malvern Hill, but who eventually took over the plantation; then Noble's grandfather, Adrian.

His reverie was broken by Catherine's return. "What are you doing way down there?" she said.

"Just looking at the book on Rembert history."

"You've seen it before," she said. "Can there be anything new?"

"Maybe ... maybe a matter of perspective."

They sat down and picked up their martinis. Neither said anything as they sipped.

Then she said, with concern, "Noble, is everything all right? Are you feeling O.K.? You look distracted."

"Err ... just thinking. Thinking about the past. Thinking about home."

"The past is gone. We need to focus on the future. Our future."

After another moment, he said, matter-of-factly, "Have you ever thought about what it would be like to be married to a judge?"

"No, it never occurred to me. I've always thought of judges as old men. The only ones I ever knew were Judge McKnight and old Judge Quigley before him."

They sipped martinis. The room was silent, except for the ticking of the hall clock. It seemed unusually loud. Noble felt a fortifying warmth building up in his stomach.

After some seconds slipped by, she said, "That's a curious question. Why do you ask?"

He didn't answer, but finished his martini. He stood up, took her empty glass and put it on the table.

Grasping her hands, he pulled her to her feet. His heart was thumping, his breathing accelerated. He pressed her against himself.

In a near-whisper, he said, "Yesterday, the Governor called me and ..."

"The Governor called you?"

"Yes. He wants to appoint me circuit judge."

She pulled back, her face beaming. "Oh, Honey, that's wonderful!"

"But I'm not sure what I should do. If I accept this appointment, what would you think?"

"Whether Noble Shepperson is a judge or a garbage collector my feeling is the same—and you know what that is."

Flashing through Noble's mind like a bolt of lightning were visions of London, of the beautiful Jennifer, of an exciting international life. But just as quickly, as he looked into Catherine's face, those visions were swept away. He took a deep breath, eyes closed, and slowly exhaled.

"Are you all right, Sweetie?"

He looked her in the eyes, pausing for a long moment, ready now for the step that would usher him into the remaining years of his life.

"Do you think the Reverend Mr. Edmunds might be available tomorrow?"

"I would guess so. Why?"

"Well, I'm just wondering whether … wondering whether, whether you would like to go with me to see him."

"See him about what?"

"Can't you guess?"

Her puzzled eyes held onto his momentarily. Then, her face lit up. "See him about us?"

He nodded. "What do you say?"

"Oh, honey." She squeezed her arms around his neck, her tear-wet cheeks pressing against his, gasping, "Yes, yes, yes!"

They heard the front door open and close and Maria calling out, "I'm home!"

END

978-0-595-46000-7
0-595-46000-3

˙ͷ the United States
004B/64-69/A